"Sending his cast to America is **a masterful touch from Hewson**. . . . Rich in characters, complex of plot, [*The Dante Killings*] is a worthy entry in **an erudite, entertaining series**."
—*Richmond Times-Dispatch*

"You find yourself catching your breath after each chapter for the next rush. **Flawless suspense**."
—Wichita Falls *Times Record News*

"With his carefully prepared stories, larded with tasty historical tidbits and spread out across the series' sumptuous Roman setting, David Hewson has created a growing clientele of satisfied readers. . . . **Shocking and satisfying**."
—*Winston-Salem Journal*

"I always have a special feeling when I begin a new book by a familiar author, especially one like David Hewson, who has never disappointed. . . . This is no exception. . . . [Hewson is] a magician with the English language. This is **a top-notch, thrilling ride**." —*Mystery News*

THE GARDEN OF EVIL

"**A dark jewel of a thriller** . . . A plot as serpentine—and suspense-filled—as the ancient Roman byways through which Costa stalks his prey."
—*Publishers Weekly* (starred review)

"**It sizzles** with grisly murders, well-drawn characters you will care about, dialogue to envy, and all in **a story not to forget.**" —*Mystery News*

THE SEVENTH SACRAMENT

"A sophisticated and original thriller that cements David Hewson's burgeoning reputation as **one of crime writing's most exciting talents.**"
—*Mystery & Thriller Club* magazine

"The interplay between Hewson's three cops—and between them and the especially rich supporting cast—lifts this novel far above the plot-driven *Da Vinci Code* and its many imitators. **A superb mix of history, mystery, and humanity.**" —*Booklist*

"Every bit as **convoluted and awe-inspiring** as the Catacombs themselves."
—The MLB News

"**Intricate** . . . A mystery whose poignant resolution few readers will anticipate." —*Publishers Weekly*

"Brimming with realism, a touch of romance (which feels inevitable given the assortment of characters), a mystery to solve, and just a pinch of the macabre. **It is always a pleasure to recommend David Hewson's series** for the sheer joy of experiencing intelligent writing plus the added bonus of the picture-postcard visits to Italy."
—*Mystery News*

"Hewson delivers once again. His ability to combine seemingly innocuous facts and characters into a well-designed and -scripted story line ensures that readers are kept guessing until the end. Those who enjoy a good mystery should certainly consider this author.... **Difficult to put down.** One of the better reads of the summer."
—Wichita Falls *Times Record News*

"Rich and intricate ... with **results you won't see coming.**" —*Sullivan County Democrat*

"**Hewson spins a compelling tale that educates and entertains.**" —*Richmond Times-Dispatch*

THE LIZARD'S BITE

#5 on the Bookseller (UK) Top 20 Fiction Heatseekers List 2/9/07

"**Told with dashing style,** in atmospheric set pieces that capture the theatrical grandeur of Venice and the pockets of miserable squalor behind its splendid façade." —*The New York Times Book Review*

"This complex novel, a journey to hell and back, is leavened with food and humor and propelled by suspense and action. The atmospherics are extraordinary—**Hewson does Venice every bit as well as Tony Hillerman does New Mexico.** The ending is particularly satisfying, like watching a multistage finale to a spectacular fireworks display." —*The Boston Globe*

"Hewson takes the story well beyond its genre-bound premise, mixing Venetian ambience and the lore of glassmaking with a multifaceted examination of his characters' dark sides. **A richly ambiguous finale** only adds to the pleasure."
—*Booklist*

"Hewson's wonderfully complex and finely paced fourth crime novel... **Hewson is particularly strong on characterization, revealing each personality subtly and naturally.**... Newcomers as well as series fans will be enthralled."
—*Publishers Weekly* (starred review)

"**Hauntingly evocative**... a suspenseful story with a surprising conclusion and characters the reader has come to treasure... **Stylish, literate entertainment.**" —*Richmond Times-Dispatch*

THE SACRED CUT

"Stunning... Hewson expertly blends historical material into the text.... All this historical detail gives the proceedings a tasty complexity comparable to Pérez-Reverte, but what really makes this novel work is the interplay between the trio of antiestablishment Roman cops.... **A masterful mix of the high-concept historical thriller and the cynical contemporary Italian procedural.**"
—*Booklist* (starred review)

"**A mesmerizing experience.**" —*Houston Chronicle*

"[With] stylish writing and his love of the city... Hewson serves up welcome snapshots of Italy much as Donna Leon does in her series set in Venice. . . ." —*The Washington Post*

"An intriguing blend of spy novel and serial-killer tale. Hewson's prose is top rate, his recurring characters even more interesting with each novel, his trademark twists as unexpected as always. *The Sacred Cut* is entertainment that challenges, **fiction that's a cut above the ordinary.**"
—*Richmond Times-Dispatch*

THE VILLA OF MYSTERIES

"**A complex and satisfying mystery from a master plot maker.**" —*Booklist*

"**An atmospheric follow-up steeped in dark ritual.**" —*Publishers Weekly*

"What happens in this titular place is so macabre and nasty it makes for **a story you won't soon forget.**" —*Rocky Mountain News*

"Hewson writes **a compellingly complex novel,** one with numerous twists. Near the end, one surprises— and a second stuns. A haunting portrayal of evil— and damaged women. *The Villa of Mysteries* will leave readers eager for Costa's third adventure."
—*Richmond Times-Dispatch*

A SEASON FOR THE DEAD

A Bill O'Reilly Book Club Selection

"A delicious and compelling view of the public art of Rome and the private intrigues of the Vatican."
—*Library Journal*

"*A Season for the Dead,* like *The Da Vinci Code,* is a thriller that takes an unflattering look at the Catholic Church, but is better written and more sophisticated than Dan Brown's phenomenal bestseller.... The books differ, too, in that Hewson, far more than Brown or most thriller writers, has a serious concern for character.... **Intelligent entertainment.**" —*The Washington Post*

"Hewson's **suspenseful, fascinating** mystery has an appealing detective and many complex characters on both sides of the law. Twisting and turning through Italian history and art, Nic Costa's first case gives the serial murder mystery a new look."
—*The Dallas Morning News*

LUCIFER'S SHADOW

A *Deadly Pleasures* Best Mystery/Crime Novel 2004

"Entertaining [and] fun." —*Kirkus Reviews*

"This intelligent and highly detailed thriller rivals Pérez-Reverte's *The Flanders Panel* in historical intricacy, complexity of motive, and multileveled storytelling. **Masterfully plotted**...Prepare for a devilish ride in which beauty masks wickedness, and righteousness is relative." —*Booklist* (starred review)

"Good mysteries set in Venice are a growth industry...and David Hewson's new book is one of the best in recent memory....Hewson has created a brave and fascinating double strand of linked plots, one set in 1773 and the other in the present....Add horribly believable scenes of violence, enough sex to ensure the city's reputation for romance, as well as great gobbets of food and scenery both splendid and squalid, and you begin to see why *Lucifer's Shadow* is **unputdownable**." —*Chicago Tribune*

ALSO BY DAVID HEWSON

THE NIC COSTA NOVELS

A Season for the Dead

The Villa of Mysteries

The Sacred Cut

The Lizard's Bite

The Seventh Sacrament

The Garden of Evil

Lucifer's Shadow

AND LOOK FOR

City of Fear in Summer 2010

The Dante Killings

ORIGINALLY PUBLISHED AS
Dante's Numbers

A Thriller

David Hewson

A Dell Book
New York

The Dante Killings is a work of fiction. Names, characters, places, and incidents either are the product of the author's imagination or are used fictitiously. Any resemblance to actual persons, living or dead, events, or locales is entirely coincidental.

2010 Dell Mass Market Edition

This book contains an excerpt from *City of Fear* by David Hewson. This excerpt has been set for this edition only and may not reflect the final content of the full edition.

Published in the United States by Dell,
an imprint of The Random House Publishing Group,
a division of Random House, Inc., New York.

DELL is a registered trademark of Random House, Inc., and the colophon is a trademark of Random House, Inc.

This work was originally published as *Dante's Numbers* in Great Britain by Macmillan Publishers Ltd., London, in 2008, and subsequently in the United States by Delacorte Press, a division of Random House, Inc., in 2009.

978-0-385-34149-3

Cover design: Tony Greco
Photo of tower: Kersti Frigell
Photo of gravestones: bridgeandtunnel.com

Printed in the United States of America

www.bantamdell.com

2   4   6   8   9   7   5   3

Midway upon the journey of our life
I found myself within a forest dark,
For the straightforward pathway had been lost.

—*The Divine Comedy, Inferno,* Canto I. Dante Alighieri,
translated by Henry Wadsworth Longfellow

PART 1

1

A LLAN PRIME PEERED AT THE WOMAN THEY'D
sent from the studio, pinched his cheeks between finger and thumb the way he always did before
makeup, then grumbled, "Run that past me again,
will you?"

He couldn't figure out whether she was Italian or
not. Or how old, since most of her face was hidden behind a pair of large black plastic-rimmed sunglasses.
Even—and this was something Prime normally got
out of the way before anything else—whether she was
pretty. He'd never seen this one at Cinecittà, and a
part of him said he would have noticed, if only in
order to ask himself the question: *Should I?*

She looked late twenties, a little nervous, in awe of
him maybe. But she was dressed so much older, in a
severe grey jacket with matching slacks and a prim
white shirt, its soft crinkly collar high up on her neck.
It was a look out of the movies, he decided. Old
movies from back when it was still a crime to be
skinny and anything less than elegant. Particularly
her hair, a platinum blonde, dyed undoubtedly,
pinned behind her taut, stiffly held head in a ponytail
that, as she walked into the living room of his

apartment, he'd noticed was curled into a tight apostrophe.

It was an effect he found strangely alluring until the connection came to him. Unsmiling, eyes hidden behind heavy shades that kept out the burning July morning, Miss Valdes—although the Spanish name didn't fit at all—resembled one of those cool, aloof women he'd watched in the downtown theatres when he was a kid in New York, rapt before the silver screen. Like a cross between Kim Novak and Grace Kelly, the two full-bodied celluloid blondes he'd first fallen hotly in love with as he squirmed with adolescent lust in the shiny, sticky seats of Manhattan flea pits. He hadn't encountered silent, fixated women like this in the business in three or four decades. The breed was extinct. Real bodies had given way to rake-thin models, exquisite coiffures to impromptu mussed-up messes. The species had moved on, and now he knew what kind of job it did these days.

It made death masks of people. Living people, in his case.

"Signor Harvey say…" she repeated in her slow, deliberate Italian accent, as if she were unsure he quite understood. Her voice was low and throaty and appealing. More Novak than Kelly, he thought.

"Harvey's a drug-addled jerk. He never mentioned anything to me. We've got this opening ceremony tonight, in front of everyone from God down. The biggest and best movie of the decade and I get to do the honours."

"It must be an honour to be in Signor Tonti's masterpiece."

Allan Prime took a deep breath. "Without me it'd be nothing. You ever watch *Gordy's Break*?"

"I loved that movie," she replied without hesitation, and he found himself liking the throaty, almost masculine croon in her voice.

"It was a pile of crap. If it wasn't for me, the thing wouldn't have made it outside the queer theatres."

He truly hated that thing. The movie was the kind of violent fake art-house junk the Academy liked to smile on from time to time just to show it had a brain as well as a heart. He'd played a low-life hood in a homosexual relationship with a local priest who was knifed to death trying to save him. When the clamour petered out, and the golden statue was safely stored somewhere he didn't have to look at it, Allan Prime decided to make movies for people, not for critics. One a year for almost three decades. Nothing that followed gave him another nomination.

The lack of Oscars never bothered Prime too much, most of the time. From the eighties on he'd become more and more bankable, a multimillion-dollar name who always brought in an army of female fans in love with his chiselled Mediterranean looks, trademark wavy dark hair, and that slow, semi-lascivious smile he liked to throw in somewhere along the line.

Except now. He'd tried, and every time he began to crease up for the famed smirk, Roberto Tonti had gone stiff in his director's chair, thrown back his hoary aquiline head with its crown of grey hair like plumed feathers, and howled long and loud with fury.

"This is what I *do*," Prime had complained one day, when the verbal abuse went too far. He was in costume, a long, grubby medieval gown, standing in front of a blue screen, pretending to deliver some obscure speech to a digitised dragon or some other monster out of a teenage horror fantasy, though he couldn't see a thing except lights and cameras and Roberto Tonti thrashing around in his chair like some ancient, skeletal wraith.

"Not when you work for me," Tonti screamed at him. "When you work for me, you…"—a stream of impenetrable Italian curses followed—"…you are *mine*. My puppet. My creature. Every day I put my finger up your scrawny, coked-up ass, Allan, and every day I wiggle a little harder till your stupid brain wakes up. Stop acting. Start being."

Stop acting. Start being. Prime had lost count of the number of times he'd heard that. He still didn't get it.

Tonti was seventy-three. He looked a hundred and fifty and was terminally ill, with a set of lungs that had been perforated by a lifetime's tobacco. Maybe he'd be dead before the movie got its first showing in the U.S. They all knew that was a possibility. It added to the buzz Simon Harvey's little army of evil PR geckos had been quietly building with their tame hacks.

Allan Prime had already thought through his performance in the director's real-life funeral scene. He'd release one single tear, dab it away with a finger, not a handkerchief, showing he was a man of the people, unchanged by fame. Then, when no one could hear, he'd walk up to the casket and whisper, "Where's that freaking finger *now*, huh?"

Or maybe the old bastard would live forever, long enough to dance on Prime's own grave. There was something creepy, something abnormal about the man, which was, the rumours said, why he'd not sat at the helm of a movie for twenty years, frittering away his talent in the wasteland of TV until *Inferno* came along. Prime gulped a fat finger of single malt, then refilled his glass from the bottle on the table. It was early, but the movie was done, and he didn't need to be out in public until the end of the day. The penthouse apartment atop one of the finest houses in the Via Giulia, set back from the busy Lungotevere with astonishing views over the river to St. Peter's, had been Allan Prime's principal home for almost a year. Tonight it was empty except for him and Miss Valdes.

"This is for publicity, right?" he asked.

"*Sì,*" the woman replied, and patted her briefcase like a lawyer sure it contained evidence. She had to be Italian. And the more he looked at her, the more Prime became convinced she wasn't unattractive either, with her full, muscular figure—that always turned him on— and very perfect teeth behind a mouth blazingly outlined in carmine lipstick. "Mr. Harvey say we must have a copy of your face, because we cannot, for reasons of taste, mass-market a version of the real thing. It must be you."

"I cut myself shaving this morning. Does that matter?"

"I can work with that."

"Great," he grumbled. "So where do you want me?"

She took off her oversized sunglasses. Miss Valdes was a looker and Allan Prime was suddenly aware something was starting to twitch down below. She had a large, strong face, quite heavy with makeup for this time of day, as if she didn't just make masks, she liked wearing them herself. The voice, too, now that he thought about it, sounded artificial. *Posed.* As if she wasn't speaking in her natural tongue. Not that this worried him. He was aware of a possibility in her eyes, and that was all he needed.

"On the bed, sir," Miss Valdes suggested. "It would be best if you were naked. A true death mask is always taken from a naked man."

"Not that I'm arguing, but why the hell is that?"

The corner of her scarlet mouth turned down in a gesture of meek surprise, one that seemed intoxicatingly Italian to him.

"We come into the world that way. And leave it, too. You're an actor."

He watched, rapt, as her fleshy, muscular tongue ran very deliberately over those scarlet lips.

"I believe you call it . . . being in character."

He wondered how Roberto Tonti would direct a scene like this.

"Will it hurt?"

"Of course not!" She appeared visibly offended by the idea. "Who would wish to hurt a star?"

"You'd be surprised," Prime grumbled. This curious woman would be truly amazed, if she only knew.

She smoothed down the front of her jacket, opened the briefcase, and peered into it with a professional, searching gaze before beginning to remove some items Allan Prime didn't recognise.

"First a little ... discomfort," she declared. "Then ..." That carmine smile again, one Allan Prime couldn't stop staring at, although there was something about it that nagged him. Something familiar he couldn't place. "Then we are free."

Miss Valdes—*Carlotta* Valdes, he recalled the first name the doorman had used when he'd called up to announce her arrival—took out a pair of rubber gloves and slipped them onto her strong, powerful hands, like those of a nurse or a surgeon.

2

AT FIVE MINUTES PAST FOUR, NIC COSTA FOUND himself standing outside a pale green wooden hut shaded by parched trees, just a short walk from the frenzied madness that was beginning to build in and around the nearby Casa del Cinema. The sight of this tiny place brought back far too many memories, some of them jogged by a newspaper clipping attached to the door, bearing the headline *"'Dei Piccoli,' cinema da Guinness."* This was the world's smallest movie theatre, built for children in 1934 during the grim Mussolini years, evidence that Italy was in love with film, with the idea of fantasy, of a life that was brighter and more colourful than reality, even in those difficult times. Or perhaps, it occurred to Costa now, with the perspective of adulthood shaping his childhood memories, because of them. This small oak cabin had just sixty-three seats, every one of them, he now felt sure, deeply uncomfortable for anyone over the age of ten. Not that his parents had ever complained. Once a week, until his eleventh birthday, his mother or father had brought him here. Together they had sat through a succession of films, some good, some bad, some Italian, some from other countries, America in particular.

It was a different time, a different world, both on the screen and in his head. Costa had never returned much to any cinema since those days. There had always seemed something more important to occupy his time: family and the slow loss of his parents; work and ambition; and, for comfort, the dark and enticing galleries and churches of his native city, which seemed to speak more directly to him as he grew older. Now he wondered what he'd missed. The movie playing was one he'd seen as a child, a popular Disney title prompting the familiar emotions those films always brought out in him: laughter and tears, fear and hope. Sometimes he'd left this place scarcely able to speak for the rawness of the feelings that the movie had, with cunning and ruthlessness, elicited from his young and fearful mind. Was this one reason why he had stayed away from the cinema for so long? That he feared the way it sought out the awkward, hidden corners of one's life, good and bad, then magnified them in a way that could never be shirked, never be avoided? Some fear that he might be haunted by what he saw?

He had been a widower for six months, before the age of thirty, and the feelings of desolation and emptiness continued to reverberate in the distant corners of his consciousness. *The world moved on.* So many had said that, and in a way they'd been right. He had allowed work to consume him, because there was nothing else. There, Leo Falcone had been subtly kind in his own way, guiding Costa away from the difficult cases, and any involving violence and murder, towards more agreeable duties, those that embraced culture and the arts, milieux in which Costa felt comfortable and, occasionally, alive. This was why, on a hot July day, he was in the pleasant park of the Villa Borghese, not far from three hundred or more men and women assembled from all over the world for a historic premiere that would mark the revival of the career of one of Italy's most distinguished and reclusive directors.

Costa had never seen a movie by Roberto Tonti until that afternoon, when, as a reward for their patient duties arranging property security for the exhibition associated with the production, the police and Carabinieri had been granted a private screening. He was still unclear exactly what he felt about the work of a man who was something of an enigmatic legend in his native country, though he had lived in America for many, many years. The movie was... undoubtedly impressive, though very long and extremely noisy. Costa found it difficult to recognise much in the way of humanity in all its evident and very impressive spectacle. His memories of studying Dante's *Divina Commedia* in school told him the lengthy poem was a discourse on many things, among them the nature of human and divine love, an argument that seemed absent from the film he had sat through. Standing outside the little children's cinema, it seemed to Costa that the Disney title it was now showing contained more of Dante's original message than Tonti's farrago of visual effects and overblown drama.

But he was there out of duty. The Carabinieri had been assigned to protect the famous actors involved in the year-long production at Cinecittà. The state police had been given a more mundane responsibility, that of safeguarding the historic objects assembled for an accompanying exhibition in the building next to the Casa del Cinema: documents and letters, photographs, and an extensive exhibition of original paintings depicting the civil war between the Ghibellines and the Guelphs which prompted Dante's flight from Florence and brought about the perpetual exile in which he wrote his most famous work.

There was a photograph of the poet's grave and the verse of his friend Bernardo Canaccio that included the line...

Parvi Florentia mater amoris.

Florence, mother of little love, a sharp reminder of how Dante had been abandoned by his native city. There was a picture, too, of the tomb the Florentines had built for him in 1829, out of a tardy sense of guilt. The organisers' notes failed to disclose the truth of the matter, however: that his body remained in Ravenna. The ornate sepulchre in the Basilica di Santa Croce, built to honour the most exalted of poets, was empty. The poet remained an exile still, almost seven hundred years after his death.

The most famous Florentine object was, however, genuine. Hidden on a podium behind a rich blue curtain, due to be unveiled by the actor playing Dante before the premiere that evening, sat a small wooden case on a plinth. Inside, carefully posed against scarlet velvet, was the death mask of Dante Alighieri, cast in 1321 shortly after his last breath. That morning, Costa had found himself staring at these ancient features for so long that Gianni Peroni had walked over and nudged him back to life with the demand for a coffee and something to eat. The image still refused to quit his head: the ascetic face of a fifty-six-year-old man, a little gaunt, with sharp cheekbones, a prominent nose, and a mouth pinched tight with such deliberation that this mask, now grey and stained with age, seemed to emphasise *I will speak no more.*

Costa was uneasy about such a treasure being associated with the Hollywood spectacle that had invaded this quiet, beautiful hillside park in Rome. There had been a concerted and occasionally vitriolic campaign against the project in the literary circles of Rome and beyond. Rumours of sabotage and mysterious accidents on the film set had appeared regularly in the papers. The chatter in some of the gutter press suggested the production was "cursed" because of its impudent and disrespectful pillaging of Dante's work, an idea that had a certain appeal to the superstitious nature of many Italians. The response of Roberto Tonti had been to rush to the TV cameras denying furiously that his return to the screen was anything but an art movie produced entirely in the exalted spirit of the original.

The more sophisticated newspapers detected the hand of a clever PR campaign in all this, something the production's publicity director, Simon Harvey, had vigorously denied. Costa had watched the last press conference only the day before and come to the conclusion that he would never quite understand the movie industry. Simon Harvey was the last man he expected to be in charge of a production costing around a hundred and fifty million dollars, a good third over budget. Amiable, engaging, with a bouncing head of fair curly hair, Harvey appeared more like a perpetual fan than someone capable of dealing with the ravenous hordes of the world media. But Costa had seen him in private moments, too, when the PR director seemed calm and quick-thinking, though prone to brief explosions of anger.

The people Costa had met and worked with over the previous few weeks were, for the most part, charming, hardworking, and dedicated, but also, above all, obsessive. Nothing much mattered for them except the job in hand, *Inferno*. A war could have started, a bomb might have exploded in the centre of Rome. They would never have noticed. The world flickering on the screen was theirs. Nothing else existed.

Nic Costa rather envied them.

3

A N HOUR AFTER THEY HAD WALKED OUT FROM the private showing, blinking into the summer sun, Gianni Peroni's outrage had still not lessened. The big cop stood next to Leo Falcone and Teresa Lupo, elaborating on a heartfelt rant about the injustice of it all. The world. Life. The job. The fact they were guarding ancient wooden boxes and old letters when they ought to be out there doing what they were paid for.

More than anything, though, it was the movie that got to him. Teresa had, with her customary guile, wangled a free ticket to the event, though she had nothing to do with the security operation the state police had in place. Early in their relationship, Peroni had realised the cinema was one of Teresa's few pet obsessions outside work. Normally he managed to pretend an interest he failed to share. Today, that was impossible.

"Roberto Tonti is a genius, Gianni," she declared. "A strange genius, but a genius all the same."

"Please. I'm still half deaf after all that racket. I've got pictures running round my head I'd really rather not have there. And you're telling me this is *art*?"

"All true art is difficult," said a young, confident male voice from behind them. They turned to see a man of about thirty in the full dress uniform of a mounted Carabinieri officer, complete with flowing cloak, shiny black boots, and a sword at his waist. "The harder it is to peel an orange, the better it will taste."

"I don't believe we've met," Leo Falcone replied, and extended a hand which was grasped with alacrity. The Carabiniere had materialised unbidden and in silence, presumably fleeing the noisy and, it seemed to Peroni, increasingly ill-tempered scrum by the cinema. The officer was tall, good-looking in a theatrical, too-tanned way, with rather greasy hair that looked as if it might have seen pomade. The Carabinieri often seemed a little vain, the old cop thought, then cursed himself for such a stupid generalisation.

"Bodoni," the man announced, before turning to Teresa and Peroni to shake their hands, too. "Please. Let me fetch you another drink. There is *prosecco*. Is this a problem on duty? I think not. It is like water. Also I have a horse, not a car. He can lead me home if necessary."

"No beer?" Peroni grumbled.

"I doubt it." The officer shook his head sadly. "Let me fetch something and then we may talk a little more. There is no work to be done here, surely. Besides . . ." He stood up very straight, inordinately proud of himself.

". . . my university degree was in Dante. All that education shall be of use at last."

He departed towards the outdoor bar, leaving Peroni speechless, mouth flapping like a goldfish.

"I love the Carabinieri," Teresa observed, just to provoke the two men. "They dress so beautifully. Such delicate manners. They fetch you drinks when you want one. They know Dante. *And* he's got one of those lovely horses somewhere, too."

Falcone stiffened. The inspector was in his best evening suit, something grey, probably from Armani as usual. After the screening, Teresa had elbowed Peroni and pointed out that the old fox had been speaking for quite a long time to a very elegant woman from the San Francisco Police Department. This entire exhibition would move on to America once the show at the Villa Borghese was over. The Californians had a team working on liaison to make sure every last precious historical item stayed safe and intact throughout. Teresa had added—her powers of intelligence-gathering never ceased to amaze him—that Leo's on-off relationship with Raffaella Arcangelo was now going through an extended off phase, perhaps a permanent one. A replacement girlfriend seemed to be on the old inspector's mind.

"I studied Dante at college for a while," Falcone noted. "And Petrarch."

"I read Batman, when I wasn't rolling around in the gutter with drunks and thieves," Peroni retorted.

"But then, I always did prefer the quiet intellectual life."

Teresa planted a kiss on his damaged cheek, which felt good.

"Well said," she announced before beaming at the newly returned Carabiniere, who now held four flutes of sparkling wine in his long, well-manicured hands.

"As a rendition of *La Divina Commedia*," Bodoni began, "I find the film admirable. Tonti follows Dante's structure to the tee. Remember..."

The man had a professorial, slightly histrionic manner and a curious accent, one that almost sounded foreign. The Carabinieri had a habit of talking down to people. Peroni gritted his teeth, tried to ignore Teresa's infuriatingly dazzling smile, and listened.

"...this is an analogy for the passage of life itself, from cradle to grave and beyond, written in the first example we have of *terza rima*. A three-line stanza using the pattern a-b-a, b-c-b, c-d-c, d-e-d, et cetera, et cetera."

Peroni downed half his glass in one gulp. "I got that much from the part where the horse-snake-dragon thing chomped someone to pieces."

Bodoni nodded. "Good. It's in the numbers that the secret lies, and in particular the number nine. Nine was, of course, regarded as the 'angelic' integer, since its sole root is three, representing the Trinity, which itself bears the sole root one, representing the

Divine Being Himself, the Alpha and the Omega of everything."

"Do you ever get to arrest people? Or does the horse do it?" Peroni demanded, aware that Teresa was kicking him in the shin.

Bodoni blinked, clearly puzzled, then continued. "Nine meant everything to Dante. It appears in the context of his beloved Beatrice throughout. Nine are the spheres of Heaven. Correspondingly—since symmetry is also fundamental—"

"Nine are the circles of Hell," Peroni interrupted. "See? I was listening. Worse than that, I was watching." He scowled at the glass and tipped it sideways to empty the rest of the warm, flat liquid on the concrete pavement outside the Casa del Cinema. It didn't take a genius to understand that last part. The three-hour movie was divided into nine component segments, each lasting twenty minutes and prefaced with a title announcing its content, a string of salacious and suggestive headings—"The Wanton," "The Gluttonous," "The Violent"—that served as insufficient warning for the grisly scene to come. "It still looked like a bad horror movie to me. *Very* bad."

"As it was meant to," Teresa suggested. "That's Roberto Tonti's background. You remember those films from the 1970s?"

"*Anathema. Mania. Dementia,*" Bodoni concurred.

"*Dyspepsia? Nausea...?*" Peroni asked. "Has he made those yet? Or does the rubbish we just saw have an alternative title? All that... blood and noise."

Bodoni mumbled something unintelligible. Peroni wondered if he'd hit home.

It was Teresa who answered. "Blood and noise and death are central to art, Gianni," she insisted. "They remind us it's impossible to savour the sweetness of life without being reminded of the proximity, and the certainty, of death. That's at the heart of *gialli*. It's why I love them. Some of them anyway."

Peroni hated that word. *Gialli. The yellows.* To begin with, the term had simply referred to the cheap crime thrillers that had come out after the war in plain primrose jackets. Usually they were detective stories and private-eye tales, often imported from America. Later the term had spread to the movies, into a series of lurid and often extraordinarily violent films that had begun to appear from the sixties on. Gory, strange, supernatural tales through which Tonti had risen to prominence. Peroni knew enough of that kind of work to understand it would never be to his own taste. It was all too extreme and, to his mind, needless.

"I hardly think anyone in our line of work needs reminding of a lesson like that," he complained, finding his thoughts shifting to Nic, poor Nic, still lost, still wandering listless and without any inner direction two seasons after the murder of his wife.

"We all do, Gianni," Teresa responded, "because we all, in the end, forget." She took his arm, a glint in her pale, smart eyes telling him she knew exactly what he was thinking.

Teresa's hand felt warm in his. He squeezed it and said, very seriously, "Give me *Bambi* any time." He and Falcone had ambled to the children's cinema earlier and seen the poster there, then Peroni had mentioned it to Nic in passing, and had noted how interested he'd seemed.

"There's a death in *Bambi*," Teresa pointed out. "Without it there'd be no story."

He did remember, and it was important. His own daughter had been in tears in the darkness when they went to see that movie, unable to see that her father was in much the same state.

"This is an interesting work also," the Carabinieri officer, Bodoni, interjected. The man was, it seemed to Peroni, something of a movie bore, perhaps an understandable attribute for a person who spent his working day indolently riding the pleasant green spaces of the Villa Borghese park. The state police had officers in the vicinity, too, since it was unthinkable they should not venture where the Carabinieri went. A few were mounted, though rather less ostentatiously, while others patrolled the narrow lanes in a couple of tiny Smart cars specially selected for the job. It was all show, a duty Peroni would never, in a million years, countenance. Nothing ever happened up here on the hill overlooking the city, with views all the way to the distant dome of St. Peter's and beyond. This wasn't a job for a real cop. It was simply ceremonial window dressing for the tourists and the city authorities.

"You can go and watch it now if you like," Falcone said, looking as if he were tiring of the man's presence, too. "It's showing in the little children's cinema. We saw the poster when we were doing the rounds."

"So did Maggie Flavier," Teresa added. "Charming woman, for a star, and a perfect Beatrice, too. Beautiful yet distant, unreal somehow. I spoke to her and she didn't look down her nose at me like the rest of them. She said she was going to try and sneak in there. Anything to get away from this nonsense. Apparently there's some hiccup in tonight's event. Allan Prime has gone missing. They don't know who's going to open the exhibition. The mayor's here. A couple of ministers. Half the glitterati in Rome. And they still can't decide who's going to raise the curtain."

"That's show business," Falcone agreed with a sage nod of his bald, aquiline head, and a quick stroke of his silver goatee.

"That's *overtime*," Peroni corrected. "That's..."

He stopped. There was the most extraordinary expression on Bodoni's very tanned and artificially handsome face. It was one of utter shock and concern, as if he'd just heard the most terrible news.

"What did you say?" the officer asked.

"There's some argument going on about the ceremony," Teresa explained. "Allan Prime, the actor who's supposed to give the opening speech, hasn't turned up. They don't know who'll take his place. The last I heard, it was going to be Tonti himself."

"No, no..." he responded anxiously. "About Signora Flavier. She has left the event?"

"Only to go to the children's cinema," Falcone replied a little testily. "It's still within the restricted area. As far as I'm aware. Personal security is the responsibility of the Carabinieri, isn't it?"

"We just get to guard *things*," Peroni grumbled.

But it was useless. The Carabinieri official had departed, in a distinct hurry, glittering sword slapping at his thigh.

4

COSTA'S EYES STAYED LOCKED ON THE POSTER for *Bambi,* outside the Cinema dei Piccoli. An insane idea was growing in his head: perhaps there was an opportunity to spend a little time in the place itself, wedged in one of those uncomfortable tiny seats, away from everything. Before he could find the energy to thrust it aside, a soft female voice asked, in English, "Is this a queue for the movie?"

He turned and found himself looking at a woman of about his own age and height. She was gazing back at him with curious, very bright green eyes, and seemed both interested and a little nervous. Something about her was familiar, though he was unsure what. Her chestnut hair was fashioned in a Peter Pan cut designed, with considerable forethought, to appear quite carefree. She wore a long dark blue evening dress that was revealing and low at the front, with a pearl necklace around her slender throat. Her pale face was somewhat tomboyish, though striking. Costa found himself unable to stop looking at her, then, realising the rudeness of his prolonged stare, apologised immediately.

"No problem," she replied, laughing. Everything about her seemed too perfect: the hair, the dress, her white, white teeth, the delicate makeup and lipstick applied so precisely. "I'm used to it by now."

The woman had "movie business" written all over her, though it took him a moment to realise that.

She returned his stare, still laughing. "You really have no idea who I am, do you?"

He closed his eyes and felt very stupid. In his mind's eye he could see her twenty feet tall on the screen in the Casa del Cinema, wearing a flowing medieval robe, her hair long and fair and lustrous, an ethereal figure, the muse, the dead lover Dante sought in his journey through the Inferno.

"You're Beatrice."

The charming smile died. "Not quite," she said. "That's the part I played. My name is Maggie Flavier." She waited. Nic Costa smiled blankly. "You still haven't heard of me, have you?"

"No," he confessed. "Except as Beatrice. Sorry."

"Amazing." He had no idea whether she was

delighted or offended. "And whom do I have the pleasure of addressing?"

Costa showed her his ID card. She merely glanced at it.

"Police," she noted, puzzled, and nodded at a couple of distant Carabinieri on matching burnt umber mares, black capes flowing, gleaming swords by their sides. "One of them..."

"They're Carabinieri," he corrected her. "Military. We're just civilians. Ordinary. Like everyone else."

"Really?" She didn't seem convinced by something. "The movie..."

Costa pointed to the Casa del Cinema. "The premiere is over there. This is just a little place. For children."

She extended her arm out towards the wall and he caught a faint passing trace of some expensive scent.

"Posso leggere," she said in easy Italian, pointing to the article about the cinema on the door, and then the poster for the cartoon, reading out a little of each to prove her boast.

"I meant this movie," she added, now in English again. "A few minutes of peace and quiet, and a fairy tale, too."

"I thought you were in the fairy-tale business already."

"Lots of people think that." She touched his arm gently, briefly. "You could join me. Two fugitives..." She nodded towards the crowd near the Casa del Cinema. "...from that circus."

She seemed...*desperate* wasn't quite the right word. But it wasn't too far wrong. He did recognise Maggie Flavier, he realised. Or at least he could now match the image of her in life with that on the screen, in the public imagination. Maggie Flavier's photo had been in the papers for years. She was a star, one who'd attracted a lot of publicity, not all of it good. The details eluded him. He was happy to leave it that way. The artificiality of the movie business made him uncomfortable. Being close to so many Americans, finding himself engulfed in such a tide of pretence and illusion, had affected Costa. He would have preferred something routine, something straightforward, such as simply walking the streets of Rome, looking for criminals. The seething ocean of intense emotion that was a gigantic movie production left him feeling a little stranded, a little too reflective. It was a relief to look Maggie Flavier in the eyes and see a young, attractive woman who simply wished to step outside this world for a moment, just as he did.

Costa spoke to the man in the ticket booth. His ID card did not impress. It was the presence of a famous Hollywood star that got the small wooden doors opened and the two of them ushered into the tiny dark hall where the movie was now showing to a small audience, their tiny heads reflected in the projector beam.

"Only for a little while," he whispered into her ear as they sat down.

"*Certo,*" she murmured, in a passable impersonation of a gruff Roman accent, and briefly gripped his arm as she lowered herself into the small, hard seat.

He started to say, a little too loudly, "But you must be back for the..."

She glowered at him, eyes flaring with a touch of amused anger, until he fell silent and looked at the screen. Bambi was with his mother, fleeing the unseen hunters' guns, racing through snow fields, terrified, shocked by this deadly intrusion. Finally the little fawn came to a halt, spindly legs deep in snow, suddenly aware that he was alone, and the larger, beloved figure of his mother was nowhere to be seen.

It never ceased to touch him, to break his heart to see the defenceless, fragile creature wandering the woods, lost and forlorn, in a series of lonely dissolves, searching, coming to realise with each solemn step that the quest was hopeless. This wasn't just a movie for children. It was an allegory for life itself, the endless cycle from innocence to knowledge, birth to death, the constant search for renewal.

Perhaps this clandestine visit wasn't such a good idea. Something about this tiny place made him feel sad and a little wretched. He glanced at the woman by his side and felt his heart rise towards his throat.

Maggie Flavier, who had seemed so quiet and self-assured when he'd met her outside the little wooden cinema, sat frozen in the tiny cinema chair, hand over her mouth, eyes glassy with tears and locked to the screen.

"I think…" Nic said, and took her hand, "…we should get out of here."

PERONI WATCHED THE Carabiniere disappear into the crowd milling around the entrance to the Casa del Cinema. The mood there didn't seem to be improving.

"Maybe they've realised people won't like it," Peroni mused. "Maybe there's—how much? A hundred and fifty million dollars and some very mega reputations?—all about to go down the toilet."

Teresa shot him a caustic look. "Stop being so bitchy. This is the biggest movie to be made at Cinecittà since *Cleopatra*. It won't fail."

"*Cleopatra* failed."

"Those were different times. Roberto Tonti has a hit on his hands. You can feel it in the air." She glanced at the crowds of evening suits and cocktail dresses gathered for the premiere. "Can't you?"

"Possibly." Falcone handed his untouched glass to a passing waiter. "The critics say it could be an unmitigated disaster, financially and artistically. Or a runaway success. Who cares?"

Peroni scanned the shifting crowd. Some of them cared, he thought. A lot. Then his eyes turned away from the milling crush of bodies and found the green open space of the park.

He was astonished to see a lone figure on a chestnut stallion, galloping across the expanse of verdant lawn leading away from the cinema complex. Bodoni of the Carabinieri didn't look the fey, aesthetic intellectual he'd appeared earlier. He'd been transformed, the way an actor is when he first comes on stage.

This Bodoni looked like a soldier from another time. He charged across the dry, parched summer grass of the park of the Villa Borghese, down towards the Cinema dei Piccoli.

High in the officer's hand was the familiar silhouette of a gun.

THEY SAT ON the wall outside the Cinema dei Piccoli.

Maggie looked a little shamefaced. "I'm sorry I went all boo-hoo. Bag of nerves, really. You're lucky I didn't throw up. I'm always like this at premieres. I took three months off after *Inferno* and it feels as if it never happened. Now I just have to do it all over again. Be someone else, somewhere else. Oh, and you dropped this in your rush to bundle me out of there…"

His battered leather wallet was in her hands, open to show the photo there. Emily, two months before she died, bright-eyed in the sun, her golden hair gleaming. It had been taken on the day they took a picnic to the gardens on the Palatine.

"No need to explain," Costa said, glancing at the

picture, then taking it gently from her. "I don't know why films do that. It's not as if they're real."

Her green eyes flashed at him. "Define 'real.' *Bambi*'s a bitch. Disney knew how to twist your emotions. It's a scary talent, real enough for me." She stared at the grass at their feet. "They all have it."

"Who?"

"Movies and the people who make them. We exist to screw around with your heads. To do things you'd like to do yourself but lack the courage. Or the common sense. It's a small gift but a rare one, thank God. Beats waiting on tables, though." She hesitated. "Your wife's lovely."

"Yes," he replied automatically. "She was."

He was distracted, watching what was coming their way from the gathering by the cinema complex, trying to make sense of this strange, unexpected sight. He knew what the park Carabinieri were like. They were indolent toy soldiers. Usually.

The woman with the Peter Pan haircut who sat next to him looked like a child who'd been placed inside her shimmering blue evening dress on someone's orders, someone who'd created her for a ceremony, or another hidden purpose. She held a damp tissue in her pale slender fingers. Her makeup had run a little from the tears.

"Did something happen back there?" he said, and nodded in the direction of the gathering. "At the premiere?"

He could hear the distant clatter of hooves as the

horse galloped towards them with a strange, stiff figure on its back. Maggie Flavier squinted into the sunlight and replied, "I don't think so. Although Allan Prime hadn't shown up to make his speech, for some reason. That's unusual. Allan's normally completely reliable." She registered the movement ahead of them, and narrowed her eyes further.

Costa stood up and said, "Go inside, please. Now."

"Why?"

He didn't like guns. He didn't like the sight of a Carabiniere in full dress uniform storming madly across this normally peaceful park in their direction.

The rider was getting closer. Maggie rose to stand next to Nic. Her arm went immediately through his, out of fear or some need for closeness, he was unsure which. Briefly, Costa wanted to laugh. There was something so theatrical about this woman, as if the entire world were a drama and she one more member of the cast.

"Let me deal with it," Costa insisted, and took one step forward so that he was in front of her, confronting the racing horse that now made a sound like an insistent drumroll, or the rattle of some strange weapon, as it flew closer. The man's insane dash across the green grass of the Villa Borghese seemed to have only one point of focus, and it was them.

The officer pointed his weapon in the air and fired. From somewhere nearby a dog began to bark maniacally.

As Costa watched, the uniformed man leaned

forward in the saddle, as if preparing for one final assault.

Nic felt as if he'd walked unbidden onto some movie set, one with a script he couldn't begin to fathom. The Carabiniere was in a crouch, racing furiously to close the distance that separated them. The sight reminded Costa of some old movie, *The Charge of the Light Brigade* maybe. Something that began as a show of bravado and ended in a shocking, unforeseen tide of bloodshed.

"Who the hell is that?" Maggie asked.

"Here's an idea. Let's not find out."

He grabbed her slender arm, both tugging and pushing her towards the closed wooden door of the tiny cinema. Seconds later, there was a thunderstorm of desperate hooves behind them and the rhythmic beat of the animal's angry snorts. He shoved the American inside, protesting still.

"Don't cops here carry guns?" she demanded, squirming out of his arms as he pushed and kicked a way in, opening up the black interior in which the movie still flickered over a handful of small heads.

"To go to the cinema?" Costa asked, bewildered. "Please..."

"Maggie! Maggie!"

The Carabiniere was screaming for her as he fought to control the horse. Costa had seen enough cowboy films to know what came next. He'd dismount. He'd come for them.

"Who *is* this guy?" she pleaded, struggling against him.

"Your biggest fan?" Costa wondered, before he snarled at the attendant to call for the police.

Of course he didn't carry a gun, Costa thought. Or even a radio. They were there for what was supposed to be a pleasant social event, and to watch lazily as someone unveiled a seven-hundred-year-old death mask. Not to encounter some crazed Carabiniere who rode like John Wayne, and seemed able to handle a weapon just as efficiently.

There was a fire exit sign on the far side. He found the light switches and turned the black interior of the cinema into a sea of yellow illumination. No more than seven kids sat in the tiny seats in front of him, each turning to blink at him resentfully.

"Go out the other side," Costa yelled at them.

No one moved.

"*Bambi*'s not finished," objected a small boy with a head of black choirboy hair. He could have been no more than five or six and didn't look as if anything would move him.

Maggie Flavier was strong. She fought as Costa dragged her over to the projection room, a place he'd visited once, when he was a child, in the company of his father. Then he kicked open the little wooden door, saw there was no one inside, and thrust her into the cubicle, ordering her to keep quiet, then shutting the door to keep her from view.

When he turned, he found daylight streaming

through the entrance again. The Carabiniere walked in, the black gun in his right hand, held at an angle, ready for use.

Costa stepped in front of him, blocking his way.

"There are children here, Officer," he said calmly. "What do you want?"

"I'm not an officer, you idiot," the man in the uniform said without emotion. "Where is she?"

"Put down the gun. Then we talk."

"I don't wanna talk."

His accent was odd. Roman, yet foreign, too, as if he came from somewhere else.

"Put down—"

The man moved swiftly, with an athlete's speed and determination. In an instant the Carabiniere had snatched the small complaining child from the nearest seat, wrapped his arm round the boy's chest, and thrust the weapon's blunt nose tight against his temple. The young eyes beneath the choirboy cut filled with tears and a fearful astonishment.

"Where is she?"

Costa thought he heard voices outside. The cinema attendant must have got someone's attention. What that meant when this lunatic had a child in his grip...

"Let go of the child—" he began.

"I'm here," Maggie Flavier said, opening the door of the projection room. "What do you want?"

She stood silhouetted in the cubicle entrance,

something trailing from her left hand, something Costa couldn't quite see.

The figure in the uniform twisted to look in her direction. He didn't relax his hold on the child for a moment.

"I want you," he replied, as if the question were idiotic. "Doesn't everyone? I want—"

Perhaps it was an actor's talent, but somehow Costa knew she was about to do something.

"To hell with everyone," Maggie Flavier declared, and tugged on whatever she held in her fingers.

It was film. Costa could hear noises coming from the projection room, frames of movie rattling, jamming, trapped and tangled inside the machine that gave them life. The showing of *Bambi* had somehow frozen on a single frame. She must have done that. She had to be in control.

Maggie Flavier yanked hard on the snaking trail of celluloid and something snapped, came free.

The Carabiniere stared at her, curious, angry, uncertain what to do next.

Bright, piercing white light, as brilliant as a painter's vision of Heaven, spilled into the room as the film fell free in the projector gate.

The boy in the uniformed man's arms squirmed and shrieked. The Carabiniere swore, a foul English curse, and tried to shield his eyes. Costa, careful to keep his eyes from the projector's beam, struck a heavy, hard blow into the man's stomach, unable, he knew, to reach the weapon, yet intent, still, on getting the child free. He punched again. There was a cry of pain and fury. His left hand closed on the child's back, his right struggled to pull the hostage free.

Then something else intervened. A large silver circular shape flashed across his vision and dashed against the Carabiniere's head. Maggie Flavier had a film can and she was using it, along with some pretty colorful language, too.

The weapon turned toward Costa's chest. The barrel barked, the black shape jumped in the man's hand.

The woman struck again, hard, with such force the firearm fell back, still in their attacker's grip. The boy wriggled free and fled the moment his small feet touched the floor. Costa closed in, seized the man's forearm, forced it back hard, sending the weapon upwards into one of the hot overhead lights in the low wooden ceiling.

There was another scream. Pain. Heat on skin. The handgun tumbled to the floor. The Carabiniere turned and stumbled out of Costa's grip, was free again, was scrabbling, half crouching, towards the gun, too close to it for anyone to intervene.

"Run!" Costa ordered, unable to understand why he was still standing, why he could feel no pain.

She didn't move.

"No. Are you hurt?"

"Run!"

"I don't need to. Can't you see?"

He could, and he didn't understand how he knew

she was correct, but she was. The individual in the Carabinieri uniform, now stained with dirt and dust from the floor of the Cinema dei Piccoli, wouldn't come back to them. It was written in his defeated, puzzled, enraged face. As if his part was over.

"Drop your weapon," Costa barked. *"Drop your weapon now."*

It was useless. The man retrieved the gun, then laughed and half fell, half ran out the door, out into a warm golden Roman evening.

Maggie Flavier started to follow. Costa put out a hand to prevent her.

"That was a mistake," he said.

He knew what happened when wild men flailed around with weapons in public, particularly in a protected, special place, full of officers determined to guard those in their care.

From beyond the door of the tiny wooden cinema came voices, loud and furious, shouts and cries, bellowed orders, all the words he dreaded to hear since he knew what they might mean, because he'd been through this kind of tense, standoff situation in training, and knew how easily it could go wrong.

"What's happening?" the American woman asked, and started to brush past him.

"No!" Costa commanded, with more certainty than he'd used in many a long month.

He stepped in front of her and stared into the woman's foreign yet familiar face.

"You never walk towards the line of fire," Costa

said, his finger in front of her face, like a teacher determined to deliver a lesson that had to be learned. *"Never…"*

He was shocked to see that, for the first time, there seemed to be a hint of real fear in her face, and to know that he was the cause, not the madman who had attacked them for no apparent reason.

Outside, the shouting ended and the staccato sound of gunfire began.

5

THEY HEARD IT FROM THE CASA DEL CINEMA. The volley of pistol shots sounded so loud and insistent it sent every grey, excitable pigeon in the park fleeing into the radiant evening sky.

"Nic's there somewhere," Peroni said instantly, alarmed.

Falcone's and Teresa's eyes were on the podium. Peroni couldn't believe their attention was anywhere but the source of that awful, familiar sound.

"It's the Carabinieri's job," Falcone answered. "Nic can take care of himself."

"To hell with the Carabinieri! I'm—"

Peroni fell silent. The dark blue uniforms of their

rivals seemed to be everywhere. Officers were shout-ing, yelling into radios, looking panicked.

On the podium Roberto Tonti, with a gaggle of puzzled, half-frightened politicians and minor actors around him, was droning on about the movie and its importance, about Dante and a poet's vision of Hell, all as if he'd never noticed a thing. The tall, stooped director looked every inch of his seventy years. His head of grey swept-back hair seemed the creation of a makeup department. His skin was bloodless and pale, his cheeks hollow, his entire demeanour gaunt. Peroni knew the rumours; that the man was desper-ately sick. Perhaps this explained Tonti's obsessive need to continue with the seemingly interminable speech as the commotion swirled around them.

"...for nine is the angelic number," Tonti droned on, echoing the words of the strange Carabiniere they'd met earlier. "This you shall see in the work, in its structure, in its division of the episodes of life. I give you..."

The movie director tugged on the braided rope by the side of the curtain. The velvet opened.

"...the creator. The source. The fountainhead."

The casket came into full view. Peroni blinked to make sure he wasn't dreaming. Someone in the crowd released a short, pained cry. The woman next to him, some half-familiar Roman model from the magazines, elegant in a silk gown and jewels, raised her gloved fingers to her lips, her mouth open, her eyes wide with shock.

The Carabinieri became frantic. They didn't know where to look—towards the children's cinema and the sound of shooting, or at the platform, where Tonti was now walking stiffly away from the thing he had revealed, an expression of utter distaste on his cold, sallow face, as if he resented the obvious fact that it had somehow stolen his thunder.

Falcone was pushing his way through the crowd, elbowing past black-suited men with pale faces and shrieking female guests.

Teresa, predictably, was right on his heels.

"Oh well," Peroni grumbled, and followed right behind, forcing his big, bulky body through the sea of silk and fine dark jackets, apologising as he went.

By the time he reached the small stage outside the entrance to the Casa del Cinema, the area around the exhibit case was empty save for Falcone and the pathologist who stood on either side of the cabinet staring at what lay within, bloody and shocking behind the smeared glass. Peroni felt somewhat proud of himself. There'd been a time when all this would have made him feel a little sick.

He studied the object. It appeared to be a severed head covered in some kind of thin blue plastic, which had been slashed to allow the eyes and mouth to be visible. The material enclosing most of what stood in place of Dante's death mask was pulled painfully tight—so much so that it was easy to see the features of the face that lay beneath. It was an image that had been everywhere in Rome for weeks, that of Allan

Prime. This was the face of the new Dante, visible on all the posters, all the promotional material that had appeared on walls and billboards, subway trains and buses. Now it had replaced the death mask of the poet himself. Sealed inside the case by reams of ugly black duct tape, it was some kind of cruel, ironic statement, Peroni guessed. Close up, it also looked not quite real—if the word could be applied to such a situation.

Two senior Carabinieri officers materialised at Falcone's side. He ignored them.

"This is ours," the older one declared. "We're responsible for the safety of the cast."

Falcone's grey eyebrows rose in surprise. He didn't say a thing.

"Don't get fresh with me," the officer went on, instantly irate. "You were supposed to be looking after the mask."

Peroni shrugged and observed, "One lost piece of clay. One dead famous actor. Do you want to swap?"

"It's *ours!*"

"What's yours?" Teresa asked. "A practical joke?"

Slyly, without any of the men noticing, she had stolen the short black truncheon from the junior Carabiniere's belt. She now held it in her right hand and was quietly aiming a blow at the blood-smeared glass.

"Touch the evidence and I will have your job," the senior Carabiniere said, more than a little fearful.

"And I'll have yours," Falcone added.

"This is evidence, gentlemen," Teresa replied. "But not of the kind you think." She looked at each of them and smiled. "We're in the movie business now, remember? Do the words 'special effects' mean anything at all?"

The short baton slammed into the top of the glass cabinet. Teresa raked it round and round. When she had enough room to manoeuvre, she reached in and, to the curses of both Falcone and his Carabinieri counterparts, carefully lifted out the head and held it in her hands, turning the thing round, making approving noises.

Teresa ran one large pale finger along the ragged line of blood and tissue at the base and then, to Peroni's horror, put the gory tip to her mouth and licked it.

"Food colouring," she said. "Fake blood. It's the wrong shade. Didn't you notice? Movie blood always is. Flesh and skin…it's all a joke." The tissue at the ragged torn neckline came away in her fingers: cotton wool stained a livid red, stuck weakly to the base of the head with glue.

Her fingers picked at the blue latex cladding around the base of the neck and revealed perfect skin beneath, the colour and complexion of that of a store window dummy. Peroni laughed. He'd known something was wrong.

"But why?" she asked, puzzled, talking entirely to herself.

She turned the head again in her hands, looked into

the bulbous eyes staring out of the slits made in the blue plastic. They were clearly artificial, not human at all. It was all legerdemain, and obvious once you learned how to look.

Then Teresa Lupo gazed more closely into the face and her dark, full eyebrows creased in bafflement. She pulled back the blue plastic around the lips to reveal a mouth set in an expression of pain and bewilderment. More plastic came away as she tore at the tight, enclosing film to show the face. There was a mask there. It had been crudely fastened to a store dummy's head to give it form. She removed sufficient film to allow her to lift the object beneath from the base. Then she held it up and rotated the thing in her fingers.

"Hair," she said, nodding at the underside. "Whiskers." Her fingers indicated a small stain on the interior, near the chin. "And that's real blood."

She glanced at Falcone. "This is from a man, Leo," Teresa Lupo insisted. "Allan Prime."

The inspector stood there, a finger to his lips, thinking. The Carabinieri couple said nothing. More of their officers were pushing back the crowd now. Peroni could hear the whine of an ambulance siren working its way to the park.

Teresa placed the mask on the podium table and rotated the pale dummy's head in her hands, ripping back the remaining covering.

"There's something else," she murmured.

The words emerged as she tore off the blue film.

They were written in a flowing, artistic script across the top of the skull. It reminded Peroni of the huckster's props they found when they raided fake clairvoyants taking the gullible to the cleaners. They had objects like this, with each portion of the head marked out for its metaphysical leanings. In this case the message covered everything, from ear to ear, as if there were only a single lesson to be absorbed.

"*'Lasciate ogne speranza, voi ch'intrate,'* " Teresa said, as if reciting from memory. "'Abandon all hope, you who enter here.'" She shook her head. "Damnation in the mind of a poet. That's what was written on the Gate of Hell when Dante entered."

A noise made Peroni glance back at the crowd. Costa was striding toward them, looking pale but determined, a gun hanging loose in his hand. By his side was the actress from the movie, her eyes downcast and glassy.

Costa nodded at the dummy's head in Teresa Lupo's hands, and asked, "What happened?"

The pathologist told him before Falcone could object.

"And you?" Falcone demanded.

Maggie Flavier was staring at the mask, shocked, silent, her cheeks smeared with smudged mascara.

Costa glanced at her before he answered. Then he said, "It seemed as if someone was trying to attack Miss Flavier. Then..."

The senior Carabinieri man found his voice.

"This is *our* case. *Our* evidence. I have made a

phone call to Maresciallo Quattrocchi, Falcone. He was called away briefly. Now he returns. You learn. This cannot—"

He fell abruptly silent as Costa lifted the handgun, pointed it at the fake head, and fired. The sound silenced them all. Maggie stifled a choking sob. There was nothing new there when the smoke and the racket had cleared. No damage. Not another fresh shard of shattered glass.

"Blanks," Costa told the man. "This was his gun. I took it from his corpse while your men danced around it like schoolgirls. They've just shot dead a defenceless man who was taking part in some kind of a sick prank. Why not go investigate *that*?"

"Th-this . . ." the officer stuttered.

"Enough," Falcone interjected, and glanced at Costa. "Assemble a team, *Soverintendente. Subito.*"

Teresa was already on the phone, and standing guard over the objects on the podium table.

"Where does Allan Prime live?" Falcone asked.

The officer said nothing.

"I know," Maggie Flavier said. "Do you think . . . ?" She didn't finish the sentence.

"You can tell us on the way," Falcone said, then called for a car.

PART 2

THEY SAT IN THE BACK OF THE LANCIA, WITH A plainclothes female driver at the wheel.

"Sir," Costa said, as they slowly negotiated the bickering snarl of vehicles arguing for space in the Piazza Venezia. "Miss Flavier . . . I don't understand why she should be here."

The woman by his side gave him a puzzled look but for once remained silent.

Falcone sighed, then turned round from the passenger seat and extended his long tanned hand. Maggie Flavier took it. She was more composed now and had wiped away the stray makeup from her face. She looked younger, more ordinary. Prettier, Costa realized.

"My name is Leo Falcone. I'm an inspector. His inspector."

"Nice to meet you. Why am I here?"

The inspector gave her his most gracious and charming of smiles. "For reasons that are both practical and political. You were the victim of some strange kind of attack. Perhaps a joke. But a very poor one, it seems to me. Allan Prime . . . Maybe it was a joke in his case, too. I don't know and I would like to. One man is dead. Prime is missing. The Carabinieri, meanwhile, are wandering around preening themselves while trying to work out which day it is. We have no need of further complications. Would you rather they were in charge of your safety? Or us? The choice is yours, naturally."

"My safety?"

"Just in case."

"What's going on here?" she demanded. "I was supposed to be at a movie premiere tonight. People shooting blanks. Fake death masks." Her bright, animated face fell. "Someone getting killed." She looked at Costa. "Why would they shoot him? The uniformed man on the horse?"

"Because they thought he was dangerous. They didn't know any better. Whoever he was..."

"Not Carabinieri, that's for sure," Falcone intervened.

"Whoever he was," Costa continued, "this is now a real case and it's not ours." He caught the dismay in the inspector's eye. "I'm sorry. That's a fact, sir. The Carabinieri were given the job of security tonight. Also, there's the question of jurisdiction. Allan Prime is an American citizen. If he's missing, someone has to inform the U.S. Embassy and allow them a role in the investigation. We all know the rules when a foreign citizen's involved. We can't just drive away with a key witness and hope it's all ours. I should never have left the scene in the first place, or taken that weapon."

The car came to a halt in the traffic in Vittorio

Emanuele. He didn't understand why they were taking this route. There were quicker ways through the tangle of alleys behind the Campo dei Fiori. A good police driver should have known about them.

The woman at the wheel turned and smiled at them. "The U.S. authorities are involved already," she said. "So don't worry about that. Captain Catherine Bianchi. San Francisco Police Department. Is there a better route than this? I don't drive much in Rome usually. I lack the balls."

She was about forty, slim, with a pleasant, bright face, Italian-looking, he would have said until he looked at her hair. That was straight and coal-coloured, with a henna sheen, tied back behind her head in a severe way that would have been rare on a Roman woman. She spoke good Italian, though with an American inflection. This was the woman he'd heard about, the one who'd caught Falcone's eye.

The inspector outlined a faster route to the Via Giulia, with a degree of patience he would never have used on one of his officers.

"Can I hit the siren?" Captain Catherine Bianchi asked.

"No," Falcone replied. "That will just give them warning."

"Give who warning?" Maggie Flavier asked.

"The Carabinieri, of course," he answered.

Costa looked out the window, at the swarming people and the tangled cars, the familiar crush of humanity in his native city.

He understood why Maggie Flavier was in the car. A man had died in the gardens of the Villa Borghese. Some strange, gruesome caricature of a human head had been substituted for the precious death mask of Dante which they were supposed to be guarding. A world-famous actor was missing, and his co-star had been the victim of an attack that seemed to be some kind of prank.

There were crimes here, perhaps serious, perhaps less so. Leo Falcone had clearly had no desire to try to go near the shooting. It would have been pointless. The man who attacked them had been killed by the Carabinieri. Only they could investigate themselves. What Falcone was quietly attempting to do was position himself to steal any broader case concerning the death mask and, more important, the fate of Allan Prime. The two principal national law-enforcement agencies in Italy usually managed to avoid turf wars over who handled what. In theory they were equals, one civilian, one military, both capable of handling serious crimes. Often the decision about which organisation handled a case came down to the simplest of questions: Who got there first?

"We will have to offer them a statement," Costa insisted. "Miss Flavier and I. We were witnesses."

"There's no hurry," the inspector observed. "Neither of you knows this man, do you? Nor did you see how he died. It's better that Miss Flavier remains in our company. For her own sake."

"Absolutely," the American policewoman insisted from the front seat. "No question about it."

Maggie Flavier leaned back in the deep leather of Falcone's Lancia, flung her arms behind her head, and sighed, "I love Italy."

She gazed at Costa, smiling wanly, resigned. He found himself briefly mesmerised by her actor's skill, the ability she possessed to turn her gaze upon someone, seize his attention, to look at him with her bright green eyes and hold his interest, make him wonder what came next. This was the way she stared into the camera lens. For reasons he couldn't quite pinpoint, he found that thought vaguely disturbing.

"Why's that?" he asked.

"Here I am being kidnapped by two charming Roman cops. And why? So you can steal some case you don't understand right from under the noses of the opposition."

At the wheel of the Lancia as they negotiated the narrow, choked lanes of the *centro storico,* Catherine Bianchi chuckled and said, "You got it."

Costa didn't laugh, however. Nor did Leo Falcone. The inspector was on his mobile phone, engaged in a long, low discussion he clearly didn't want anyone else to hear.

They rounded one more corner, past a house, Costa recalled, that was once supposed to have belonged to the mistress of a Borgia pope, Alexander VI. An image flashed through his head: Bartolomeo Veneziano's subtly erotic portrait of Alexander's bewitching daughter Lucrezia, ginger hair braided, a single breast bared, catching the artist's eye with an unsmiling sideways glance, just exactly as Maggie Flavier regarded Roberto Tonti's camera, and through it the prurient world at large. It was a strange memory, yet apposite. Lucrezia, like Beatrice, the character Maggie played in Tonti's movie, was an enigma, never quite fully understood.

The Lancia turned into the Via Giulia, one of the smartest streets in Rome, a place of palatial apartments and expensive antiques stores. A sea of blue state police cars stood motionless ahead of them. There were dark blue vans of the Carabinieri in among them. Traffic was backed up on the Lungotevere by the river which ran above the street. A battle was looming.

Maggie nodded at a house in the centre of the tangle of the vehicles. "It's that one there."

"You know it well?" Costa asked.

"Allan threw parties," she said with a shrug. "A lot." She looked at him, her smile gone. "Everyone likes a party from time to time, don't they?" She paused and looked, for a moment, very vulnerable.

"You don't want me to come in, do you?" she said, and the question was asked of Falcone.

The inspector seemed puzzled. "Would you rather stay here?"

"If that's OK." She put a hand to her close-cropped hair, tousled it nervously, the way a child did. "You'll think I'm crazy but I get a feeling for things sometimes. I've got one now. It's not good. Don't make me go in there. Not unless you know it's all right. I need the bathroom. I need a drink."

"Soverintendente Costa," Falcone ordered.

"Sir."

"Find two women officers who can take Miss Flavier to the wine bar round the corner. Then you come with me."

2

GIANNI PERONI HAD ENJOYED STANDOFFS WITH the Carabinieri before. Just never over a dummy's head with an apparently genuine death mask attached to it. He had four plainclothes state police officers with him to form a physical barrier between the evidence and the grumbling crowd of smart uniforms and surly faces getting angrier by the moment. The small police forensic crew had, meanwhile, gathered what passed for some of the strangest evidence Peroni had ever seen.

What really took his breath away were the movie people. Roberto Tonti, storming at anyone within earshot, grey hair flying as his gaunt frame hobbled around the stage. The producer Dino Bonetti, who'd pass for a mob boss any day, stabbing his finger at anyone who'd listen, demanding that the evening proceed. And, more subtly, some quiet American publicity man backing the two of them up during the rare moments either paused for breath. Even the Carabinieri balked at the idea everything could go off as planned. While the arguments ensued, Teresa and her small team worked quietly and swiftly, placing items very quickly into evidence bags and containers, trying to stay out of the melee. Peroni hadn't told her they didn't have long. He hadn't needed to.

"There's been a death," Peroni pointed out when Tonti began threatening to call some politicians he knew. "And..." He gestured at the bloodied fake head. "...this. The entertainment is over, sir. Surely you appreciate what I'm talking about?"

The publicist took him by the arm and requested a private word. Glad to have an excuse to escape the director's furious bellows, Peroni ordered the plain-clothesmen not to move an inch and went with the man to the back of the stage.

He had seen Simon Harvey on their visits to Cine-città to discuss arrangements for the exhibition. The American seemed professional, obsessed with the job as much as the rest of them, but, perhaps, with some rare degree of perspective. Peroni recalled that, on one occasion, the man had even given them a brief lecture on Dante and the origins of *Inferno*, as if somehow needing to justify the intellectual rationale behind the movie. He'd even declared, "This will be art, promise." This had struck him as odd and unnecessary at the time. But then the movie industry was rarely predictable, for ordinary human beings anyway. That day in the film studios he'd watched hideously disfigured ghouls sipping Coke, smoking cigarettes, and filling in crosswords during their time off camera. After that, he'd been glad to get out into the dull suburb surrounding the studio and breathe the fume-filled air.

"Listen," Harvey went on. "Forget about Roberto and Bonetti bawling you out. That's how they work. The point is this. There's big money at stake here. *Italian* money."

Peroni stared at the man, wondering what to make of this strange comment. "Italian money?" he asked. "What does that mean?"

Harvey cast a backwards glance to make sure no one was listening. "Do I need to spell it out?"

"For me you do."

The publicist placed a conspiratorial hand on Peroni's arm. "You're a cop," he said with a sigh. "Please don't act the innocent. And God knows it's been in the papers anyway. Bonetti has all kind of friends. Government friends." He winced. "Other . . . friends. There's more than a hundred and fifty million dollars running on this horse. Money like that creates debts that need paying. This is your country . . . not mine, Officer. We both know there are people neither of us want to piss off, not for a three-hour private screening in front of a handful of self-important jerks in evening dress, anyway. All I ask is you give us a break. Then we're done. It won't get in the way. I'll make sure. That's a promise."

Peroni couldn't believe what he was hearing. "Someone's been shot. They heard it. We all did. There's also the question of a death mask which, in case you've forgotten, is not only a national treasure. It also seems to resemble your missing movie star."

He pointed at the head, which was now on a plastic mat on the podium table, being prodded and poked by Teresa and her deputy, Silvio Di Capua. She caught Peroni's eye; he got the message instantly. It was time to get the evidence out of there as soon as possible, before the Carabinieri grabbed it. The dark blue uniforms seemed to be breeding around them, and some of them had fancy stripes and medals on their jackets that denoted the arrival of more-senior ranks.

"Ever heard the saying 'The show must go on'?" Harvey retorted.

"Don't tell me: it's what this missing star of yours would have wanted."

"Precisely. Imagine. All these people can go tell their friends tomorrow they still got to the premiere, even after all this mess. This is the world I live in, friend. It's about status and money and one-upmanship. *Inferno* is the biggest release of this summer, worldwide. They get to say they saw it first. We get to keep our backers happy. You escape the phone calls from on high. Please."

"This is a police investigation—"

"No, it's not," Harvey interrupted. "Let's speak frankly. I oversaw those security arrangements. By rights, this belongs to the Carabinieri. Not you. All you guys had to look after was the stuff."

"The stuff," Peroni repeated.

"No fun doing the menial work while others get to stand in the spotlight, is it?" The American smiled. "I forget your name, Officer."

"Gianni Peroni," he answered. "Like the beer."

Harvey stuck out his hand. Peroni took it.

"Simon Harvey. Like the sherry. Here's the deal. You let this little show go on tonight. I'll do what I can to ensure this investigation comes your way. The Carabinieri won't argue. Not until they've phoned home, and by then you and your friends will be away with the goods."

Peroni thought about this. Harvey had no idea how these matters worked. The probability was that the Carabinieri would get the investigation in any case, however hard Falcone tried to steal the job. The men from the military had been given cast and crew security from the beginning. Murder or no murder, this was their call.

"Why would you want to give me a deal like that?"

The American nodded in the direction of the dark blue uniforms. "Because I've had a bellyful of those stuck-up bastards for the past few months and they won't cut me a deal on anything. Is that good enough?"

Peroni discreetly eyed the opposition. Some boss

figure had emerged and was now bravely taking on the police forensic team, not even blinking at Teresa's increasingly desperate attempts to shout him down. There was strength in numbers, particularly when it came backed up by medals and rank. It was definitely time to leave.

"You must have seen that film a million times," Peroni observed.

"A million times is not enough," Harvey replied. "Roberto Tonti's a genius. I'd watch it a million times more if I could. *Inferno* is the finest piece of cinema I've ever worked on. I doubt I'll ever have the privilege to get my name attached to anything better. What's your point?"

"My point, Signor Harvey, is I'm willing to let you have your little show. Provided you can help us get out of here the moment my colleagues are ready."

"It's done," Harvey said immediately. "You have my word."

"And I want someone to come along with us. Someone from the studio. Bonetti, Tonti . . ."

The man waved his hand in front of Peroni's face. "Don't even think about it. They don't *do* menial."

"In that case, you. Seen inside many police stations?"

Harvey's pleasant demeanour failed him for a moment. "Can't say I have. Is this relevant?"

"Not at all."

"Then what am I supposed to talk about? Dante? I've got a degree in classics." Harvey caught Peroni's

eye and nodded at the fake severed head. "That...
thing. It's about Dante, you know. The line they
wrote on the skull...'Abandon all hope, you who
enter here.'"

Teresa had what she wanted. He could see the
boxes and bags ready to go. The pathologist took a
break from bawling out an entire line of Carabinieri
officers to issue a sly nod in his direction.

Harvey wriggled, a little nervous. "You know something, Officer Peroni? We've been getting strange
anonymous e-mails. For months. It happens a lot
when you're making a movie. I never thought too
much about it."

"Strange?"

"They quoted that line, always. And they said..."
Harvey tugged at his long hair. "...they said we were
living in limbo. I never took it literally."

"What do you mean?"

The American grimaced. "I mean *literally*. The way
it appears in Dante." He sighed. "Limbo is the first
circle of Hell. The place the story begins."

Just the mention of the film revived some memories Gianni Peroni hoped had been lost. Things
seemed to be happening from the very opening
moment in Tonti's version of the tale. Not good
things either.

"And then?" Peroni asked. "After limbo?"

"Then you're on the road to Hell."

3

THE DOOR TO ALLAN PRIME'S APARTMENT opened almost the moment Falcone pushed the bell. Nic Costa felt as if he'd stumbled back through time. The woman who stood there might have been an actress herself. Adele Neri still looked several years short of forty and was as slender and cat-like as he recalled. She wore designer jeans and a skimpy white T-shirt. Her arresting face bore the cold, disengaged scowl of the Roman rich. She had a tan that spoke of a second home in Sicily and a heavy gold necklace around a slender neck that carried a few wrinkles he didn't recall from the case a few years before, when she had first come to the notice of the Questura. That had taken them to the Via Giulia, too, to a house not more than a dozen doors away, one that had been booby-trapped with a bomb by her mob boss husband, Emilio, as he tried to flee Rome. Adele Neri was an interesting woman who had led an interesting life.

"I thought I was past getting visits from the likes of you people," she said, holding the door half open. "Do you have a warrant? Or some reason why I should let you into my home?"

"We were looking for Allan Prime," Costa replied. "We thought he lived here."

"He does. When he's around. But this is my house. All of it. Several more in the Via Giulia, too. Do you mean you didn't know?"

She gazed at Falcone, thin arms crossed, smiling. Costa recalled seeing the intelligence reports after Emilio's death. They said that Adele had taken over leadership of her husband's local clan for a while before selling on her interests to a larger, more serious mob and, if rumour was correct, removing herself from the murky world of Roman crime to enjoy her vast, illicitly inherited wealth.

"Inspector Falcone. The clever one."

"Signora Neri," Falcone said pleasantly, nodding. "What an unexpected delight."

"Quite. So tell me. Why didn't you try to put me in jail? After Emilio got shot?"

"Because I didn't think it would stick," Falcone replied, looking puzzled. "Isn't that obvious? I'm a practical man. I don't fight lost causes over trivia." He got one foot over the threshold and tried to look around. "This is nothing to do with you. We merely wish to locate a lost Hollywood actor."

"Join the club," she sighed, then stepped back. "I'll let five of you in here and they'd best have no dirt on their shoes. This place rents for eight thousand dollars a week. For that, people don't expect muddy cop prints on the carpet."

Costa issued some orders to the officers left

outside, then began to prowl the vast, airy apartment. There was a spectacular view of the river and the busy Lungotevere through long windows, with a vista of the dome of St. Peter's in the distance, and by the external terrace a circular iron staircase to what he took to be a roof garden. To their left stood a large open kitchen with the kind of fittings only the rich could think about.

He sat down on a vast leather sofa. Falcone joined him and they waited. She wanted to make an entrance, a point. Adele Neri slipped briefly into the kitchen and came out with a glass of blood-orange juice, a *spremuta* freshly pressed, probably from one of the stalls in the Campo dei Fiori. The drink was almost the colour of her hair, which was now longer than he recalled, clipped bluntly against her swanlike neck. Emilio Neri had been one of the most important mob bosses in Rome until his past caught up with him. Adele, more than thirty years his junior, with a history in vice herself, had been complicit in his downfall, though how much of that was greed and how much hatred for her husband they had never been able to decide. The gang lord was dead, his empire shattered, soon to be disposed of by his guilty widow. One crime clan left the scene, another took its place. Life went on, as it always would. He'd felt happy about Neri's fate at the time. A man had died at Costa's hand in pursuit of the answers Adele Neri had held in her smart, beautiful head all along.

He had never quite shaken off a misplaced sense of guilt over that particular outcome.

"Where's Allan Prime?" Falcone asked.

"You tell me. I was supposed to have lunch with him today, at noon. I came over, rang the bell. No one answered, so I let myself in. Then some people phoned from the studio. They said he hadn't turned up for the premiere either." She took an elegant, studied sip of the scarlet drink. "This is my place. I can do what I damned well like."

"You and Mr. Prime..." Costa asked.

"Landlady and tenant. Nothing more. He tried, naturally. He's the kind who does that anyway, just to see who'll rise to the bait. It's a form of insecurity, and insecure men have never interested me."

"You have no idea where he might be?"

She made a gesture of ignorance with her skinny, tanned arms. "Why should I? He pays the rent. I indulge him with lunch from time to time. It's a kindness. He's like most actors. A lot less interesting than he thinks. A lot less intelligent too. But..." She gazed at them, thinking. "This isn't like him. He's a professional. He told me he was going to that premiere tonight. He moaned about it, naturally. Having to perform for free." The woman laughed. "Allan's an *artist*, of course. Or so he'd like to pretend. All that razzmatazz is supposed to be beneath him."

"Girlfriends—" Falcone began.

"Don't know, don't care," Adele interrupted. "He had women here. What do you expect? He had a few parties early on, and I had to get someone to speak to him about that. There are some nice old people living in the other apartments. They don't like movie types wandering around with white powder dripping from their noses. It's not that kind of neighbourhood. Also…"

She stopped. There was something on her mind, and she was unsure whether to share it with the police, Costa thought.

"Also what?" he asked.

"Why should I tell you people anything? What do I get in return?"

The inspector frowned. "Some help in finding your tenant, perhaps. Does he owe you money?"

"Three months outstanding. Show business people never pay on time. They think we should be grateful they're here at all. That we should put up a plaque on the wall when they're gone."

"Twenty-four thousand dollars," Falcone observed. "A lot of money."

"Don't insult me. I spend more than that in one day when I go to Milan. I'll tell you one thing, though. For free. Prime and his cronies had interesting friends. I came to one of his parties. Him and that evil bastard Bonetti. The company they kept." She smiled. "It was like the old days. When my husband was alive. The same dark suits. The same accents bred in cow shit. A bunch of surly sons of bitches from the south who think they own you. That kind never changes. They just put their money in different places. Legitimate places. And movies, too, not that they're the same thing."

"You seem to know about the movie business."

"I've made my contribution. Shits like Bonetti know how to screw you. 'It's only a million. Think of the tax write-off. If the worst comes to the worst, you get your money back anyway.' Then . . ." She clapped her skeletal hands. The loud noise rang round the room like a gunshot. "It's gone, and Bonetti or one of his creatures is phoning from L.A., full of apologies, promising that maybe a little of it will come back one day. After everyone else has taken their cut." Adele Neri leaned forward and her sharp eyes held them. "Allan moves in dangerous circles and he doesn't even know it. I told him, but he isn't the kind of man who listens to anyone else. A woman least of all. That's the truth. You don't honestly think I'd be sitting here waiting for the doorbell to ring if I'd done something, do you?"

"Do you read Dante, Signora Neri?" Falcone asked.

The unexpected question amused her. Adele Neri looked human, warm and attractive and perhaps even a pleasure to know at that moment.

"Dante?" she asked, amazed. "I'll go see the movie sometime. Preferably when Allan gets me some free tickets. But reading?" She finished what remained of the *spremuta*. "I'm the merry widow now, Falcone. I shop, I spend, I travel, and when I feel like it, when I see something that interests me, I take a little pleasure. Life's too enjoyable for books. Why leave this world for someone else's? Reading..." She leaned back and closed her eyes. "...is for people without lives. No. I know no more of Dante than you."

"Actually, I know quite a lot," Falcone replied almost apologetically. "Not that it matters."

"It doesn't?" she asked. "Why?"

"Because I find it hard to believe that anyone would commit much of a crime over poetry. However much they might wish us to think otherwise."

"You really think something's happened to Allan?"

"He's missing. We have some very strange evidence. One man is dead. Perhaps there's no connection. Perhaps..."

She cut the air with her hand and said, "This does not involve me. If you want to talk any more, we need to do this with a lawyer around."

Taccone, the old soverintendente Falcone liked to use, had returned from looking around the apartment and stood waiting for the inspector to fall silent.

"You need to see this," he told them.

The two men got up and followed him into what appeared to be the master bedroom. Adele Neri came in behind them. Somewhere along the way she'd picked up a packet of cigarettes and was quickly lighting one.

"What is it?" Falcone asked Taccone.

Costa walked forward to stand a short distance from the bed. He looked at Adele Neri and asked, "Didn't you come in here?"

"Why would I want to sneak around his bedroom?"

"Call in forensic," Falcone ordered. "Let's not touch anything. Did you find any signs of violence?"

Taccone shook his head. "We didn't find anything. Except this."

The bed was covered with a green plastic ground sheet of the kind used by campers. The shape of a man's body was still visible on it, set deep enough to imprint itself on the mattress below. Around the outline of the upper torso there was a faint sprinkling of pale grey powder which grew heavier around the head.

Taccone reached down and, using a handkerchief, picked up the handle of a brown bucket that had been hidden on the far side of the bed.

"It looks like clay or something," he said.

Costa's phone was ringing. The doorman who had been on duty that morning had gone home at lunchtime. It had taken a while to trace him. Costa listened to what the officer who'd finally found the man, in a Campo dei Fiori café, had to say. Then he asked to be passed to the *agente* who had handled the second inquiry.

"Seal off this room," Falcone ordered. "Assume we have a murder scene."

"We don't," Costa said simply. "There's no CCTV in this building, but we've found one of the staff who was on duty. There are details in the visitors' book."

He looked at Adele Neri and asked, "Is the name Carlotta Valdes familiar?"

She drew on the cigarette and shook her head. "No. Spanish?"

"A woman calling herself that arrived to see Allan Prime at eight-thirty this morning. They left together around ten. Mr. Prime looked very happy, apparently. Expectant even."

Falcone shook his head in bafflement, lost for words for a moment, as if the investigation were slipping away from them before it had even begun.

"A man *is* dead," Costa reminded him.

"His death is the Carabinieri's problem, as you have made very clear."

"Also..."

"Also the death mask we were supposed to protect is missing," Falcone went on. "I am aware of that. It may be all we have. A case of art theft."

Costa struggled to see some sense in the situation. It was impossible to guess precisely what kind of case they had on their hands. The loss of a precious historic object? Or something altogether darker and more personal?

"The man who was killed in the park," he persisted, regardless of Falcone's growing exasperation. "He's been identified. We were told by the Carabinieri as a matter of course, at the same time they put in a formal request for an interview. I need to report to them with Signora Flavier."

"Well?" Falcone asked.

"His name was Peter Jamieson. He was an actor, originally from Los Angeles. The man moved to Rome a decade ago, principally playing bit parts, Americans for cheap TV productions at Cinecittà."

"Tell me. Did he have a part in *Inferno*?" Falcone looked ready to explode.

"Nonspeaking. Barely visible. There's no reason why anyone from the cast should have recognised him at all."

The inspector pointed a bony finger in Costa's face, as if he'd found the guilty party already.

"If this is some kind of publicity stunt gone wrong, I will put every last one of those painted puppets in jail."

"If…" Costa repeated, and found himself staring again at the powder on the bed, and the silhouette of Allan Prime's head outlined there.

4

MARESCIALLO GIANLUCA QUATTROCCHI WAS furious on several fronts. The screening had begun without his permission. Key pieces of evidence had been removed from the scene by the morgue monkeys of the state police, under the supervision of Teresa Lupo, a woman Quattrocchi had encountered, and been bested by, in the past, on more than one occasion. And now Leo Falcone had placed a team in Allan Prime's home without consulting the Carabinieri, though the state police inspector knew full well that security for the film cast was not his responsibility and never would be.

As a result Quattrocchi's bull-like face appeared even more vexed than normal, and he found himself sweating profusely inside the fine wool uniform he had chosen for an occasion that was meant to be social and ceremonial, not business. He stood at the back of the projection room, temporarily speechless with fury, not least because his principal contact within the crew, the publicist Simon Harvey, appeared to have been spirited away by Falcone's people, too. All he got in his place was the smug, beaming Dino Bonetti, a loathsome creature of dubious morality, and two young ponytailed Americans with, it seemed to him, a hazy grasp of the seriousness of the situation.

While everyone else wore evening dress, the two young men had removed their jackets to reveal T-shirts bearing the name *Lukatmi*, with a logo showing some kind of oriental goddess, a buxom figure with skimpy clothing, a beguiling smile, and multiple arms, each holding a variety of different cameras—movie, still, phones, little webcams of the kind the Garabinieri used for CCTV—all linked into one end of a snaking cable pumping out a profusion of images into a starry sky.

Quattrocchi peered more closely. There were faces within the stars, a galaxy of Hollywood notables— Monroe, Gable, Hepburn, James Stewart, their heads floating in the ether.

"Note," the skinny one identified by his shirt as *Josh Jonah, Founder, Ideologist, Visioneer,* ordered, "the absence of noise."

"I can hear *you,*" Quattrocchi snapped, to no avail.

"If we were in an ordinary projectionist's room," Jonah continued, "we wouldn't be able to have this conversation. There would be film rattling through the projector. Physical artefacts. Needless expense. Time and money thrown away without reason."

"I am an officer of the Carabinieri. Not an accountant."

"We're all accountants in the end." It was the other American, a big muscular man with a boyish face and a ponytail of long wavy dark hair. Quattrocchi peered at his T-shirt. It read, *Tom Black, Founder, Architect, Corporate Conscience.* Black seemed younger than his partner. A little less sure of himself, too. "In the sense that we pay for things. You'd like to get movies quicker, cheaper, easier, wouldn't you?"

"Right now," Quattrocchi blurted out so loudly that he felt sure his voice had carried into the cinema beyond, with its audience of VIPs, "I would like to know where Allan Prime is, why we have a dead actor in the park out there, and what the hell is going on around here." He glowered at their shirts. "Who is Lukatmi anyway? Some Indian god? And who the hell are you?"

The two men looked at each other and Tom Black smiled.

"That was kind of the positioning we were looking for. Three million dollars got blown there. Worth every penny," he said.

"We're backers," the skinny one boasted. "We've got money in this thing. Without us, this movie would never have got made."

"What—" Quattrocchi began to say.

"Lukatmi's got nothing to do with India," the quieter American interrupted. "Lukatmi. 'Look at me.' It's a philosophical statement about not hiding away, about being a part of the digital lifestream, a star in your own right, out there for everyone to see."

"Like YouTube," Bonetti added, and Josh Jonah howled, "No, no, no, no, *no*! How many freaking times do I have to say this? YouTube is *yesterday*…"

"When Google bought them…" Tom Black shook his head. His broad, young face was so sorrowful it looked as if someone had died. "…it was all over. They don't understand the whole mash-up thing. The behemoth days are past."

"Lukatmi is just the medium, not the message," Jonah added, taking over, clearly the boss. "Except for the paid-for content, we don't own a damned thing. It's not for us to dictate to human beings what they create or what they see. If you have a problem with that, don't watch."

Quattrocchi suddenly realised he'd read about these people in the newspapers. They'd found some loophole that allowed them to be absolved of any legal responsibility for what was, on the surface, carried by their network. They were, if he understood this correctly, like a dating agency. Their computers put someone wanting something in touch with someone offering it. The relationship was consummated in a way that had, so far, allowed them to escape the attentions of the law, on the simple grounds that they never published anything directly themselves. If the material that people found on Lukatmi turned out to be copyrighted, blasphemous, or, with very few restrictions, pornographic, they weren't to blame. It was anarchy with a listing on NASDAQ. Millions and millions of people had flocked to their site since it had gone live less than a year before. The two founders had become paper billionaires as staid investment houses and international banks poured vast sums of money into a company that seemed to be little more than two geeks with a big and possibly dubious idea.

One thing still puzzled him. "What on earth has all this got to do with the movie business?"

"Everything," said Bonetti. "This is a revolution. Like when silent movies got sound, when black-and-white turned to colour. It means we can finally reach people direct, any way we want, without getting screwed by the distributors or anyone else." He cast a sour glance at the Americans. They saw it, as the Italian producer intended. "Except them."

Quattrocchi massaged his temples. There was a persistent, low ache there and had been ever since the shooting. An internal investigation team was now overseeing that, following the procedures after the deaths of civilians at the hands of a Carabinieri team. He wasn't looking forward to having to face the investigators. He'd been absent from the Casa del Cinema when the killing took place on highly spurious grounds, a call of a personal nature. That was one more secret to keep under wraps.

"Who'd want to watch a movie on a phone?" he demanded, unable to take his eyes off the screen beyond the room. It seemed to be on fire. The flames of Hell licked everywhere, and through them burst the faces of grinning, leering demons, their green and purple mouths babbling profanities and obscenities at the stricken, cowering figure of Dante, who shrank back at the horrific sight, the beautiful Beatrice at his side.

"Millions of suckers everywhere," Bonetti crowed. "A dollar a clip. A monthly subscription for twenty. And then they go to see it in the theatre anyway. And buy the DVD. Then the director's edition. Then the collector's…" The Italian producer's fleshy face beamed. "It's a dream. You sell the same old junk over and over again."

"With absolute efficiency," the skinny one, Josh

Jonah, emphasised. "Not a wasted piece of celluloid. Not a single cassette or DVD in inventory. And this"—he patted the silver box streaming light into the theatre beyond—"is ours. Every last piece gets streamed straight here for less money than it costs to produce a single cinema print. The crap the masses turn out gets fed from PC to PC for free. The people that junk brings in become the movie audience of the future, and we serve them direct, same price they'd pay in a theatre, but at a fraction of the delivery cost." He clicked his fingers. "Voilà. Big money."

"Big money," Bonetti insisted.

Quattrocchi shook his head and grumbled, "So much for art. Also..."

This had bothered him all along. The picture on the screen didn't look right. It wasn't as sharp, as detailed, as engaging, as he'd expect of a movie like this. It felt wrong, however smart the toys these kids used to fool Bonetti and anyone else throwing their hats into this particular ring.

He stopped, unable to believe what he was seeing.

"What on earth is that?"

The scene was dissolving in front of their eyes. The flames faded. The faces of the demons, Dante shrinking in terror before them, now gave way to something else. Quattrocchi had seen Roberto Tonti's movie that afternoon, at the private screening. He knew for sure that what was now emerging on the screen in front of a selected audience of some two hundred international VIPs, politicians, and hangers-on had never been there before.

It was Dante again, still terrified, his face frozen in dread. Or rather, it was Allan Prime. In close-up, grainy, as if from some CCTV camera.

An open-faced black metal mask, ancient, medieval looking, enclosed his head, one band gripping his mouth. Behind its bars, the man's horrified features seemed exaggerated. His eyes were locked and rigid with terror.

There was utter silence in the projection room and in the theatre beyond. Then, nervously, someone in the crowd laughed, and another coughed. A voice rose. Quattrocchi recognised it: the furious, coarse bark of Roberto Tonti complaining about something yet again.

Josh Jonah wiped his skeletal forearm over his eyes. "Was this an outtake or something?" he asked no one in particular. "I don't recall seeing it. Tom. *Tom?*"

The other American was staring at his silver machine, punching keys, watching numbers fly up on the monitor.

"This isn't coming from us." Sweat was starting to make dark, damp stains across his burly chest. He looked almost as frightened as Allan Prime. Or Dante. Whichever, Quattrocchi thought. "I don't know where it's coming from."

"Cut it," Jonah ordered. "Stop the frigging thing. If someone else has got hold of the stream..."

"Sure . . ."

"No," Quattrocchi ordered, and found he had to drag the American away from his strange projector.

They both stared at him. Bonetti, too, though there was no expression Quattrocchi could read on the producer's dark, lined face.

"This isn't part of the show," Josh Jonah stated firmly. "It's not supposed to be up there."

"Yes, it is. Your star's missing. Someone has taken control of your toy. What if they're trying to tell us where he is? Or why? Or . . ."

He was about to say *Or both*.

But the words never reached his lips. Two things had happened on the screen. In the right-hand corner a digital stopwatch appeared, counting down from the hour. *59:59, 59:58, 59:57 . . .*

As it ticked away, an object entered from centre left, first in a sudden movement that darted in so quickly he was unable to see what had happened, only the result, that it had inflicted yet more pain and fright on the trapped man struggling on the screen in front of them, and that blood was now welling from some fresh wound that had appeared on Allan Prime's left temple.

The image vanished. After a long break the picture resumed. A narrow, deadly spear, the shaft as shiny as a mirror save for the bloodied tip which had just stabbed the trapped man's face, had slowly emerged, sharp and threatening, aimed directly at Prime's temple.

The stopwatch flicked over from 58:00 to 57:59. The spear moved on a notch towards Allan Prime's head, as if attached to some machine that would edge it forward, minute by minute, until it drove into the actor's skull.

Quattrocchi stared at this gigantic, real-life depiction of a captive man waiting to die. There were hints to be found in this sight, surely. Clues, keys to unlock the conundrum. Otherwise why broadcast it at all? Simply to be cruel? Behind the head, he could just make out some shapes in the darkness, paintings perhaps, images, ones that might have been familiar had he possessed some way to illuminate the scene.

Beyond the projection room, out in the cinema, Tonti ceased roaring. Someone moaned. Another voice cried out in outrage. A woman screamed.

Bonetti threw open the door and bellowed at an attendant, "Clear the room, man! Everyone!"

Then he returned and stared at Quattrocchi, shocked, finally, babbling, "Find him, for God's sake. *Find him!*"

"But where?" Quattrocchi asked, to himself mostly, as he held down the shortcut key for headquarters on his phone, praying that there was someone there who was good at riddles.

He got through. The wrong man answered. Morello. A good officer. Not a bright man. Not the one

Quattrocchi hoped for, and there was no time to locate others. He had to work with what he had.

"Are we listening to our friends?" Quattrocchi asked.

There was silence on the line. The Carabinieri weren't supposed to eavesdrop on the police. And vice versa. But it happened. In both directions.

"We can be. Are we listening for anything in particular?"

"I would like to be informed of any mention of the actor Allan Prime, from any source whatsoever."

"Of course."

"Good," Quattrocchi said, then got himself put through to forensic.

While waiting he caught the attention of Tom Black. The young American stood back from his silver machine, staring at the flashing monitor with concern.

"I need my scientific officers to see what's happening," Quattrocchi told him.

The American winced, as if afflicted by a momentary pain. "Tell them to find a computer and tune in to Lukatmi," he answered glumly. "These bastards are putting it out to the public, too. Through us. We can stop them, but the only quick way would mean we lose the stream here, too..."

"Touch nothing!" Quattrocchi roared. He pointed through into the cinema, where Prime was screaming on the screen again. The small, deadly spear had moved closer to its destination. "If we lose that, we lose him."

Josh Jonah walked up to the machine and peered calmly at the monitor. "I can read off the URL," he said. "Are you ready?"

5

ONE KILOMETRE AWAY, IN THE FORENSIC LAB OF the *centro storico* Questura, the same word was puzzling another law enforcement officer, though one from a very different agency.

"Url? What's a URL?" Peroni asked.

He thought they were in Teresa Lupo's morgue to stare at the head of a store window dummy and the curious death mask that had been attached to it. And to talk to Simon Harvey. At the age of fifty-one, with an understanding of the cinema industry which extended to no more than a few security duties at the Cinecittà studios over the years, Peroni felt it was time to become better acquainted with the working methods and mores of the movie business, such as they were. He had an inexplicable feeling they might come in useful, and that Simon Harvey was a man who could impart much worthwhile information on the subject if he felt so minded.

No one answered his question. Harvey and Silvio Di Capua had exchanged a brief conversation, and the whole game plan seemed to disappear in smoke. While Teresa and her two young white-coated trainee assistants played halfheartedly with the head and mask—finding no new information—Di Capua and Harvey had gone over to the nearest computer and started hammering the keys, staring at the gigantic monitor as it flipped through image after image.

"Will someone please tell me what a URL is?" Peroni asked again.

"Universal resource locator," Di Capua grumbled. "What I'm typing. Any the wiser?"

"No. Enlighten me. How is this helping exactly?"

"Gianni," Teresa said. "If I'd been allowed to set up some kind of a crime scene on that stage . . . If we were in control in any shape or form . . ." She opened her hands in a gesture of despair. "We have nothing to work with. Nowhere to begin. If staring at a computer helps, I'm all for it. What else is there?"

"This is my fault," Harvey apologised. "I didn't mean to start an argument. It was only a suggestion."

The suggestion being, Teresa explained patiently, that they use the strange, unexplained Internet service owned by two American geeks who'd helped finance *Inferno* to try to find out what people at large were saying about Allan Prime.

"Think of it this way," Harvey went on. "Would you like to be able to tune in to every TV newscast around the world that was covering Allan right now? Every little net TV channel, every vidcast, too?"

Peroni shook his big, grizzled head. "Every what?"

"If it gave us a clue…" Di Capua said. "I'd take anything. This thing…" He blinked, incredulous at the flashing series of moving pictures on the monitor. "…is unbelievable. I never realised…"

"They bring stuff online before announcing it," Harvey said. "It's all part of the hype. You never know what they'll turn up with next. You just have to tune in to check."

Teresa had her head bent towards the screen. Peroni felt like an unwanted intruder from a different century.

"How the hell do they do it?" Di Capua asked, still in a state of awe.

Harvey sighed. "I don't really understand it myself. From what they said, it's a mixture of reading keywords, transcribing speech, recognising faces…All the TV stations are now online and streaming. Add to that new video material. Blogs. Small web stations. I guess they have some way of consuming it all as it appears, reading it, then serving everything up. Google for video and audio, only ten times bigger, ten times faster, and deadly accurate. That's why they're worth a billion or so each."

Peroni cleared his throat. "This is *so* interesting. Is anyone going to find something for me to look at?"

Teresa stepped back and gestured at the screen. "Take your pick."

What enthusiasm he had left swiftly dissipated. The monitor was crammed with moving pictures the size of postage stamps, each with odd graphs and a geographical location.

"Allan Prime's a star," Di Capua observed. "When someone like him disappears, it's a big story."

Peroni leaned forward and found himself wishing he could rewind the clock to enter a simpler, more straightforward universe. Each postage-stamp video represented a TV channel, usually news, seemingly issuing some kind of bulletin about the Prime story. The BBC in London. CBS in New York. A channel in Russia. Somewhere in Japan, Australia, the Philippines... "This can't all be live..."

Harvey nodded. "Pretty much. With Lukatmi, if it's going out real time, it's being relayed by them that way. With maybe a few seconds' delay, that's all."

Peroni felt he could soon start to lose his temper. "This is of no use to me whatsoever. How many channels are there, for pity's sake?"

Di Capua hammered some keys and said, "More than four hundred sources have run a story on Prime in the last hour."

Peroni watched as the monitor cleared again, then very slowly came back to life, painting a set of new tiny videos on the screen at a snail's pace.

When the images returned, they were all the ones Peroni expected. Local and national news channels, familiar presenters reading from their scripts, all with images of the missing actor and shots from the park and the production of *Inferno*. A counter by the side of the screen was some kind of popularity meter. The audience seemed to be running at seven figures and rising, most of them for a single video channel, one that was blacked out at that moment.

"Why can't we watch the one that's top of the list?"

"It won't load for some reason," Di Capua said, trying something with the keyboard. "Too many people watching it, I imagine. Or maybe their fancy computer system can't cope."

"I want to see it..." Peroni began, and then fell quiet. Teresa's deputy had made the black window occupy the full screen of the path lab monitor. As he watched, the empty space filled, line by line, with a real moving image.

They all crowded round to see. It was a man in fear for his life, trapped inside some cruel and ancient cast-iron head restraint. The digital stopwatch imprinted by his neckline turned from *28:31* to *28:30*, and the seconds kept on ticking. Allan Prime's eyes were as large as any man's Peroni had ever seen. He looked ready to die of fright even before the bright, shining spear with the blood-soaked tip reached his head, which surely would happen soon. Within less than thirty minutes or so, this strangely hypnotic little movie, the most personal Prime had ever made surely, seemed to be saying.

Teresa leaned over Di Capua and said, "Get me more detail."

Harvey's eyes were glazed, filling with tears. Peroni

looked at him and said, "You don't have to watch this. Why not go and sit somewhere else? I'll come for you when there's news."

"I've got to watch it," the movie man croaked, then dragged up a chair.

There was no caption. Only the image of the terrified actor, the time ticking away, and, by the side of the video, the digital thermometer that was the popularity counter. It was now flashing red. Peroni stared at it. Allan Prime's dying moments seemed to be the most sought-after thing in the world at that instant. A real-life drama being watched by a global audience that was growing into the tens of millions and swelling by the second.

He pressed a finger against the screen and indicated the area behind Prime's quaking head. "There's something there, Silvio. Can you bring it up?"

The pathologist's hands raced across the keyboard. Prime's features began to bleach out. From the dark background it was now possible to make out some kind of shape. Di Capua tweaked the machine. It was a painting, strange and old and, Peroni thought, possibly familiar.

"Get that to the art people straightaway," he ordered.

Teresa was staring at him. He knew what she was thinking.

"Has Nic got one of those new video phones?" he asked.

"You all have them," she said, and folded her arms. "Even you if you bothered to look."

"I deal in people, not gadgets," Peroni replied, then called Costa on the fancy new handset the department had issued to everyone only a few months earlier.

"Silvio," he said, listening to the ring tone.

"Yeah?" the young pathologist answered absent-mindedly, still punching away at the keyboard, trying to improve any recognisable detail in the swimming sea of pixelated murk that now filled the screen.

"Best give me the URL, please."

6

THEY WENT BACK TO THE LANCIA IN THE VIA Giulia. The forensic team would go through the clay dust and any other evidence they might find in the apartment Adele Neri had rented Allan Prime. It felt better to be outside. Something about the information they had gleaned from Neri's widow depressed Costa. The movie world was not all glitter. Allan Prime, along with the producer Dino Bonetti, kept the company of mobsters and thieves. Costa wondered why he was surprised. There had been plenty of scandals in Italian show business over the years. It shouldn't have come as a shock to discover they spilled over into something as important and lucrative as the comeback blockbuster for one of the country's most reclusive directors.

Maggie Flavier came and stood next to him by the wall beneath the Lungotevere. The traffic made a dull, physical sound through the stone that separated them from the busy road and the river beyond. She was smoking and had the sweet smell of Campari on her breath, a lightness that might have been the onset of drink in her eyes.

She smiled at him and said, "We all lead different lives. What's yours?"

"Being a police officer. It's enough."

She drew hard on the cigarette, then tossed it to the ground and stamped out the embers with her shiny, expensive-looking evening shoe.

"In my line of work you become more conscious of words," she said quietly. "You used the past tense when you talked about your wife..."

He nodded. He liked her directness. Perhaps it was an actor's trick. Perhaps not.

"She died six months ago." He thought of the mausoleum of Augustus, less than ten minutes away on foot, and the terrible events of the previous December.

"I'm sorry. Was it unexpected?"

"You could say that."

She breathed in deeply, quickly. "I don't know what to say. I felt something, that's all."

"'Sorry' is just fine." There isn't a lot else, he

thought. People died all the time. Those who survived got on with their lives.

She turned to look at the building housing Prime's apartment, now surrounded by blue police cars, with only a handful of Carabinieri vehicles in the street.

"Do you know where Allan is yet? Is he OK?" she asked.

"He was fine when he left here this morning." His eyes rested on Falcone, serious and intent by the door, busy on the phone. "Perhaps he's just gone walkabout."

She shook her head. "When he's due to open the premiere for the biggest movie of the summer? I don't think so…"

The thought wouldn't leave Costa's head. "Could this all be some publicity stunt?"

She stared at him in disbelief. He caught the bittersweet aroma of Campari again.

"Someone died, Nic. The premiere's been cancelled. A publicity stunt?"

"The man who attacked you was an actor. His name was Peter Jamieson. He was an extra on the set of *Inferno*. Did you know him?"

Maggie Flavier didn't blink. "A movie set's like a football crowd. The only people I see are the ones I'm playing a scene with. I don't even notice Tonti. Just hear him. You couldn't miss that." She gazed directly into his eyes, to make the point. "I didn't recognise that poor man. I've never heard of someone named

Jamieson. If I had, I would tell you. I may be an actor, but I'm a very bad liar."

His phone rang. It was Peroni, excited, trying to explain something he clearly didn't understand himself. Nic heard Teresa snatch the thing from him at the other end.

"Nic," she said anxiously. "Don't ask, just listen. Allan Prime is captive somewhere and it's being broadcast on the web. He's in danger. It looks bad. We need you to see the pictures and tell us if you recognise anything."

"Pictures?"

"*Live* pictures," she emphasised, then told him how to find the Lukatmi page.

Costa had to cut the call to try to get the web on his phone. When he did, and keyed in the address she gave him, all he got was a blank page and a message saying that service was unavailable. He called Teresa back. There was a brief exchange between her and someone who sounded like Silvio Di Capua.

"Nic, forget that idea," she ordered. "Silvio says the network must be breaking up under the strain. Everyone's watching this poor bastard trying to stay alive. Listen. It's possible there's a hint about where he might be. The background to the picture is blurry, but it seems to contain some kind of painting. We think we've captured some of it. We're trying to circulate it to the art people here to get their opinion, but they're all out taking tea with their maiden aunts or something. Look at it for us. Please."

A beep told him there was an incoming e-mail. Costa opened it, looked, thought for a moment, then told her, "It's just smudge and ink. I'm seeing it on a phone. Tell Silvio to get more detail and blow the thing up until it's breaking."

There were curses and shouts on the end of the line. Two more images arrived on Nic's phone, each little better than the first. Falcone came over. Costa told him what was happening, while Maggie stood by his shoulder, trying to peek at what was on the phone. It was impossible to recognise anything on the tiny, pixelated screen.

"Bigger, brighter, louder," he ordered.

They waited. One more e-mail arrived.

He looked at it and thought of a bright day the previous autumn when he and Emily had bought ice cream from the little café near the Piazza Trilussa, then gone on a long stroll to the Gianicolo, past the house that was supposed to belong to Raphael's mistress, La Fornarina, through the still-quiet part of Trastevere the American tourists rarely found.

The image was cruelly disfigured by both Silvio Di Capua's digital surgery and the distorting electronic medium through which it had been relayed. But he recognised those lovely features all the same, and could picture the figure beneath the face, half naked, racing her scallop shell chariot over the surf, surrounded by lascivious nymphs and satyrs.

"This is from a painting called *Galatea*," he said with absolute certainty. "It's in the Villa Farnesina in the Via della Lungara in Trastevere. It's just a small museum and art gallery, not well known. Quite deserted at night, and in secluded grounds." He thought of the way there across the river. It was perhaps four minutes if they crossed the Mazzini bridge.

"Four cars," Falcone ordered, walking back to his Lancia. "Leave Miss Flavier under guard here." He opened the driver's door and beckoned for Catherine Bianchi to move. "In the passenger seat, please," Falcone ordered. She obeyed immediately. Costa followed.

From somewhere came the wail of a siren. Falcone looked surprised, and more than a little cross. More so when it became apparent from the timbre that it was the sound of the Carabinieri.

7

ACROSS TOWN, IN THE CONTROL VAN MARES-ciallo Gianluca Quattrocchi had positioned outside the Casa del Cinema, there was excitement and amusement.

Quattrocchi put down the mike and, with the same coded instruction to Morello that he had used earlier, ordered an end to the eavesdropping. Then he closed his eyes and pictured the layout of his native city, the place where he'd grown up, where he felt he knew every brick and alley, every corner and battered statue. Falcone and his team were in the one-way streets of the Via Giulia, trapped in the sixteenth-century warren that had once been created as a wealthy suburb for the Vatican across the river, a little way along from Trastevere itself.

Quattrocchi had ordered officers and cars to all of the key crossings in the centre of the city, a trick he had developed and perfected in the past. The Tiber would once more be his ally.

"Close the Mazzini," he ordered. "And the Vittorio Emanuele. There will be only one easy way left to the Via della Lungara then. We go south to the Garibaldi. Falcone will never reach there. Not till sometime tomorrow."

This was a Carabinieri case and it would stay that way.

8

I T WAS THE SMALLEST CAMERA ALLAN PRIME HAD ever worked with. The device hung in front of his face, dangling from a flickering light in the ceiling, a wire trailing off somewhere to the computer he'd seen on the way in. Prime never did understand technology. It was tedious, even now. Nothing had ever really mattered except the monocular glass eye that watched him, never blinking, never ceasing to pay attention. In his head it had always been there. Even in the dim, dark, noisome movie theatres of Manhattan when he was a sweaty teenager dreaming of stardom, determined to achieve it, whatever the cost.

Whatever the cost.

The idea provided some amusement in his present odd predicament. He wanted to laugh even as sobs came rippling up from his body, physical reactions, tricks of the trade, not conscious, personal responses. He was able to divide the self from acting. That was always the first deceit. And this *was* acting. He kept reminding himself of that. This whole exercise, once complete, would be an end to things. A wiping out of all debts, financial and otherwise, with a considerable prize in private, too.

It hadn't been the decent lunch and a little afternoon delight he'd been hoping for following Miss Valdes's work on the clay mask. She had turned somewhat coy, to his surprise. Long term, though, maybe it was for the better. Hide away for the day. Miss the premiere, stoke up some publicity. Then let her put him in some weird, sadomasochistic rig set up in a tiny museum that had been closed for renovation. The camera came out. A fake kidnapping, an act of terror played out in front of millions. A world-famous star in a one-man show that would make headlines everywhere. Hell, she sold it so well Allan

Prime thought for a moment he would have paid to be in the thing. This one stupid prank would set up queues outside movie theatres everywhere, sell millions of pieces of merchandise, bring a flood tide of money into the coffers of *Inferno*, a cut of which, after producer fees, would come his way. And the rest...

The performance was what really mattered, though. It was always about the performance.

So he had allowed himself to be strapped into the black metal frame, worked with her to perfect the focus on the tiny, bug-eyed camera, and sat patiently while she faked the spear thrust into his skull—plastic point, stage blood—that was used for the opening sequence.

He'd done this kind of thing a million times and, given the swift, smooth professional way she went about her business, he assumed Carlotta Valdes—or whoever she really was—had too.

After that, she actually called "Action" and he was on, moaning and writhing for the tiny white light that sat blinking on top of the camera, unwilling, and unable, to focus on anything but the tiny lens for the next sixty minutes, an hour which, Carlotta promised, would make him the biggest, most talked-about star in the world.

And then the cops would come. Rescue him. One more piece of deceit, of acting, was required to explain his abduction. This was, Prime thought, a piece of cake. He was used to faking it for millions. By comparison, fooling a few dumb Italian cops would be child's play.

The movie business was weird sometimes. It ran in uncertain directions, was diverted by fate and circumstance and, on occasion, pure luck, both good and bad. The debts were worth losing. So was the rape complaint still hanging over him from that weekend in Rimini three months before. What the dark suits behind Dino Bonetti surely promised—he assumed Carlotta came from them, though she never said—was a fresh start, a vast private payoff, and a mountain of free publicity and global sympathy that would make him bigger even than *Inferno* itself. Plus the fringe benefits only a few—Carlotta among them—understood.

The unseen clock *tick-tock*ed once more. The device to his left moved another notch towards his face. It would stop, she said, when the rubber tip reached his cheek, before the supposedly razor-sharp blade bent beneath the pressure, revealing the legerdemain, exposing the lie. That couldn't be long now. He felt he'd been trapped in the rig for hours. It was starting to become painful. He couldn't wait for this scene to be over, for the cameras to die, and for her next trick: his astonishing, headline-grabbing rescue.

Prime was wondering how he could vary the act, too. Sixty minutes of writhing and yelling would be boring. He'd be marked, rated, critiqued on this performance, just as on every other.

So he stopped crying, made an effort to appear to

be a man struggling to recover some inner resolve and strength. Then, trying to find some way round the awkward iron bar over his mouth, he began to bellow, as loudly as his lungs allowed.

"Carlotta," he cried, not minding he was yelling out her name to millions, since it could only be a sham, like everything else. *"CARLOTTA!"*

There was no reply. None at all. Not a footstep, not a breath, not the slightest of responses. In some chilling, inexplicable way, Allan Prime came to understand at that moment that he was alone in the small, dark museum to which she had taken him in the early evening after eating ice cream together in a secluded corner of the Gianicolo.

And something else. He remembered where he'd heard her name before, and the recollection made his blood run cold.

Carlotta Valdes was a ghost from the past—vengeful, vicious.

The unseen clock must have ticked again somewhere. The invisible device to his left lurched another ratchet, ever closer. As it did so, it made a heavy, certain clunk, quite unlike that of a stage prop, which would have been cheap, throwaway stuff, its own soft, revealing sounds covered by the insertion of a Foley track dubbing menace and the hard clash of metal to lend a little verisimilitude to flimsy reality.

This is for real, Allan Prime realized.

Real as pain. Or blood. Life. Or death.

A warm, free flow of stinging liquid was spreading

around his crotch. He stared at the bug-eyed camera and began to plead and scream for help, for release, with more conviction than he'd ever possessed in his life.

Somewhere at the back of his head he heard Roberto Tonti's disembodied voice.

Stop acting. Start being.

It sounded as if the vicious old bastard was laughing.

9

FALCONE SCREAMED OUT OF THE OPEN LANCIA window, not at anyone in particular, but the world in general. They hadn't moved more than fifty metres in the Via Giulia, and traffic was backing up in every side road around. Sirens blaring, lights flashing, it didn't make a blind bit of difference. These were medieval cobbled streets, made for pedestrians and horses and carriages. There was nowhere left for the civilian cars stranded in them to move to allow another vehicle past. They were trapped in a sea of overheating metal.

Costa called the control room and asked what was happening. He looked at Falcone.

"The Carabinieri have thrown up roadblocks on the bridges. They won't even let pedestrians across."

"I will crucify those stuck-up bastards for this—"

"They think it's their case," Costa pointed out. Then, before his superior exploded, he added, "We can get there across the footbridge. The Ponte Sisto. Go over, turn right, and find the Via della Lungara. It's the long way round—"

"How long will it take?" Catherine Bianchi wanted to know.

But Costa was getting out of the car already, signalling to two of the younger men in the vehicle behind to come with him. "That depends how fast you can run."

He began to backtrack along the Via Giulia, towards the shallow uphill slope that led to the Lungotevere and the old footbridge crossing, setting up a steady pace, aware he'd be well ahead of any of the men behind him. Since Emily had died, Costa had got back into running, spending long hours pounding the stones of the Appian Way near his home. It helped, a lot sometimes.

He was at full pace by the time he got to the bridge, pushing past the importunate beggars and their dogs, the hawkers with their bags and counterfeit DVDs. On the Trastevere side, he had to leap across the hoods of the cars which were so tightly and angrily backed up along the river they didn't leave space for a pedestrian to get through. Costa ignored the howls of outraged drivers. He was sprinting through the Piazza Trilussa, turning in towards the Via della Lungara.

There were Carabinieri everywhere, but no barriers within the road itself yet. They were still getting into position, leaving some movement in the area to allow senior officers to decide their tactics.

Costa pulled out his police ID, held it high, and kept on running. The sight of him took them by surprise so much he managed to get through the gates of the Farnesina and into the beautiful, secluded garden before anyone stopped him.

Finally a large, gruff minion stuck out his arm and immediately launched into the customary litany of excuses that were trotted out, on both sides, when some conflict occurred in public.

"I don't have time for this and nor do you," Costa interrupted him. "Look at the card, see my rank, and tell your superior officer. I know the Farnesina. It's got a history he needs to understand. If you don't take me to him now, I will make damned sure afterwards he gets to understand you kept me away." Costa pointed at the small, elegant villa that had been built five centuries before on the orders of some wealthy Roman noble as a salon for artists and gamblers and beautiful, occasionally dubious women. "There are things he needs to appreciate."

"Get lost," the idiot said, waving him away. "This is nothing to do with you."

A large, ruddy-faced man in an immaculate uniform swept past. Costa was never good at Carabinieri ranks, but something in the officer's face spoke of seniority.

"Sir, sir..."

He ran into the individual's path, waving his police ID. The man looked at him as if this were an act of the utmost impertinence. Costa could see his own colleagues, who had followed him from the Via Giulia, being apprehended at the villa gates, along with a furious Catherine Bianchi.

"My name is Maresciallo Gianluca Quattrocchi. This crime scene is in our possession. Go away."

"I know this building," Costa insisted. "Do you?"

"When I wish the opinion of civilians, I will ask for it. Now stand aside..."

Two sets of strong arms pulled Costa away. Quattrocchi marched forward, flanked on either side by half a dozen uniformed officers. An elderly civilian was unlocking the doors, seemingly shaken by the fuss.

"It's all about illusion," Costa yelled. "*Trompe-l'oeil*. A trick of the eye. What you see is not what's real!"

Just like the movies, he thought, as he watched the group of men stomp towards the villa's elegant entrance. Under the harsh white floods, the building looked like a sketch from Piranesi scribbled into life with the crayons of a giant.

Quattrocchi turned and, to Costa's astonishment, grinned sarcastically. Then he made a coarse and sexual street gesture not normally associated with senior military officers.

Very little in the Farnesina was as it appeared, Costa recalled, as the dark uniforms of the Carabinieri vanished through the doors. Inside, there were paintings masquerading as tapestries, a cryptic horoscope depicted as a celestial relief, artificial views of a lost Rome that may never have been quite as real as they suggested. The villa was a temple to both illusion and the sensuality of the arts.

He turned on his heel and headed for the gate. It was quieter now. Falcone was there, and for once the inspector wasn't shouting. The game, for them, was surely lost.

10

"MAKE NOTES," THE *MARESCIALLO* ORDERED AS they entered. "Take photographs. Video. I wish a record of everything. We will release it to the media when we're done."

He glanced at his large gold watch, then at Morello, who already had pad and pen in his hands.

"How much time do we have left?" Quattrocchi demanded, walking on.

"Seven minutes and…" The Carabiniere held up his phone to try to see the picture there. "No. It's gone again. Seven minutes at least. Ample time."

"You!" Quattrocchi said to the elderly caretaker they had jerked away from the TV soccer in his tiny apartment adjoining the villa. "Take us to *Galatea*."

"This is the Loggia of the Psyche," the little man said with pride, immediately falling into a fawning tourist-guide voice. "You will note, sirs, the work of Baldassare Peruzzi and Raphael. These fruits, these flowers... once this would have opened onto the garden, hence the horticultural theme. And the so-called tapestries, which are painted, too. The Council of the Gods, Cupid and Psyche's wedding banquet—"

"This isn't a damned social visit," Quattrocchi snapped. "Where's *Galatea*?"

"We don't get many visitors at night," the caretaker replied, hurt. "Not from officers of the law."

"Where—" Quattrocchi snarled, then stopped himself, realising the man had been leading them there all along. Now they had wandered into the loggia, which connected with that of Psyche.

He stared ahead. The painting was there, and many others, too. There was nothing else. The place was empty.

The *maresciallo* muttered a curse under his breath and found himself briefly wishing he hadn't shooed away the young police officer quite so quickly. What had he said? *This is a place of illusions.* The images on the web had guided them—or, more accurately, the state police—to this building, and this room. But one more trick, one more sleight of hand, still stood between them and Allan Prime edging towards death.

"Someone told me," Quattrocchi said, "that this villa was a place of tricks. What does that mean?"

The caretaker rubbed his hands with pleasure. "There are many, sir. Allusions. Illusions. Codes and cryptograms. References to the stars and alchemy, fate and the fleeting, intangible pleasures of the flesh."

"Spare me the tourist chat. Where do I look to find them?"

"Everywhere..." The old man spread his arms.

"Where more than any?"

"Ah," he replied, and nodded his head as if something had been suddenly revealed. "The Salone delle Prospettive. But it's closed for restoration, and has been for many months. I'm sorry. What visitors we have...they always ask. The matter is out of my hands..."

The Salon of Perspectives. Quattrocchi knew it was the place the moment he heard the name. This was part of the cruel game. Playing with viewpoint. Changing a familiar aspect of the world through a trick of the light, a twist of the lens through which one saw the scene.

"Show me."

"It's closed. No one enters except the restoration people."

"Show me!"

Morello had found a sign to the place and was pointing to it. Quattrocchi brushed the caretaker aside and led the way up a flight of marble stairs, breath rasping.

The younger officer was staring at his phone again. He had a picture back.

"Time?" Quattrocchi asked.

"Less than five minutes."

The door was locked. They bellowed at the caretaker until he came up with the key. Then, with Quattrocchi in the lead, they went in.

It was dark and church-like. The only illumination came from a low light in the ceiling which was focused on a mass of tangled wires, mechanical contraptions, and constricting devices near the end of the room. A man—Allan Prime—was at the heart of this ganglion of metal and cable, strapped tightly into an upright frame, the open iron device around his head. A tourist print of the painting of Galatea fluttered behind him, animated by the breeze from an open window. On the floor, connected to the whole by a slender cable, sat a single notebook computer, its screen flashing a slow-moving image of something so unlikely it took Quattrocchi a moment to recognise what it was . . . the Golden Gate Bridge in San Francisco.

From behind, the caretaker, unaware of what lay before them, chanted, "You will note, sir, the perspectives of another Rome . . . Trastevere and the Borgo . . . the *centro storico* . . . painted as if real views from real windows. Also—"

Coming in last, he finally saw, and stopped.

Allan Prime whimpered. Pain and relief mingled with the tears on his sweat-stained face.

Quattrocchi walked forward, as close as he dared, and took a good look around the mechanical apparatus into which the actor had been strapped, checking carefully for traps or some kind of light signal device that might have been set to warn of an intruder's approach, and perhaps trigger the mechanism early.

He saw none, but the gleaming sharp point had now edged its way to within a centimetre of the actor's left temple.

The mechanism that held the deadly device was hidden in the deep, dark shadow outside the garish, too-bright overhead light. Carefully, barely breathing, Quattrocchi took out a penlight and shone it on the space there. A low, communal gasp of shock ran through the cluster of officers behind him. A full-size crossbow, of such power and weight it could only be designed for hunting, stood loaded, locked inside some ratchet mechanism that shifted it towards its victim with each passing minute. It was not just the spear—which he now saw to be an arrow—that was moving in the direction of Allan Prime. It was an entire weapon, ready to unleash its sharp, spiking bolt straight into the man's skull.

"Four minutes," Morello said, and sounded puzzled.

"We will release you immediately," Quattrocchi said calmly. "You have nothing to fear. Four minutes is more than enough—"

"Sir..." the young Carabiniere interrupted.

Quattrocchi turned, annoyed by this intrusion.

"Something is happening," the officer pointed out.

He walked carefully towards the *maresciallo* and showed him the phone.

The picture was changing. Quattrocchi grappled for the correct term. Finally it came. *Zooming*. The camera was zooming out of the scene. He looked at the single grey eye of the device that had been set up in front of Allan Prime. Its glassy iris was changing shape, as if trying to focus on something new.

When he returned to Morello's phone, Quattrocchi saw himself there, looking surprised, angry, red-faced, and, to his dismay, rather old and lost as he stood next to the terrified actor strapped into the deadly frame.

From a place Quattrocchi couldn't initially pinpoint came the deep, loud, disembodied rattle of a man's laughter, cruel, uncaring, determined, too. Someone gasped in shock and, perhaps, terror.

A lilting, laughing voice, male, probably American, issued from the computer, and spoke in English.

"Say cheese. Say…"

There was a sound like water rushing through air, then a scream that was strangled before it could grow into a full-throated cry.

Quattrocchi turned his back on the apparatus, not wishing to witness what was happening to Allan Prime. On the floor of the Salone delle Prospettive, in a sixteenth-century nobleman's version of an illusory paradise, he saw instead an elderly caretaker who was on his knees, crossing himself, turning his eyes to heaven and starting to pray.

Something had been written on the dusty tiles in multicoloured aerosol paint, letters a metre high, the way teenagers sprayed graffiti on the subway. Maresciallo Gianluca Quattrocchi gazed at the message and remembered his lessons on Dante from college some thirty years earlier. The letters were ragged and rushed, but the words were unmistakable.

The Second Circle. The Wanton.

"What next?" Morello asked, unseen by his side.

"The third circle, of course," Quattrocchi answered numbly.

11

COSTA AWOKE WITH A START. HE'D SLEPT IN LEO Falcone's Lancia, which, after much argument, had been allowed to enter the secure area created by the Carabinieri in the Via della Lungara and the streets beyond and park close to the Farnesina. The Lungotevere was closed to traffic, which explained the strange silence. There would be media everywhere, cameras and reporters, crews from around the world, switched from the year's grandest movie premiere to a terrible death, and eager for a story that would surely occupy the headlines for weeks to come. But none of the morning hurly-burly of commuters fighting to get to work.

Beyond the window, he could see Falcone, Peroni, and Teresa Lupo talking to Catherine Bianchi near the villa's entrance. Maggie Flavier was joining them, a seemingly uncomfortable Carabinieri officer by her side. He couldn't help but notice the young actress glanced in the direction of the car after she spoke to them. He looked at his watch. It was nearly seven in the morning. Costa turned on the car radio and listened to the news. There was only one story, and one law enforcement agency to tell it. Not the Polizia di Stato.

No one had been apprehended. The idea that *Inferno* would receive its world premiere in Rome had been abandoned. Instead, the entire cast and security operation would bring forward their planned move to California. The exhibition created for the Casa del Cinema would be rebuilt instead at the Palace of Fine Arts in San Francisco. Once that was complete, *Inferno* would be launched there, leaving Roman filmgoers to wait weeks for a domestic public release, a decision that was already creating fury among local fans.

The name of the place rang a bell. Costa closed his eyes and recalled Emily, then unknown to him, in a room in the American Embassy displaying a picture of a beautiful, half-ruined classical building by a lake as part of the investigation that had brought them together.

Then he was brought to earth by the gruff Roman voice of Gianluca Quattrocchi giving the news his somewhat overdramatised version of events. Allan Prime, he claimed, was beyond rescue from the very beginning. The videos of the actor on the web—and his savage demise, which was now on many millions of computers and phones around the world—were all part of a sadistic murder plot played out with heartless deliberation over the Internet. Why? Quattrocchi had the answer. The clues were there throughout. In the message scribbled on the dummy's head—*Lasciate ogne speranza, voi ch'intrate.* In the words written on the floor in front of the trapped actor, which had been shared instantly with the world as the webcam panned the scene. In the constant stream of hate mail and dark threats sent to the production for months and now released to the Carabinieri by the movie's publicist, Simon Harvey, who had—unwisely, Quattrocchi suggested—kept them quiet out of a mistaken belief they came from a crank.

"Cranks they may be," the *maresciallo* went on, playing for the cameras, "but they are also killers." He lowered his voice to make sure there could be no mistaking the seriousness of his message. "Killers obsessed with the works of Dante. They wish to punish those who made this movie for what they see as some kind of blasphemy. The star is dead already. We are redoubling security for everyone else involved—cast, crew, all of them. We will cooperate with the American authorities in this, and, since Italian citizens are under threat, participate in the operation in California as well."

"Nice work if you can get it," Costa muttered. Quattrocchi had never mentioned that the unfortunate Peter Jamieson had been carrying a gun loaded with blanks. He wondered how that awkward fact could possibly fit in with such strangely histrionic theories.

Feeling stiff and hungry, he got out of the car. Two more state police vehicles were set close to the far side of Falcone's Lancia like a wagon train surrounded by a sea of dark blue Indians. He ambled over to the discussion Falcone was conducting. Maggie Flavier looked pale and pink-eyed as if she'd been crying. When she saw him, she turned to the Carabiniere and ordered him to fetch coffee and *cornetti*. The man slunk off with a mutinous grunt.

"Be kind. He's only doing his job," Costa suggested.

"If I want protection, I choose who does it," she retorted. "And I choose..." Her slender finger ranged over the four of them, before adding Catherine Bianchi, too. "...*you.*"

"Oh no," the American policewoman responded, half amused. "I'm just the captain of a little San Francisco precinct, and one that won't be there much longer either. If the Palace of Fine Arts didn't happen to be around the corner, I wouldn't be here at all. All the important stuff gets assigned to the people downtown at Bryant Street. Frankly, they're welcome to it. Guarding celebrities is out of my league."

"There are protocols here, Miss Flavier," Falcone added. "You must do as the *maresciallo* says. He seems very sure of himself."

"People don't murder for poetry," Costa reminded him. "You said it yourself."

"Allan Prime's death is none of my business. Our business. That…" Falcone's bright eyes shone with some inner knowledge. "…has been made very clear to me indeed by people with whom I am not minded to argue. Besides, Quattrocchi has created for himself a very certain picture of what is happening, one that seems to fit well with his own theatrical ambitions. Far be it from us to disturb his reveries."

"Leo…" Teresa interrupted. "We have some interesting material from that place in the Via Giulia. Get us a little time. Perhaps we could get something useful."

The inspector shook his head. "You must hand it over. It's theirs now. All of it. Everything pertaining to Allan Prime and that American actor they shot dead in the park. Besides, whoever is responsible is surely gone from Rome already. That circus trick they performed with Prime…It could have been run from anywhere. America even. If Quattrocchi is correct and this is connected with the film—and I do believe this to be true—their attentions will surely follow that, too, across the Atlantic, far from Rome."

Costa waited. He recognised that glint in Falcone's eye.

"All we have," the inspector went on, "is a missing

death mask. A priceless historical object. And several other similar exhibits that will shortly be crated up and air-freighted to America." He scratched his chin. "Is it possible they might also be at risk? If so, would it be fair to add to the Carabinieri's burden by asking they take responsibility for that role, too ...?"

Peroni laughed.

"I'm not sure it's a possibility I can ignore," Falcone went on, then pointed a commanding finger at Costa.

"Your English is good." He peered at Peroni. "What about yours?"

"Mine? Mine?" the big man replied, aghast. "I spent six months on assignment with the Metropolitan Police in London, eating nothing but pies and fried potato. In some place called..." He thought about this. "The Elephant and Castle."

"A bar?" Teresa asked.

"No," he replied, outraged. "A place."

"How long ago?" Falcone demanded.

Peroni shrugged. "Fifteen, twenty years...They were first-class police officers. And also good..." He searched for the word. "...blokes."

"Your English, Gianni," Teresa wanted to know. "How is it?"

Peroni drew himself up and looked officious.

"*Ecco!*" he declared, stabbing a finger straight into Costa's face. With his scarred and beaten-up face, he suddenly seemed remarkably threatening. "Consider yourself well and truly nicked, sonny," he roared in a thuggish London accent that Costa thought comprehensible—just.

The volume of this outburst caused the Carabinieri man newly returned with the coffees to tremble with shock and spill the hot liquid, cursing quietly under his breath.

"Works for me," Costa murmured with an admiring nod.

"We fly out in two days," Falcone announced. "I have reservations already. You must fly economy, I'm afraid. Budgetary restraints. Now go home and pack, both of you."

Teresa danced a little dance, sang a short burst of "America" from *West Side Story*, and twirled around on her large feet with an unexpected grace.

Then she checked herself and prodded the inspector's chest. "When you said 'we'..."

"Happily, the financial affairs of the forensic department are none of my business," Falcone declared, and began walking off, turning only to add, "Since there is no death on our files, I doubt even you can persuade someone upstairs to foot the bill for that. Of course, if you have vacation owing and the money for a ticket..."

"I have to pay my own way?" she shrieked.

"Perhaps we can fit you in at the accommodation Catherine is arranging," Falcone added, barely pausing. "The choice—and the expense—are both yours."

Costa watched the two of them walk into the street bickering, both understanding neither would change his or her position, and that Teresa would be on that flight, even if she had to buy the ticket herself.

Maggie Flavier took a coffee from the silent Carabiniere's hands and passed it over to him. "Will they find who did this?"

"They'll try." He didn't want to pry. He knew he had to. "Was Allan Prime a friend of yours? A good friend?"

"No," she answered with a shrug. "He was just a man I worked with. He tried his . . . charms, if you can call them that. Welcome to acting." She stared at him and he knew: she had been crying, and was now allowing him to see, to understand. "It's a solitary business. Being other people. The really odd part is you get to be alone in the presence of millions."

"I can imagine," he said.

She looked at him with a sharp, engaged interest that made him feel deeply uneasy.

"Can you?" she asked.

PART 3

1

NINE DAYS LATER THEY FOUND THEMSELVES surrounded by a sea of storage boxes fighting for space inside a gigantic tent by the lake in front of the Palace of Fine Arts, San Francisco. Home had become a small, two-storey rented house a short walk away. It was in the oddly named district of Cow Hollow, on a quiet corner on Greenwich Street, just a few blocks away from the police station of which Catherine Bianchi was captain, head of a dwindling team, slowly running down for the unit's eventual closure at the end of the month.

Hundreds of chests and cases had been shipped by air from Italy over the preceding week. Item after item was being patiently lined up on serried lines of tables under the scrutiny of U.S. police, private security guards, and Leo Falcone, who was clearly torn between a duty he found tedious and a desire to impress the amiable but apparently unyielding Captain Bianchi.

There was, in Peroni's words, an awful lot of stuff to unpack. Paintings, sketches, cartoons, letters, manuscripts, reviews, personal artefacts, mostly genuine, many of considerable value. Costa was, by now, used to the painstaking cycle of work that went into as-sembling any moving exhibition. He had worked several in his career. Each was different. This, set in a different country, to be housed in tents during the day, guarded at night in secure warehouses nearby, was more unusual than most.

"I'll say one thing for you lot," Teresa declared, watching Peroni hover over a set of eighteenth-century Florentine ceramics being unpacked by a pretty young woman from the museum in Milan. "You certainly know how to treat a woman. I blew al-most two thousand euros getting myself here. And what happens when I arrive? You spend days unpack-ing all this junk at the speed of a maiden aunt. And as for him..." She nodded at Peroni, who was still, in spite of the weather, dressed in thin summer slacks and a polo shirt, though the temperature was dis-tinctly nippy, even in the tent. "There ought to be a law against some people being allowed out of the country."

"Your liberal tendencies are slipping."

"I'm bored, Nic. And this is a very long way to come for that."

She had a point. Gianluca Quattrocchi had swiftly seized control of all the key aspects of the investiga-tion into Allan Prime's murder, sharing what infor-mation he had only with the senior San Francisco Police Department homicide team that had been brought into the case. The local force had a direct in-terest: Prime had owned a home in the city, a palatial house in Pacific Heights, part of a small community of Hollywood professionals who preferred the bohemian atmosphere of northern California to the frenetic commercialism of Los Angeles. Maggie Flavier was a long-term resident, too, with an apartment in Nob Hill. Roberto Tonti lived in a grand white-painted mansion in the Marina, opposite the Palace of Fine Arts, where his film would now receive its world premiere. *Inferno*, it seemed, was a local, almost family, affair.

Falcone and his team had become outsiders in a crime which, in some ways, they had witnessed. Briefly interviewed by Quattrocchi's surly plainclothes Carabinieri officers, they'd been left to take responsibility for the tasks they had originally been handed in Rome. This was strictly confined to ensuring the security of the remaining historic items for the Dante exhibition.

Costa was determined not to allow this to get under his skin. This was his first visit to America. San Francisco was a city of delights. The mundane work they had been left by Quattrocchi's team was both straightforward and easily managed. Not that any of them felt entirely relaxed about the coming round of public events.

"You bore too easily," he told Teresa. "There are at least ten items in this exhibition equivalent in value to that missing death mask. If we lose one more, Leo could be looking for another job."

The inspector was with Catherine Bianchi again,

finger on chin, listening to her as if she were the only person in the world.

"Try telling him that. Leo's mind is elsewhere, not that it's doing him any good. The man needs a case. A real one, not babysitting antiques. There's a murder investigation here. It should be ours. Not that idiot Quattrocchi's."

Costa was inclined to agree. With the assistance of officers in the *centro storico* Questura, he had pieced together more information about Peter Jamieson, the bit-part actor who had seemingly attacked Maggie Flavier and died because of it. While the Carabinieri busily briefed the media and gathered together Dante experts and criminal profilers, Costa's men had patiently tracked Jamieson's movements the day he died. They could place him at a rehearsal for a play at the Teatro Agorà in Trastevere only forty-five minutes before he appeared outside the Casa del Cinema. Jamieson was a skilled horseman, and had performed stunts when acting work was hard to find. The uniform he wore when he rode at them outside the Cinema dei Piccoli was stolen from the Teatro Agorà, as was the stage gun loaded with blanks that had brought about his end. CCTV clearly showed him travelling by bus and tram directly from Trastevere to the Villa Borghese park shortly before the strange interlude that led to his death, in uniform and with no obvious possessions. It was inconceivable that he could have found the time to replace the real Dante mask with the fake one. Even if he had, someone else must have taken the genuine object away. The entire park area had been searched and no trace of the original found.

There the information ran out. Jamieson lived alone in an inexpensive apartment not far from Cinecittà, had few possessions and even fewer friends. There was nothing on his computer or mobile phone to indicate an e-mail correspondence with anyone inside *Inferno*, apart from his minor role as an extra. His agent described him as a strange, melodramatic individual prone to fantasies and deeply in debt. In other circumstances, the police would have assumed that he'd been acting alone. Only one unusual fact stood out: the day before he died, twenty thousand dollars had been deposited into his bank account through an Internet money wire service which hid the identity of the sender. Peter Jamieson, it seemed, had been hired for a single expensive performance, one he doubtless knew would cause trouble with the police. The money—perhaps a down payment on some promised balance—seemingly made it worthwhile. Had he behaved less rashly and dropped the gun in the children's cinema, he would simply have been apprehended as a troublesome gate-crasher and probably released with a simple caution or a minor fine for public nuisance.

It seemed clear to Costa that only someone inside the exhibition or movie production teams could have exchanged the masks. Someone directly involved in the dreadful fate meted out to Allan Prime, given the verse scribbled on the dummy's head and its link with the message on the floor of Farnesina. These facts, however, appeared to be of little interest to Gianluca Quattrocchi when Costa raised them after the much-delayed interviews he and Maggie gave to the Carabinieri shortly before flying to California. They were merely awkward, minor details in a larger conspiracy.

Costa's second anxiety was more personal. Maggie Flavier had abruptly shaken off the attempts of the Carabinieri to dog her footsteps, and seemed very good at doing the same with the exasperated officer from Catherine Bianchi's station who had been assigned to take care of her security here in San Francisco. She had also developed a habit of finding Costa, sometimes when he least expected it, rapidly discovering the address of the house on Greenwich Street and knocking on the door to invite him for a coffee or lunch, keen to talk of anything and everything except the movie business and the continuing furor around *Inferno*.

He was flattered. He was amused.

The large form of Gianni Peroni, Falcone and Catherine Bianchi at his side, brought him back down to earth.

"Are you two going to do anything?" Peroni wondered.

"I'm on holiday," Teresa protested. "Also, apart from you, I try to stay away from old, dusty things."

"Thanks. Soverintendente?"

"I was thinking."

"About what?" Peroni asked.

"About the fact there's not a lot more we can do here."

Costa had spent two days going over the CCTV surveillance systems and the various alarm arrangements for both the exhibition and the storage areas. They were among the most thorough and technologically advanced he'd ever seen. There was so much in the way of surveillance hardware in the vicinity, he half wondered whether human beings were really needed.

Teresa looked Peroni up and down. He wasn't shivering, quite.

"Why on earth are you wearing those flimsy clothes?"

"It's California, isn't it?" he complained. "In July."

" 'The coldest winter I ever spent—' " Catherine Bianchi began.

" '—was a summer in San Francisco,' " Peroni interrupted. "Mark Twain. If someone paid me every time I've heard that since we arrived . . ."

"Sorry," she apologised.

"No problem. It's a myth anyway."

The American policewoman laughed. Falcone couldn't take his eyes off her. She was in plainclothes, a dark blue jacket beneath an overcoat most Romans would have chosen for autumn. Her long hennaed hair was loose around her face. With her bright eyes and dark, constantly engaged features, she appeared more relaxed, more certain of herself, than she had seemed in Italy. A fitting match for the elegant, upright Roman inspector, with his tanned, gaunt face and silver goatee, and love for expensive clothes. A fitting match in Falcone's mind at least.

"It's not a myth, Gianni. I grew up in San Francisco. This is what summer's like. You should come back in September." Catherine glanced at his polo shirt. "Then you'd be dressed for the weather."

"I wasn't talking about the weather. I was talking about Mark Twain."

They all looked at him. Everyone seemed to throw this quote at visitors the moment the subject of the climate came up.

"It's a myth," Peroni insisted. "Twain never really said that. I looked it up. I Googled it. Isn't that what you're supposed to do out here?"

"You're kidding me." Catherine Bianchi looked astonished.

"A myth people take for granted," Peroni added. "Like killing people over poetry, perhaps." He stared at Falcone. "So are you going to tell us, Leo? Or do we just pretend to be museum guards for the duration in the hope that some miraculous revelation will put us back in charge? Or even help us find that stupid death mask?"

Falcone bristled. "The mask of a legend like Dante Alighieri is anything but stupid."

"Don't be so pompous," Teresa scolded him. "It's a piece of clay depicting a man who died seven centuries ago. You're chasing moonbeams if you think you're going to get it back, and you know it. There's a market for art that can't be sold in public. It's a black hole. They disappear down it, and unless we recover them very quickly, the odds are they will never reappear again, not in our lifetime." She stared hard at him. "We're not really here for that, are we, Leo?"

"I suspect we won't see the mask again," he agreed.

"Here's something else," she added. "The Carabinieri's fantasies. Is it possible some bunch of nutcases will travel the world going to great lengths to murder a well-known actor simply out of revenge for a movie they despise?"

Catherine Bianchi said, "This is California. I've known people to kill someone over a can of Bud and a hot dog."

"That makes more sense, doesn't it?" Teresa responded. "It's instant fury, not premeditated murder. Human emotions like that are real. Poetry. History. Art. Much as I love them...they're not. Not in the same way. Quattrocchi has his reasons for showboating like this. He likes the movie business. It's glamorous. These people flatter him. Also these fairy tales deflect attention from the pathetic way he handled the case in Rome. But as an answer..." She shrugged.

"So where do you look?"

"This is a project with more than a hundred and fifty million dollars floating around inside it," Costa said. "At least some of which seems to have come from criminal sources."

"That is a distinct possibility," Falcone concurred. "But I would be grateful if we didn't trouble Quattrocchi and his men with this thought. They're busy enough already. When we meet..." He glanced at his watch. "...and we must be going soon, we're there to listen and nothing else. Catherine? Agreed?"

"I'm an officer of the SFPD," she answered, astonished. "Not one of you."

"Of course you're one of us!" Falcone insisted with heat. "Think of it. You're snubbed by those men from downtown, since they regard a homicide as above you. Your station will close at the end of the month out of... what?"

"Centralisation," she hissed. "Rationalisation. Putting good officers behind desks downtown, in front of computers, instead of out on the street where they're supposed to be."

Peroni chuckled and muttered, "We *are* in the same business."

Falcone pointed at Costa and told him to stay with the exhibition. From the look on his face, it was clear there was no point in objecting.

"I don't want anything else disappearing," the inspector insisted. "There are thirteen incunabula, a good number of rare books, and what's supposedly the finest copy of the original manuscript of the work in existence, from Mumbai of all places. The Indians will have our hide if that goes. Make sure it doesn't happen, Nic."

"And me?" Teresa wondered.

"How you spend your holiday is your business. If you happen to be passing a store, could you kindly buy some decent coffee? That stuff in the house is disgusting."

She took a deep breath and glared at him. "So what am I supposed to do with my brain? I was on holiday when we were in Venice, if you remember…"

"Venice was a different place."

"Damned right. I saved your life there."

"Grazie mille," Falcone said nonchalantly. "We must get this out of the way because I don't wish to keep repeating it. You are here of your own volition, on your own time. You're a pathologist. We're not investigating a murder. Nor will we ever be allowed the opportunity. It's hard enough for me to argue a way in to eavesdrop on the investigation. I cannot do that for you. I won't waste my breath trying."

A chill wind engulfed them at that moment, and it wasn't simply the lively sea breeze gusting in from the nearby shoreline.

The Palace of Fine Arts was a beautiful, quiet spot. Not what Costa had expected of the city of San Francisco, any more than was Cow Hollow, the small district neighbouring the Marina and the houses of the rich and famous, Roberto Tonti among them. They had landed in a quiet, genteel oasis of affluence tacked to the side of the larger grey urban metropolis from which the Carabinieri team and the local officers Catherine Bianchi simply referred to as "downtown" were running the investigation. And keeping their cards very close to their besuited chests.

2

To GIANNI PERONI'S MILDLY JAUNDICED EYE IT seemed as if Maresciallo Gianluca Quattrocchi and Captain Gerald Kelly, his counterpart in the SFPD Homicide Detail, might have been made from the same mould, one customarily used to turn out military action figures for reclusive adolescent boys. Both men were of similar age—late forties—similar heavy build, and possessed the same kind of sullen, heavy, clean-shaven face, that of a boxer or field sergeant perhaps, or some burly priest with a taste for communion wine. Now both sat with their respective teams, three officers each, all male, behind facing tables in the largest room the modest Greenwich Street Police Station could offer, which wasn't very large at all. But at least the American threw Quattrocchi the occasional doubtful look from time to time when the Carabinieri man's language got a little too over the top. There might be hope there, Peroni thought. If only they had the chance to speak frankly...

Falcone, Peroni, and Catherine Bianchi were

perched on the end like bystanders. It was chilly outside but this overcrowded chamber at the rear of the little station was stifling and beginning to fill with the musky odour of men in business clothes. Peroni wondered, briefly, how much of his life had been passed in meetings, and atmospheres, such as this, then reminded himself that for once there was a variation from the norm.

Quattrocchi had found himself an expert. Or rather *the* expert, if the Carabinieri were to be believed. Professor Bryan Whitcombe had flown from Toronto, where he divided his time between teaching Dante and writing about the man and his work, to join the team Quattrocchi and Kelly had assembled inside the Hall of Justice. The purpose, Quattrocchi had let it be known in a fulsome round of newspaper and television interviews, was to gain precious insight into the mentality and intent of the Dante-fixated murderers of Allan Prime, killers who might now be stalking remaining members of the *Inferno* cast and crew right here in San Francisco. The media, naturally, loved this story, and had come to adore the handsomely uniformed, English-speaking Carabinieri *maresciallo*, a man who seemed like an actor himself and was only too happy to play up for the cameras on any occasion.

Peroni and the others had watched Quattrocchi introduce Bryan Whitcombe on the TV the previous night. The man was thirty-five, according to his personal web site, though his manner spoke of someone much older. He was extremely short and slender, bird-like in appearance, with darting, expressive hands and a pinched, pale academic's face half hidden by enormous horn-rimmed spectacles. His curly dark brown hair seemed to shoot straight out of his scalp in any direction it fancied, in the manner of a 1970s rock musician. Whitcombe clearly enjoyed the attention and the cameras as much as his Italian patron, frequently stuttering off into academic dissertations, often peppered with obscure quotes in medieval Florentine, and never tiring of dealing with the most basic and idiotic of questions.

"He wants his own show," Teresa had observed perceptively. The professor also seemed extremely well informed about the case, given that he'd only been in San Francisco a day. The TV reported that the Dante expert had been following the story since the dreadful night of Prime's death in Rome, and had been taken onto the team after the Carabinieri had identified him as one of the world's leading authorities on the interpretation of *The Divine Comedy*.

Falcone had cleared his throat at that point and revealed something the TV station hadn't. Thanks to Catherine Bianchi, the inspector knew Whitcombe had approached Quattrocchi personally to offer his assistance after seeing the Carabinieri officer on CNN the morning following Prime's murder.

"Toronto is six hours behind Rome," Falcone added. "He must watch television in the early hours."

Seeing Whitcombe in the flesh now, Peroni didn't

doubt it. The little man had the nervous energy of a squirrel.

Gianluca Quattrocchi made the nature of the meeting clear from the outset.

"You're here to listen," he told Falcone and Peroni as they arrived. "Not talk. I have a duty to share with you any information I feel may enable you to carry out your guard duties professionally. Nothing more. This is an ongoing murder investigation. The less chatter, the better. Professor?"

Whitcombe nodded as if in approval and added, in an oddly nasal accent that was not quite English and not quite American, "I have examined the notes and they support the thesis that these people are intelligent, informed, and knowledgeable in their subject. They know Dante—"

"These people?" Peroni interrupted. "I know you think the man shot dead in the park was one of them. What makes you think there were ever more than two, one of them dead?"

"Because I am assuming we're dealing with normal human beings," Quattrocchi said with a sigh. "Not Superman. Now will you kindly sit and listen without interrupting?"

Peroni shrugged and caught Falcone's eye. Catherine Bianchi scratched her ear and smiled down at the table.

"These *people*," Whitcombe emphasised, "clearly know and appreciate the subject matter. They understand this is a cycle, with form, direction, and purpose. I must assure you my opinion is this: they will regard their work as only begun, not even half finished. There are nine circles of Hell, and their notes indicate only two have passed...."

Falcone raised a finger. "I'm sorry. This is my first and last question. Why would anyone kill another human being over a movie, even some so-called blockbuster that half the world seems to be panting to see? What does it matter?"

Quattrocchi began swearing again. The academic bristled, then adjusted his glasses.

"No, no, please," Whitcombe continued. "Let me handle this." He fixed Falcone with a glare, one Peroni found more daunting than he might have expected. "If I were the killing kind, *Ispettore*, I would murder over this. With as much brutality as I could muster. It's blasphemy."

"Not according to any dictionary I know," Peroni objected. "If Roberto Tonti is insulting anything— and he's adamant he's not—it's some ancient piece of poetry. Not the Church."

"For anyone who admires Dante," Whitcombe emphasised, "this *is* blasphemy. I sat through that drivel a week ago. They flew a group of experts to London hoping we would gild their vile nonsense with praise." His small fist thumped the table. "Not a man or woman among us would say anything but the truth. It's rubbish. Like defacing the Sistine Chapel." He turned and glanced at Kelly and his men. "Or painting the Golden Gate Bridge black."

"Neither of which is worth killing for either," Peroni observed mildly.

Catherine Bianchi's light fingers caught his arm, and he found himself looking into her bright, attractive face.

"Remember what I said, Gianni. This is America. A Bud and a hot dog. Sometimes that's all it takes."

"Let's get to the point," Kelly cut in brusquely. "This is all we have. If it's not some lunatics offended by what's up there on the screen, what else could it be?"

Falcone frowned at Peroni, who was about to open his mouth.

"In the absence of any better suggestions," Kelly continued, "we've got to run with what we have, and for the life of me this *does* sound convincing. I watched that movie. The thing's creepy and obsessive. Just the kind of crap that can push the buttons of any number of screwballs out there."

"Someone hijacked that computer system," Falcone suggested. "Someone made Allan Prime's death an international event. That's evidence, isn't it? Not poetry."

One of Kelly's men leaned forward and said, "It's evidence that confirms there's probably a link in this geographical area, sir. Nothing more. They didn't *hijack* Lukatmi, by the way. They simply hacked into the DNS servers so that particular stream got pointed to some place they were hosting it in Russia, not that we'll ever discover much from them."

Peroni felt his head start to thrum. "How many people could pull off that kind of trick?" he asked. "Surely it's got to be someone from the company? Or someone Lukatmi fired?"

The men from Bryant Street looked at one another as if these were the most idiotic questions they'd ever heard.

"This is San Francisco," Gerald Kelly said with a shrug of his big shoulders. He looked a little apologetic. "Ninety percent of the world's geek population lives between here and San Jose. These people don't breed or have girlfriends. Their principal romantic relationship is with their iPhone. They barely eat or talk. They spend their time frigging around with their little laptops, earning a living one moment and destroying someone else's the next. Any big-name start-up like Lukatmi gets hackers going for its throat the moment someone picks up the *Wall Street Journal* and reads they've got seed capital. It's part of the game." He stared hard at Peroni to make his point. "We can give you more detail later if you want it."

"No clarification needed." Gianluca Quattrocchi was intent on reclaiming the conversation. "This is none of their concern. We are naturally investigating employees and ex-employees in both Lukatmi and Tonti's own production company. That's all you need to know. That's *more* than you need to know."

"Maybe," Kelly agreed. "But understand this. Any one of a million pathetic nerds out there could have hacked into that system. Whoever it was could have done it on their laptop sitting in a Starbucks downtown sipping their double-foam latte while that poor bastard was breathing his last in Rome. This stuff is global."

One of the younger American officers jumped in. "We have experts in the FBI trawling the web spoor."

"The what?" Peroni asked.

"Any traces they've left in their wake on the Net," the officer explained. "We've gotten officers down at Bryant Street working this. There are other agencies involved, too, in the U.S. and in Rome..."

"Enough," Quattrocchi barked.

Falcone stifled a laugh and glanced briefly at the ceiling.

"How many officers do you have knocking on doors, staring in people's faces, and seeing if they look guilty?" Peroni asked.

The Carabinieri glanced at their watches. Gerald Kelly wriggled in his seat.

"Listen," the SFPD captain responded, "we all came up that way. Those of us over the age of thirty-five. Go head-to-head, yell at people, watch what happens. Let me tell you guys. First, even if we did have a face to yell at, those days are over. In this town there'd be a lawyer in the way before you got to the second sentence. Or the civil rights people if their name's unpronounceable. Those days are past. Intelligence, analysts, profiling..." He patted Whitcombe's arm.

"Expert insight based upon years of knowledge…welcome to the future."

Peroni nodded and leaned forward. "And when you find them, will you have anyone left who still knows how to bring them in?"

"You just watch," Kelly replied with no small amount of menace. "We called this meeting to tell you the direction this investigation is heading. If those of you working the exhibition team see any suspicious individuals or come across any possible evidence, however small, we expect to hear of it, immediately. Your job is to keep those museum exhibits all together in one place. I suggest this time you get it right. It shouldn't be too hard, should it?" He pointed at Falcone. "And stop that young cop of yours from hanging around with Maggie Flavier. She's under our protection. Not yours."

"Miss Flavier goes where she wishes," Falcone answered mildly. "You know that as well as we do. Speak to her. Put her in protective custody if you like. The media will love that."

"Falcone…" the Carabinieri officer warned.

"What?"

"Do not get in our way. One more question. Then we go."

"I doubt our paths will cross much, Maresciallo. I will be happy to comply with your wishes."

"And the question?" the man in the smart uniform added.

Falcone screwed up his face. "You haven't found

anywhere that sells decent coffee, have you? The stuff we have in our house is simply disgusting."

"Good day," Quattrocchi snorted, and stood up.

The tiny room emptied in a flash. Catherine Bianchi opened every window, letting in some welcome fresh air. Peroni was pleased to notice that he could detect the scent of the ocean. Did the Pacific smell different from the Mediterranean? He thought so.

Catherine Bianchi looked at Falcone and said, "Gerald Kelly is a good man. He's only swallowing that bullshit because he's got nothing else to work with."

"I believe you," Falcone insisted.

"So do you intend to tell him anything? You guys go home when this is over. I've got to keep a career, and it just might wind up on Bryant Street once they close up this place."

"I can't think without coffee," Falcone complained. "Real coffee. Not with chocolate in it. Or cinnamon. Or anything else. Just coffee."

She looked at Peroni, and he wished she hadn't.

"There's a store around the corner," she said. "They take orders. Not me."

Then she walked out of the room.

Falcone watched her go, quite speechless. Peroni found himself a little misty-eyed with mirth.

"They do things differently here, Leo," he said quietly. "Best remember."

3

TERESA LUPO KNEW SHE WOULD END UP GRAVI-tating to Chestnut Street. The house on Green-wich was comfortable and pretty and…boring. One neighbourhood store on the corner. A couple of bars and restaurants a block along. That was it. She han-kered for noise and people and the bustle she associ-ated with Rome. More than anything, she craved intellectual activity. Chestnut provided the first three, and perhaps the fourth, if she was lucky, though she felt sure that, by the time this self-assigned trip was over, she'd know every last book-store, delicatessen, restaurant, and café there as well as any back home.

At three o'clock on this chill San Francisco after-noon she found herself in a small and spotless café trying to summon the energy to walk along to the stores. Distances in this city were deceptive. From the nearby waterfront the Golden Gate Bridge itself seemed not much more than a stroll. She'd checked on the map she'd bought. The truth: it was a long, long haul, past West Bluff, Crissy Field, then Fort Point, and on to the bridge's great arching span, thrusting out like some metal giant's arm, reaching over the water. San Francisco was deceptive, a metropolis posing as a set of villages, or a set of villages posing as a metropolis, she wasn't quite sure which. Perhaps if she went downtown... But the Marina and Cow Hollow were comfortable, and given that she seemed to be expected to fall into some kind of mental torpor while the men got on with being jumped-up museum guards, there was, perhaps, no better place to be.

The café owner was Armenian. His list of Italian "specialities" contained several items which Teresa not only failed to identify, but also found quite difficult to categorise. The coffee was fine, though: a strong *macchiato*, from a proper Italian machine, good enough for her to ask him to grind some to keep Falcone happy. Though why she did that...

A long, low, and somewhat scatological Roman curse escaped her lips.

One of two men seated at the next table shook his head and said, "Tut, tut. We are shocked."

She hadn't really noticed them before, and now she realised that was odd. The pair appeared to be at the latter end of middle age, average height, dressed in the same fawn slacks and matching brown shirts with military-style pockets. Each had a good head of greying brown hair receding at the front, leaving them with prominent widow's peaks. Their broad, friendly faces were tanned and adorned with walrus moustaches that nestled beneath florid, bulbous noses that spoke of beer and a bachelor lifestyle. They had the same eyes, too: deep set, dark, yet twinkling with intelligence and, perhaps, mischief.

"I'm sorry," she apologised. "I didn't realise anyone here would speak Italian."

"We don't," the second one said. "A curse is a curse in any language. It's the intonation."

"The force and the manner of speech," the other added.

"Observation is everything," his counterpart continued, then dashed a vicious look across the street. Teresa's own powers in this field were clearly on the wane. Both men were staring, with some degree of malevolence, at the fire station opposite. The doors were open, revealing the largest fire engine she had ever seen, a gigantic monster of gleaming red paint and mirror-like chrome that looked eager to burst upon the world seeking some blaze to extinguish merely by the force of its looming, glittering presence.

A young fireman, handsome in heavy industrial trousers, suspenders over a white shirt rolled up at the sleeves, was sweating over the front of the machine with a bucket, a sponge, and a chamois cloth, making it sparkle even more.

"That spot's on the fender still, I'll wager," the first one declared. "Dirt on the front left mudguard. Tire walls grimy as hell."

"Not that *he'll* notice," the other chipped in. "Sloppy, slutty, careless, or perhaps uncaring. Who knows?"

Both sets of beady eyes turned on her.

"Do you agree?" they seemed to say in unison.

"It seems a very shiny fire engine to me."

"Surface shine, nothing more," the first announced. His voice had a firmness, both of opinion and tone, that she was coming to associate with San Francisco. She liked it. "That's all anyone requires for the twenty-first century. People don't notice detail anymore. What you don't see is what you don't get. The powers of observation wane everywhere. And as for deduction..."

"Who said deduction was dead?" she objected.

Their eyebrows rose and the other said, simply, "We did."

It was a challenge and she never ducked one of those. Teresa Lupo looked at the two of them and was relieved that someone was, albeit in ignorance, asking her to exercise a little professional judgment.

"You're identical twins," she said.

They peered at her wearing the same dubious expression, then picked up their coffee mugs, each with a different hand, and took a long swig.

"Fruits of the same zygote?" the nearer commented. "That's quite a far-reaching conjecture. A similarity of features suggests relationship, I'll agree. Little more."

"No," she said firmly. "It's more than that. You share the same facial features. The same build, hair colour, and a shortness of breath that would indicate some inherited tendency towards asthma. Also, hardly anyone but a scientist or an identical twin would know the word 'zygote.' Most people think babies come straight from the embryo."

"So," the further one said pleasantly, "you surmise we share the same DNA and fingerprints?"

"Oh no. You can cut out the trick questions. The DNA is identical at birth. Fine details such as finger-prints ... individual."

"A doctor?" the same man asked.

"Once. A criminal pathologist now."

The other one raised his coffee mug in salute, and was followed by the second.

"Any more?" the first wondered.

"You're mirror twins." She pointed to the one who had just spoken. "You're right-handed. You part your hair on that side and it curls clockwise at the crown. He..." She indicated the second, who was listening intently, fist beneath chin, a posture his brother adopted the moment he saw it. "...is the opposite in every respect."

They applauded. The Armenian barista, who had been eavesdropping avidly, came over with free cake by way of a prize.

"One other thing," she went on. "Don't take the DNA thing for granted either. If one of you is think-ing you can get away with something by blaming it on the other, I've got news. DNA changes. It's called epigenetic modification. You start off the same, but DNA's plastic. Different environments change it over the decades. I'd know."

The near twin leaned forward on one elbow. "We've never had different environments. We were born around the corner on Beach Street sixty-one years ago. We've lived there all our lives. Before we re-tired..." He nodded across the road and added, though this was no surprise, "...we worked there, keeping every engine that came through that place spicker and spanner than any of those indolent young bloods know how to today."

Two large, identical hairy hands, one right, one left, extended her way, and their joint, booming voices announced in unison, "Hankenfrank."

Teresa blinked and asked, "Do you run to first names?"

They sighed. Then the one with left-turning curls said, "I'm Hank Boynton." And the other added, "In case you hadn't worked this out, I'm Frank."

"Oh... Teresa Lupo."

Their grips were warm and soft and, though mir-rored, very much the same.

"When did you retire?" she asked. "From over there?"

"It's been thirty-three weeks, two days and..." Frank looked at his watch. "A few hundred minutes. That poor damned engine hasn't been properly cleaned since."

"And so we pass the time," Hank declared with a flourish of his arm. "We read. We think. We talk with intriguing and exotic strangers in cafés. About DNA and... epigenetic modification."

"Do you read the same books?" she asked out of curiosity.

They erupted in spontaneous, deafening laughter. When it had subsided and they'd wiped away the tears, still saying nothing, she persisted.

"Well?"

Hank flourished his hand and declared, "My specialty subjects are the history of this rich and wonderful city during and immediately after the gold rush in 1849—"

"He stole it all from Herbert Asbury," Frank cut in. "Blood-and-guts nonsense..."

"—as well as the works of Gilbert and Sullivan, nineteenth-century Japanese woodcuts, notably Hokusai, and, in literature, anything by or related to Sherlock Holmes."

"Note the recurrent theme," Frank suggested. "Lowbrow posing as high. My...*things* are bebop, Edgar Allan Poe, the Impressionists, and American film noir from the 1940s on. These are lists in summary, you understand. The full catalogue is much more horrendous, on both our parts. We won't even breathe a word about philately."

"As I'd expect," she declared, pleased with herself. "You choose opposites."

Hank gave her a humbling look and said, "Not really. It just gives us something different to talk about at night. There isn't a smart explanation for everything, you know. Some things just are."

"Good point. I forget that sometimes."

"So what do you want to know?" Hank asked. "A little bloodcurdling local history? Where to go to hear music, not Muzak? Two crumpled old men's advice on the last yuppie-free place to get a cold beer in the Marina?"

The question made her feel pathetic. She had no good answer. The ticket to San Francisco had cost a fortune. It was bought on a whim without a thought as to why she had to come. The four of them worked together as a team now, or at least they had since Nic had arrived. She hated feeling excluded.

"What I'd really like to know," she murmured, half to herself, "is where I can find Carlotta Valdes."

Hank and Frank looked at one another briefly. Then Frank tapped his forefinger on his watch and declared, "If you've got ten minutes..."

"...we can show you," Hank added.

4

THE LOCATION FOR THE *INFERNO* EXHIBITION had proved to be a visual delight so unexpected that, when he first saw it, Costa felt he ought to rub his eyes to make sure it was real. The Palace of Fine Arts was a purpose-built semi-ruin set by an artificial lake with fountains and swans. It was set a short distance inland from the beachfront that led to Fort Mason, home to Lukatmi, on one side, and on the other, after a long and pleasant walk by the ocean, to the Golden Gate Bridge. The exhibition was slowly being assembled during the day in a series of peaked Arabic tents which had been erected around the central construction, a high, dome-roofed rotunda open to the elements. The tents stretched in a curving line through the trees along the lakefront to a group of Romanesque colonnades on the northern side, close to a children's museum housed in a set of unremarkable low square blocks.

For days the area had been overrun with workmen, security guards, uniformed police officers, and members of the *Inferno* cast and crew inspecting the temporary theatre, in the largest tent of all, that would be used for the movie's premiere. For Costa, the event had the feel of a travelling circus. The collection of rare objects—documents, letters, the manuscript from India, and, arranged in haste, an authentic replica of the original death mask—was arriving in San Francisco crate by crate. The mandate for Falcone's team was clear and limited: monitor the security arrangements before the opening to ensure they were satisfactory. Then, when the exhibition became public after the premiere, to hand over all responsibility entirely to the Americans and return to Rome. No one mentioned the missing death mask of Dante. The assumption was that this had now entered the global black market for stolen art and was probably long gone.

Costa had soon grown tired of checking the security system set up by the American organisers. So he took the time to wander through the tents and the teams of individuals milling around delivery vans and crates, building the stage for the premiere, trying out lights and projection systems, playing with shiny and seemingly very expensive toys he could not begin to comprehend. He also, at Peroni's bidding, spent some time with the publicist, Simon Harvey. The man's purview appeared to run far beyond dealing with the media. Harvey had taken a keen interest in every aspect of the security arrangements, insisting that if another item went missing, or there was a second violent incident affecting the crew, it would be his job to deal with the fallout. It was Harvey's opinion that the replacement death mask would prove one of the most popular items in the show, for its macabre connotations. The man had even suggested that what the public really wanted to see was the actual death mask of Allan Prime, now sitting in the Carabinieri's labs in Rome.

Costa had listened to the American and said nothing. It seemed a cruel thing to think, let alone say. Yet he had to acknowledge that the idea contained some truth. Actors of the stature of Prime—and the beauty of Maggie Flavier—were no longer fully in control of their own lives, or deaths. In return for fame and wealth, they surrendered their identities to the masses, who would dissect, reshape, and play with them as they saw fit. Celebrity came at a terrible price, he felt, one that was made acceptable to those it affected only through their own ability to pretend they were unable to see its costs.

Costa was, however, sanguine about the security arrangements. The only way the original death mask could have been switched for the fake severed head of Prime was by someone on the inside, probably within the two hundred or more individuals who worked for the exhibition companies, the caterers, the crew, and the various arms of the production company: publicity, accounts, still and movie photographers, makeup artists, and a variety of hangers-on who appeared to fulfill no particular function at all. These people seemed even more numerous in San Francisco. But the items on show were to be heavily guarded and under constant CCTV surveillance.

It was difficult to see what more could be done. If some improvements were advisable, Costa felt sure that he would be the last person who could bring them about. An expensive private security company had been brought in to deal with the handling of the exhibits from the moment they arrived by truck, and to provide personal security for key members of cast and crew. Catherine Bianchi's dwindling band of officers from the Greenwich Street Police Station was being sidelined, too. Only one, a sullen young man named Miller, with bright blond hair and a curt, sharp tongue, remained at the Palace, and he seemed to take little interest in proceedings. Like the Italians of the state police, the local cops were spectators, ghosts walking in the shadows of the men of the Carabinieri and Bryant Street.

This he found deeply vexing. After checking the arrangements once more, he spent a pleasant few minutes peering at a rare Venetian incunabulum of the *Comedy*.

"Incunabulum," Miller grunted. "Sounds like witchcraft."

"You're thinking of 'incubus,'" Costa replied. "Incunabula are just very early printed books. Before 1501."

"So why don't they call them 'very early printed books'?" the young cop shot back.

"For the same reason people call this the Palace of Fine Arts, even though it's a pointless folly made out of plaster and chicken wire. It makes life more interesting."

"You clearly don't have to deal with the kind of shit we do if you've got nothing better to do than learn stuff like that."

"I didn't know until now," Costa replied, indicating the exhibit case. "I just read the label. The same goes for the chicken wire. It's all there if you take the time to look."

"Yeah, well…"

"No worry," Costa said pleasantly. "Sometimes it takes a stranger to show you something that's sitting right beneath your nose. It happens to us all. If you ever visit Italy, come and see me. You can return the favour."

It had happened in Rome, with Emily, experiencing the city through different eyes. Perspective was good, as a cop—and as a human being.

He walked outside to see Simon Harvey, Dino Bonetti, and Roberto Tonti engaged in a huddled conversation beneath the dome of the rotunda. Costa went over, watched as they became silent, noting his approach.

"Something you need, Officer?" Harvey asked.

"Introductions. I've seen these two gentlemen in Rome and now here. We've never met." He extended his hand. Tonti simply stared at it. "Soverintendente Costa," he added. "If there is ever anything…"

"Such as?" Tonti asked.

"I don't know. You tell me."

Close up, the director looked even more grey and sick. He sighed. "What matters lies with Quattrocchi and Kelly. These security guards who are eating into what's left of our promotion budget take care of the day-to-day work. Everything else is irrelevant. Including the state police of Rome."

"Yet you have the SFPD outside your own house, sir," Costa remarked, nodding at the three-storey white mansion, with gold crests and handsome bowed windows, across the street from the palace. "Not a private company."

"I am an exception," Tonti replied, his expression hidden behind the dark sunglasses. "They regard me as a local celebrity, to be protected. Besides, who would want to end the life of an old man when nature is doing that for them?"

"I'm sorry to hear of your illness," Costa said.

"Why? You don't know me."

"To have spent so long without directing anything. It must be..."

The glasses came off and Costa fell silent. Two grey, watery eyes, physically weak yet full of some unspent intellectual power, stared at him.

"Must be what?"

"Frustrating."

"You know nothing about this industry, young man. It's the invisible people like me who make it work. Over the past twenty years I've written, produced, developed TV series..."

"Is that why you came here? TV?"

"I came here for freedom," the old director snapped. "For money. For life. Compared to this, Rome is a village. Cinecittà is a peasant's pigsty compared to Hollywood. I would have made *Inferno* there if it weren't for..." Tonti stopped. His gaunt cheeks were bloodless. His breath seemed laboured.

"For what?" Costa asked.

Bonetti laughed and nudged the director with his elbow. "If it weren't for the money, Roberto. Hollywood didn't want to give it to you. Italy did. And your generous friends at Lukatmi. Tell the policeman the truth. More importantly, tell it to yourself."

"Dante was Italian. It could be made nowhere

else." Tonti rubbed his eyes, then returned the sunglasses to his face. "I could have made it here if I'd wanted."

"Of course you could!' Bonetti declared. "*Inferno* is the kind of project Hollywood adores. The pinnacle of commercial art..."

"Popular. *Popular* art," Tonti screeched. "How many times do I have to say this?"

"Popular," the producer corrected himself. "Like me."

"Still, a hundred and fifty million dollars," Costa wondered. "So much money to reclaim before any of your backers makes a penny profit. Even with all this...unwanted publicity. That's a mountain to climb. Isn't it?"

Tonti waved him away with a feeble, bloodless hand. "My movie is made. Those who matter have been paid. The rest is meaningless."

"Money is best left to those of us who understand it," Bonetti muttered, scowling. "Why are you wasting our time, Soverintendente? Do you have nothing better to do? No idea where to find this mask of yours?"

"I—"

"Perhaps one of your own stole it. Have you thought of that? Who had better opportunity? You're as rotten as the rest of us. Don't pretend otherwise. At least with us they get entertainment. And from you?"

"Very little, sir. But at least we never promise any."

He looked Bonetti straight in the eye. "Adele Neri told me you invited some of her late husband's friends to dine in Allan Prime's apartment."

"What friends?" Bonetti snarled. "What are you talking about?"

"Emilio Neri was a *capo* in Rome until he was murdered. I'm talking about criminal friends. Perhaps from the Mafia or the Camorra. Or the Russians or the Serbs. We live in international times. If you knew Neri's friends, then some might assume..."

Harvey was coughing into his fist. Roberto Tonti, in his dark suit, behind his black sunglasses, was stiff and silent, like an arthritic crow waiting for something to happen.

"I am a congenial man in a congenial business," Bonetti said bluntly. "When you wish to raise money for a creative enterprise, you meet all kinds. Our little business is merely the world writ large. You should get out more, Costa. It might make you less of a pain in the ass."

Costa leaned forward and touched the director's thin, weak arm, and said, "Should you need any help...I know that breed of people better than you."

The man shrank back, murmuring a succession of bitter Roman curses, then finished—Costa was not quite sure he heard this—with the low, mumbled words, in Italian, "I doubt that."

It was enough. Costa walked to the mobile van set up by the caterers, thinking that even a poor cup of coffee that had been stewing in an urn for hours might help take away the taste of that encounter. Bonetti dealt with crooks. At least some of the money—perhaps a large part—that paid for the production of *Inferno* surely came from criminal sources. Roberto Tonti appeared not to care less whether they got their investment back, although he seemed to be aware that this nonchalance carried with it some risk. All useful intelligence ... if they had been working on a murder case.

Costa got a coffee, closed his eyes, gritted his teeth, and took a swig. It was as disgusting as he expected.

When he turned, she was there, smiling, bright-eyed in a white sweater and blue jeans, looking younger than ever.

"Well?" she asked. "What do you think?"

His mouth felt dry. His head was spinning. Maggie Flavier had become a different woman. Her hair was fuller, longer, and had lost its chestnut hue. It was no longer an expensive, straggly impersonation of an English page boy's. Through some process he could not begin to comprehend, it had become a pure golden shade of yellow, and had straightened into a serious, slightly old-fashioned cut falling down to her shoulders. She was changed. No, he corrected himself. She was transformed, almost into someone else altogether.

What took his breath away were the memories, the connections. Maggie's hair vividly resembled that of Emily in the photograph in his wallet the actress had briefly seen in the Cinema dei Piccoli. The similarity both shocked and fascinated him. She didn't look like his late wife. Her eyes were a different colour, her neck more slender, her skin a subtle shade darker, and her face possessed a more classical, timeless beauty. All the same...

"I hate it," Maggie said, reading his mind. "But I have no choice. I'm testing for some new part. Some 1950s mystery. I'm a waitress in a diner."

"You look beautiful," he said, without thinking.

She blushed, and seemed even younger. "Please..."

"No," he said, laughing, shaking his head. "I'm sorry. It was just such a...surprise. How do you do this? Where does it come from?"

"Fake," she replied, and put one hand up to her long, soft locks, then tugged out a length with her fingers. "Everything's fake that's not flesh and blood, and there may come a time when I can't even say that."

The familiarity between them was strange, and had been from the start. It was as if there had never been a point of introduction, a border that was crossed between their being strangers and their being... friends.

"Now look what you've made me do," she complained, holding up the hank of golden hair. "I can't put it back myself. Nic?"

She turned. He found himself staring at the back of her neck, which bore the lightest olive tan, so dissimilar to the pale northern skin of Emily. They weren't alike. Apart from the single physical resemblance, and the same directness and utter lack of self-consciousness.

He took the bunch of hair and found some way to pin it back in place. His hands shook.

She noticed but didn't mention it.

"I can show you," Maggie said, turning to face him.

"Show me what?"

"Where it comes from. If you like." She moved closer and whispered, "If we can shake off the goons. I want to get away from this place. I need to. I feel like a dummy in a shop window. Please..."

She turned to the man working behind the counter of the catering van and asked, "Do you have any fruit?"

It took a moment but from somewhere a shiny red apple appeared. She took it, rubbing the skin against her sweater, and made as if to eat, then stopped.

"Food is one of life's great pleasures," Maggie said, her green eyes holding Costa. She held up the apple. "I'll eat this on the way. So? Do you want to see a secret or not?"

5

HANKENFRANK—SOMEHOW SHE THOUGHT OF them as a single entity—led her across Chestnut, past the fire station—where a few gruff words were exchanged with the poor young officer who was unlucky enough to be cleaning the engine—then down the street towards the stores a few blocks away. As they walked, Teresa saw a building rise in her vision ahead and knew somehow that this had to be their destination.

An old and probably defunct neon sign on the side read *Marina Odeon*. It was attached to a grimy bell tower that rose three storeys above the low line of houses and shops on the street. Like the building itself, the tower was clad in rough white adobe plaster.

It was a cinema. More than that, it was somehow familiar, in a way that was nagging her, exactly as the name of Carlotta Valdes had.

The two men in identical brown clothing got to the entrance. Hank hammered on the shuttered ticket booth. Frank stood stock-still and yelled, "Anyone home?"

She caught up with them.

"What do you mean, is there anyone at home?" she demanded. "The place is derelict."

"Derelict?" Hank objected vociferously. "*Derelict?* This is San Francisco. Dereliction is a trait of character, not a notice of death. This old Odeon's just a little careworn. That's all."

"It's a dump," Frank added. "The young guy who's got it inherited the thing from his uncle or something. He opens it up when he feels like, so he can show ancient movies to ancient people like us. Good old movies, in wide-screen Technicolor, with just a couple of speakers for sound, not some goddamned rock band's racket machine like you get in the new theatres."

"Is the popcorn good?" she asked.

"We are not children," Hank pronounced, folding his strong arms. "But yes. It is. Do you want to see Carlotta Valdes or not?"

"I do! I do! And I want to know about this place. I've seen it before."

Frank shook his head. His walrus moustache bristled with the pride of superior knowledge.

"No, you haven't. You just think you have. In spite of appearances, this is not San Juan Bautista. That's ninety miles south, and you won't find the bell tower there either. That was a lie as well. We're dealing with the movies, Teresa. Remember? Everything worthwhile usually turns out to be an invention. You don't sit in those hard, bald seats for the *truth*."

She stared at the stumpy white tower. It was all

coming back. An old, old film, one she'd loved when she was a teenager, juggling dreams of getting a job in Cinecittà, following in the footsteps of the greats: Fellini, Bertolucci, Pasolini. Even Roberto Tonti, for one brief teenage summer spent spellbound by a horror flick mired in gore.

The title of the movie eluded her but she could picture it now *and it was here*. In San Francisco, an earlier incarnation of the city but one still recognisable. Some sights—the Palace of Fine Arts, the city streets, the view towards Fort Point and the Golden Gate Bridge—were scarcely changed. The colours were the same: the bright, sharp sun, piercing, relentless.

The name danced in the shadows at the back of her head.

"There's no one around," Frank announced. "They won't mind if we walk around the back. Hell, if they didn't want visitors, they wouldn't have something like that in the garden, now would they?"

There was a particular colour that mattered, Teresa recalled, in a way she never quite understood. It was a dark yet vivid green, the colour of a vehicle, and of a woman's flowing, elegant evening dress, all somehow iconic of a lost and deadly desire.

"Garden?"

They were already pushing their way through a battered wooden gate by the tower side of the cinema. She looked up and got a momentary fearful ache in her stomach. That was a memory, too. Of a man staring down from just such a campanile as this,

his face creased in misery, as if all the cares and tragedies in the history of the world had fallen on his shoulders at that moment.

"Here it is," one of the two brothers—she couldn't see which—was shouting. "There's a donation box. We could put something in it."

Even for her, a Roman pathologist well used to stepping off the straight and narrow, this seemed strange. To be following two complete strangers, eccentric old firemen, well read, self-educated probably, into an unkempt backyard—it was no garden, not in her judgment—of an odd little rotting cinema in a lazy, sunny suburb of San Francisco called the Marina.

"Just like I remembered," Frank said. She recognised his voice this time. It was a little higher, exactly half a tone. Mirror twins. Identical in most ways. Differently similar in others.

Teresa Lupo walked through what looked like a small junkyard, with an old white sink stained with rust, an abandoned refrigerator, and a snake-like morass of ancient piping, and found herself in a patch of open ground a few metres out of the shadow of the bell tower above them. Pansies and miniature dahlias ran around the border of a bed of pale marble chips and gravel. A grey stone urn stood in the centre, filled with fresh scarlet roses. A green silk sash—the colour sent a shiver through her, it was so accurate, so familiar—was wrapped around the neck of the vase, new and shiny.

She stared at the headstone that stood over what could only have been a fake grave and felt her head might explode.

The inscription, worn by the years and only just visible, read, *Carlotta Valdes, born December 3, 1831, died March 5, 1857.*

"You're supposed to pay a couple of dollars to see that," said a man's voice from behind.

She must have jumped. She wasn't sure. This all seemed so curious: real, yet dreamlike, too.

"Sorry," she stuttered.

There was concern all over his young face. He was pleasant looking, in his early thirties, wearing workman's overalls, and sturdily built.

"You look like you've seen a ghost." He smiled at them apologetically. "Sorry. I didn't mean to scare you."

"It's our fault," Hank said, taking out a ten-dollar bill. "Blame us. The lady came all the way from Rome to see this. There was no one in, but the gate was open."

"You mean Rome, Italy?" the young man asked, amazed.

"There are others?" she wondered.

"Oh yeah," he answered, nodding. He had a vigorous, simple demeanour, like that of a farmer. "Georgia, for one. Not that I've been there either. You came all this way to see *that*?"

"Not really." Not at all, now that she thought about it. "I just wanted to put a name to a memory."

She looked at the tower again. "It was in *Vertigo*, wasn't it? Hitchcock. Nineteen fifty..."

"Shot in '57," Frank said, tapping his right temple. "Released the following year."

"Sounds right," the man in the overalls agreed. "I'm not a movie fan, to be honest with you. I just inherited all this stuff. If it keeps people happy and doesn't cost a fortune, it can stay for all I care. I work construction for a living and it doesn't get in the way. Besides, the last thing Chestnut needs is another yuppie bar. My uncle was a good old guy. He claimed he was a carpenter on the set, hand-picked by Hitchcock. That's why we got to pick up a couple of props. Then he got the movie theatre when it went bust, built that stupid bell tower on it...Unique selling point, he always said. He was right about the unique part. I keep a few flowers on that fake grave there for any fans who turn up. Caught three this week, not including you."

He leaned forward and, in a stage whisper, added, "Tell you the truth. My uncle was a terrible liar. I reckon the whole thing's a fake. But what the hell. It's the movies. Does it matter?"

"Are you showing it again soon?" Teresa asked hopefully.

"*Vertigo*? I only open the place up when someone comes up with the money. Too expensive to keep it open every day. We've got a little festival of fifties noir coming soon. John Huston. Nicholas Ray. Billy Wilder, Sam Fuller, Fritz Lang. Some bank is backing it, with a little help from the arts people. Those arts guys produce the program. They love this place for some reason. I just smile and hand over the keys."

"I shall be here every night," Frank insisted, then elbowed his brother. "He can go slurp beer and fart alongside his bar buddies."

"Great." The young man hesitated. He shooed away a couple of wasps buzzing around the place. "Damned yellow jackets. I came around 'cause one of the arts guys thought we had a nest somewhere. Guess he's right. Anything else I can help you with?"

"I really need to see *Vertigo* right now," Teresa said hopefully. "Tonight, if possible. Maybe a DVD. Or..."

Lukatmi, she thought suddenly.

"...I could download it off the web or something?"

Frank put the forefingers of his two hands together to form a cross, then pointed it in her direction, hissing all the time, like someone chasing down a vampire. "Jimmy Stewart would be turning in his grave."

"I rather doubt that, sir," the young man said very seriously, and removed the ten-dollar bill from Hank's fingers. "I don't know much about the movie business, but I'm guessing he'd rather be watched than ignored. No idea about all that Internet stuff. But there's a Blockbuster down the street, if that's any use."

6

THE PRIVATE SECURITY MEN WERE EASILY shaken off. Maggie led Costa around the rear of the Palace, past the children's museum, to a parking lot where she climbed into a dark green vintage Jaguar, then fired up the throaty engine with visible enthusiasm. He got into the passenger seat and felt himself sinking into soft, ancient leather.

"What kind of car's this?" he asked.

"It's a Betsy. That's my name for her anyway. She's a loan from some company trying to sell something or other. I dunno. Corporate bonds. Doughnuts. Who cares? She turned up yesterday morning. My agent said I can keep her for a week as long as I do a photo shoot at the end. It's all by way of thanks for some romantic slush that came out a couple of months ago called *On a Butterfly's Wing*. The boss liked me, apparently. Did you see it?"

"No."

"Ever hear of it?"

"Vaguely..."

She slapped the leather steering wheel and giggled in disbelief. "You are the world's worst liar, Nic. Here I am chauffeuring some foreigner around my hometown and he's never even seen my movies. Will someone please explain to me why? Where's the adulation? What's my ego supposed to survive on?"

"It's nothing personal. I just don't go to the cinema much."

She crossed the busy highway leading to the Golden Gate Bridge, then pulled off to enter the pleasant open space of the Presidio. Soon they began to climb uphill, winding through a network of narrow, empty roads, past a cemetery and both modest and palatial homes, mostly set against a backdrop of lush forest.

The windows were down. The ancient engine growled and roared as the vehicle tackled the steep inclines. Costa felt as if he'd stepped back fifty years into the frame of some old movie.

"Some stranger *lent* you this car? It must be worth a fortune."

"That's what I said. And yes, I guess it must be worth a fortune."

"Isn't that odd?"

"This life is odd. Haven't you figured that out yet? I get given stuff all the time. I could have had three new kitchens last year if I wanted. And a condo in Orlando. Yuck. It's business, not kindness. People hope the stardust will rub off and leave a little money behind. Occasionally it's some kind of trick from some sleazeball who figures it's the price of a date with a movie star. If that's what I am…"

"I will watch every movie you've ever made," he promised fervently. "When I have the time."

That amused her, though in his heart he meant it.

"No need. Most of them are junk. No one's called about Betsy yet, mind, so perhaps I'll be spared that particular ordeal. What would *you* do? Send her back?"

He patted the upholstery and ran a finger along the gleaming polished burl walnut of the dashboard. "I'd still wonder why he really did it."

She burst out laughing. "God, Nic. Don't you ever relax? I checked. This is a Jaguar Mark Eight. She was made in 1957. Only in production for two years. Allow me one indulgence, please. It came with these, too. I should have put them in water but I forgot. I'm not house-trained. Not really."

She reached over into the backseat and retrieved an odd-looking bouquet.

Pink roses set among blue violets, tied inside a star-shaped arrangement of white lace.

"That's the strangest bouquet I've ever seen," he said. "They look so ... old-fashioned."

Maggie shot him a pitying glance, then threw them on the rear seat.

"Flowers are flowers. Beautiful whatever ... Why don't men understand such a simple idea?"

He leaned back, put his hands behind his head, and closed his eyes, enjoying the cool breeze, with the tang of the nearby ocean, and the peace of the Presidio.

"It's genetic," Costa murmured over the burbling lowing of the engine. "Where are we going?"

"I told you. To see a secret. Where this all comes from. Where *I* come from."

He recalled the file he'd examined, guiltily, in the Questura before catching the plane.

"I thought you came from Paris?"

"When I was a child. But when I got older, became…" A coldness entered her voice. "…*saleable,* my mother moved me here. Not L.A. That was too… nouveau riche for her. We spent a year living off fast food and flying down to studios for auditions. The week I finally got a part was the week they told her she had a spot on her lungs that would kill her in a couple of years. All that smoking while she sat outside auditions. Was it worth it?"

"What was the part?"

"I doubt it reached Italy. Big here for a while, though. It was a corny TV comedy, *L'Amour L.A.* Sort of *The Partridge Family* but with foreigners. I was Françoise…" She glanced upwards, as if trying to recall something that was once important. "…the rebellious teenage daughter of a handsome French widower pursuing an on-off relationship with an ordinary Californian divorced mom. Ran for three seasons. Made me. Killed everyone else. My catchphrase—and I had to deliver this in a really stupid French accent—was, 'But 'oo can blame Françoise?' Usually uttered after I'd done something really bad. Ring a bell?"

"I think you're right. It didn't reach Italy."

She smiled at the view. It was hard for him to believe they could have moved from the city so quickly. Everything was so lush and quiet and beautiful.

"Why did I come the scenic route, not the easy one?" She sighed, slapping her forehead. "Oh, right." She pointed at him. "Because of *you*."

"San Francisco..." he said, returning to the subject.

"This is where I come from," she said, serious all of a sudden. "The real me. Not the child. I grew up juggling movie parts, smiling for the camera, even learning to act sometimes. Watching my mother waste away to nothing. I was born here. I guess I'll die here, too. Not that I like that idea. I don't want to die. Not ever."

She pumped the pedal so that the spirited engine dropped a gear and the car lurched forward into the darkness of a eucalyptus glade.

Their route through the Presidio and beyond ran up and down, steadily climbing along empty narrow roads that belonged in deep, isolated countryside, not on the edge of a great city. Costa found himself trying to crook his neck so that he could see in the mirror, glancing back through the Jaguar's rear window from time to time.

They were not alone. In the distance, briefly glimpsed as the ancient Jaguar wound its way through the forest of the Presidio, then on into Lincoln Park, past solitary golfers swinging clubs in the golden sun of late afternoon, Costa could see the same car following them, a yellow sedan, maintaining a constant distance, dogging their tracks.

7

WHILE TERESA LUPO TRIED TO WATCH HER new Hitchcock DVD, Falcone and Peroni bickered in the kitchen over whose turn it was to provide dinner.

"I cooked yesterday, Leo," Peroni complained. "And the day before."

Falcone remained adamant. "I told you. If you want me to get food, I will. But in the way I choose."

"I am not eating that fried chicken crap again! How fat do you want me to get?"

"I like the fried chicken. It's different. You can't get it like that in Rome. Or we could have pizza. Or Thai. Or Chinese. Or..."

"Just cook some pasta, put the damned sauce on it, then grate some cheese," the big man yelled. "Have you never, ever cooked for yourself before?"

"No..." The inspector sounded dejected. "What's the point if there's only one of you?"

"There are three of us now. And I happen to be as hungry as a horse."

This was impossible. Teresa turned up the volume on the huge flat-screen TV and bellowed, "Shut up, the pair of you, and come and look at this."

There must have been something in her voice, because for once it worked. Or perhaps they were just taking a break between rounds. The two men came and sat meekly on either side of her on the deep, soft sofa. Teresa worked the buttons, keying to the scenes so conveniently tagged on the DVD.

"Here's Carlotta Valdes," she said, and showed them the scene in the graveyard of Mission Dolores. "Or rather the headstone."

"Where is this?" Falcone asked. "Mexico?"

"The original location is about a fifteen-minute cab drive over there." She pointed back towards the city. "Mission Dolores was one of the Spanish missionary outposts set up in the eighteenth century when California was being colonised. It's still there."

The two men glanced at each other, their faces full of puzzlement and surprise.

"Rome doesn't hold the copyright on history," she reminded them. "Other people have their own bits, too."

"So Carlotta Valdes is buried in some old missionary cemetery in the middle of San Francisco?" Peroni asked.

"No. It's not the middle exactly. And she was never buried there. It was a fake grave and headstone they made for the movie."

"What was she like?" he added. "The character, I mean?"

"Impossible to say. All you see is a painting of her, and a brief glimpse of someone in a dream. Hitchcock had the canvas made. Like he did the headstone. Which now, by the way..." She waved towards the window. "...is sitting in the garden behind some crazy little cinema three blocks or so over there."

Falcone looked uninterested. "People choose false names in all sorts of ways. Newspapers. Phone books. Perhaps the woman was a movie fan. It hardly proves anything."

"Movie obsessive," Teresa insisted.

"Movie obsessive. So what?"

"So it's interesting! Quattrocchi thinks this is all to do with Dante. You think it's about the mob getting restless over their investment in *Inferno*. What if you're both wrong? What if...?" She stopped. She knew it sounded ridiculous. Then she said, "What if it's to do with an old movie somehow?"

They both tried not to laugh.

"Teresa," Falcone replied, placing a sympathetic hand on her shoulder, "it's no more likely someone would kill over a piece of cinema than they would over a piece of poetry. Adele Neri told us all we needed to know. There's black money, from the Sicilians or someone, in this thing, and they're determined they'll get it back, with interest, one way or another. Or leave a reminder that they don't like being squeezed."

She stared at him. Then she said, in a deliberately censorious tone, "You are becoming shockingly literal in your dotage, Leo. Keep quiet, watch and listen. Please."

They did, and they stayed silent, too, as she showed them, by flicking through Hitchcock's eerie masterpiece, places they now knew—the Palace of Fine Arts, the waterfront at Crissy Field leading to Fort Point, beneath the great bridge, and so many of the narrow downtown alleys through which they'd wandered in delight, jet-lagged, when they'd arrived and had a little time for rubbernecking.

"In short," Falcone summed up, "this movie covers many of the locations we've seen, and a few that appear to have connections to Roberto Tonti, or his cast, his crew, and his movie."

"That and the rest," Teresa went on. She announced, "Tonti worked on *Vertigo*."

She watched their faces. They didn't seem surprised, or interested.

"He was a second cameraman! In America illegally, trying to pick up experience. It's in his biography. Tonti didn't know a thing about directing until he came and saw Hitchcock at work here, in San Francisco, in the autumn of 1957. If you look at the movies that made him famous in the seventies, the influence is obvious. *Vertigo* made Roberto Tonti. This city left its mark on him."

The pair of them folded their arms, an identical

indication of boredom that would have made HankenFrank proud.

"Also," she added desperately, "he came back and got married when his career in Italy began to hit a brick wall."

Falcone's tan face creased in a scowl. "It didn't work, did it? What's the man done for two decades? How's he managed to live?"

That question had also occurred to her.

"It's all listed on the Internet. Directing commercials. Developing TV programs. Jobbing work. Lecturing. Writing. Consulting. There are always crumbs to be picked up if you once had a name."

"And then," Peroni ventured, "he bounces back from the dead and picks up one of the biggest jobs around. One hundred and fifty million dollars and rising. How does that happen? Why didn't they give it to Spielberg or someone?"

"Because," Falcone suggested, "of the risk. It's a movie based on an obscure literary masterpiece everyone's heard of and no one's read. That's why the mobsters who put up the money are getting worried."

She wriggled on the comfy sofa. It had to come out, however much she hated the idea. But the revelation she was about to make obscured her principal point.

"You're very quiet all of a sudden," Falcone noted.

"Don't get fooled by the obvious," she warned

them. "I got the office to do some discreet checking. No footprints back to us. That I promise."

Falcone cleared his throat and gave her a filthy look.

She pulled out the sheets she'd printed on the little ink-jet that came with the apartment. Her assistant, Silvio Di Capua, had risked no small degree of internal conflict by calling in some favours from the anti-Mafia people in the DIA and asking them to run a few names through their system. Somehow what he'd found came as no surprise to her. Still, it didn't mean it was relevant.

"Tonti got married thirty-two years ago, here. His wife was Eleanor Sardi. Born and bred in San Francisco. Daughter of the Mafia *capo* for northern California at the time. There have been a few...corporate takeovers since then. But Roberto Tonti knows the mob. Probably better than he knows Dante. The dark suits run in the family."

"Family. So that's how Bonetti raked in the emergency financing when he needed it," Falcone declared, suddenly animated.

Peroni looked puzzled. "Why wouldn't Tonti get the money himself?"

"Because he's a director," Teresa pointed out. "Money's beneath him. Supposedly. Producers find money. Directors direct."

"Where's this wife now?" Falcone demanded.

"It hasn't made the newspapers for some reason, but they separated nine months ago, not long after

Inferno got a lot of bad publicity saying it was in trouble over financing. She's living in Sardinia. In a very well-guarded villa on the Costa Smeralda. Doesn't go out much. Her father died years ago. His clan's now part of some Sicilian conglomerate."

She saw that familiar glint in Falcone's sharp eyes.

"The wife's hostage for the mob money that went in to rescue the movie," the inspector surmised. "Either Tonti comes up with the goods, or she pays the price. That gives him a great motive for making sure *Inferno* grabs all the publicity—good or bad—he can find."

"You could say that about Dino Bonetti," Peroni pointed out. "If he tapped Tonti's mob relatives for money. Also, remember Emilio Neri's lovely widow said *he* was the one mixing with the crooks at Prime's place. Not Tonti."

"You could say that about Simon Harvey, too," Teresa added.

"He's just the publicist!" Falcone cried.

She picked out another piece of paper that Silvio had found. "Harvey's a substantial investor in *Inferno*. He took a profit share instead of a full fee. It's all in *Variety*. And he's a scholar, of both literature and the cinema. Someone who's familiar with Dante and Hitchcock. Don't forget those two odd little geeks, Josh Jonah and Tom Black, either. They've put in a stash of money too, which, contrary to popular opinion, they can't afford. There are lawyers hovering around Lukatmi trying to screw them for breach of copyright, inciting racial hatred, suicide...you name it. And where exactly do they come from? Just over the road. A two-minute walk from Roberto Tonti's mansion. If you want to go down that path..."

"I still don't like the way the video of Prime got onto that site," Peroni complained. "It's all very well for Gerald Kelly to claim there's a geek on every corner here. It can't be that easy. Also, think of the publicity. The publicity they're all getting. Every last one of them, even Maggie Flavier. It has to be worth millions. They could all be in it together."

Falcone looked cross. "Oh, for pity's sake. You're starting to sound like Gianluca Quattrocchi, both of you. There may well be an attempt to make everything that's happening appear complex. That doesn't mean it is. Two men are dead, a fortune hangs in the balance, and everything depends on Roberto Tonti's movie being a success, which it might not be on its own merits. The more we lose sight of those basic facts, the further we are from some resolution."

"It's not our case, though, is it?" she reminded him. "You didn't even know this stuff about Tonti and his marital background, Leo. Don't play games. You're desperate. Best admit it."

To her astonishment he allowed himself a brief, childlike grin.

"Touché," the inspector murmured. "But...I hear things."

"From Catherine?" she asked outright.

"Possibly."

"Is telling you stuff her way of diverting the conversation from all these pathetic invitations to dinner?"

"I have no idea what you mean," Falcone complained.

"Dammit, Leo. I'm not giving dating lessons here, too. I told you before. This is California. Not some middle-aged playboy's cocktail shack on the Via Veneto."

"I know for a fact that we are no more and no less in the dark than Quattrocchi and Gerald Kelly," Falcone insisted, trying to steer the conversation somewhere else. "It's a level playing field."

"Not exactly," Peroni snapped. "They've got weapons."

That had been a source of discontent from the outset. The rules of their security assignment precluded their carrying guns. Costa liked that idea. Peroni wasn't so sure. Falcone was of much the same opinion.

"Does anyone want to hear about this movie I found?" Teresa cried, before the gun debate could start again.

"A summary in no more than three sentences," Falcone ordered.

She shook her fist in mock fury. "You have to watch it. I don't want to spoil things for you."

The two men made a show of looking at their watches.

"It's a work of art. This is ridiculous…" She'd only

managed to flick through the DVD before they came home bickering about dinner. Most of what she did know was dimly remembered from two decades before.

She closed her eyes and in that moment could picture where she first saw it, on the screen of the dusty little cinema in the corner of the Campo dei Fiori, on the arm of a hirsute Milanese economics student with exquisite manners and dreadful taste in clothes.

"John Ferguson, a police officer known to everyone as Scottie, afflicted by vertigo, off duty after a terrible fall that killed his partner, agrees to tail Madeleine Elster, the wife of a former acquaintance who believes she is acting oddly, possibly suicidal, and possessed by the spirit of Carlotta Valdes, an ancestor. The cop falls in love with the woman, who appears to kill herself. He has a breakdown, and afterwards meets another woman whom he rebuilds in her image, only to discover that she was the original Madeleine Elster he met, taking part in a complex murder plot to kill the villain's true wife. In the end he loses her, too." She clapped her hands. "There!"

"That was four sentences. And what's this got to do with Dante?" Peroni asked.

"Nothing! Everything!" she screeched. "I don't know. You work it out. I'm on holiday, aren't I? The woman whose spirit was supposed to possess the victim was named Carlotta Valdes. The story played itself out here, in San Francisco, and Roberto Tonti worked on the film. I do not believe in coincidences."

"I'm not in the mood for a movie," Peroni grumbled. "I'm hungry."

Falcone took out a coin and said, "Heads it's chicken, tails it's pizza."

Peroni's large scarred head fell into his hands and he groaned.

"Chicken it is," Falcone declared, after briefly flipping the coin and letting no one see the outcome. "I'll go."

Teresa swore bitterly beneath her breath, then passed them a piece of paper with her scribbled handwriting visible on it.

"This is a list of real-life locations from the film. My prediction is that if something happens, it will happen close to one of these. We are being led down a merry little path, gentlemen. But not the one you think."

She skipped through the chapter points she'd set on the DVD. A bouquet of pink roses, set with blue violets in a star-shaped lace bouquet, came on the screen. Then the camera panned up to the painting of a serious, intense Hispanic woman in Victorian dress, dark eyes staring directly out of the canvas. In her hands sat an identical bunch of flowers.

"Meet Carlotta Valdes. This scene was shot in an art gallery called the Legion of Honor in Lincoln Park, which you will find on my list. Also..."

She switched to a new scene, one of several hypnotic, dreamlike sequences in which Jimmy Stewart's Scottie followed the troubled Madeleine as she drove apparently aimlessly across the city, along narrow urban streets, quieter neighbourhoods, and then through endless, dark, unidentified woodland.

The two men became quiet. Falcone reached for the remote control and paused the playback. He pointed to the dark metallic green car frozen as it wound its way downhill, somewhere, it seemed, near the Golden Gate Bridge.

"I saw one just like that this morning. Maggie Flavier was getting into it."

He scratched his narrow jutting chin.

"Where's Nic gone?" he asked.

8

THEY PULLED UP OUTSIDE A BUILDING THAT seemed like a mirage emerging from the faint Bay mist. Flat grey lines of weathered stone, perfectly placed columns, an American version of a distorted Palladian dream transplanted from some country estate in the Veneto to a green Californian hilltop running down towards the Bay and the great red bridge below. The two of them got out of the Jaguar. Costa stopped and stared and smiled.

"I know this place..."

"You've been to Paris. I was a child there. I knew it,

too. The home of the French Legion of Honour opposite the Quai d'Orsay. This is a copy. San Francisco always did look to Europe, you know. Why do you think Tonti is so at home here? The pace of life. Buildings like the Palace of Fine Arts..."

"Piranesi should have drawn that."

Her sharp, incisive eyes peered at him. "Why are you a police officer? Not an artist or something?"

Costa shrugged. "I can't paint."

"Does that bother you?"

It seemed an odd question. "No."

"It would annoy the hell out of me. I'd *try*."

"I did. That's why I know I can't do it. What else should I be? Why are you an actress?"

"Because it lets me be other people, silly."

She took his arm and dragged him past a large, familiar statue, towards the entrance.

"And because I get paid a lot for it. That really is Rodin's *Thinker*, by the way. One of the early casts."

It was almost empty inside. The gallery had such space, such light, such apparent modernity. It was nothing like Rome. All his favourite places there—the Doria Pamphilj, the Borghese—had more the feeling of palatial homes decorated with pictures. The Legion of Honor was cold and clean, organised and... dead. A memorial, Maggie told him, to the fallen American soldiers of the First World War.

Faces lined the walls, portraits of men and women, some in the flush of youth, others in failing old age.

Maggie seemed to know every last work in the place, every feature, every personality.

"The cruelty of man," she declared as she guided him to a fifteenth-century tapestry that depicted peasants trapping and killing rabbits with ferrets and dogs.

"Presumably they were hungry."

"You're a vegetarian! You're supposed to disapprove."

"When someone's hungry…"

She harrumphed and took him to another canvas. It showed a young girl in poor country dress, seated by a grubby stone well. He looked at the notice next to it: Bouguereau, *The Broken Pitcher*. Late nineteenth century.

"Had you seen my movie debut, the Disney epic *The Fairy Circle*," Maggie announced with mock pomposity, "you might have recognised this."

"I didn't."

"I know that. Well, this was me."

It was impossible for him to imagine her as this lost, sullen creature. "How?"

Her strong hands beat the front of her sweater.

"Because I stole her!" Then, more thoughtfully, "Or she stole me. The hair. The surly, sad look. The determination. Which won the day in the end, naturally, since this was Disney."

He looked at this sophisticated blonde woman by his side and laughed.

"Ridiculous, am I?" she demanded. "Watch."

She snatched the extensions out of her hair and thrust them into her bag. Then she did something with her hands, put her head down, shook it, as if getting rid of something bad.

When she looked up at him, Nic felt briefly giddy, just as he had the day they first met.

Costa switched his attention between her and the painting. There was the same life, the same identity in the fierce, hard stare, the set features, the reproach to the viewer as if to say: *Can you see now?*

"Point taken. You're a good actress."

A mild curse escaped her lips. She was back. Herself again in an instant. "No. I'm a good vampire of paintings. Or an easy vessel for some ghost. This is what I do. It's what I learned, when my mother was down in L.A., doing whatever it took to get me auditions." Her face turned stony for a moment. "So I came here. I studied these women on the walls. I imagined them into me. It's not hard, not when you try. Whenever I needed them, they showed up. Look..."

She led him to another pastoral canvas, this one more lyrical: a young shepherdess next to a brook, gazing wistfully out of the frame as her flock wandered in the background. French again, of the same period.

"This was two years later. *The Bride of Lammermoor.* Walter Scott. Classic stuff. Here..."

Another portrait. French again, but clearly earlier, from the romantic style and of a rather vapid-seeming aristocrat. He examined the notice: *Hyacinthe Gabrielle Roland, later Marchioness Wellesley*. It wasn't easy to imagine the woman's round, naive face, with its flush of curls and gullible stare, succumbing to Maggie's talents.

"I had to put on weight for that. You need puppy fat for Jane Austen. That took me, oh..." She placed a finger against her cheek. "...three weeks to hit the mark. You can't hurry gorging. First time I got to take my clothes off." She cleared her throat. "But at least it was art. Ha-ha."

The discomfort inside her was distant but discernible.

"Why do you do this?"

"Because I like it. Do you need another reason? Being someone else. It's...distracting."

She was taking him to another canvas, one he knew he would dislike the moment he saw the familiar, neurotic swirls beginning to take shape as they approached.

"This is me when I'm older," she went on. "Maybe not a movie at all. Maybe *me*. Whoever that happens to be."

It was a woman in her late thirties, posed like a siren on a dreamy sea, her face tilted at an awkward angle towards a Mediterranean sky, her full body half clothed in a revealing, swirling dress that flowed over her flesh with the liquid sinuousness of the waves beneath. In the background nymphs and mythical creatures revelled in some impenetrable diversion. It was reminiscent, vaguely, of Raphael's *Galatea* in the Far-nesina.

"I never much liked Dalí," Costa admitted. "He doesn't seem to like the people he paints."

"Agreed. She looks like a bad actress being forced to smile for the audience. If I'm still getting paid for that when I turn forty, I'll be happy."

"So this is where you come for inspiration?"

"No. I told you. I come here to possess, or to be possessed. By a dead girl in a French painting. Or a forgotten English aristocrat. Anyone, as long as it works."

She leaned towards him, as if he were a child. "You don't honestly think they go to the movies to see *me*, do you?"

"Where's Beatrice?" he asked, avoiding the question.

Without a word she took him to another canvas. He stood in front of the work and felt, finally, at home.

"Dante came before Raphael, remember," Maggie whispered. "So what do you expect?"

It took him back to Italy in an instant. The simple beauty, the placid tempera colours, the classical, re-laxed posture of the figures: a winged Cupid with his bow, a young woman, in long medieval robes, reclin-ing opposite him, staring at his tender face, in antici-pation, perhaps in fear. They were in the kind of garden that might have been found in many a canvas adorning the walls of the museums of Florence: thick with trees, dark in places, shot through with light in others. In the distance three muses turned around each other, dancing.

The centuries passed, some ideas stayed the same. Costa leaned down and looked to see its origins. Maggie was right: Pre-Raphaelite, John Roddam Spencer Stanhope, from 1877 but fired directly by the Renaissance, and Botticelli in particular.

He turned to Maggie Flavier, now blonde, looking much, as she had first said, like an attractive young waitress from a 1950s TV show. When she wore the guise of Beatrice on the screen, under the directorial control of Roberto Tonti, she was someone different entirely: this woman from another time, a different now pretending to be a different then.

"I knew you'd ask," she said as she retrieved some ribbons out of her bag. Costa watched as she wound the coloured strands through her hair, loosely styling them, after a fashion, in the manner of the braids on the figure in the painting. He could see her Beatrice still, beneath the dyed blonde tresses, beneath the tan she'd acquired somewhere along the way.

"You were perfect," he whispered.

"I *am* perfect," she corrected him. "When I want to be."

He looked at the nameplate: *Love and the Maiden, 1877.*

"I have nothing else to show you here," she said. "But there's a view. If we wait long enough, we could see the best sunset in the world. Well, in San

Francisco anyway. I used to love it when I caught the bus, waiting for my mother to get back from the studios, wondering what she'd say."

"Where?"

"Through the woods," she murmured, her green eyes never leaving his face for a moment. "Where else?"

9

IT WAS A SHORT DRIVE. THEY STOPPED IN A deserted car park next to a stand of eucalyptus. Nearby there was a group of picnic tables and a site for tents alongside a campfire pit. He'd almost forgotten about the yellow car he'd seen on the way to the Legion of Honor. No one seemed to have followed them, though it was impossible to be certain in the narrow, winding pathways they drove along, the old green Jaguar swaying on its ancient suspension as if it were some ageing vessel navigating a rolling hilltop sea.

They got out and the smell of the trees—strong and medicinal—was everywhere. The grey trunks, shedding bark like bad skin, ranged around them, disappearing into the hazy blue distance. He'd read the signs on the Presidio when he'd walked in the lower reaches. The forest was the creation of man, not nature, planted by the military who had once occupied this narrow stretch of territory to the north of the city. He liked this idea, the notion of a land that was made, not simply inherited. To him it seemed novel.

"Down there," Maggie said, pointing, "lie Baker Beach and the Pacific Ocean. Call this a city? Four miles behind us there's Union Square and Market and all that crap. Here." She made a circle around herself, eyes closed, smiling, face pointed to the sky. "Here is peace and paradise. I used to spend the night here sometimes when my mother didn't come back from L.A. It's a *world*."

"Isn't that dangerous?"

"Do you know something worthwhile that isn't?"

"Quite a lot of things, to be honest."

"Did your wife feel the same way?" she asked nervously. "She was an FBI agent once. She must have..."

He stayed silent, wondering.

"It was in the papers," Maggie said. "Sorry. I looked. I had to. None of us has secrets anymore, you know."

"You could have asked."

She shook her head. The blonde locks, exactly Emily's colour, fluttered in the wind.

"No. You don't want to talk about it. I don't want to make you. All the same, I had to let you understand I know. Otherwise it would hang over us both. Me wondering whether to ask. You wondering whether to tell."

He gazed past the trees, trying to guess how far it was to the beach and what they might find there.

"She wasn't afraid of danger," Maggie said simply. "That was what killed her. Didn't it?"

"No. A man killed her. A deranged man I should have stopped. But I didn't. I was too slow. Too...indecisive. I thought..." This knowledge would never go away. "I thought I could negotiate some solution in which no one got hurt."

That failure almost nagged him more than anything. It was a curiously indeterminate kind of guilt.

"So you want everything to be safe from now on. You want everyone close to you to wear some kind of armour that stops them from being touched by what's bad."

"If I could find it..."

She stood closer to him. "If you found that, Nic, they'd be someone else. Not who they really are." She sighed. "Unless of course you're in my business, in which case you have to be other people. God, I wish I could still use the word *actress*. Katharine Hepburn. Kim Novak. Bette Davis. It was good enough for them. I can't stand in their shadow. But maybe one day."

"I promise to see one of your movies. Soon."

"I didn't mean that."

The wind quickened. It ruffled her hair. For a moment she looked like the urchin, a very elegant and well-kempt one, he'd first seen in Rome. She took a deep breath of the clean, sweet air.

"I love this place. The ocean. These trees. When I was a girl, I used to imagine I was a bird, a gull or something. That I could fly off this headland, over that beach, head west, on and on, free forever. Where do you think I'd wind up?"

"Hawaii?"

"Shame on you. Are all Italians bad at geography?"

"This one is. I've never been out of Europe before. What do you expect?"

"Better. Head that way, my boy…" Her long, strong, purposeful arm stretched out into the wind. "…and you will, after a very long journey, end up in Japan."

She bowed like a geisha and said, *"Konbanwa,"* then paused to enjoy his bafflement. "It means 'good evening.' I can do small talk in a million languages. Helps when you're on tour." The forest of slender, upright eucalyptus made a whispering sound, leaves rustling in the breeze. The scent seemed stronger. Night was on the way.

"What did you do?" he asked. "When you camped here. As a girl."

A different expression on her face now, amused, mock angry. "On a warm San Francisco night…" she sang. He dimly recognised the song. "What do you think? I smoked pot. Fell into the sleeping bag of any passing stranger. The usual."

"I didn't mean that." It was true and had to be said. "I didn't think it. For a moment."

"Why? You might be right."

"It's none of my business."

"Oh." She raised her finger in front of his face, in a way that Teresa Lupo might have done. "So you do believe in intuition. When it suits you. But you're not far wrong." The shadow he was coming to recognise flickered across her face. "That all came later. Do you really want to know what I did?"

"If you want to tell me."

"I ran."

This was California, he reminded himself. "You jogged?"

Her green eyes lit up with indignation. "*Jogged?* I ran. Like the wind. Not your kind of running. Peroni told me about *that*. Long-distance stuff. Marathons. I sprinted. Pushed myself until I could feel my heart ready to burst. And then..." She raised her shoulders in a gesture of self-deprecation. "...I curled up alone in my sleeping bag with a bunch of Twinkies, feeling alive, watching the moon until I fell asleep. All alone. I liked it that way. I still do."

A part of him wanted to touch her. A part of him wanted to resist.

"I'll count to five. Give you a start." She nodded across the campsite. "There's an information sign with a map a hundred yards over there. I'll still beat you to it."

"Too old...too tired..."

"Get running, damn you!"

He turned, not quite thinking right, and happy with that idea, the release of sanity, the embrace of something less rational. He could see the sign she spoke of in the shade where the trees became denser.

Costa didn't move as quickly as he could. He felt a little giddy. He wanted her to win, wanted her to overtake him, laughing, childlike, racing in front of him. And then ...

He didn't know. San Francisco was a million miles from home. None of the old rules—the old cares, the old burdens—existed here. He was free of them, for a while anyway.

When he got to the sign, he wasn't even out of breath.

"Maggie ..." he said as he turned.

There was no one there. Just a forest of grey trees standing like petrified soldiers, unmoving except for the dark fluttering diamonds of leaves, rippling their aroma into the land breeze that was running through the forest, down to the ocean.

He stood and thought, realising, with the old head he used in Rome, that he'd acted like a fool. Then, in the distance, where the light was failing, he saw a figure flit through the grey trunks.

It was a man, heavily built, carrying something low in his right hand. Something black and made of metal.

"Maggie!" Costa yelled again.

There was the faint echo of her laughter from

somewhere. A shape in a white sweater slipped through the glade ahead to the right, not far from the man he'd seen. Not far at all.

Costa raced towards her, at full speed this time, half tripping over the rotting branches and the carpet of crisp dry leaves at his feet, bellowing into the thin night air, summoning up all the threat and force he could muster.

A voice wasn't much against a weapon but it was something. In the distance, a little down the hill, just off the road, stood the yellow car he'd seen earlier. Trying to stifle the fury he felt with himself, he ploughed on, half stumbling into a crater full of ferns and moss and trash, fighting to keep his balance, yelling all the time.

He didn't catch sight of the man anywhere. But the third time he called he heard her laugh again, a calm, musical sound, followed by a mild French curse directed at his masculinity.

"This is not a game!" he roared.

A flock of birds rose unseen in a noisy, squawking gaggle. The suddenness and the sheer physical noise of their presence made him jump.

"Not a game . . ." he whispered to himself, trying to still his thoughts.

Something white emerged briefly from behind a silvery trunk ten steps or so to his right.

He didn't say anything. He walked straight there. When he was close, she stuck out a foot to make sure he saw.

Costa rounded the tree and found her. She was smiling, looking like a guilty schoolgirl. The apple she'd gotten from the catering van in the car park at the Palace of Fine Arts was in her hand.

"We're going," he said, and took her arm, more roughly than he'd intended.

"Why? What's the rush? Oh, come on, Nic. Loosen up. Help me. Just a little. This is new to me, too, you know. I'm starting to feel like I'm fourteen again. Only this time, I'm happy."

"There's someone here," he warned, glancing around, seeing nothing.

"What? A Peeping Tom? Who cares? I don't. I've had those since forever."

"Well, I haven't." He reached for her arm. She stepped back, away from him. "I'm taking you home. You're supposed to have security."

"Not from you, mister! You know, I could lose patience with all this. I don't usually have to beg."

"I'm sorry." He was still scanning the grey trees for the lone individual who was surely stalking them. "Let's go back to the city. We can find a restaurant. Have dinner."

"I don't need dinner, thank you very much." She waved the apple in his face. "I have this. Got it myself." She took a huge, greedy bite of the fruit and screwed up her face as if it wasn't so good. "I don't need anything from anyone. Ever."

"Fine. So can we go? Please?"

She didn't say another word. But she moved,

striding in front of him, long steps, trying to make a point. In other circumstances he might have laughed. There was a theatrical quality to her petulance. It was a performance, one that was deliberately comic.

They were just a couple of steps from the car when she fell. Costa rushed to her side. The ground was treacherous: leaves covered potholes, snarled roots of the stiff military trees lurked hidden, waiting to trip the unwary.

"Let me help you up," he said, and offered her his hand.

Maggie Flavier rolled over on the earth in front of him. Her face seemed strange. Taut, a little swollen. Her mouth flapped open as if out of control. Her lips were a vivid shade of red, and her green eyes stared up at him in terror.

"Ow, *ow*, OW…" she screamed, and gripped her stomach in agony.

The apple tumbled from her hand, half eaten. Costa bent down. Stupidly, automatically, he picked up the piece of fruit and sniffed it. A strange, unexpected aroma rose from the flesh. *Almonds,* he thought, and the word caused alarm, for reasons he couldn't place.

A physical tremor gripped her thin body. She stiffened. Her head jerked back, golden hair thrusting into the dank leaves and earth, then rolled sideways. A cry of pain and astonishment and anger emerged from her lips. Then a thin stream of bile began to trickle from her mouth onto the ground, her breathing became short and laboured, her body started to arch in harsh involuntary spasms.

Someone was approaching, fast and deliberate.

His hands held hers until the last moment. Then Costa rose, turning, saw the powerful, muscular shape of a man in a red-checked lumberjack shirt, with something black and threatening in his hand, closing on them.

There wasn't time to think anything through. He took one step forward and lashed out with his right fist, caught the intruder on the chin, punched hard again, was satisfied to see the corpulent frame start to fall backwards, the object in his hand tumbling into the dead leaves.

It was a camera, a big black SLR.

Costa blinked, felt hopeless, uncertain where his attention ought to lie.

The man on the ground started swearing at him. Costa didn't listen. He turned and looked at the stricken woman, crouched next to her again. Her eyes were starting to roll back under the lids. She seemed barely conscious. Her breathing appeared dreadfully fast and shallow. The convulsions had fallen into a terrifying regime, one that was slowing with each diminishing lungful of air.

They trained a police officer for this kind of event. But that was on a different continent, in a different language.

Whoever the man was, he wasn't a threat. Not an obvious one at that moment.

All the same, as the hulking figure in the red shirt retrieved his camera and began to scuttle away, firing off shots all the time, Costa took one quick step towards him, kicked hard at his arm as it held the camera, heard the snap of fracturing bone.

There was a scream. The figure was on the ground again, still trying to scramble crab-like through the desiccated leaves covering the forest floor. Costa turned, stepped forward, and stood quite deliberately on his shattered limb for a moment, then waited for the cries of agony to subside a little.

"Dove..." he began, then shook his head to clear it. "Where are we? I need to know the location. Now. Before this woman dies."

"You saw the sign," the man in the red shirt spat at him, clutching his arm and the camera as if each was of equal value.

"Where?" Costa bellowed, and lifted his foot again, eyeing the tortured, crooked arm.

The photographer shrank back in fear. "Rob Hill Campground. Now leave me alone."

Nic was only dimly aware that the man was crawling off somewhere. And that the sound of the camera was there again, diminishing as the paparazzo retreated, like the chirp of some electronic bird fading into the lowering dark.

Costa got down on the ground next to her, held her damp, sweating, twitching hand, leaned into her head, ignoring the foul smell rising from her agonies. He put his lips to her ear, then, not knowing whether she could hear, he began to murmur, over and over again, "Stay with me, stay with me, stay…"

Her breathing seemed to stop for a moment. Her eyes opened. Maggie Flavier's face was puffy and soaked in sweat and tears. But her right hand was jerking towards something. He looked into her eyes. They were calm, determined. As if she'd been here before.

She was pointing at the bag. He picked it up and turned it upside down, emptying the contents onto the forest floor.

The kit was there, with a red cross on the outside, and inside it were instructions and a primed syringe that looked like a pen. The drill he'd learned from the medical trainers flooded back. He tore open the pack, withdrew the needle, removed the cap, bent down, and in one sure, forceful move thrust the injector into her right thigh, through the fabric of her jeans.

Maggie half screamed, half sighed, and her head fell back hard, hitting the ground.

Still he held the pen there firmly, and kept his left hand in her hair. After ten seconds, as gently as he could, he eased the needle out of her flesh before checking that the drug had been dispensed. Then he threw the thing into the spent dry leaves.

She was sobbing. He cradled her in his arms, making comforting, wordless sounds, grappling for the phone, fighting to find the right language to use in this strange, foreign country.

From somewhere, finally, the words came.

He dialled 911, waited an agonisingly long time, then said, knowing the name would make a difference, not caring about whether that was right or wrong or just plain stupid, "I need an ambulance at the Rob Hill Campground, near the Legion of Honor, *now*. I have an actress here, Maggie Flavier. She's in anaphylactic shock and we need a paramedic team immediately. I've given her…" The words danced elusively in his head until he snatched up the discarded syringe package and examined the label. "…epinephrine. It's serious. She needs oxygen and immediate transfer to hospital."

The line went quiet.

Then a distant male voice asked, "You mean *the* Maggie Flavier?"

"I do," Costa answered calmly, and tried to remember something, anything about CPR.

PART 4

1

CATHERINE BIANCHI SAT AT THE WHEEL OF HER Dodge minivan looking as if she were worried about her career. Falcone was by her side, Peroni and Teresa Lupo in the back. Ahead, like ancient aircraft hangars at a decayed military installation ranged along the Bay shoreline, rose Fort Mason. Three buildings were bright with recent paint. Above the central one, a good ten metres high, stood the waving, multiarmed logo of Lukatmi. Its neon flashed in the dazzling morning sun.

The American police captain took a deep breath. She muttered, "You guys are going to get me into real trouble, aren't you?"

They had an appointment with Josh Jonah and Tom Black inside Lukatmi headquarters. If Bryant Street got to hear of it, there'd be plenty of awkward questions. It was difficult to see how interviewing the bosses of a digital media firm, albeit one heavily involved in financing *Inferno*, could possibly be justified given their tight and supposedly unbreakable orders: watch over the assembly of the exhibition, nothing more.

"You don't have to join us if you don't want,"

Falcone told Catherine. "I do think we have the right to be here."

That got him a fierce look in return.

"The Palace of Fine Arts, with all your precious stuff, is that way. There's not a single thing in those Lukatmi buildings that concerns you, Leo. There's nothing there but geeks and computers. We should be back where we're supposed to be." She seemed as exasperated as the rest of them. "Twiddling our thumbs and waiting to be told what to do next."

Falcone leaned back in his seat and sighed. "What we do next is look for the money."

Teresa Lupo realised she didn't have the energy to engage in that particular argument again. The same circular bout of bitching had rumbled on all morning, in between the inquiries to the hospital and the calls from an infuriated Quattrocchi and an equally livid Gerald Kelly of the SFPD. It was now two days since the attack on Maggie Flavier. The temperature hadn't cooled.

And yet Falcone stuck obstinately to his guns; somehow, somewhere, he insisted, this case was about nothing more than cash. Not a piece of poetry. Not an old movie. Money was at the root of everything. Maybe it was Josh Jonah and Tom Black protecting their investment. Maybe it was Roberto Tonti or Dino Bonetti trying to make sure the heavy mob who bankrolled *Inferno* got payback before they turned ugly. Or maybe it was the mob themselves doing just that. Those, as far as the inspector was concerned, were the only avenues worth exploring, not that they were supposed to.

Once the arguments began again, made yet more shrill by the howls of outrage from the Carabinieri and the suits in Bryant Street over Nic's close involvement with the actress they were supposed to be protecting, no one even bothered to ask much about Maggie Flavier's condition, which did nothing to calm Teresa Lupo's temper. A severe anaphylactic shock was a truly terrible experience. If Nic hadn't been there, it might have taken her life. Not that he was going to get much credit on that front. The media had fresher blood to excite its appetites.

She picked up that morning's copy of the *San Francisco Chronicle* from the vehicle's floor. They'd printed only one photo, of Nic bent over the stricken woman, stabbing the epinephrine pen into her thigh. It wasn't the worst. Some of the less fussy rags had felt no such restraint. In spite of his broken arm—now the subject of a police investigation on the grounds of assault—the paparazzo had hung around long enough to capture a series of images of the actress being taken into the ambulance by paramedics, with Nic, face grim and eyes steely, holding her hand.

While Teresa fumed over the paper, Peroni studied a couple of the grosser tabloids. Splashed over the front pages, alongside the shots of a woman in the throes of a dreadful allergic reaction, they carried photos of Maggie Flavier. She sat close to Nic, propped against the silver form of a grey, ghostly tree, smiling, a look on her face no one could mistake. It was one step away from a kiss, and everyone who saw it would surely have wondered what came after.

"If she'd died," Peroni pointed out, "they'd never have run these. Not for a day or two anyway. They'd call it 'respect.'"

That was probably true, Teresa thought. Allan Prime had been treated like a lost genius for a short while after his murder. Then the reporters had started to find other stories. Of his financial wranglings, his debts, his association with known criminals. And the women. Young, too young sometimes. Often vulnerable. Sometimes paid off for their "troubles." It took less than a week for the dead actor to tumble out of Hollywood heaven and into the gutter. Teresa had read enough about Maggie Flavier's past, a very typical tale of broken love affairs, tussles with the law, and the occasional drug and booze bust, to understand that the young woman would doubtless have followed the same path had she wound up on a morgue table.

"OK," Catherine Bianchi said. "I shouldn't be telling you this but I will. Nic isn't going to be charged over that guy's broken arm. He might get yelled at. No—he *will* get yelled at. But that's it. The SFPD doesn't like that kind any more than you."

"What do you know about him?" Falcone asked. "The photographer?"

"I can't possibly tell you that, Leo. You shouldn't even be asking."

"What if he's not just a photographer?" Peroni wondered. "What if he's involved?"

The woman's smart, dark face creased with fury. "We're not idiots. Don't presume you have some kind of monopoly over proper police procedure. We will investigate the man." She swore under her breath. "Hell, we *have* investigated him. He's a lowlife. He's been accused of harassing five young actresses over the last two years. He's a jerk and a creep and probably ought to get taken into some dark corner somewhere and taught a lesson he won't forget. But he is not a murderer."

The big man folded his arms and asked, "Where does he live?"

"You must be joking!"

"His name is Martin Vogel," Falcone announced, taking a scrap of paper out of his pocket. "He has an apartment somewhere called SoMa. I have the address. An art district or something, I'm told. Good restaurants apparently."

"What..." Catherine snarled. "Restaurants? What?"

"I thought we might go out for dinner somewhere."

"*Dinner?* Screw dinner, Leo! Are you seriously thinking of approaching a witness who claims—with some justification—that he's been assaulted by one of your own men? How the—"

"His name was in the paper. You have these things called phone books."

"Visit that man and you are on your own," she snapped. "God knows you're pushing my limits already. Martin Vogel's screaming that Nic attacked him. Some lawyer will be coming at us all for millions. Things are complicated enough already. I will not allow you to make them worse."

Falcone tapped his fingers on the dashboard, thinking. Then he said, "Martin Vogel was in the right location, though, wasn't he? Not an obvious place either."

"He's freelance camera scum," she pointed out. "Jackals like Vogel will follow someone like Maggie Flavier for days, weeks, just to get one photograph. Don't you have any idea how much he'll get for those photos? Thousands, probably. Not bad for an evening's work."

"The Legion of Honor was on my list," Teresa pointed out, ignoring the American policewoman and talking to Falcone. "The *Vertigo* list."

He scowled. "Nothing happened at the Legion of Honor. It was a mile away in the woods. Stop clutching at straws, please."

"But you said..." she protested. "About the car."

"It was just an old car. Perhaps the company that sent it had a movie buff on the staff. Where's the *real* link?"

"Carlotta Valdes!"

He had that foxy look in his eyes. One she both

loved and hated, because it was both a rejection and a challenge.

He gazed out the window in the direction of the Lukatmi studios and said, "If we can understand who benefits, who feels cheated, and, ultimately, who loses . . . there lie the answers."

"You're a philistine," Teresa announced. "And if you hope to understand the financing of modern movies, you'll be here for years." She waved a hand at the Lukatmi building. "I'll bet you even *they* don't understand it, and a stack of their money has already disappeared into Dino Bonetti's pockets. I'm a pathologist. I look for traces. So should you."

Falcone was unmoved. "You've no laboratory, no staff, no jurisdiction. Most of all you've no job. You're nothing more than a tourist here. Don't forget it."

"As if I could! You remind me every hour on the hour. So tell me. How did someone know that Maggie was vulnerable like that? Could Lukatmi's computers have told them she was allergic to almonds?"

"Any computer could have told them that," Catherine Bianchi said. "She had some kind of attack at the Cannes film festival three years ago. All the papers covered it. That one wasn't so severe, thankfully. But that's why she carries that syringe all the time." She eyed Teresa nervously. "You won't tell anyone I gave you that lab report, will you? They'd fire me. They'd have every right."

"Of course I won't!"

"So? What did it tell you?"

"You have a forensic department. What did it tell them?"

"Nothing more than you read in that report. Just...facts."

"And I'm supposed to give you more than that? Me? The *tourist*?"

All three of them stared at her in silence. And waited.

2

CAPTAIN GERALD KELLY LOATHED PRESS CONFER-ences. Particularly, he had come to realise, those press conferences that involved a police chief from another country, one who loved the limelight and seemed incapable of going anywhere in public without the presence of a similarly media-obsessed Canadian professor who never knew when to shut up.

Kelly had looked at Leo Falcone's odd pair of side-kicks while bawling them out the day before, one huge and old and ugly, the other slight and dark and handsome, and wished, with all his heart, that they had been on this case with him. Gerald Kelly had long ago learned to live with the nagging sense of doubt and uncertainty that went with everyday police work, so much that, at times, he came to regard these feelings almost as friends, ghosts on the shoulder reminding him to ask the impertinent, awkward, important questions he might otherwise have forgotten. On occasion the science people came up with tangible proof—a blood or semen stain, a fingerprint or a string of genetic code. But when science failed them, the answers almost always lay in lacunae, what was missing or unknown. Kelly had lived with that slippery reality for years, as had Falcone's men, he was certain of it. Not so the artificially erudite Gianluca Quattrocchi, a man who seemed to harbour very few doubts about anything, himself most of all, shunning the interesting if difficult Falcone for the diminutive Bryan Whitcombe, who was constantly at his side, tossing out obscure and useless literary references at any opportunity.

If this strange, tangled, and seemingly impenetrable case went on much longer, Kelly decided, he'd tell Quattrocchi that he was bringing Falcone and his men on board, no matter how loudly the Carabinieri back in Rome howled. He could live with the squeals. This was San Francisco, not Italy. It was his call. The SFPD needed all the bright help they could get on this one, and Kelly's instincts told him Leo Falcone and his men could provide it.

Kelly grunted an inaudible curse as the TV men swarmed forward, raising their cameras. Nic Costa, who was more than Falcone's right-hand man, Kelly could sense that in the bond between them, was at that very moment the quarry of a thousand prying lenses. California's dread legions of showbiz hacks and cameramen were seeking photos and interviews with Maggie Flavier. Second best would be the man who had saved her life, not long after he had seemingly entered it in a way half the male population of America envied as they pored over the photos in that morning's papers. Maggie Flavier in her prime, Maggie Flavier in her agony. And gazing adoringly at some lowly Italian cop. This ravenous pack usually saved its activities for L.A.; now Kelly had them on his doorstep in San Francisco. It did nothing to improve his mood.

Kelly had seen enough of show business to understand that when stars and the movie trade came into play, every key aspect of an investigation had to be approved by the tin gods above him. Slowly, ineluctably, this homicide investigation was starting to follow the familiar path from a tight, well-ordered police case to a public circus, one played out daily in the papers and on the TV. He had seen this happen often enough to know there was no way of turning back the clock.

The conference room was packed. Standing room only. The event was, naturally, going out live, through the networks, and, he saw to his amazement, over the web, too. The crew at the very front wore bomber jackets bearing the logo of Lukatmi.

"Wait a minute," Kelly whispered to the police

public affairs officer who was watching her minions trying to keep some kind of order in a rabble of more than a hundred assorted newspaper, TV, radio, and web hacks. "Josh Jonah's got himself a TV station now?"

"Since last month," the woman whispered back. "Don't you read the news?"

"Only the stuff that matters. Who the hell let his ponytails in here? And why are they sitting up front like they own the place?"

"I did. How am I supposed to keep them out? They're media. They've got an audience bigger than ten local news stations. Besides, Lukatmi is backing that movie. They're using this footage for some program on the 'making of...' or something."

Kelly stared at the woman in disbelief. "This is a homicide investigation. Not a reality show."

"You have your job. I have mine. We both report to the commissioner's office. You want to sort this out there?"

"Listen—"

"No, you listen. Josh Jonah and Tom Black have been on all the networks, prime-time nationwide TV, telling the world what great pals they were with Allan Prime. They've delivered flowers by the truckload to Maggie Flavier. How do you think it's going to look if we throw their TV crew onto the street?"

"I don't care about how it looks..." Kelly was aware his voice was rising. The lights came up just then and he found himself stared at by a multitude of faces in a sea of shining artificial suns. "And frankly," he muttered, "I am starting to care even less with every passing minute."

"That's your problem," the public affairs woman snapped, then thrust an envelope at him. "They asked me to give you that."

"Who?"

She looked a little guilty. "The commissioner's office. After Bonetti and the Lukatmi people got in there. Via the mayor's office, I ought to add. The governor's been on the line, too."

Kelly blinked. The public affairs woman added something he didn't quite catch, then waded into the audience, trying to instill some order. Gerald Kelly fervently wished he were anywhere else on the planet but in this room, with these people, knowing that, in between the crap and the prurience, there'd be a few good, decent, old-fashioned reporters who knew how to ask good, decent, old-fashioned questions. Ones he couldn't begin to answer.

He didn't have the time to look at the sheet of paper the infobabe had handed him. The room had exploded in a frenzy. The media was hungry and demanding to be fed. Besides, the first question was prearranged: some guy from the *Examiner*, primed to ask the obvious. Was there any proven connection with Allan Prime's death? Kelly liked to seed the openers. It gave him a slim chance to keep a handle on things. Normally.

"Any connection is supposition at this moment..."

he began, after the plant rose to his mark. He faltered. He was astonished to see Gianluca Quattrocchi reaching over to take the mike from him, talking in his florid English, saying the exact opposite. Kelly sat, dumbstruck, listening to the stuck-up Italian blathering on about poetry and motivation and the damned movie that seemed to overshadow one bloody murder and now a near-fatality, too.

As he reached some obscure point about the relationship between the crimes and the cycle inside the book, the pompous Carabinieri man fell silent. He gestured to the Canadian at his side to finish the answer.

"The links are implicit, obvious, and ominous," Whitcombe announced, in his weedy, professorial voice. "In Dante's Hell, the punishment fits the crime. Allan Prime died in the second circle, that of the wanton. He was led to his death by a woman, and the publicity we have since seen seems to indicate that Prime's private life merited this description. The third circle is that of the gluttonous. Ergo..."

Kelly muttered to Quattrocchi, "Ergo what? Maggie Flavier was eating an apple. This is not what we agreed."

"Listen, please," the Italian replied, shushing him, almost politely, "the man is a genius."

"He's a frigging..." Kelly began, and then shut up.

The PR woman was actually pointing at him from the audience, her long finger erect in the bright lights of the camera, then running across her upper lip, as if to say "Zip it."

In the front row, McGuire, the crime reporter for the *Chronicle,* had started to snigger.

Kelly picked up the envelope the infobabe had given him, ripped it open, and read the contents with growing disbelief.

3

TERESA LUPO WISHED THE AMERICAN POLICE-woman hadn't asked about Maggie Flavier's poisoning. Teresa hated imprecision more than anything.

So she simply said, "The poor woman met her wicked stepmother. Or stepfather. Who knows? Unless your people find the man who gave her that poisoned apple."

"Mobile caterers..." Catherine Bianchi sighed. "They're minimum-wage businesses. What do you expect?"

"Not much. The thing is..." She felt as if she were trying to analyse a scene from a movie, one that had been ripped out of context. Without knowledge of what preceded the event, she couldn't begin to pull some logic out of what might follow. "...it's a very

strange way to try to murder someone. If that's what
it was. Particularly given the way they killed Allan
Prime. A crossbow bolt through the skull. A poisoned apple given to someone with a food allergy. It
doesn't even sound like the same person to me. What
they did to Maggie was horrifying. But…"

The more she thought about it, the more convinced she became. "If I were a betting person, I'd lay
money against her being badly affected by a cruel
stunt like that, much less killed. She spends most of
her time near lots of people. She knows she has that
allergy and she's prepared to deal with it. Yes, she was
at risk in the woods, alone with Nic. But who could
have predicted she'd be there? The chances of her
dying should have been quite slim."

Falcone finally took his attention away from the
Lukatmi building. "You mean they *weren't* trying to
kill her?"

"I don't know what I mean. I just think it was a
very odd way to go about it if that's what they
wanted. Perhaps they just planned to hurt her. They
certainly managed that."

She tried to put the problem succinctly. "What
bothers me most of all is the style. Allan Prime had no
chance of survival whatsoever. He died from violence
of the most extreme sort, the kind of brute force we
see ten, twenty times a year because that's the way the
human race tends to go about eliminating one another. It's quick. It's easy. You don't have to do much
in the way of preparation. But poisoning…it's rare.

And tricky. I've only dealt with one case of willful poisoning in my entire career and that worked only because the victim was dying from heart disease already. Why now? Why here of all places?" One more thing bothered her. "Do they grow almonds in California?"

"Of course," Catherine answered. "Millions of them. Merced County. About an hour south. I go at the end of February, when the blossom's out. You can do a tour. It's beautiful."

"Farmed almonds? For sale?"

"Sure. But you don't need to go out and buy almonds to get almond essence. It's on sale in any grocery store."

"Not this kind," Teresa answered, wishing she had her lab and Silvio Di Capua. "Whatever was injected into that apple was homemade. There were traces of fibre. You don't get that in essence. Also, there was a small but noticeable amount of prussic acid."

That silenced them.

"Cyanide," she explained.

"Cyanide smells of almonds," Peroni pointed out.

"Or almonds smell of cyanide, whichever way you want to look at it. The native wild almond contains a substance that transforms into hydrogen cyanide when the flesh is crushed or bruised. Domesticated varieties have had that mostly bred out of them, though they retain the smell. That's not what Maggie Flavier got. She was poisoned with the crushed fruit of a wild bitter almond. You can still buy bitter-almond essence in Rome. We use it, very carefully, in cooking. But it's banned in the U.S., except in medicine, which is why I guess he had to make it himself."

"So she had cyanide poisoning, too?" Catherine asked, bewildered. "And you still think they weren't trying to kill her?"

"Not with cyanide. It was a minute amount. You can get exactly the same effect using standard almond essence from a grocery store. It was the allergic reaction that put Maggie in hospital. There wasn't enough cyanide there to do much of anything. I don't get it."

Falcone yawned. Details that went nowhere always bored him.

The clock on the dashboard ticked over to one-fifteen. They were due inside Lukatmi.

"That supermarket over there," he said, reaching into his wallet and pulling out a fifty-dollar bill. "We need some shopping."

Teresa took a deep breath in an attempt to calm herself. "Are you going to do this to me every time there's someone interesting to talk to?"

"We scarcely have reason to be in that place," Peroni said apologetically. "You certainly don't."

"So I'm supposed to shop? While you question the Lukatmi guys?"

"A suggestion only," Falcone cut in. "I would never presume to give you orders. It would be impertinent. And also..." He mulled over the words.

"...somewhat counterproductive. You fare best left on your own. Think about old films and bitter almonds, please. Just do it out of my earshot."

Muttering something obscene in which the phrase "stinking cops" was one of the milder rebukes, she got out of the car, slamming the door as hard as she could behind her.

It was a bright, cold summer day. The chill of the strong sea breeze soon began to make her teeth ache. She thought of walking out to Fort Point, a mile or so towards the bridge, and trying to find the exact location for the haunting scene in which Jimmy Stewart rescued Kim Novak from the ocean. Much, it seemed to her, as Nic had apparently saved the stricken Maggie Flavier. Life imitating art. Quattrocchi believed that was happening. So did she, but in a different way. While Leo Falcone...

Teresa Lupo wasn't sure she was right. But she was certain they were wrong, at least in part.

She walked back towards the Marina, thinking. Naturally, she'd keyed their number into her phone, under the single name HankenFrank.

"Pronto!" said a voice on the other end.

"What the hell are you doing talking Italian, Frank?"

"What the hell are you doing being ignorant of caller ID?" the voice on the other end demanded. "And how did you know it was me, not zygote two?"

"Because you sound different, even if you don't know it. Can I buy you two coffee?"

"Only if you have some interesting questions with which to entertain us."

"That," Teresa said, pocketing Falcone's fifty-dollar bill, "I can guarantee."

4

BRYAN WHITCOMBE WAS DRONING ON ABOUT poetry again, things a homicide cop could never, Gerald Kelly felt, be expected to understand or take seriously. About how the fourth circle was to do with the avaricious and the prodigal. About how they should expect, given the rigid adherence to the subject matter of the structure of *Inferno,* that any next intended victim should somehow have fallen guilty to these sins.

"That narrows it down in the movie business," Kelly muttered. He didn't mind that a couple of people in the front row got to hear, the furious-looking public affairs woman among them.

Someone put up their hand and asked the kind of obvious question hacks always wanted to bring up: "And after that?"

Whitcombe launched into the list. The fifth circle, the irascible. The sixth, the heresiarch, which he defined as the leader of some dissenting movement.

Then the seventh, the violent. The fraudulent and the malicious, the eighth. Finally the last, the traitors.

"And after that?" the same reporter asked.

Kelly snatched the microphone and barked, "After that, there's not a living soul left in the whole of California. Gentlemen. Ladies. I leave you with our Italian friends and their pet professor. Some of us have work to do."

He stalked out and went straight to his office three floors above. The conference was still going on. Quattrocchi and Whitcombe were fielding questions. The harpy from public affairs had press-ganged poor, meek Cy Fielding, one of Kelly's oldest and softest detectives, onto the podium in his place. Not that anyone seemed remotely interested in what the man might say.

Kelly looked at the letter from the commissioner's office again and swore. The phone on his desk rang.

"Yes!" he yelled into it.

It was Sheldon from the commissioner's office, all sweetness and sympathy.

"Calm down. We would have told you beforehand, but you weren't around."

"That's because I was out doing my job. Believe it or not, murderers rarely walk into the office on their own or turn up as attachments in an e-mail."

Kelly hit the keyboard on his computer and brought up the video of the press conference. It was live on the screen in front of him in an instant, naturally. Geeks ran the SFPD. Like they ran the world. At that moment just about every police officer inside a station in San Francisco was doubtless watching this piece of vaudeville instead of walking the street looking for bad guys.

"When a big movie company wants to drop a million dollars on the table as a reward for finding the bastards who butchered one of their stars and tried to kill another, we listen," Sheldon said calmly. "We have no choice. These people have clout. Especially Quattrocchi. You have to work with them."

"A million-dollar reward," Kelly spat back at the phone. He put on an accent he thought came close to Quattrocchi's dainty English. "For information leading to the arrest and conviction of anyone threatening the life or security of any cast members or associates of Roberto Tonti's *Inferno*. Jesus. Hollywood's writing the script for *us* now. Don't you see that? They're turning this into a freak show."

"Enough—"

"No. Not enough. I won't shut up. You've just taken away half my manpower. Maybe more. 'Cause now we have to field the phones listening to kooks who think their neighbour's a star-killer."

"Enough!"

That was loud, and Sheldon didn't normally do loud. So, reluctantly, Kelly kept quiet.

"I say this once and once only, Gerry. You're too damned good to throw away your career over this. And it could happen. Believe me."

"Someone murdered Allan Prime. Maybe they tried to murder Maggie Flavier. We are not dealing with an episode of *Columbo* here."

"Maybe?"

"You heard me."

"That's your problem. These guys have got money. They've got clout. They've got the ear of the governor, the mayor, and God almighty for all I know. Deal with it, Kelly. Otherwise, these guys will eat you alive."

Captain Gerald Kelly slammed down the phone, then rolled his executive chair around and stared out the window.

The worst thing was, Sheldon had a point.

5

"PONYTAILS," CATHERINE BIANCHI GRUMBLED AS they walked through the wide central hall of Lukatmi Building Number One. Three galleries ranged around the sides, each housing cubicles lit by the glow from ranks and ranks of computer screens. In the centre of the hall were scattered vast soft sofas in bright primary colours, pinball and foosball machines, places to eat and drink coffee. The staff, all around twenty-five, rarely more, wore jeans and

T-shirts and either lolled in the play area or dashed about looking deeply serious, often tapping away at tiny handheld computers. To Peroni, it seemed like a kindergarten for people who would never grow up. Except for the flashing sports-style scoreboard at the end of the vast interior, set against a window overlooking San Francisco Bay, with a rough grey chunk of Alcatraz, a lump of uninviting rock and slab-like buildings, intruding into the corner.

High above the office the electronic scoreboard displayed the Lukatmi stock price in a running ticker alongside a host of other tech industry giants: Microsoft, Apple, Google, Yahoo.

A skinny individual with greasy shoulder-length hair had been deputed to meet them when they arrived. He said very little and did so eating a sandwich that looked as if it were stuffed with pond weed. When he saw what had caught Peroni's attention, he tapped the big Italian cop on the shoulder and nodded at the scoreboard.

"Watch the totals. Dinosaurs down five percent average over the year. Lukatmi . . ."

The numbers kept on flickering. There was a big "up" arrow next to the symbol that had the multi-armed logo by its side.

"Sixty percent and rising."

Catherine Bianchi eyed him and said, "The dinosaurs have still got more money than you. They could buy out Lukatmi tomorrow if they wanted. Or invent something that kills you stone dead overnight. Beware old people. They don't harbour grudges, they nurture them."

The geek shrugged. "You know, lady, when you're living inside the *e*-conomy you soon get to realise there are some things people *outside,* old people in particular, never ever come to comprehend."

"Does that mean you're up for sale or not?" Falcone asked.

"I code," he replied, after a bite of pond weed. "Nothing else. My old man told me anything's for sale if the price is right. But I earn more in one year than he ever got in a lifetime. So who do you think I should listen to?"

"Perry Como," Peroni suggested. " 'Hot Diggity, Dog Ziggity Boom.' "

Their guide looked bewildered for a moment, then pointed. "Josh's and Tom's offices are over there. I will leave you three now before whatever time machine you own drags me back to the Ice Age, too."

The big cop watched him leave.

"What's the kid's beef? Pierino Como was a fine Italian American."

"The kid belongs to a superior race," Catherine guessed, then held out her hand to Josh Jonah and Tom Black. Both were approaching, Black a foot or two behind his partner.

Neither looked welcoming.

"What's this about?" Jonah wanted to know.

"Security," she said, promptly. "Yours. Ours. The movie. The people." She smiled. "And the stuff. You do understand the stuff is important, too, don't you, Josh? My Italian friends have lost a very important museum exhibit already. They don't want to lose any more."

Peroni considered this strange couple. Skinny, moody, arrogant, with his long, carefully coiffured fair hair, Jonah seemed to be just the type who'd be running a company like Lukatmi. Student on the outside, shark on the in. Tom Black, though...he wasn't so sure. They'd run through some profiles before arriving. The two of them had met at college, Stanford. Black was the coding genius, Jonah the business visionary. A complementary mix, left side of brain meets right side, or so the glowing profiles claimed. Untold wealth ensued. But did that mean they liked one another? Peroni saw no sign of it. These two men had just turned twenty-three and were, at that moment, worth more than a billion dollars each, with much, much more in prospect if they managed to "grow the company," as the papers put it, or sell the business on a high. Not that it seemed to be making them happy just at the moment.

"How's Maggie?" Tom Black asked.

"We know no more about Miss Flavier than you've seen on TV," Falcone told him.

"Don't give me that," Jonah moaned. "That was your guy with her."

"When they..." Black added, before stopping awkwardly.

"If you don't know about Maggie," Jonah went on, "what the hell are you here for?"

He barked at a passing female employee to fetch him a coffee. Lukatmi didn't look much like a new-age politically correct do-no-evil-to-anyone corporation to Peroni. He'd seen bosses in Italy treat women staff that way—and get their heads chewed off in return.

"Sorry," Tom Black told them. "This is a bad time for us. Allan's murder... The movie. How it got out onto the web... We're working to make sure it can't hit us again."

"How did it happen in the first place?" Peroni asked.

Jonah stepped in to field the question. "In ways you people never could understand. Ask the SFPD tech team. It was no failure on our part. Not even on our network. Some dumb third-party supplier. Bryant Street and the Carabinieri have their names. We'll wind up suing the shit out of them. Or taking their business." His hand made a dismissive sweep through the cold office air. "That crap could have happened to anyone. Microsoft. Google. We were not to blame, and if anyone says so, they can talk to our lawyers."

He took the coffee off the woman who brought it and didn't even acknowledge her presence.

"Lukatmi is a busy corporation," Jonah insisted. "All that old junk at the exhibition... that's got nothing to do with us. We're investors in *Inferno*. We have a fiduciary interest in its success. That does not extend to any crap you brought with you from Italy." He glanced at his watch, theatrically. "Now if you don't mind...I'll have someone show you out."

"What do the investors think?" Catherine Bianchi asked.

Josh Jonah's face froze. "Our investors are looking at a return on their money of between sixty and a thousand percent, depending on when they came in," he replied sharply. "How would *you* feel in that situation?"

"Nervous. That's paper money. The only way you can get your hands on it is to sell now. If you do that, you lose on any upside that comes after. You guys are getting big. Maybe you're the next Google..."

"Google..." Black sighed. "That comparison is getting *so* tired."

"Why?" Catherine Bianchi demanded. "Because they're *not* in the red?"

The two young men stayed silent.

"You're buying yourselves Ferraris on dream dust," she went on. "I talked to an analyst buddy. He told me you're four, six quarters away from reporting anything close to a real profit. And even that's just speculation."

"Analysts..." Jonah mumbled, and scratched his head.

Black cleared his throat, like someone starting a lecture. "You can't apply old-world economics to what we do. You can't gauge our value on a spread-sheet. Those days are past. Those people are past."

She wasn't budging. "Even in the new world, you have shareholders, Tom. They'll still want to recoup their investment at some point, and after the last crash, they know they can't do that out of thin air."

Peroni realised he was starting to like Catherine Bianchi a lot. She hadn't mentioned a word of this before they went in.

"That's your real fiduciary duty," she persisted. "To the people who own your stock. That's your *legal* duty. Unless you think the law's just so..." She waved her hands, did a woozy hippie look. "...like twentieth century, man."

"Your analyst buddy tell you anything else?" Jonah asked.

She walked up and stood very close to him. "He said there's a bunch of shareholders looking at a class action right now. Seems they didn't know about you investing their money in a movie. They claim it was unapproved and illegal to cut a deal like that from the funds you were raising to develop Lukatmi. When that lawsuit lands on your desk, your stock could go forty, sixty...maybe two hundred percent *south*. If that happens, anyone could stroll through the door and pick you up for a song. You're walking a tightrope and I think you're hoping *Inferno* will keep you upright. Maybe it will. Maybe not."

Josh Jonah pointed to the exit. "You can walk there or I can get someone to walk you."

With that he turned on his heel, and Tom Black, stuttering apologies, did the same. They watched the two men return to their gigantic executive fish tank overlooking the Bay.

The geek who'd been eating the pond weed sandwich showed them to the door without saying a single word. The day was a little warmer when they got outside.

"So that's why you made captain," Peroni declared, and shook Catherine's hand.

Falcone was beaming like a teenager in love. "It's nearly two. Time for a late lunch," he announced. "Somewhere good. Fish, I think. Perhaps even a glass of wine. Then I have to call Nic."

"That would be nice, Leo. But I have a police station to run."

"Dinner then."

She looked at him. Then she said, "You can be very importunate sometimes."

Peroni watched in awe as the merest shadow of a blush rose on Falcone's cheeks.

"It was just an idea. I'm on my own. You ..."

"I have a million friends, some of whom think they're more than that." She wrinkled her nose. "OK—you're on for dinner. But you behave. No wandering around SoMa. No getting near Martin Vogel. That's the deal. Gerald Kelly is a good guy. He might do you a favour one day. If you don't jerk his chain again. Agreed?"

"That's the deal," the inspector replied with a little

too much enthusiasm, then glanced back at the Lukatmi building, with its vast multiarmed logo over the hall. "They're desperate, aren't they?"

"They're a couple of naive kids drowning in so much money they can't count it. They don't know what's around the corner. Of course they're desperate. It doesn't mean..."

She reached into her handbag and took out a band. Then she fastened back her hair. Catherine Bianchi looked more serious, more businesslike, that way. It was her office look, the signal that she was preparing to go back into the Greenwich Street Police Station and get on with the job.

"My dad worked in a repair shop. He taught me that mechanics matter. A lot sometimes. Arranging for Allan Prime to be abducted. Getting all that equipment into that little gallery where he died. Sure, these two geeks could point a camera in his face and put it on the web. But the physical part... finding that penniless actor and getting him to threaten Maggie in the park. Coming at her again here with a poisoned apple. I don't see it, somehow."

"Jonah could do it," Peroni suggested.

"He'd like to think so. But then, he'd like to think he could run the world. I'd hate to be around if he got the chance to try. Now you go guard your old 'junk.' And stay out of trouble."

"This analyst?" Falcone asked tentatively. "He's a... friend? Nothing more?"

Catherine threw her head back and laughed.

"He's an imaginary friend. I made it all up just to see what happened. Companies like Lukatmi come and go. If they don't have someone preparing a class somewhere, they're probably out of business anyway."

"Oh," Falcone said softly, then put a finger to his cheek and fell silent.

"Can I drop you somewhere?" Catherine asked. "Such as the Palace of Fine Arts and that exhibition you're supposed to be guarding?"

"We can walk," Falcone answered. "We need the fresh air. But thank you."

6

THE PARK HILL SANATORIUM WAS LOCATED IN AN old mansion on Buena Vista Avenue, opposite a quiet green space overlooking the city. Costa drove lazily through Haight-Ashbury to get there, then parked two blocks away on a steep hillside street. The staff entrance was around the corner. From the ground-floor hall, he could see that the front of the building was besieged by reporters and cameramen, the road choked with live TV broadcast vans. Baffled residents of this wealthy, calm suburb walked past shaking their heads, many with immaculately trimmed pedigreed dogs attached to long leads. This wasn't the kind of scene owners or animals were used to witnessing. They probably preferred it on TV, beamed from somewhere else, distant, visible but out of reach. Costa felt grateful that Catherine Bianchi had called ahead to make arrangements for him to enter by a different door. Otherwise, he knew, he'd have been forced to run the gamut of the media mob.

Maggie had been transferred to Park Hill Sanatorium after several hours in the ER of a private hospital in the centre of the city. The corridors resembled those of a fine hotel, not any medical institution he'd entered. Vases of fresh flowers stood in every corner and alcove, piped music sang discreetly in the corridors. Smiling white-clad staff wandered around nonchalantly. He found it impossible to imagine anything more distant than this place from the chaos and crush of a Roman public hospital. The rich and famous lived differently. Somehow that thought had not occurred to him during the brief time he had known her. Beauty and fame apart, Maggie seemed... *ordinary* was the word that first occurred to him as he walked to her room, carrying a twenty-dollar bouquet of roses.

Yet he couldn't get out of his head the image of her standing in front of the paintings in the Legion of Honor, choosing which one—which woman from the past, from someone else's imagination—she would select for her next role. Maggie Flavier enjoyed being possessed in this way because for a few months or, in the case of *Inferno,* more, she no longer had to deal with the difficult task of defining her own identity. In the skin of others, she was free to escape the drudgery of everyday existence, the old, unanswerable questions: who am I, and why am I here?

The questions Costa asked himself every day. The ones that made him feel alive. He couldn't begin to understand why she avoided them with such relentless deliberation. All he felt sure of was that she was aware of this act of self-deception, acutely, for every minute of the performance.

She was beneath the sheets of a large double bed, propped up on pillows next to a wall filled with flowers. The room was large and flooded with light; the window behind her opened onto a gorgeous vista of the skyline of downtown San Francisco and the ocean beyond. Simon Harvey sat on a chair by her side, holding her hand, staring into her tired green eyes with an expression that managed to combine both sympathy and some sense of ownership. Her hair was still blonde, though it now seemed dull and shapeless.

"Nic," Maggie said, smiling warmly at his appearance.

"I didn't mean to interrupt."

"You didn't," Maggie said quietly. "Simon's an old friend. We did a movie together in the Caribbean. When was it …"

"Five years ago," Harvey answered, releasing her hand, still not looking in Costa's direction. The publicist seemed different in America—more at home, more powerful. In Rome he'd appeared a tangential, almost servile figure, running round the set at Cinecittà doing the bidding of anyone who called, Tonti or Bonetti or even Allan Prime. Here, in Maggie's room, he didn't look like the kind of man to take orders. "Piece of derivative pirate crap posing as art-house. It bombed. At least we got paid. Not everyone did."

Harvey stood. He seemed bigger somehow in the bright, hard California light streaming through the long windows.

"I don't know whether I should shake you by the hand or punch you in the mouth. If it wasn't for you, Maggie might not be alive. And she might not have gotten into this situation to begin with. What do you think?"

"I wouldn't advise the second. It would be impolite, and I can't imagine anyone in the publicity business would want that."

"You're a smart-ass, Costa. Maybe you can get away with that in Rome. You won't get away with it here. Remember that when you need me."

"Simon," Maggie protested, "will you stop being so rude? I told you a million times—it was *my* idea to play hooky from all that tedium at the exhibition. If you want to blame someone, blame me."

"I do. And him. The pair of you." He extended his hand to Costa. "But Maggie's alive and I'm grateful for that. And now the two of you are all over the papers. So I have a professional interest, too."

His grip was firm and powerful.

"Not in me you don't," Costa said.

"Please," Maggie implored him. "Sit down, Nic. Hear Simon out." She looked at him and Costa couldn't interpret what was in her eyes. Dependence? Fear? "He's my publicist, too. Not just the movie's. My advisor. I need you to listen to him."

Costa sat down on the end of the bed and said, "But first I need you to tell me how you are. That's why I came here."

The actress leaned back against the pillows. Her face fell into the shadow cast by the long drapes.

"I'm exhausted, my head hurts, I'm full of dope and glucose. I've had worse hangovers." A scowl creased her half-hidden face. "It was an allergy, that's all. All I needed was a shot—and thanks to you, that happened—and I'll be fine. They say I can leave here soon. The premiere's next Thursday. I'll be fine for that."

"Why the rush?"

"What kind of business do you think this is?" Harvey demanded. "Get up at ten, work for an hour, then go home and party? Celebrity never stops. Not for weekends. Not for sickness. Not for anything."

"I understand that."

Maggie shook her head. "No, you don't. No one can. Not until it happens."

"You don't even escape it when you're dead,"

Harvey said. "Josh Jonah's people are looking at out-take footage of Allan Prime right now, seeing what they can CGI for the sequel. That's going to be an interesting one for the money men. Who gets the fee?"

"What?" Costa was unable to comprehend what he was saying.

"There's going to be a second *Inferno*," Maggie told him. "They'll work up Allan's outtakes on computers."

"God knows what the story line's going to be," Harvey barked with mirthless laughter. "How many circles can Hell have? Mind you, Roberto didn't bother so much with that for the original. Why worry now? After what's happened, all the publicity, the interest... *Inferno*'s no longer just a movie. It's becoming an obsession. And that could mean a franchise. A brand. Like Sony or McDonald's or Leonardo da Vinci. They could get eight years, maybe even a decade out of this. With or without Tonti. Or any of us. When something's this big, no one's indispensable."

The publicist took Maggie's hand again. "And she—my friend and my client—is going to be a part of that brand. I'm going to make sure of that. A precious and important part. If we handle this story about the two of you right, it works in everyone's favour. Maggie's. Yours. The movie's—"

"I am not your client," Costa interrupted, suddenly angry. "I am not in your business."

"You are now," Harvey retorted. "Don't you get it?

The moment those pictures of you two appeared in the papers, you lost everything you ever had. Your privacy. Your identity. Your *soul*. It's all out there..." He pointed to the window. "You've just become the livelihood of people you wouldn't wish on a dog. They feed their kids off you, they take their wives and their mistresses out to dinner on what you make for them. Break that deal..."

"There is no deal. This has nothing to do with me."

"As if you have a choice! It's too late for that. You're part of the story. Screw with my client's ability to fulfill her potential and"—Harvey bunched a fist and shook it in Costa's face—"you will answer to me. *Capisce*, Soverintendente?"

"An intelligent man spends a year in Rome," Costa observed without emotion, "and still your accent sounds like that of a bad actor in a cheap gangster movie."

"Don't push me..."

"Will you both shut up! *Will* you...?"

She had her hands to her ears. Her face spoke of pain and fatigue. Costa felt something elemental tug at his heart, an emotion he hadn't known since Emily was alive. Guilt mingled with a deep, intense sense of misgiving about what might lie ahead.

"I was beginning to feel better until you two started screaming at each other," she moaned, real tears in her eyes. "What the hell gave you the right to walk in here and start bawling each other out like a couple of teenagers?"

"Nothing," Costa answered, and placed the bouquet of roses on the bed. It suddenly seemed insignificant next to the gigantic displays of orchids and garish, gigantic blooms he couldn't begin to name ranged against the wall.

"Is this what you want?" he asked softly. "Another year with Roberto Tonti? Another year of being someone else?"

She turned to Harvey, squeezed his hand, and said, "Leave this to me, Simon."

The American left without a word, just a single threatening glance in Costa's direction.

Maggie beckoned to Nic to take the empty seat. She held his hand, looked into his face. He wanted to ask himself who it was that he saw before him. Her? Or someone else, someone stolen from a painting?

Costa felt oddly, reluctantly detached. As if someone were watching, directing this scene, one that was happening in some place that was apart from all that he regarded as reality.

"I'm sorry," she whispered, looking so pale, so frail and fallible and human, eyes moist with fatigue and emotion.

"There's nothing for you to be sorry about, Maggie. Just rest. Take your time. Think things through."

She laughed through her tears. "Time. I don't have any, Nic. I never have any. There are a million actresses out there screaming to take my place, most of them younger, smarter, better than me. Dino Bonetti wants to make this sequel. There's a lot of money at

stake. I have to sign now, to commit. Otherwise…"
She wiped her face with the sleeve of her dressing
gown. "Let's face it. Nobody knows who the hell Beatrice is anyway. All she does is stand there looking
transcendental, promising Dante they'll be together
one day, if only he lives a good life. Any actress in a
blonde wig could play her. I'm thirty-one years old. If
it wasn't for all this publicity, they wouldn't even be
offering me the part. I'll be thirty-four, thirty-five before the movie even appears. In this profession that's
ancient. I can't say no."

Her eyes stared into his. "Also…" She hesitated.
"I'd be in Rome, too. For the filming. I thought…
you might like that idea."

"I'd like that very much," he answered honestly.

She reached down and took the modest bouquet
of roses, smelled them, and said, "These are the nicest
flowers anyone's ever given me."

"The ones in Rome…" he said, and that instant a
picture entered his head, of the two of them walking
through the Campo dei Fiori, hand in hand, past the
flower stalls, with not a single photographer in sight.

"Tell me about it, Nic," she urged. "About you.
About where you live. Your family. About who you
are."

He held her hand in a room that seemed like a
suite in a hotel he could never hope to afford, staring
down towards the city and the distant blue Pacific
Ocean, and he told her. Nic Costa talked, as much to
himself as to her. Of a quiet, difficult child taking

lone bicycle rides on the Appian Way, of grapes and wine, of the countryside and the ruins, the tombs and the churches, the simple, modest rural life that his family had enjoyed as he grew up, watching their close-knit love for each other fall apart through sickness and age, however much he tried to hold back time, however hard he fought to paper over the cracks.

Some things were inevitable, even for the young.

He'd no idea how long he spoke, only that she never said a word. When he was finished, his own eyes were stinging from tears. He felt as if some immense inner burden had lifted from him, one so heavy, familiar, and persistent he had long ago ceased to notice its presence.

She was sound asleep against the pillows, her mouth open, snoring softly.

Costa picked up the roses from the coverlet and placed them next to the bed. Then he let himself out of the room.

The staff were no strangers to celebrity. They guided him back to the side entrance, where he strode out into the bright, cold July sun.

A sea of bodies surrounded him immediately. Reporters jabbed mikes in his face. Photographers with cameras roared his name.

They followed him down the street. Across the road stood Simon Harvey. As Costa passed, Harvey tipped an imaginary hat and smiled sarcastically.

This was his work, Costa realized. A publicist's way of saying, "Do as I say or pay the price."

Costa said nothing, simply smiled for the cameras and tried to look as pleasant and as baffled as he could.

When he reached the car, he drove down the hill into Haight-Ashbury, found the nearest empty café, and ordered a coffee. It was nearly four in the afternoon. He'd achieved nothing all day.

His phone rang.

"How is she?" Falcone asked.

"Recovering."

"Good. You should find that photographer you hit and apologise."

"I am so very much in the mood for that right now."

"Excellent. I'll give you the address."

7

TERESA LUPO RECOGNISED THE PLACE THE MOment HankenFrank's ancient Buick pulled up outside. Mission Dolores had changed very little in the fifty years since Hitchcock chose the church for a short but significant role in his movie. Not that the twins seemed much interested in that idea. All the way from Cow Hollow they talked of Dante and his numbers. Nothing else.

"So this guy of yours…" Frank went on. "Quattrocchi…the snooty one we saw on the TV…"

"He's Carabinieri," she declared from the rear seat. "Not one of ours."

Hank, who was at the wheel with his brother next to him, eased the old car into a parking spot, then leaned back to look at her. "A cop's a cop."

"What about the FBI?"

"They're not cops," Hank pointed out.

"Neither are the Carabinieri!"

"Yeah, well, they look that way to the SFPD and that's what matters."

"Hank," she said, taking his hand over the seat back and looking into his large, watery blue eyes. "Try and understand. You're not reading a book now. This is not Sherlock Holmes versus Inspector Lestrade of Scotland Yard. Real life isn't fiction. It's all much more complicated and ragged at the edges. There are rarely neat symmetrical resolutions. People like me, the police, the Carabinieri…we just blunder around in the dark, hopefully with a little skill, creativity, and luck, praying there's light somewhere around the corner. But don't quote me on that. Ever. It's supposed to be a secret."

Frank let out a warm, throaty chuckle. "Worst one you people have. We read newspapers, too, you know. If it wasn't for the scientists…"

"Science isn't everything. Trust me. I know. Did

you ever read of someone getting murdered over poetry?"

"This is America. You *need* a reason to get killed?"

"But *poetry*?"

Hank perked up and punched his brother playfully on the arm. "On the other hand, this isn't our case, is it? The whole thing began in Rome. In Europe. Maybe that's where it all comes from. And in Europe…"

"In Europe we don't murder people over poetry either."

With his fondness for Victorian fiction, Hank relished the Dante story for the same reason Quattrocchi and the media did. It was colourful. It engaged the imagination. It told people that this involved more than low cunning, naked violence, and one instance of vicious, heartless homicide. There was, as Quattrocchi was trying to say, reassurance in the idea that some intellectual puzzle lay behind everything, a riddle waiting to be solved. This put an attractive skin on something ugly and old and familiar—simple, brutal violence. Which was all very well for a book, or someone who couldn't face up to reality…

Frank was looking at her, full of sincere curiosity. "What do you murder people over back home?"

"The usual. Jealousy. Rage. We're not a different race; we just talk a different language. People everywhere kill each other for the same reasons they always have. We make the same mistakes, over and over again. It's always something personal. A slight, an offence, even another crime, against ourselves or someone we love or feel responsible for. As a species we're selfish, vengeful creatures at heart. When something hurts us, we like to hurt back."

"Lots of people love Dante," Hank pointed out. "Some of them feel hurt by that movie."

Frank looked dubious. "But not many murderers, surely. And didn't I read somewhere that usually it's people you know? Family. Friends. Some guy around the corner. Those are the ones you need to worry about."

"Usually," she murmured. "Whatever that means."

"It's a ridiculous theory," Hank announced. "This stuck-up Quattrocchi guy's a professional. How can he believe such garbage?"

"For the same reason you believed it," Frank said. "It sounds fun, and he's got that tame little Canadian monkey at his elbow reminding him of that fact. It doesn't mean he's a bad cop."

Teresa bristled and pointed the wagging finger at them. "He's not a cop. And if he was, he wouldn't be a good one. Real cops are honest. They're honest with themselves, sometimes to the point of self-loathing." She thought of Peroni, Nic, and Falcone, and the way they couldn't ever really let go of anything until they'd shaken the thing into its component parts, however messy and painful that might be. "It's not a talent to be envied or coveted. Honesty's painful. But without it . . . what have you got?"

A curious sideways glance passed between the two

of them, Hank in the driving seat, Frank next to him. It was a look of self-knowledge, of something fresh and different and challenging occurring between two people who knew each other better, surely, than most men knew their wives.

She stared into their nearly identical faces and asked, "Is there anything you two have been wanting to say to each other?"

"Yes," Hank and Frank said simultaneously, then fell silent.

"OK," she said after a while, pointing at Frank. "You first."

"That stupid fire engine is as clean as it ever was," he blurted out. "And we both damned well know it."

Hank coughed and stared out the window. "Not *quite* as clean..." he muttered.

"Clean enough. Why don't we get off those guys' backs? It's their job now. Not ours."

Hank cleared his throat again, then turned to look at him. "I've been trying to say that to you for months. I thought...maybe you'd have been offended. You started the whole thing. I wondered what we'd have without it."

"I know I started it. And maybe I would have been upset. Stupid of me."

Teresa Lupo was briefly speechless. For the first time, she finally saw them as two individuals, no longer the single identity HankenFrank she had first met the day before. Their vivid mirror personalities, their almost exact physical resemblance, the near-identical clothes they wore...these visual cues had thrown her. It was a movie director's trick, one worthy of Hitchcock. The eye saw what it wanted to see. Just as Gianluca Quattrocchi and Professor Bryan Whitcombe looked at the events surrounding *Inferno* and beheld nothing but Dante, she had been fooled into thinking that Hank and Frank both thought and behaved as one. And in some ways, so had they.

"You know, I would love to show you two around Rome sometime. Will you come?"

"That's a date," Frank replied, his voice a little cut up. To distract her—and Hank—from noticing, he turned and glanced at the church. It appeared to be divided into two parts, one relatively modern and grand, the second white, adobe-style, and visibly older than anything she had ever seen in America. "So why are we here?"

"To blunder creatively. And to see where Carlotta Valdes was really buried, before your friend on Chestnut Street stole her headstone. I want to see what's become of the grave of a ghost."

8

MARTIN VOGEL WASN'T AT HOME. SO COSTA
drove around the city, meandering through
the long, grey urban streets, up and down hills that
seemed too steep for the automobile, dodging buses
and cable cars, getting lost from time to time, then
always finding something—the stretched silhouette
of the Bay Bridge, the upright outline of Coit Tower,
the Transamerica pyramid, the line of the ocean—
that could give him some bearings. The previous
night he'd sat alone until three watching the movie
he'd found lying on the coffee table next to the TV.
Teresa had mentioned it briefly and received a fierce
look from Falcone when she tried to expand on her
theory that it might somehow have something to
tell them.

Now, as he cruised the city a day later, thinking of
Maggie and a case that was not just baffling but also
off-limits, he found it impossible to shake the memories of the movie from his head. It wasn't just that so
many of the locations—the Legion of Honor, the
Palace of Fine Arts, the same mundane landscape of
small stores and offices—were places he'd visited with
her. There was an atmosphere to the film, a sense of

motion without obvious progress, yet with a hidden direction just out of reach, that was beginning to haunt him.

Teresa had every right to be intrigued. There were obvious links. The car some stranger had loaned Maggie was the same model and colour of that driven by the principal female character in the movie. Costa had tried to find the vehicle but the studio security people said it had been taken away the morning after she'd been poisoned. Not by the police either. The Jaguar had disappeared, and when he phoned her agent, who seemed both fascinated and appalled by the fact her client had been pictured in the papers gazing adoringly at a mere Roman cop, he'd discovered there was no paperwork, no trace of where it had come from or gone. Only a phone number, which turned out to be fake.

Something else bothered him. He was never good at flowers. But he was certain the oddly old-fashioned bouquet on the rear seat of the Jaguar had been a copy of the ones in the movie, held by the dead Carlotta Valdes in a painting and Madeleine Elster in real life. Not that it was the real Madeleine Elster. Or real life, for that matter.

Everything about this case seemed steeped in the cinema. Roberto Tonti, Teresa said, had learned his craft in the employ of Hitchcock as the director was making *Vertigo* in San Francisco. Everyone from Dino Bonetti to Simon Harvey, and even the young men in control of Lukatmi, had some kind of obsession with the moving image. A dependence—financial, perhaps, or something more personal—gripped them all.

He recalled Rome and a strange young actor dressed as a Carabinieri horseman, running through a performance that would lead to his death. And the end of Allan Prime, in the beautiful little Villa Farnesina. The links to Dante were everywhere, in the deadly cycle of numbers, the written warnings. The *evidence*.

Supposition and guesswork were dangerous friends. In Hitchcock's movie, the tragic detective Scottie had toyed with them and lost everything in the end.

Costa's rented Ford kept nosing aimlessly over the city, from the tourist dives of Fisherman's Wharf to backstreets and rich residential areas, and semi-abandoned industrial districts that looked as if they hadn't changed in years. He knew what he half hoped to see. An old green Jaguar with a blonde woman at the wheel, pulling into a dark corner, a dusty dead end where he might meet her and find some answers.

Somewhere along the way, he wasn't sure exactly, he stopped in a gleaming 1950s diner. A young Asian girl in a white hat and anachronistic smock served him a weak milky coffee. She wore a badge that said *The Philippines* and a broad toothy smile. San Francisco seemed possessed of multiple personalities, all of them jumbled up together, one running into the many.

He looked at his watch. It was close to seven. A decent enough time to call. He phoned the Park Hill Sanatorium and waited as a woman who sounded like the smartest of hotel receptionists put him on hold.

"Miss Flavier discharged herself an hour ago," she reported after a long wait.

"You mean she's OK."

"We can't discuss a patient's condition, sir. You appreciate that."

"Where did she go? Who with?"

"I really can't add to what I've said. Good night."

The line went dead. Costa realised he didn't know where Maggie lived. An apartment somewhere on Nob Hill. That was all she'd told him.

He called the agent and got an answering machine. He tried Falcone. The inspector listened to him, then said, "If Maggie Flavier wants to go home, it's none of your business."

"She nearly died . . ."

"It was an allergic reaction. One she's had before. If she was really ill, they would never have let her leave the hospital. She'll have security. Relax."

"I don't even know where she lives. Can you find that out?"

"Yes. I can."

Then nothing.

"Leo . . ."

"Leave it. You're fortunate the police haven't charged you with assault over that photographer. Don't tempt fate."

He could feel his temper rising. "You asked me to go and apologise to the man."

"So why didn't you?"

He wasn't in, Costa told him. No one was around. The place looked deserted. But that was three hours before.

"Then try again. That's what we do, isn't it? No more phone calls, Nic. I'm off-duty."

"Yes . . . sir."

Costa cut the call and uttered a short, meaningful Roman curse.

The Filipino waitress was beaming at him. She had a plate in her hands.

"Here you go. Veggie burger and fries," she said, and the sight of it dispelled his appetite for good.

He gazed at the shining chrome and, plastered on the walls throughout the diner, posters for movies and stars he'd long forgotten. Marlon Brando in *The Wild One*. Robert Mitchum in *Cape Fear*. Cinema attempted to define modern life through allegory and mystery, in much the same way Dante sought to define his own medieval world. Fundamentally, they were looking for the same unreachable goals: happiness, peace, and a few good answers.

Then a familiar voice came over from the TV in the corner.

He picked up his glass of plain water and sat in the

steel seat directly beneath the screen. Roberto Tonti was on some news interview program. It seemed to be live. A long clip from the movie—Allan Prime as Dante, spellbound as Maggie, ethereal, otherworldly, strode through a nightmare universe of monsters and flame.

The waitress stopped work and watched it with him.

"Who's the boring guy?" she asked. "What's he got to do with big stars like that?"

He told her the director's name. She looked puzzled.

"Never heard of him. He looks sick. Oughta be in the hospital."

"He directed the movie. It's his show."

"No, it's not. I don't go to the movies to see guys like that. I wanna see stars. Don't you?"

"They're just people. Like you and me."

She stared at him, then burst out laughing.

"Not like me, mister. Not in a million years." Her eyes shone with amusement. "No offence but...not like you either."

9

THEY HAD SPENT MORE THAN AN HOUR WANDER-ing around Mission Dolores. She couldn't have hoped for better guides. Hank and Frank were in love with their city. They seemed to know every last corner. For Teresa Lupo, who had no fondness for religion, the mission was a revelation. In Rome, the Church was omnipresent, and seemed to have been that way forever. Seated in the small adobe chapel of Mission Dolores, she was, for the first time in her life, conscious of a world that existed before God, at least the one she'd grown up with. This had been a different, virgin environment, one conquered by a foreign host bringing what it saw as enlightenment and civilisation, just two hundred and fifty years before, at a time when Rome regarded itself as the modern capital of a civilised, fixed universe in which everything was labelled, recognised, and known. In Italy, history seemed either distant or a part of the living present. Here the past existed just out of reach, tantalisingly near yet untouchable, alive yet gone, too.

The place fascinated her so much that she forgot,

for a while, why they'd gone there. Then Frank asked, "So you really want to see Carlotta's grave?"

"Oh. Of course."

They walked outside. It was getting cold and late. She wondered how much longer they could stay here. How much she could put off going back to Greenwich Street and admitting she had nothing to report, or suggest. A green car, some locations, a few possible coincidences . . . it added up to nothing and she knew it.

The cemetery was beautiful, hushed and peaceful, filled with roses, bold spikes of yellow cannas, and flowers she couldn't identify.

The statues of dead monks ranged across the graveyard, pensive heads bowed over their own tombs, the long foreign grass rising up to their frozen grey waists. Misshapen conifers rose among the forest of headstones against the white adobe walls where two unequal towers, like decorations on a wedding cake, pointed to a fading blue sky above floods of purple and red bougainvillea tumbling down from the roofline.

The names on the graves seemed to come from everywhere: Spain and Ireland, England and the east coast of America. Some tombs were grand, most modest. Death and the relentless maritime climate were slowly reducing them all to crumbling stone.

She wandered through a grove of roses and came upon a small dome-shaped reed hut, recently erected. A sign said it was designed to show the original kind of dwelling place used by the Ohlone, the indigenous people of the area before colonisation. She closed her eyes, thought of the scene in the movie: Scottie, in a brown suit and a 1950s gentleman's hat, skulking by the overhang of the mission walls, watching from the shadow of a sprawling tomb, furtively spying on Madeleine as she gazed down at a grave, a curious bouquet of roses in her hand.

"She knew you were there all along, Scottie," Teresa murmured.

"That she did," Frank agreed.

"You like the movie, too?" she asked.

His eyes clouded over with doubt. "It's not easy to forget and I don't know why. Or what it means, if it means anything, or needs to. There's something…" He chose his words carefully. She noticed how Hank watched him, a quiet look of admiration in his near-identical face. "…there's something not quite right about it. Something…obsessive. The way everyone seems to be watching that woman. Not just Scottie. The camera, too. Us. The audience. It's unnatural and it's supposed to be that way. The thing draws you in, and if you think about it, that makes you uncomfortable."

"It's voyeuristic," she suggested.

He grinned. "The very word! You know, for a foreigner, you're very good with English."

She shrugged. "I've got the time. I'm off the case. Just another tourist. Words are all I have."

Teresa put out her hand and touched the dry reeds

of the Ohlone structure. "It was here, wasn't it? Carlotta's gravestone? Before they moved it to that little cinema in the Marina?"

"*If* they moved it to that little cinema in the Marina," Frank cautioned. "You heard that guy. His uncle was a rogue. Movie crews always are. Do you know *no one* has any idea where the painting went? The one of Carlotta? It'd be worth a fortune now. They think it just got scrapped. Thrown out with the junk. One more prop. That was Hitch. Finish one movie, get on with the next. Never look back. Only the present matters. Do you think people like Roberto Tonti treat the job that way?"

"Not for a moment. They've got egos the size of a whale. They're interested in their legacy."

"Which is nothing more and nothing less than the movies they leave behind," Frank insisted. "I think Hitch got it right."

His brother intervened. "It was actually a little to the left." Hank pointed to a rough patch where a few low flowers were struggling to flourish in the dry earth. "They couldn't use somewhere there was a real grave, for sure."

"You saw it?" she asked them. "When it was here?"

"We were kids," Hank replied. "It was fun to go somewhere movie stars had been. To stand on the same spot. Like touching the hem of God. Not that we would have put it that way back then." He nodded at the mission. "Much more fun than that place, anyway."

"The funny thing is," Frank went on, "they left that fake gravestone there for a while. It was a tourist attraction. The mission needed the money. You can't blame them. Then…" He glanced back at the little chapel again. "…someone said it was *disrespectful*. An insult to the real dead people here."

"As if they're going to complain," Hank added. "No one's been buried here in years."

"Does that matter?" she wondered.

Frank shuffled, uncomfortable. "When you're dead you're dead. Only fools and children believe in ghosts."

She felt the same way, usually. "That's what Scottie thought. Was he right?"

Frank nodded earnestly. "Yes. He was bang on the money, even if it did cost him. Is there anything else you need to see? Churches give me the creeps, to be honest with you. Also, if we're in time, we can hit the happy hour at a little bar we know…"

"No. I don't think so…" she began, and then her eye caught the tree.

What was it Catherine Bianchi said? In California, almonds flowered at the end of February. That would mean they would bear fruit during the summer.

Next to the place where the grave of the fictional Carlotta Valdes had once stood was an old, crooked almond tree, little more than the height of a man. Its leaves fluttered weakly in the early evening breeze; its feeble, arthritic branches were black with age and dead fungi. On each, visible, still a little green from their newness, stood lines of nuts in their velvet, furry shells.

She took two steps towards the tree, reached up, and tugged one from the nearest branch.

"You're going to get us in trouble," Hank warned.

"Perish the thought..."

Teresa crouched down and found a stone. Then she placed the nut on its surface and cracked the shell open with a rock. There was a loud bang that ricocheted around the walls of the tiny graveyard. She studied the shards of the inner fruit, white and mashed against the stone.

There was no lab in San Francisco she could use. So she picked up the largest piece and put it in her mouth.

Even before she got to her feet, she was coughing. It was painful. Someone—she couldn't see who—was thumping her on the back. There was a new voice, a woman's voice.

With no grace whatsoever, she spat out every last piece of the almond she could. Even so, the taste lingered.

It was the most bitter thing she'd ever known.

"What are you doing? *What are you doing?*" The face of a severe, dark-skinned Mexican-looking woman hove into view and began castigating her.

"It was..." She started coughing, gagging for breath.

Another woman, a nun, with a blue headdress,

arrived, carrying a plastic cup with water in it. Teresa drank greedily and found herself spitting out more pieces of almond.

"I'm sorry," she said, and found herself coughing again.

"Why did you do that?" the nun asked. "This is a cemetery. Not an orchard."

"I was curious. The fruit was very...harsh."

The two women were silent.

"It's a bitter almond," Teresa asked, "isn't it?"

The nun crossed her arms in anger. "They say the first priests planted it. Two hundred and fifty years ago. Do we need to put up a sign saying 'Don't steal the almonds'?"

The Mexican woman touched the branches. "It's dying. We feed it. We try to care for it. Nothing helps." She shook her head. Her eyes were sad. "Perhaps it's for the best. If people keep coming here and taking away what's not theirs..."

Teresa felt her heart skip a beat and prayed it wasn't a side effect of the bitter nut she'd just eaten. "Someone else ate the almonds?"

"A man," the Mexican woman said. "And he had a bag! He took many, and wouldn't give them back when we caught him."

Hank and Frank were looking at her and licking their lips in anticipation.

"This man," Teresa asked, "do you know who he is? I really need to know."

The nun took the plastic cup and gave her a

withering look. "We don't know his name. We told the police, of course. This is a nice neighbourhood. We don't want people coming in and stealing things. The police said we were wasting their time. There are worse crimes in this city than stealing almonds from a graveyard."

The Mexican woman waved her fist in the air. "But we had a photograph! *A photograph!*"

Teresa wanted to laugh. She still felt giddy. The nasty taste wouldn't go away. "Can I see it?"

The two women stared at her and said nothing.

"Please. It may be important."

"The *parroco* has it," the Mexican woman said. "The pastor. He is out for a little while."

"Then I'll wait."

"Not here," the nun ordered. "In the basilica, please." She patted the trunk of the withering almond tree. "Out of the way of temptation."

10

MARTIN VOGEL'S APARTMENT WAS PAST UNION Square, the department stores and gift shops, the cable cars and the constant presence of street people pestering for money. It lay in a nondescript commercial building down a dark, dank lane. SoMa,

Nic learned from the guidebooks, was a trendy part of the city, up and coming, aspiring to be cultural, in much the same way as Testaccio in Rome. In parts it had the same tough, rough, urban aspect, too.

He found a discreet, half-hidden set of nameplates by a set of side doors. One, number 213, which he took to mean the second floor, had the scrawled name *Vogel* by it.

His finger lurked over the bell push for a moment. Then Costa chose another name, a few doors along, pressed the button, and waited.

A woman's voice, taut, angry, and hurried, barked out of the speaker.

"Pizz—" he began to say.

"Jesus Christ!" the woman screeched.

The buzzer on the lock bleated. He pushed the door open and found himself inside a spare, cool atrium that smelled of bleach.

Without thinking, he patted his jacket. There was no gun there. He was just another civilian.

He walked upstairs, trying to think of what he'd say. He hadn't just broken the photographer's arm. He'd stood on it. This didn't worry him any more now than when it had happened. Vogel had been stalking them for reward and the paparazzo had been determined to get out of there without helping once he had his pictures. Costa had needed to know where they were, to extract from him the exact location so that an ambulance could find them. Costa felt he'd had little alternative.

There was a sound from the floor above. A dog barking. A woman's cry. Music. From somewhere the shriek of a baby. There was the smell of stale food and rotten trash. Down the stairwell fell the noise of people arguing several floors up.

When he got to the top of the staircase, he found himself in near darkness. Two of the strip lights in the corridor ceiling had failed. A third flickered sickly, on and off.

The baby wailed again, its cries echoing off the walls so much he had no idea from which direction the sound came.

Each door had a little light behind the bell push. The nearest read 256. He walked along. The next read 257.

The wrong side, and the wrong direction. It was turning out to be one of those days.

He wondered whether this was a good idea at all. Then he thought about what Falcone would say if he came back and admitted he'd pulled out at the last moment. The good mood that the presence of Catherine Bianchi instilled in the inspector was, like most things surrounding Falcone, transient. The inspector's private life consisted of a series of short, intense relationships followed by periods of mute, surly celibacy. The pattern was well established now. Costa didn't want to bounce it out of phase prematurely.

He recrossed the stairwell and strode down the opposite corridor. Only one light was out here. As he walked, the sounds of the apartment block receded. There were no crying babies in this part of the building, no angry voices.

Costa reached the door of apartment 213. It was ajar, just a finger's width, enough to let a shaft of orange artificial light stumble through and fall on the tiled floor of the apartment in an eccentric shape.

Decisions, he thought.

He edged his foot forward until it reached the cheap painted wood that was supposed to keep Martin Vogel safe from the world beyond. The door moved steadily inwards at his touch, on hinges that needed a touch of oil.

11

THE LATER THE HOUR, THE MORE UNCOMFORT-able Hank and Frank became. Churches really didn't suit them and the bar was calling. Finally, just before eight, she lost patience and sent them on their way. She could ride a bus home. One went from the street outside all the way down to the waterfront at the Marina. She liked buses. They put you in touch with people.

Predictably, the priest appeared moments after the two brothers departed. She took one look at the man in the familiar black frock and felt her heart sink. He had a long pale face, pockmarked cheeks sagging with age. His eyes were sad and rheumy, as if they'd seen rather too much. A drink with the twins might be welcome relief after a little time in the gloom of Mission Dolores. She was glad she'd made a note of their favourite bar.

Then she told him who she was and where she came from. The priest opened his mouth and her opinion changed instantly. His voice did not match his appearance in the slightest. It was bright and young and engaged, as if some lively inner spirit was trapped inside an older, more fragile frame. The *parroco* introduced himself as Dermot Gammon, originally from Boston, but a resident of Rome for several years before returning to the U.S. and ending up in San Francisco.

"Where do you live?" he asked her.

"Off Tritone. The Via Crispi."

He rubbed his hands together and a beatific expression put fresh light in his eyes. A comprehensive list of local stores and restaurants and wine bars streamed from his lips.

"You know Rome well," she said sincerely.

They spent a few happy minutes discussing her home city. Finally the priest asked her why she was there. She told him a little about the case and the movie, then said, "They told me you had a photograph. Of the man they found stealing something in the cemetery."

His long, sad face fell into a frown. "A bag full of almonds. The ladies…" He sighed. "Sometimes their desire to protect this place goes to extremes. We exist to cater to souls, not bricks and mortar. They saw the man, they took some photos. I showed them to the police. Our local captain was not, I have to say, terribly interested or impressed." He edged forward, as if making some statement in confession. "Which pleased me greatly. I don't wish to see the mission in the newspapers. Only for births and marriages and deaths, and a few charitable occasions. Certainly not as part of something as serious as this dreadful investigation you mentioned. Am I making myself clear?"

"I'll be discreet. I promise. Besides, it's probably nothing. I'm shooting arrows in the dark, hoping one will land somewhere sunny."

"That's work for a priest. Not a scientist."

"I wouldn't presume to teach you your job, Father. Science and religion aren't enemies."

"Really?" He didn't look convinced. "I must disagree. Nothing wonderful that I recall of Rome has to do with science."

"Not the Sistine Chapel? Michelangelo thought himself more an architect than a painter. And Bernini. Those statues. How could he create them without knowing anatomy?"

"I was always a Caravaggio man myself. I like real human beings, frail men and women, not make-believe perfect ones. Without the fallible…" The priest opened his hands and looked around the dark interior of the mission. "...I'm out of a job."

"Without mysteries we both are. Please, Father. The photographs. Just to satisfy my curiosity."

He excused himself for a few minutes. When he came back, he sat down by her side and retrieved a snapshot from the inside of his gown. It was too dark to see much of it, so she went and stood beneath the electric candles close to the altar.

The priest followed, looked over her shoulder, and said, "The gardener told me to chop that tree down two years ago. He said it's dying. Too old."

She peered at the figure in the picture. The man was holding a supermarket bag that, from its bulging shape, appeared to contain a good collection of nuts. He was arguing with the Mexican woman she'd seen earlier.

"I told them all, 'It's a tree,'" the priest went on. "'Not a human being. The thing is insensate. It feels no pain, has no consciousness of its impending end, or its present feeble state. We can wait a little while,' I say. Not thinking..." His glassy eyes stared into hers. "I've been here thirteen years, Ms. Lupo. We've never had a single person take something from the cemetery. Not something supposedly edible anyway. Now two in a matter of weeks."

"It's not edible. It's a bitter almond. Poisonous in quantity."

He looked shocked. "That's why the man took those nuts? Because they're poisonous?"

"Someone with a little knowledge might know, I imagine. Most people would simply see an almond tree…"

Its gnarled, failing form stood next to the patch of ground where the imaginary Carlotta Valdes's grave had been created for the film, and stayed, for a few uncertain years, in real life, too, until someone deemed it unsuitable for a real cemetery. It was a link, one that, like the rest, seemed to lead into some opaque and unrelenting San Franciscan fog.

"Do you know this man?" the priest asked.

She gave him back the photograph. "He's wearing sunglasses, Father. And he's turned away from the camera…"

He took the snapshot from her. "I'm sorry. I gave you the wrong one. Here. There's a better picture."

Father Gammon scrabbled again in his clothes. A crumpled packet of cigarettes fell to the floor. He apologised and looked a little guilty, then picked them up. In his other hand was a new photo.

This was clear and distinct, even in the fusty yellow light of the electric altar candles.

"Do you know him now?"

"I believe so," she answered. "Will you excuse me, please?"

Falcone was furious at being interrupted halfway through what sounded like a nervous dinner with Catherine Bianchi. But not for long.

12

COSTA PUSHED THE DOOR AS FAR AS IT WOULD go. It was pitch black in the apartment.

There was a smell, though. Something familiar: the harsh odour of a spent weapon and behind it the faint tang of blood. From a tinny radio in a room beyond the entrance came the sound of music. *Tannhäuser.* He thought of the burly photographer squealing as he stood on his shattered arm. The man hadn't looked like an opera fan.

He stopped and listened. Not a sound except the music, but that was so full and insistent...Costa found the wall inside the entrance, making sure he stayed inside the shadow as much as possible. It wasn't a good idea to be a silhouette in a doorway. He couldn't see a thing. Then, in the middle of a line, the music stopped abruptly.

"Police," he said quietly into the dark.

All he could hear was his own voice in the dark of an apartment where the smell of spent ammunition was so strong it seemed like the mark of some murderous feral cat.

When it came, the racket made him jump. The electronic wail of the mobile phone cut through the black interior of Vogel's apartment like the scream of a child.

It was the tone he'd set for Falcone. Costa swore, ducking further back into the pool of gloom by the door, desperate to avoid becoming an easy target.

He yanked the phone out of his pocket and killed the call.

There'd been another noise, though. Someone moving in the blackness ahead of him. A new smell, too, one he couldn't place.

Costa stared at the bright blue screen in his hand, got Falcone's number, and texted four words, URGT VOGEL APT NOW.

Then he threw the phone across to the other side of the room and pressed back against the wall. The ring tone went off seconds after. The space in front of him was briefly filled by sound, the bellowing roar of gunfire fighting to escape the confined space that enclosed it.

He froze where he was, cold and sweating. Someone was scrabbling around on the floor, maybe three or four strides to the right, struggling to say something. The unseen figure's breathing was laboured, words unintelligible. He sounded sick or wounded, in some kind of trouble. But he was a man with a gun. The strong, noxious smell was beginning to overwhelm everything.

Finally he worked out what it was. Petrol.

Down the corridor someone screamed. The baby

was wailing again. Lights were coming on, voices were rising.

He wanted to kick himself. They'd called the police *before*. The woman had let him in immediately, not because she thought he was a pizza deliveryman, but because she thought he was the police. The gunfire had started before he'd blundered onto the scene. That was why everything was so quiet, so deserted. Sane people stayed out of the way.

As he moved a fraction further into the room, Costa stumbled, found his fingers encountering the familiar hard metal frame of a photographer's tripod. He pushed it over, heard it clatter.

There was no shooting this time. He fell to the floor, rolling, turning, turning, out into the corridor, scrabbling on hands and knees to get out of the deadly frame of the doorway.

Breathless and sweating, but outside the apartment, finally, he heard nothing more. As he started to scramble upright, he found himself staring into the barrel of a gun. The man who held it was black, stocky, and wore the uniform of an SFPD cop. He looked terrified. The weapon trembled in his hands.

"I'm a police officer," Costa said, slowly, carefully raising his hands. "My ID's in my jacket pocket."

The gun was sweaty in the young cop's grip. He passed it from one hand to the other, then back, the barrel staying straight in Costa's face. He nodded at the open doorway. "You gonna tell me what I might find in there? And why you was looking?"

"There's a wounded man with a gun. I just came here to apologise. There was an incident. With the actress. Maggie Flavier. Maybe you read about it..."

The gun lowered a little. A flicker of recognition crossed the young cop's face. "That was you? You looked bigger in the papers."

"Thanks..."

There were more people behind him. The cop swiveled nervously, waving the gun everywhere. Costa wanted to shout at him but it didn't seem a good idea.

He didn't need to anyway. Catherine Bianchi was marching down the corridor, police ID held high, Falcone behind her with a face like thunder. She was bellowing at the young cop to get his weapon down, in a voice that wasn't easy to ignore.

"Captain Bianchi...?" the cop faltered.

She was wearing a short cocktail dress with a scarlet silk scarf over her shoulders. The badge in her hand looked incongruous next to it.

She ignored him, stared at Costa, and asked, angrily, "What the hell is going on?"

"There's a wounded man inside with a gun," Costa said quickly. "I urge—"

Caution, he was about to say, but the word stayed in his mouth. Someone was screaming, a high-pitched shriek of terror and pain. Inside Martin

Vogel's apartment a light had appeared, a grim and familiar orange.

Costa scrabbled to his feet and raced down the corridor, away from the apartment.

Catherine Bianchi let out a piercing yell as a man stumbled out of the door, his body a bright, burning torch of flame from head to foot, leaping around like a victim of Saint Vitus's dance consumed by fire.

Costa snatched the fire extinguisher he'd seen earlier from the wall and ran towards the blazing figure.

"He's got a gun," Catherine shouted, standing in the way, blocking any chance he had to move forward.

Sure enough, there was a weapon in the burning man's right hand, which now appeared blackened and useless, gripping the familiar black shape out of nothing more than fear.

Costa pushed her to one side and triggered the extinguisher.

A crowd was gathering. The spray doused the shrieking figure, which staggered and fell to the floor. His skin was black with soot, red with livid burns.

He was recognisable, just.

"Medics," Costa said, dropping to his knees beside the man, wondering if there was much life left in him. Blood was beginning to seep through the scorched clothing. He was wounded, perhaps more than once. "They're coming. Hold still. It will be all right…"

A noise escaped the blackened lips, a long, painful

groan that blew the stink of burnt petrol straight into Costa's face. It was the final breath. He knew it. So did Josh Jonah, dying in his arms.

They were around him now, looking, unable to speak.

Costa didn't wait. Two steps took him to the door to Vogel's apartment; he found the light switch, tried to take in what he saw.

The place was wrecked. There'd been a fight, a bloody one. Money—fifty- and one-hundred-dollar bills—was scattered across the table in the living room. A lot of money. Thousands, surely.

Falcone and Catherine Bianchi weren't far behind him.

"Let's put out a bulletin for Vogel," she said, pulling out her radio. "Then we figure out how the hell I'm going to explain all this to Gerald Kelly and keep my job."

Costa tried to take in what he was seeing. "I wouldn't make any hasty decisions. There were three people in here. I heard them."

He walked on through the scattered mess on the floor, into the bedroom.

The smell he'd first noticed, that of blood, hung heavy in the air, mingling with the harsh chemical stench of petrol. There was something else, too...

A single naked bulb swung lazily over the bed as if someone had recently brushed against it. Martin Vogel didn't live in style. Or die that way either. The corpse was on the bare mattress. Vogel wore nothing but a pair of boxer shorts and the plaster cast on his arm. A gaping wound stood over his heart like a bloody rose poking its way out from the inside.

"You can hold the bulletin," Costa said, mostly to himself.

The window was open, just a fraction. He walked to it. There was a fire escape outside. Someone could have escaped undetected.

Maybe they did kill each other—Vogel and Jonah. Or maybe it was meant to look that way.

Catherine Bianchi walked over to the table, picked up some of the notes and let them drop through her fingers. Costa watched Falcone biting his tongue, wanting to tell her not to touch a thing.

"What was it the Carabinieri's pet professor said?" she asked. "Next we'd get the Avaricious and the Prodigal?"

She shook her head and cast a brief glance at the bedroom, and then the corridor, where Josh Jonah's corpse lay like a burnt and bloodied human ember escaped from some recently extinguished bonfire.

"How do you tell which one was which?"

The stink of petrol drifting into the room from around Vogel's bed was becoming overpowering. It must have been in the carpet, the curtains, everywhere.

So Josh Jonah intended to set fire to the place and had been caught by his own misdeed, shot by the wounded Vogel. Costa's mind struggled with that idea. Jonah was ablaze when he died. If he'd been close to the petrol trail he'd been laying, that would have ignited, too. There was a gap in the scenario somewhere.

"I think we should get out of here until the fire people take a look," he began to say. "This isn't a safe—"

Something hissed and fizzed in the corner and finally he managed to place the last unknown smell. It was one from childhood. Fireworks on the lawn of the house, bright, fiery lights in the sky. A fuse burning before the explosion.

In the corner of the room, safe on a chair above the fuel-stained carpet, sat an accordion-style jumping firecracker. A long length of cord had been attached so that it wound across the seat of the chair, lengthening the burn time. Most of it was now charred ash. Scarcely half a finger of untouched material remained, and that was getting rapidly eaten by the eager, hungry flame working its way to the small charge of powder that would take the incendiary and fling it into the room.

It was a perfect homemade time bomb and it was about to explode.

Costa shoved Catherine Bianchi back towards the door, bellowing at Falcone and the baffled young cop to join them.

Then the soft roaring gasp of the explosion hit.

13

AN HOUR AND A HALF LATER COSTA FOUND himself standing outside next to the engines and the emergency vehicles as they wound down their pumps and reported the entire building evacuated, without a single casualty.

Gerald Kelly had arrived, disturbed at dinner in formal dress, just like Falcone and his companion. The SFPD captain listened in quiet fury to a report from Catherine Bianchi and the firemen. After that he took the two Italians to one side to demand an explanation—any explanation—for Costa's presence in Martin Vogel's apartment.

"I came to apologise," Costa said simply. "That was all."

Falcone stood his ground. "I asked him to do this, Kelly. I thought it might help."

"Oh, right. That's what you were doing. Helping." He looked at them, desperation in his eyes. "Well? Did it?"

"This isn't our case," Costa said, before his superior had the chance to intervene.

Kelly eyeballed him and stifled a single, dry laugh. "You guys really are something. I know it's not your case. If it was . . . what would you think? What would you do?"

Costa glanced at the narrow, badly lit street that fed back into the bright, busy district around Market Street.

"I'd be looking for a third man," he said.

PART 5

THREE DAYS LATER COSTA AND TERESA LUPO SAT at the door of the principal exhibition tent in the temporary canvas village erected by the Palace of Fine Arts, watching Roberto Tonti and Dino Bonetti strut around the area as if they owned it.

The question had been bothering him for days. He knew he had to ask.

"What's the difference between a producer and a director?"

She stared at him and asked, "Are you serious?"

"Deadly. I was never addicted to movies like you. I just see the finished thing. Actors. Pictures. I've no idea what goes into it."

"What was the difference between Caravaggio and Cardinal Del Monte?"

Costa frowned and replied, "One was an artist and the other was the man who made his art viable. By paying for it, or finding others to come up with the commissions."

"One provides the art. The other provides the wherewithal. There. You answered your own question."

He thought about that, and the nagging doubt

that had been with him since the conversation with the Asian waitress in the diner.

"If you'd been Del Monte, would you have loved Caravaggio or resented him? So much talent in one human being, something you couldn't hope to achieve yourself?"

"I think I'd feel lucky to have known a genius," Teresa replied. "And a little jealous, too, from time to time." She nodded at the two Italians. "You think Bonetti might resent Tonti in some way?"

Bonetti was striding past the huge marquee that was destined to house the audience for the premiere the following evening. Tonti was at his side, listening. Thirty years separated these men. One was in his prime: strong, both physically and personally. Tonti was dying; his face seemed bloodless. His walk had the slow, pained determination of an old man resenting his increasing infirmity.

"Directors win Oscars," Costa said. "Producers don't win anything."

"The kind of money they make, they don't need to. Someone like Bonetti dips his beak in everything. He's Del Monte with a twist. He gets to sell the paintings he commissions and keep a share of them in perpetuity. What's some stupid little statue next to that?"

Something, he thought. But perhaps not much. Dino Bonetti was a powerful, confident man. It seemed far-fetched to think he would be offended by any fleeting fame attached to cast or crew.

"The question you should really be asking," she added, "is how much someone like Tonti resents his stars. I've read his biography. It's full of bust-ups with his cast. For some people that's a trademark. Tonti..." She frowned. "He treats his cast as if they're just puppets. It's a shame he's so old. All this digital stuff they have nowadays...It can't be long before real actors become irrelevant for directors. Just one more piece of software they can manipulate on-screen—so much more manageable than flesh and blood."

Lukatmi was never far away from the story, Costa thought. The Italian director had been involved with the digital video company since the outset. The papers said that Tonti had even provided seed capital for its founding. Not that it was going to be worth much now. Lukatmi's shares had entered meltdown after the death of Josh Jonah. In seventy-two hours the company had gone from star of the NASDAQ to one more discredited and busted dotcom. The very day that the news channels and papers devoted huge amounts of coverage to the deadly inferno in Martin Vogel's SoMa apartment, twelve lawsuits had been filed in the courts in California and New York. Given the speed with which they appeared, it was clear lawyers had been hovering at the edge of the company for some time, just as Catherine Bianchi had predicted. All accused the dead Jonah and his partner Tom Black of everything from stock option irregularities to misuse of shareholder funds. The newspapers claimed the district attorney was mulling over a formal probe into the company for fraud, money laundering, and racketeering. The share price that had seemed so buoyant only four days before had fallen through the floor until, that morning, trading had been suspended amid expectations of an impending bankruptcy announcement. Predators—old-school companies, the ones Lukatmi treated with such contempt—were hovering, ready to snap up what few worthwhile pieces might be salvaged from the corporate corpse on the waterfront at Fort Mason.

It was a juicy story for the media, one bettered only by a more astonishing revelation: as well as being a corporate crook, Josh Jonah had turned out to be a real-life criminal, a man who'd been willing to murder a Hollywood movie star in a desperate attempt to save his company from collapse. The case was closed, or so Gianluca Quattrocchi, with Bryan Whitcombe in tow, had declared to the cameras. Gerald Kelly seemed somewhat muted in front of the press. But the arguments presented by Quattrocchi appeared solid: in spite of Costa's protests, the evidence appeared to point to there being only two individuals in Martin Vogel's apartment in SoMa. Forensic believed that Jonah had fatally wounded Vogel, who had returned one shot before he died. That had crippled the billionaire as he started to spread petrol around the apartment to destroy any evidence.

"I still think I heard a third person there," Costa said quietly.

Teresa watched him; he was aware that he had, perhaps, protested this point too much.

"It was dark. You knew something was wrong. When people are under stress…"

"I know what I heard…"

"Enough! If you were sitting in Bryant Street now, which way would you be leaning? Be honest with yourself."

Costa didn't have a good answer for that. All the available facts suggested a failed murder attempt on Jonah's part. Cell phone company records showed that, shortly before Costa's arrival, the stricken man had tried to call his partner Tom Black from Vogel's apartment, presumably seeking help. That was speculation, though. Black had disappeared completely the evening his partner died. Kelly had let it be known to Catherine Bianchi that he thought the man was out of the U.S. already. There were huge black holes in the Lukatmi accounts. The missing money could easily fund a covert flight from the country, enough to last a lifetime if Black was smart enough to keep his head down and choose the right, distant location.

Quattrocchi's theory was, predictably, one the media was growing to love. Jonah and Black had hatched the plot to hype *Inferno,* employing Vogel as their legman. A phony passport recovered from the wreckage in the photographer's apartment had a stamp proving he'd flown to Rome one week before Allan Prime died, and left the day after. The picture snapped in the cemetery clearly revealed Vogel to be the man who had stolen the almonds that had very nearly ended Maggie Flavier's life. Josh Jonah and Tom Black had enough access to security arrangements to provide Vogel with the means by which Maggie might be poisoned. His job as a paparazzo had proved the perfect cover to follow her afterwards. Records in Rome showed that he had also managed to obtain media accreditation there using his forged passport, giving him the opportunity to enter the restricted area by the Casa del Cinema and replace the genuine death mask of Dante with the fake one taken from Allan Prime that morning. Quattrocchi's team had, in what Falcone declared a rare moment of investigative competence, discovered that Vogel's alias was in an address book belonging to Peter Jamieson, the actor who had died in the uniform of a Carabinieri officer at the Villa Borghese. It seemed a logical step to assume that Jonah had recruited the actor to scare Maggie Flavier, perhaps as a way of distracting the police from Allan Prime, perhaps calculating, too, that his act might provoke a violent response the unfortunate Jamieson had never expected.

The case remained open. Tom Black was still at large. There was still no sign of the woman calling herself Carlotta Valdes. Moreover, from the point of view of the state police, the genuine death mask of Dante was still missing, and causing considerable internal ructions with the museum authorities in Italy. But a kind of conclusion had been reached in terms of Allan Prime's murder. As far as Quattrocchi was concerned, nothing else really mattered. Josh Jonah had used the cycle of Dante's numbers as a code for his attacks on those associated with the production, knowing that this fed the idea the movie was either somehow cursed or stalked by vengeful Dante fanatics seeking to punish those associated with the perfidious Roberto Tonti. It was all a desperate publicity stunt, one engineered by Lukatmi. It had worked, too. *Inferno* was on every front page, every news bulletin.

The pace of the investigation—one which had hung on the assumption that yet one more attack lurked around the corner—had slackened as the principal focus moved to the financial mess inside Lukatmi. They were now one day away from *Inferno*'s world premiere. Once that had occurred without incident, the cast and crew would hand over security arrangements entirely to the private companies. For Costa and his colleagues, Italy would beckon.

Maggie Flavier had left innumerable messages imploring him to visit. He'd made a series of excuses, some genuine, some less so. In the hectic aftermath of the deaths of Jonah and the paparazzo Vogel, Costa had come to realize that he was beginning to miss Italy, miss Rome, with its familiar sights, the street sounds, the easy banter in cafés, the warm, comforting embrace of home. San Francisco was a beautiful, interesting, and cultured city, but it could never be his. Rome was part of his identity, and without it he felt a little lost, like Maggie Flavier attempting to find herself in the long-dead faces of the women in the paintings in the Legion of Honor. A movie was a temporary caravan, always waiting to disperse. If she came to Rome for some sequel, she would be there six, nine months, perhaps no more. And then . . .

Life was temporary, and its briefness only given meaning by some short, often clumsy attempt to find permanence within the shifting sands of one's emotions. He knew that search would never leave him. He knew, too, that Maggie Flavier would struggle to feel the same way. She would seek as she did character after character, personality after personality, through the constant round of work.

"I can't believe you're not even up to an argument over this," Teresa complained, jolting him back to the present.

"We could be home in a few days. I'd like that. Wouldn't you?"

She screwed up her face in an awkward, gauche expression. "Not yet. Not till it's over."

"You just told me I was wrong to think there was more to this case than Gianluca Quattrocchi would have the media believe."

"No. I merely said your supposition for the existence of a third party in Martin Vogel's apartment was difficult to prove. I do wish cops would listen more carefully sometimes." A familiar sly smile appeared. "May I remind you of some things we do know? One chief suspect is missing. Thanks to the gigantic amount of publicity this has generated, a stack of money has been thrown up in the air and no one knows where it's going to fall. And you don't have your precious mask."

Two points he appreciated. The third puzzled him.

"What do you mean about the money?"

"You should talk to Catherine Bianchi more. She has a firm grasp of finance. How you go about backing companies like Lukatmi. She even seems to understand how to raise money for movies, as much as anyone outside the business can."

He watched the private security guards working on the installation of CCTV cameras on the nearest tent. The place was bristling with the things. There were enough cameras to catch a squirrel sneezing. But the tempo of the investigation had changed. It felt... if not over, then at least more manageable, to some anyway.

There was a minor commotion. Roberto Tonti strode through the door of the tent, followed by Dino Bonetti speaking in low, confidential tones by his side. Bonetti didn't look his usual bouncy, arrogant self. This was surely going to be the most extraordinary and potentially lucrative movie he had ever produced. The newspapers were talking about a posthumous Oscar nomination for Allan Prime. The industry rags were predicting that *Inferno* could be the first movie to break a two-hundred-million-dollar weekend gross at the box office when it went nationwide.

Perhaps it was the strain, but neither man looked like someone on the verge of breaking every entertainment industry record in the book.

2

THE TWO BROTHERS STOOD AT THE ENTRANCE to the main hall of the Lukatmi building. Bulky individuals in blue overalls appeared to be gutting the place. Furniture and phones and computer equipment were disappearing out of the door and into moving vans at an astonishing rate.

There was a supervisor by the entrance, his rank emphasised by the fact that he was so scrawny he couldn't lift a thing except the clipboard in his hands. Hank Boynton tapped the man on the arm.

"Didn't these guys own *anything* themselves?"

"Maybe a paper clip or two. But we're taking them, too. This place stinks of rotten debt. I'll have anything that's not nailed down."

"The cops won't like that," Frank suggested.

"The cops are in Building Two, where all the accounting and e-mail stuff got kept. We're just taking the dweeb items they used to mess around with while they were pretending they were Fox or something."

"Computers..." Hank said.

"Workstations," the man emphasised.

"I was gonna ask if you had one going cheap," Frank intervened. "Not so interested now."

"You guys want something? Or you just here to yank my chain?" he asked, and not nicely.

Hank pulled out an ID. "We're safety officers here on an official visit. We'd like to check for fire hazards from any stray discarded ponytails left behind after the train wreck. You know the kind of thing. Just routine."

The man eyed the card and said, "That thing expired a year ago. There's laws about impersonating a city official. Isn't there a bingo parlour or somewhere you two could go and while away the hours?"

Frank put his broad muscular arm around the little man's shoulders and squeezed. "You know," he confided, "I could say you'll live long enough to feel old and useless one day. But maybe I'd be lying. We're looking for a friend who quit the fire department for the joyous pastures of private enterprise. Jimmy Gaines. He did security here. We'd like to commiserate with him on the sad and premature loss of his stock options. Find him and we go away. Try to pretend we don't even exist..."

He caught Hank's eye, removed his arm from the supervisor, and said, "Slip me some skin, bro."

Then the two of them grazed knuckles and made rapper-like noises.

Mr. Clipboard watched, looking worried.

"Folks keep going on about the young people these days," Frank told him. "Why? It's the old guys they got to worry about."

The removals man walked into the front vestibule and yelled, "Is there anyone here called Gaines?"

To everyone's relief, a sprightly upright figure in a dark uniform which contrasted vividly with his bright, bouncy grey hair emerged. He looked in their direction, then started to dance up and down with glee.

"The old days," Jimmy Gaines squealed as he came to greet them. "It's like the old days." He hesitated. "Are they cleaning that engine good and proper yet? Like we used to?"

"Stop living in the past, you stupid old man," Frank ordered. He watched the clipboard guy barking at his brutes to hurry up stripping the building. "What the hell are you supposed to be guarding anyway, Jimmy? This place is going to be bare in an hour or so."

"Nothing," Gaines replied cheerfully, setting up a brisk pace away from the vast hall that had once been home to Lukatmi. "Come around the corner. There's a café. A real one. No ponytails. No geeks or people drinking crushed wheatgrass. If it was later and I didn't have a uniform, I'd buy you a beer."

"Coffee will do," Hank said quietly.

"You look serious," Gaines declared as he cut behind the building, heading for a small door with the sign of a coffee cup above the threshold.

"We need to give a nice Italian lady a present," Frank said as the brothers struggled to keep up.

"Chocolates," Gaines suggested. "I'm told they come with a guarantee."

Hank caught up with him and placed his hand on Gaines's arm. The man stopped and looked at them. They were alone now. No one could hear.

"We want to find her a better present than that, Jimmy. We want to hand her Tom Black."

Jimmy Gaines gave them a hard stare. "And I thought this was a social call! Half of SFPD is looking for Black. I tried talking to them, but they looked so bored having an old fart like me wheezing away I gave up in the end. What makes you think you can find someone they can't?"

"Because six, maybe nine months ago," Frank said, "we saw you and Mr. Black out together. Him looking at you as if he had stars in his eyes and all manner of that fancy exploration gear you love in the back of your station wagon. You looked like good friends going somewhere remote. Two and two going together the way they do…"

"Hiking," Jimmy Gaines snapped. "We both belong

to the Sierra Club and a couple other things. You suggesting something else?"

"Not for a moment," Hank insisted. "You always did love the wild side of life. The great outdoors." The Boynton brothers liked Jimmy Gaines, mostly, though not so much they wanted to see him more than a couple of times a year. "I remember you reading Henry David Thoreau on those long, empty night shifts. Things like that stick in the memory."

"If more people read Thoreau, we wouldn't be in the shit we're in now. The simple life and a little civil disobedience from time to time. You boys ever take a look at *Walden* like I told you to?"

"I'm allergic to poison oak and air that doesn't have a little scent of gasoline in it," Hank confessed. "Wild things don't agree with me. Was Tom a Thoreau fan, too?"

"Damned right. *Walden* was his favourite book after I showed it to him. He isn't a murderer either. Don't care what those stupid cops say. That Jonah bastard . . . nothing would surprise me about him."

"That's what we heard," Hank said, urging him on.

"Tom's a decent human being. Just a little lost kid with too much brains and money and too little life. Didn't have an old man. His mom was half crazy. Did you know that? Did you read that in the papers?"

"I guess we didn't," Frank replied.

"No. Kind of spoils the story, doesn't it? So what do you really want?"

"We want to find him," Frank replied. "We want to

know the truth. If it's what you think it is—and our Italian friend believes that, too—we'd maybe hope we can help get him off the hook. So where is he, Jimmy?"

Gaines shook with fury. He was fit and strong for his age. Sometimes, when much younger, he had been a touch free with his fists in a bar after work.

"I don't know! Why would he tell me where he was going? I'm just an old security guard he used to talk to about the mountains and the woods. When he wanted some new place to go, usually. He liked being on his own. Poor kid thought he was soft on that actress for a while, not that *that* was ever going to go anywhere. She was a tease. Led him on. Tom never should have gotten mixed up with that Hollywood crowd in the first place."

Hank and Frank looked at one another.

"We need you to talk to us about those places you showed him," Hank said.

Gaines nodded in the direction of the great red bridge along the Bay and the wooded Marin headlands beyond.

"Why? You think he's up there somewhere? Scared and hungry and him a billionaire only four days ago?"

Frank folded his arms. "I don't think he's in Acapulco. Do you?"

Jimmy Gaines swore. "It was Josh Jonah, all on his own, I swear it. Tom was just a starstruck idiot. Kid didn't understand the first thing about money.

He actually believed all that new-world crap Lukatmi used to spout."

"We're sorry, Jimmy," Frank apologised. "Truth is, you can insure against anything these days except stupidity, can't you?"

Gaines stared at them and asked, "Insurance? What the hell are you talking about?"

"You know exactly what we're talking about," Frank replied. "Sorting this thing out once and for all. Please. Just tell us where to look."

There was a short, unpleasant moment of laughter. Then...

"Oh, what the hell, this was my last day anyway. I guess I get to leave early. You two got good boots?" Gaines was stripping off his jacket. He was still a big man, all muscle under the cheap white security guard shirt.

Hank and Frank looked at each other.

"Just the old ones from the station," Hank confessed.

"Better go get them. And something for poison oak. Where we're headed, things bite."

3

COSTA AND TERESA LUPO GOT TWO CUPS OF foul coffee from the food truck, then headed for a bench by the lake in front of the Palace, listening to the ducks arguing, glad to be away from the ill-tempered crowd.

"Here's something to think about," Teresa declared as she sat down. "Josh Jonah told anyone willing to listen, including the papers, that fifty million dollars of Lukatmi money went into *Inferno*."

"I know that."

"Good. Well, it's not there."

"They've spent it, surely."

"No. The SFPD can't find any proof much Lukatmi money went into the movie in the first place. All they can track is a measly five million in the production accounts at Cinecittà. The rest of it doesn't exist. Not in Rome anyway. They've located some odd currency movements out of Lukatmi, substantial ones into offshore accounts, in the Caribbean, South America, the Far East. But not to Rome. Not to anything that seems to go near any kind of movie production. They think that was just

Josh Jonah thieving the bank to put something aside for a rainy day."

Costa found himself wishing he understood the movie industry better. "If they didn't have the money, how did the thing get finished? What did they pay people with?"

She shrugged. "I don't know. Bonetti's the lead producer and he refuses to discuss the matter with the Americans. He says it's none of their business. Strictly speaking, it isn't. *Inferno* got made by committee. A string of tiny production companies, all set up specifically for the purpose of funding the movie, all based in places where the accounting rules tend to be somewhat opaque. Cayman. Russia. Liechtenstein. Gibraltar. Even Uzbekistan."

"The company was Italian," Costa insisted. "I saw the notepaper. I saw the name on the posters. Roberto Tonti Productions."

"Tonti put up half a million dollars to assemble a script, a cast, and a budget. That's all. The real money came from ordinary investors, the mob, Lukatmi, God knows where else. We'll never find out. Not unless the offshore-banking business suddenly decides to open itself up to public scrutiny."

Costa struggled to make sense of this. "Someone must have paid the bills at Cinecittà. They couldn't have worked for six, nine months or so without settling at least some of what was owed."

She grinned. "Catherine says the SFPD have checked through the Carabinieri in Rome. The urgent bills were settled by all those little co-production companies. One from Liechtenstein would handle catering, say. One from Cayman would pick up special effects. I'd place a bet on that being how the mob money got there. They like these places. None of it came from Lukatmi direct, and the Lukatmi accounts show just that five million I told you about going into the production to pay two months' studio fees at Cinecittà. Nothing more." She paused. "And for that, they got exclusive world electronic distribution rights and stacks of publicity. Something that ought to have been worth, well, not fifty million dollars, but maybe twenty-five."

Teresa had a habit of springing information on people this way, Costa thought.

"Why's Catherine confiding all this to you and not Leo?" he asked.

"Because Leo, being Leo, is utterly fixated on this idea that the real story lies in that rotten money from the men in black suits. He's not the world's greatest listener, in case you never noticed. I am. Also I think Catherine likes stringing him along. He's getting nowhere with her and it's driving him crazy."

"Ah."

Costa had gathered this from watching the two of them together. He'd never seen Falcone fail to get something he wanted in the end. It was an interesting sight, and an experience the old man himself clearly found deeply frustrating.

"Enough of Leo," Teresa went on. "Here's something else . . . Josh Jonah *hated* old movies."

"How can you possibly know that?"

"He told everyone! In a million media interviews. Anything that wasn't invented in this bright new century of ours simply didn't matter to him. There are three long articles a couple of friends tracked down for me. In them he gets asked to name his favourite movies of all time. They're all the same stupid, violent, computer-generated crap that passes for entertainment these days. Not a human emotion in any of them. No *Citizen Kane*. No Eisenstein. Nothing Italian. I doubt he'd even *heard* of Hitchcock."

The director's name conjured up the cartoon image of the man, in profile, lips protruding, and that funny old theme tune he'd heard so often on the late-night reruns put out by the more arcane Italian channels.

"If he'd never heard of Hitchcock, who invented Carlotta Valdes?" Costa asked.

"Who sent Maggie Flavier a green '57 Jaguar?" Teresa shot back. "And told Martin Vogel to pick bitter almonds from a tree next to that fictional grave at Mission Dolores?"

She turned around and pointed to the huge white mansion across the road that was the home of Roberto Tonti. "He knows all about Hitchcock. So does Bonetti. His first movie in Italy was a cheap Hitchcock knockoff. Simon Harvey knows, too.

Maybe there's a movie fan among those mobsters Bonetti tapped for cash."

"The Carabinieri say it's over."

"We can argue about whether this was all about Dante. Or a bunch of Sicilian money from some people who were starting to feel they've been taken for a ride. Or a movie an old English movie director made here—*here*—half a century ago. But there's one thing even Leo can't argue about..." Teresa watched him, waiting.

"Josh Jonah didn't know about any of these things," Costa said.

"He could—and probably did—fix that awful snuff movie that made Lukatmi so much money when Allan Prime died. But that's about it," she agreed. "Whoever started this circus is still out there. Maybe they're going to go quiet now the SFPD want to lay the blame at the door of a dead computer billionaire. Maybe they feel the publicity they've got is enough. Maybe not."

She looked at him. "So what are you going to do now? Every case is unpacked. Every item accounted for." She nodded towards the tents. "You're surely not needed in there and you know it."

He'd been warned to steer clear of Maggie Flavier, by both Gerald Kelly and Falcone, who was concerned that whatever little cooperation they could still count on from the SFPD was about to disappear.

"I'm supposed to behave myself."

"Call her, Nic. Go and see her. No one's going to

miss you. Even Leo and Peroni don't feel the need to hang around this place. Why should you?"

He hadn't been able to get Maggie out of his head for days. That was why he had hesitated.

Teresa reached into his jacket pocket, pulled out his phone, and dangled her fingers over the buttons.

"Don't make me do this for you," she warned.

4

IT WAS ALMOST THREE IN THE AFTERNOON BY THE time Jimmy Gaines parked his station wagon in the Muir Woods visitor centre and pointed them up the hiking route signposted as Ocean View Trail.

"You ever watched *Vertigo*, Jimmy?" Hank said as he tied on his old fireman's boots.

"Couple of times."

"Some of it was shot here. They give her a famous line. 'I don't like it... knowing I have to die.'"

"One more folk myth," Frank cut in. "Hitch shot that somewhere else."

The two men turned and looked at him.

"You sure of that?" Jimmy Gaines asked. "All them big sequoias. I'd assumed..."

"It's the movies," Frank insisted. "I've been reading up on things. The buffs call that part 'the Muir

Woods sequence.' But it wasn't even filmed here. It was shot at Big Basin, eighty miles south. Hitch liked the light better, apparently." He watched Gaines pulling on a backpack with three water bottles strapped to the outside. "Did Tom Black like *Vertigo*, too?"

Gaines heaved more gear out of the car. "Not that I know. He never talked about movies much. Just books. Thoreau, *Walden*. All that stuff Tom used to spout to the press about how we could build a different world, one in tune with nature, with no real government and some kind of weird pacifism when it came to dealing with authority…it all came from Thoreau. That old nut wasn't just a tree hugger, you know. He was an anarchist, too."

He stared into the forest of gigantic redwoods ahead of them. "I never much liked to talk to Tom about that. He was so young and naive, there wasn't much point. Josh Jonah was the opposite, except when he wanted to appear that way to keep Tom happy. Josh liked movies where people died. We had a brief conversation once about *The Matrix*. When I told him I couldn't figure which way was up, he looked at me like I was brain-dead. We didn't talk movies or much else ever again." He stopped and scratched his grey mop of hair. "Why are we talking about Hitchcock?"

"It's just some crazy theory our Italian friend has. You know what Europeans are like."

"Not really."

They steered clear of poison oak and listened in

silence as Jimmy Gaines talked as they walked, mostly to himself, about the forest around, the redwoods and tan oak, the madrone and Douglas fir.

Frank Boynton caught his brother's eye after half an hour and knew they were both thinking the same thing. Or rather two things. This didn't seem the kind of place a fugitive would hide. The Muir Woods were popular. At weekends and on holidays, it could be difficult to find a space in any of the parking lots dotted around the park.

And Jimmy Gaines looked like a man who knew where he was going.

After a while he diverted them onto a side path deep in the thickest part of the wood. Frank glanced at the sign at the fork: they were on the Lost Trail.

It seemed well named. They began to descend through deep, solitary tracts of fir that merged into deeper, thicker forest. The sun was so scarce the temperature felt as if the season had changed. For some reason, that line of Kim Novak's refused to leave Frank Boynton's head.

After what seemed like an hour of punishment, Jimmy Gaines led them off the barely visible path and directly into the deep forest. Here there was no discernible track at all. They stumbled down a steep mossy bank, further and further into the dense thickets where the massive redwoods stood over them like ancient giants. Gaines's eyes flickered constantly between the dim path ahead and a small GPS unit in his hand.

"They got animals here?" Frank asked.

"Chipmunk and deer mainly," Gaines said without turning round. "Snakes. Lots of snakes. Don't believe the stories you hear about mountain lions. They're close but not that close. Too smart to come near humans mostly. We got ticks that carry Lyme disease. Rat shit with hantavirus. Some of them mosquitoes might have West Nile Virus, too." He stopped and watched them standing there, uncertain where to put their feet. "It's dangerous in the wild woods. I figured you knew that."

Gaines removed his backpack, pulled out the water bottles, and handed two over. The Boynton brothers gulped greedily.

"Doesn't feel like we're wandering around aimlessly," Frank said. "If I'm being honest."

Gaines shook his head. "You boys always were too clever for your own good, weren't you? Too greedy, too. You just had to know what was going on." He swigged at his own water bottle and eyed the redwoods around them. "I remember one time when there was a fire in some little baker's on Union. You two weren't even on duty. Didn't stop you coming around and watching, telling us what we were doing wrong while you stood there looking all know-it-all from the sidelines."

He opened up the backpack and took out a large handgun, old, with a revolving chamber. A Colt maybe, Frank thought. He was never great at weapons.

The Boynton brothers' former colleague from the San Francisco Fire Department pointed the barrel in their direction and said, "Tom and I are a little more than friends, if you really want to know. I never had a son. Never had a wife either. Just like you two." He leaned forward and grinned, a little bashfully. "Didn't you ever wonder?"

"Yeah," Frank said. "But we didn't think it was any of our business. Still isn't. What's with the gun, Jimmy? We've known each other thirty years. You don't need that."

There was a noise from behind them. Frank Boynton didn't turn to look. He refused to take his eyes off Jimmy Gaines and the weapon in his hands.

A dishevelled figure stumbled down through the high ferns of the bank by their side. The newcomer looked like some street bum who'd been homeless for a long time, not a fugitive ex-billionaire who'd only a few days before kept the company of movie stars.

"Hello, son," Frank said, extending his hand. "My brother and I are here to help."

The young man turned and stared at Jimmy Gaines, fear and desperation in his eyes. And deference, too. Maybe Jimmy bossed him around in the open air the way Josh Jonah had inside Lukatmi's grim brick fortress by the water.

"You got food?" was all Tom Black asked.

Gaines threw him the backpack. "I showed you

how to find things to eat in the woods," he said, sounding cross. "I can't be here for you all the time, Tom. That would just make them suspicious."

"Can't stay here forever, either," Hank cut in. "Sooner or later you've got to come out."

The young man ripped into a pack of trail mix, poured some into his throat, and looked at them unpleasantly, as if they weren't quite real.

"What if we could make it sooner?" Frank added. "What if we could make it safe?"

Black glanced at Jimmy Gaines, seeking guidance.

"Take their phones and throw them in the forest," Gaines ordered. With his left hand he retrieved some rope out of the backpack. "Then tie them up good and tight."

5

THE BROCKLEBANK BUILDING WAS OLD AND elegant and hauntingly familiar. Costa parked outside the grand entrance and talked his way past the uniformed concierge at the door. There was money on Nob Hill. History, too. The connection came to him as he stood in the elevator, waiting for it to rise to the third floor, where Maggie's apartment was situated.

In the movie, Madeleine Elster had lived in this

same block. The detective Scottie had watched her leave the forecourt in a green Jaguar, identical to the one some unknown stranger had briefly loaned Maggie Flavier.

He went through a cursory ID check when he reached the floor—the movie company's security men were all flash suits and earpieces and very little in the way of brains—and then she let him in.

Maggie looked as if she'd come straight from the shower. She was wearing a bright emerald silk robe and nothing else. Her blonde hair was newly dried and seemed to have recovered its gleaming sheen. It was still short, without the extensions that had caused his heart to skip a beat at the Palace of Fine Arts. She looked incredibly well, as if she'd never suffered a day's illness in her life.

"I wish you'd come when I asked," she said. "No need to explain. Help yourself to a drink, will you?" She pointed at the kitchen. "I've got a vodka. I need to get dressed."

He watched her walk into the bedroom and close the door. Then he found some Pellegrino in the refrigerator, returned with it, and stood in front of a marble fireplace and the largest TV screen he'd ever seen. The place wasn't as big as he'd expected. A part of him said movie stars needed to live somewhere special, somewhere different. From what he could see, there was just the one living room, a kitchen, the bedroom on the inner side of the building, away from the noise of the street, and a shining stone-and-steel bathroom next to it.

When she returned, she was wearing a short pleated skirt, the kind he associated with teenage cheerleaders at sports matches, and a polo shirt with the number seven on the front. No makeup, no pretence, no borrowed character from an old museum canvas. She looked little more than twenty.

"How long have you lived here?" he asked.

"Forever. My mother found it not long after we came from Paris. We rented back then. Not that she could afford it. There were . . . standards to be maintained. If you read the bios, they'll tell you she spent our last thousand dollars trying to find me a break. That's not quite true. Not quite."

"So that's . . . what? Ten, fifteen years ago?"

"Seventeen years in October. I remember how warm and sunny it was when we arrived. I thought San Francisco would always be like that. You should come in the autumn. It's beautiful. Different. What you'd expect of the summer."

"You don't know how she found it?"

She shook her head and ran her fingers through the ragged blonde locks. "No. Why should I? It was a good choice. When she was gone and I had the money, I bought the apartment. It's just a one-bedroom bachelor-girl pad. I'm not here more than two or three months of the year anyway."

"And when you're travelling?"

"Then the agency rents it. I hate the idea of an

empty home. A place should be lived in. Why are you asking all this?"

"I've seen it before. This apartment block. It was in a movie."

"It was?" she asked, wide-eyed, curious.

"*Vertigo*. Hitchcock."

Maggie closed her eyes and fought to concentrate. Then she opened them, picked up her glass from the table, and gulped at it.

"No. I don't think I've seen it. Hitchcock isn't really that fashionable these days, to be honest with you."

"The woman in it lived here. She died. In the end."

Maggie raised her drink in a kind of toast. "Women in movies often do. You should congratulate me, by the way. Dino Bonetti came by earlier. He offered me the part of Beatrice in the sequel."

"Did you agree?"

"What, on a social visit? I don't think so. All that stuff goes through Simon and then my agent."

"Do they take a cut?"

She laughed, exasperated. "This is show business, Nic. Everybody takes a cut of everything. I feed thousands..."

"How much?"

She hesitated. "You're very curious. I don't know. I don't really want to. They put together some deal, I sign it when I'm told. Money goes in the bank." Her eyes darkened. "At least it's supposed to. Apparently, I'm missing something from *Inferno*. My accountant was whining about something or other. It's no big deal. I'm..." She threw a hand around the room. "...rich, aren't I? After the first couple of million, you stop counting. Any problems, I guess I can still do a hair ad. I'm not proud." She hesitated. "Why are you looking at me like that?"

"There's money missing in the production company accounts. A lot of money. And you haven't been paid?"

"Not everything. It's not the first time. Sometimes it takes months. They wait for the exchange rates to get better or something. That's why I didn't want to waste any time talking to Dino when he started pressing me to sign a new contract. Why should I? They can't screw me out of what they owe me for *Inferno*. It looks like it's going to be the biggest-grossing movie I've ever made. I'll get what I'm owed." She glanced at the window. "I want to live to enjoy it, too. Are we all still supposed to be on someone's hit list?"

He tried to sound convincing. And convinced. "I don't think so. Still, it makes sense to be careful."

"No rides through the Presidio? No visits to strange art galleries?"

"Not for the moment."

She stood a little closer. Her perfume was subtle and mesmerising. Close up, she didn't look so young, and he liked that.

"I have to do the premiere tomorrow. Then launch some old movie festival in the city over the weekend. After that..." The glass bobbed up and down, a touch nervously. "I have a villa for three weeks in Barbados. No one but me. Private estate. Nearest house half a mile away. Is that safe enough for you?"

"I'd think you'd be fine."

"What I meant was . . ."

Another edgy shot of vodka disappeared. She was coughing hard, her hand to her mouth. Her eyes were wide open again with astonishment. His mind began to race, recalling her terrible collapse in the park.

Maggie fell back on the sofa behind them. He was beside her instantly.

"Damned drink," she swore, still struggling to speak. "Went down the wrong way. Must break that vodka habit. Tomorrow. Definitely. Wait, I forgot something, Nic. Dino Bonetti! That movie! *Vertigo!*"

"What?"

"The first time he came here. He told me to watch it. He recognised the location." She looked at him. "Now you're saying the same thing. What's going on here?"

Costa told her a little of Teresa's ideas, and how the woman who had first approached Allan Prime had introduced herself as a character in the movie.

She sat on the sofa, bare, slender legs tucked beneath her. "Well, I guess it's time I followed everyone's advice. Will you watch it with me?" She closed her eyes and looked exhausted. "I've been on my own so much since all this craziness began."

"Where's the movie?" he asked.

She picked up the phone, called someone, and

ordered a DVD. "It'll be an hour or so. Are you hungry?"

"Starving."

"I can order some food, too."

He got up. Costa knew he needed activity, something that would take his mind off Dante Alighieri and Alfred Hitchcock, Dino Bonetti and the shattered corpse of Josh Jonah, prone on the floor of a run-down SoMa apartment block.

Maggie followed him and watched as he rifled through the kitchen drawers and cabinets.

"You have food," he said. "That's a start."

"*Old* food. One of the rental people must have left it."

He found a small envelope of dried porcini, a packet of arborio rice, a couple of shallots in the vegetable rack along with a chunk of Parmesan wrapped in foil. Five minutes later he had the makings of a risotto. It felt good to cook again. It felt even better to have Maggie Flavier leaning on the threshold of the door, looking at him as if she'd never seen anything like this in her life.

"Any wine recommendations?" she asked, nodding at the floor-length chilled cabinet filled with bottles that looked a lot more expensive than anything he usually drank.

"I'll leave that to you."

She opened the glass door, peered inside, and pulled out a bottle. "I bought this in Rome. Is it any good?"

He looked at the 2004 Terredora Greco di Tufo and said, "It'll do. Can I leave you to set the table?"

"Men!" she exclaimed, and went to the kitchen drawers, where she removed a tablecloth and place settings.

"After that . . ." he shouted through the open door, ". . . we need some cheese grated."

It wasn't the best risotto Costa had ever made. But he didn't want someone else's food. Not with her.

They ate and talked. Towards the end she looked at him and asked, "Did you used to cook? For Emily?"

He had to force himself to remember. There was now a distance between the present and the past. Perhaps it was San Francisco. Perhaps it was Maggie Flavier. Or both. But he could now see the winter's nightmare with some perspective, could stand back from it and feel apart from the pain and despair it had brought.

"Sometimes. Sometimes she did. Emily wasn't a vegetarian. If I was working nights, I'd come home occasionally and I could smell steak in the kitchen." He looked at her. "Or bacon and eggs."

"Were you upset?"

"Of course not. It was her home, too." He could picture the two of them together, inside the house near the Appian Way. "It used to smell good, if I'm honest. If I ate meat . . ." He shrugged. "But I don't. And I didn't like the smoking much. She went outside for that."

Maggie held up her hands. "I won't smoke inside either. Promise."

"It's your home," he said.

"No, it's not. It's just somewhere I live from time to time. Did you think about it? Being together? Did you ever . . . question whether it was right?"

"Not once. Not for a second," he said immediately. "We had arguments. We saw things different ways. None of that mattered. I can't explain. It happened." A flash of recollection, of a cold, hard winter's day by the mausoleum of Augustus, ran through his head. "Then it was over."

She reached out and touched the back of his hand.

"I could feel something. Your sadness. Outside that little children's cinema. Before we went inside. Before I even knew who you were. It was like something tangible."

"Not good for a police officer."

"I wouldn't worry about it. I'm freaky Maggie Flavier. I see things other people don't. Lucky them."

He got up and started to take the plates.

"No," she insisted. "You cooked. I load the dishwasher. Sit. Make yourself comfortable."

She went back into the kitchen. He walked to the bathroom and looked at himself in the mirror, wondering what he saw, what he felt.

When he returned, she was tipping the video deliveryman at the door. After that she put the disc in some machine by the fireplace and turned the TV on.

They sat next to each other, opposite the gigantic screen. She picked up a couple of remotes. The curtains on the apartment closed themselves slowly; the light fell.

The black-and-white credits ran: the logo of the Paramount peak, the awkward, jarring music he had come to associate with the movie. Then a brutal close-up of a woman, zooming into her eye with a cruel, unforgiving honesty, monochrome turning to bloodred, a swirling vortex spinning out from the black, unseeing pupil.

He felt cold. He felt lost and he'd no idea why.

6

IT GOT COLD QUICKLY IN THE WOODS. AT LEAST, Frank Boynton assumed the way he felt was due to the temperature of the out-of-the-way patch of the sequoia forest, not some innate primeval sense of dread on his part. He'd read more noir books than he could count, watched the entire school of movies in the genre. He'd thought he understood a little about fear from all that dedicated study, but now he realised he was wrong. There was a world of difference between theory and practice. Reality was a lot less complicated. It also seemed to happen a lot more quickly. He could almost feel the minutes slipping away from them.

So he sat there in silence, thinking, seated on the damp, cold ground, his hands tied behind his back, the two brothers bound together so securely there really wasn't much point in contemplating escape. He couldn't run as well as either of their captors even if it was a level playing field, without ropes, without a slippery dark forest where the light was fading and he hadn't a clue which way to turn.

The Muir Woods weren't the overrun tourist destination he'd believed, not in this part anyway. Here, the woods felt vast and timeless and desolate, an army of identical redwood monoliths stretching towards a darkening sky in every unfathomable direction. A place where a man could lie dead for months and maybe never be found.

Jimmy Gaines and Tom Black had gone off to a small clearing. They'd been there a long time, talking out of earshot. Making a phone call or two. Frank could hear the distant electronic beep of a phone and envied the way it communicated so easily, so swiftly with the outside world.

If he could just find his own ...

They'd be dead by the time anyone came. The idea of rescue was one confined to the pages of fiction. In the real world there was no escape, except perhaps through meek, obedient submission. The brothers had told Jimmy Gaines and Tom Black what they knew: an Italian woman they both liked believed

Tom was innocent and might be able to help if only he'd get in touch. Then she'd pass him on to a friendly cop who, for once, didn't come with a bunch of preconceptions about presumed guilt. Frank had taken the lead, as he usually did in such situations, offering to make the call, promising he'd do nothing to compromise their location, or Jimmy Gaines's identity.

They'd listened, then left. Something in the way they walked hadn't filled him with optimism.

Frank wriggled, trying to get a little more comfortable. He wished he could look at his brother eye-to-eye. He wished he could understand what might be going on in Hank's head. Closeness could make you deaf and blind to things that sensitive, observant people spotted instantly. Over the decades, their relationship had settled into an easy, unspoken rhythm. Frank was the practical one, the right-brainer, as Teresa Lupo had so cannily noticed. Frank handled the money and the day-to-day problems of keeping the house in the Marina going: bills and taxes, repairs and improvements. Hank was the dreamer, the would-be poet, more interested in the San Francisco of yesterday than now, more obsessed with the cerebral puzzles of Conan Doyle than the gutter reality of Dashiell Hammett that Frank preferred. Neither had much real preparation for their present quandary. Sherlock Holmes and Sam Spade were myths, ghostly actors in tales that chose entertainment over mundane, prosaic reality.

There weren't any favorable ends when it came to men with guns. Not in the Muir Woods. Not anywhere. Jimmy Gaines, when he wanted, would simply walk over and pop them, one after the other, straight in the head as they sat, tied together in a place that stank of moss and rotting vegetation. A jerk of the trigger was all it took. He'd been thinking of Jimmy a lot in the hour or so since Tom Black had appeared from behind the sequoias, like a lost forest creature in search of salvation. Jimmy Gaines taking them to bars where they didn't really feel comfortable. Jimmy Gaines swinging hard and viciously at a stranger who'd said the wrong thing, thought the wrong thought, looked the wrong way.

Like the idiots they were, he and Hank had walked straight up to him at Lukatmi based on that single sighting of Gaines with Tom Black weeks before, when they had, now Frank thought of it, seemed the very best of friends. That was the trouble with the Marina. It was a community, a little village full of smart, engaged, occasionally difficult people, all living on top of one another. It was hard to keep secrets. Jimmy Gaines, a solitary bachelor who quietly declined to go to some of the bars the other guys did after duty, had never really kept his. People were simply too polite—too uninterested, frankly—to mention it. So when a secret became big, became important, a man just passed it by like all the others. Familiarity didn't breed contempt. It bred a quiet, polite ignorance, a glance away at an awkward, embarrassing moment, a cough in the fist, then, after a suitable pause, a quick smile while glancing at the ground and formulating a rapid change of subject.

All of which led them to the Muir Woods while a line from an old movie kept running and running and running round his head like some loose carnivore circling the big, dark forest of his imagination.

I don't like it . . . knowing I have to die.

Hank's elbow nudged him in the ribs. He felt his brother's bristly cheek rub up against his.

"How are you doing?"

"Never felt better."

"This is my fault. Sorry."

"No need to apologise. We are jointly responsible for our own stupidity."

Hank cleared his throat. "May I remind you I am the junior here?"

Frank so wished he could look his brother full in the face at that moment. "By seven minutes, if you recall," he pointed out, thinking it was a long time since they'd had this conversation. Maybe five decades or so.

"Seven minutes, seven years. It doesn't matter. It still makes me younger. Still makes you the old one. The serious one. The one who does things the way you do 'cause you think that's what's expected."

They never argued. If there was cause for complaint, they simply fell into silence and waited till the cloud lifted. It had worked this way for almost sixty years, since they learned to speak.

"So what?" Frank asked.

"So we're clever and stupid in different ways. Normally, I'd say you were the cleverer and me the stupider. But this isn't normal, is it?"

Tom Black and Jimmy Gaines were on the phone again. Frank was glad of that. They weren't taking any notice of the two old men they'd tied up next to a redwood tree.

"I am inclined to concur," he said. "Your point being?"

Hank shuffled round a little. They could just about catch the corner of each other's eye.

"The point being," Hank went on, "whether this is a left-brain or right-brain situation. Whether it's one best handled by me." The nudge in the ribs again. "Or by you. And you think it's you. Because you're like that. No offence, brother. You are. That's fine."

"Hank," Frank said very calmly, "this could be difficult. We might have a lot of talking to do. Talking's something best left to me. We've always worked that way."

"There you are wrong, brother." There was anger and determination in that lone, bright eye. "This is not about talking at all. Did they look remotely interested when you offered to call Teresa? Well, did they?"

Frank thought about that. He'd been a little scared when Jimmy Gaines had demanded the Italian pathologist's number. He just wanted to give the man anything he could if it kept that big old gun out of their faces.

Jimmy Gaines and Tom Black never asked them to do a damned thing once they had Frank's address book.

"No. They didn't."

"Another thing," Hank added. "I can hear better than you these days. They weren't talking about Teresa. They kept using that cop's name, the one whose number she gave us. Costa. Seemed like Black knew who he was already."

"That's good."

"No, it isn't. That Italian cop doesn't know us from Adam."

Frank felt scared again. Very.

"Listen to me, Frank. I don't know who they've called already but pretty soon they're going to call the Costa guy. Then Tom's going to go to see him and cut some kind of a deal. You know the routine. You read it a million times in all that stupid pulp fiction of yours: 'I didn't know what was going on, Officer. I just got scared and ran away. I got your number sometime. You seemed a nice, gullible guy.'" He took a deep, wheezy breath. "Whatever. And then..."

Hank's single eye peered at him. Frank marvelled at the fact he'd learned more new stuff about his twin brother this last week than at any time in the last twenty years.

"Then it's just Jimmy Gaines and us," Frank

replied. "And us knowing that was all a pile of crap, and that he was in there with them, too, which Costa won't get told because Jimmy Gaines doesn't want to go to jail, not for anybody."

"You old guys," Hank muttered with some sly amusement. "You get there in the end. Just listen to your little brother and do what he says."

"OK," Frank said, and was amazed how odd the concession sounded.

"Good. They're working out their story. Their plan. Pretty soon Tom Black's going to make that final call, then he's going to get out of here. After that, Jimmy Gaines is going to walk over, say a brief apology, and blow our brains out." He sighed. "Or so he'd like to think."

Frank Boynton watched his brother's lone eye wink the way it did when they were children.

"Good thing the stupid, head-in-the-clouds kid brother had the gumption to bring a knife, huh?" Hank asked lightly.

After that, Frank didn't say a word. He stayed still and silent, hustling up a little closer to his brother so that the two men locked in conversation by the trees didn't get suspicious about what Hank was doing with his hands.

A little while later they heard Tom Black make one more call, and the name Costa came into that. It didn't last long. Then he left without once looking back.

Jimmy Gaines stayed by the big redwood and lit a cigarette. He smoked it slowly.

At least he seemed a little reluctant. Frank Boynton gave him that.

7

VERTIGO LASTED JUST OVER TWO HOURS. They watched in silence, Costa upright, Maggie reclining, her head on his shoulder, hair brushing against his cheek, sweet and soft and full of memories of another. They had nothing to say, nothing to share except the same sense of fearful wonder watching what was taking place on the screen, a fairy tale for adults imagined long before they were born.

The day started to die beyond the curtains. The lights in the streets and adjoining buildings began to wake for the evening. He scarcely noticed much except the movie and the presence of the woman by his side, so close she was almost part of him, and equally rapt in the strange, disjointed narrative playing out in front of them, one which meshed with their identities and the city beyond.

Maggie let out a sharp, momentary gasp at the scene outside the Brocklebank, with the green Jaguar pulling away, Kim Novak at the wheel, made blonde by Hitchcock. Some parts made her shiver against him: Madeleine falling into the Bay at Fort Point, not far from the Marina, and Scottie rescuing her, an act which was to establish the bond between them; again when she was wandering among the giant redwoods, lost, uncertain of her own identity; Madeleine in the Legion of Honor, staring up at the painting of Carlotta Valdes, seeming to believe this long-dead woman somehow possessed her own identity, in her hands a bouquet identical both to the one in the painting and to that left in Maggie's borrowed car.

Most of all she seemed affected by what happened at the old white adobe bell tower of San Juan Bautista, erect in a blue sky like some biblical monument to a warped sense of justice, the place where the real Madeleine fell to her death, and where the woman who usurped her identity—and Scottie's love—followed in the cryptic, cruel finale.

Her eyes were wide with shock at that final act. Unable to leave the screen. Together they watched Jimmy Stewart, tense and tragic, frozen in the open arch high above the mission courtyard, his own vertigo cured, but at a shocking price: the life of the female icon—not a real woman—whom he'd come to love, obsessively, with the same voyeuristic single-mindedness with which Hitchcock himself pursued her through the all-seeing eye of the camera.

When the credits rolled, she got up anxiously and took her glass into the kitchen. She hadn't touched it for the entire duration of the movie. Maggie returned with a fresh cocktail, full of ice and lime and booze, in her left hand, and a glass of wine for him in her right.

"I need a drink after that," she announced, and sat down, putting just a little distance between them. "Don't you?"

"I don't know what I need." He didn't reach for the wine.

Maggie gulped at the vodka, let her head drift back onto the sofa, breathing deeply, as if to calm herself.

"What does it mean?" she asked, her green eyes suddenly alive with interest.

That question had never left him from the moment the spectral figure of Madeleine Elster walked across the screen, through a world that seemed so like the one they now inhabited.

"Perhaps it's what Teresa said all along. Someone, somewhere is using the movie as a template for what they're doing. A riddle; a reminder, a taunt...The way the Carabinieri think that Dante is being used. Maybe they're both right."

There was a half smile on her face, and an expectant look. Costa knew he hadn't said enough.

"There's nothing here that could possibly interest the SFPD. I'm a cop like them. We don't think along these lines. We don't watch movies for inspiration. Or read books of poetry. We do something real, something concrete and direct. It's all we know. If a case gets inside your head, that's usually when it all starts to go wrong."

There was another problem, though he didn't want to say it. There had to be more. Some link, some individual inside *Inferno* who was the catalyst. Whether what had happened was a simulacrum of *The Divine Comedy* or *Vertigo*—or both—some event, some conversation, perhaps recent, perhaps long forgotten, must have given life to the dark, convoluted story that began in the park of the Villa Borghese.

She moved closer. "Like it went wrong for Scottie? They said he was a good cop. Then along comes a woman who isn't what she seems..."

"You could put it that way."

"Nic." Her green eyes shone with bright intelligence. "I was really asking about the movie. What does *that* mean?"

"Next to a murder investigation? Nothing."

She sighed, disappointed. "What I wanted was for you to tell me about Scottie. About Madeleine. The woman he thought he loved, the woman who didn't really exist. Then that sad little thing who did exist, who pretended she was Madeleine just because that was what Scottie wanted. That could make him happy, so that he would love her in return."

"I don't know what it's about," Costa confessed. "It's supposed to be enigmatic. Art's not there to give you answers, not always. Sometimes it's enough simply to ask a question."

"What question?"

He thought about Scottie and the way he looked at the woman he believed to be Madeleine Elster.

How he'd undressed her while she was unconscious after rescuing her at Fort Point. How he waited expectantly by his own bed until she woke, naked, beneath his sheets.

"I don't know," he said again. "Scottie can't extricate himself from his desire for Madeleine, even though a part of him knows it's not real. The way he's always following her, watching, thinking. Hoping. It's the pursuit of some hopeless fantasy. Like…"

He felt cold. He felt stupid. He felt more awake—more alive—than at any time since Emily had died.

"It's like Dante's *Inferno*," he said, and could feel the revelation rising inside him. "Scottie and Madeleine Elster. Dante and Beatrice. It's the same story, the same pilgrimage, looking for something important, the most important thing there can be. The big answer. A reason for living."

Costa shook his head and laughed. "Why couldn't I see this before? *Vertigo* is *Inferno*. It's just a different way of looking at the same question. Scottie… Dante… they're both just Everyman looking for something that makes him whole. Some reason to live."

" 'I don't like it… knowing I have to die,' " Maggie Flavier said, quoting from the movie in the same quiet, lost voice, one so accurate she might have been the woman they'd just watched on the screen.

"Do you know what Simon told me once?" she asked in a whisper. "When I asked him what *Inferno* was really about? Not Tonti's movie. The poem."

"What?"

"He said it was about knowing you never got to see the truth, to get a glimpse of God, until you're dead. That everything up to that point is just some kind of preparation, a bunch of beginnings. You live in order to die. One gives meaning to the other. Black and white. Yin and yang. Being and not being." She snatched at the glass. "But none of it's up to us, is it?" she asked, and there was a quiet note of bitterness in her voice. "That's for God, and if we play *that* role, we lose everything. Scottie tried to make the woman he wanted out of nobody. He tried to play God. In the end, that killed her. A man's just a man. A woman can only be what she is."

"What did you say? When he told you that?"

"I damn near slapped his face and told him not to be so stupid. I don't believe in anything except here and now. Don't ask me to trade that for some kind of hidden grace I only get when I'm dead. Don't *ever* do that."

The blonde hair extensions he'd seen at the Palace of Fine Arts were there on a low coffee table. She picked them up and held them to her head. There was a movement in her eye, an expression she had somehow picked up from that photo in his wallet, something else he couldn't define because, unlike her, he'd never consciously noticed . . .

Instantly the associations rose for him, ones that were both warm and worrying.

She wasn't Emily. She could pretend to be, though. If he wanted.

"I'm just like the woman in the movie, aren't I? I can be anything you like. That's what I do."

He felt uneasy; he wondered whether it was time to leave, whether that was even possible.

"Is that what you'd like, Nic? Would it make things easier?"

"I want you to be you."

She threw the false hair onto the table, brusquely, as if she hated the things. "That's very noble. What if I don't know who I am?"

"Then it's time to find out."

"Doing what? Commercials? Too cheap. Theatre? I'm not good enough. Get them to revive *L'Amour L.A.* so I can stare into the camera one more time and say, 'But 'oo can blame Françoise?'"

Her eyes were glassy. This was a conversation she both needed and feared. "Or become one more suburban housewife who used to be something. Getting pointed at in supermarkets while I buy the diapers. Getting pitied. I don't think so."

"Doing whatever you want."

She took a deep breath, looked him in the eye, and said, "The only thing I want right now is you. I've wanted that ever since the moment I saw you in the park, Nic, looking lost and so sad, not knowing who the hell I was and still wanting to help me, protect me, in spite of all that pain you had inside. That's never happened before. Something so selfless. Not anything like it. And I've seen them all, Nic. The filthy rich, the astonishingly beautiful." She pushed away the glass on the table. "I've been drunk on this shallow little existence since I was thirteen years old. It was only when I got to know you I realised I might as well have been dead all that time. Or a creature from someone's imagination. Like that woman who pretended to be Madeleine Elster."

It had to be said. He couldn't avoid it. "I'm just a Roman police officer. I do what I do in the place that I know. That won't change. Not ever. That's me."

"I know," she replied, still staring at him. "But that's not what scares you. *I* scare you. What you think I am. Some being from a different planet. Out of your reach."

He felt the need for a drink and reached for the glass of Greco di Tufo. It tasted warm and a little too complex. There were cheaper wines he preferred. Cheaper places than this luxurious apartment in a city where he didn't belong. He'd lost track of time. He'd no idea where any of his team were, or whether they'd simply given up on him.

"I was never much interested in anything that couldn't last," he said, and found he couldn't look at her when he spoke those words.

"Because of what I am?" she asked. "Some perfect untouchable movie star? Listen to the truth." She lifted her hands to her face. "This is an accident and maybe not a lucky one. I'm the most flawed, most damaged human being you're likely to find. I've been off the rails more times than you could imagine. I've woken up in the wrong place, the wrong bed, so often I don't even have to blot out the memories anymore, there are so many they do that for themselves. I'm weak and pathetic and stupid. Someone can even poison me with an apple. Remember? Without you I might be dead."

"I remember."

She got on her knees on the sofa next to him and hitched up her skirt. "Does this look like perfection to you?" she demanded.

The mark of the hypodermic pen was still livid on her thigh, darkening purple at its centre, yellow at the rim.

"If I was naked on a set, with a million men pointing lights and cameras at my body, they could cover that with makeup. It doesn't mean it isn't there."

She took his head in her hands. Her eyes were wide and guileless, her fingers felt like fire on his skin. "I bruise, I bleed. I weep. I ache . . . I need. Just like you."

His fingers reached and touched the mark on her leg. Her skin felt soft and warm, like Emily's, like anyone's.

She leaned forward, took his head more firmly, pulled it towards her.

Her breath was hot and damp in his ear. "You can kiss it better if you want, Nic."

His hand spread over her leg without a single, deliberate thought.

"Please," she whispered.

Costa bent down and brushed his lips gently against the mark, then let his tongue touch the warm flesh. She tasted of something sweet: soap and perfume. His fingers ran around her torso and felt the taut, nervous strength there.

Then he got off the sofa, picked her up in his arms, and carried her into the bedroom. Her frantic kisses covered his neck, his face; her hands worked at his shoulders. Gently he placed her slender frame on the soft white cotton coverlet. She looked at him, pleading in silence, unmoving, arms raised.

He removed her shirt with a slow, deliberate patience. She was naked beneath. Her hands tore anxiously at his clothes. In the shadows of her bedroom they found each other, not seeing anything else, not caring.

There hadn't been many women in his life, and all of them had mattered. But not like this. Maggie Flavier sought something in him he'd never been asked for before, in ways that were utterly new to him.

He lost count of the times they struggled with each other in the half darkness on a bed so gigantic he couldn't hear it creak, however physical their efforts. There would never be a time, he thought, when he could forget these moments, the sight of her sighing beneath him. The gentle curves of her legs with their moist dark triangle at the apex, the dark corona of the areola of her breast as she arched above him, straining with a gentle insistence, seeking to prolong the sweetness between them.

Eventually Costa rolled to one side, closed his eyes, threw back his head against the deep pillow, and laughed.

She was on her elbow at his side when he looked again, poking at him with a long fingernail. "So it's funny, is it?"

"No. It's ridiculous."

"I like the ridiculous. I feel at home there. So will you, one day." She rolled over and looked at the bedside clock. "It's nearly ten. What do we do now?" She ran a finger down his navel to his thigh. "Chess?"

"I haven't played chess in years..." he began to say.

The phone rang from somewhere.

His jacket was strewn on the floor with all his other clothes. He struggled to find it.

"Oh God," she groaned. "You really are a cop, aren't you? I suppose I should be glad this didn't happen ten minutes ago."

"Or ten minutes before. Or ten minutes before *that*."

Costa picked up the phone, sat down on the bed, and said, without thinking, *"Pronto."*

"What?" asked a young, uncertain voice on the other end. "Who is this?"

"I'm sorry. My name is Nic Costa. I'm Italian. I wasn't..." He glanced at Maggie, who sat upright with her arms folded, watching him with an expression of mock anger. At least he thought it was mock. "I wasn't thinking straight."

"Please start, Mr. Costa. I need your help."

"Who are you?"

"My name is Tom Black and someone wants to kill me. Be at the viewing platform above Fort Point. Eleven, on the dot. Be alone and for God's sake tell no one or I'm as good as dead."

The call ended abruptly. Costa hit redial. The number was withheld.

"Who was it?" Maggie asked.

"He said he was Tom Black. Wants to meet me. The viewing platform above Fort Point."

He'd glimpsed the old brick fortress when they'd been sightseeing. The building was half hidden beneath the city footings of the Golden Gate Bridge, like some ancient toy castle discarded by a lost race of giants. It was there that Scottie had fished the supposedly suicidal Madeleine Elster out of San Francisco Bay. The spot seemed so remote and shut off by the great red iron structure above, he'd no idea how it could be reached.

"How do I get there?"

"You don't," she said very severely. "You tell the police and let them do it. This isn't Rome. This isn't your investigation."

"I know that. Tom Black's no idiot. He won't give himself up if he sees the police there. He's scared and he wants to talk. With me for some reason."

"Nic…"

"If he disappears this time, we may never see him again."

She swore and gave him an evil look. Then she

said, "Get on 101 as if you want to go over the bridge. Just before you do, there's a turnoff to the right with a parking lot."

"How public is it?"

"You're right next to the Golden Gate Bridge. There'll be traffic." She hunched her arms around herself. Naked, she seemed smaller somehow, and vulnerable. "But not much if you turn off the road, I guess."

She took his hand. "Nic—don't go. Stay here with me. We can drink wine and play chess. Leave this to someone else."

"Who?"

"Anyone. I don't care."

He couldn't read the expression on her face.

The hot, human scent of sex hung around them, along with that sense of both embarrassment and elation he'd come to recognise when life took a turn like this. Something had changed in a subtle and mysterious way. The barriers were tumbling down, like leaves caught in an autumn storm. A part of him, he knew, wanted to run.

Costa gripped her fingers, then kissed her damp forehead.

"Stay here, Maggie. I'll call," he promised.

8

JIMMY GAINES SMOKED THREE CIGARETTES BY the redwood tree, none of them quickly. As darkness fell, a waxy yellow half-moon began to emerge above the forest, and the dense wilderness became drowned in a cacophony of new sounds: birds and animals, insects and distant wild calls Frank Boynton couldn't begin to name. He and his brother watched everything like hawks. More than anything, they sought to measure every breath of the man by the tree. Or perhaps, he reflected, they were simply counting away their own.

Without Gaines noticing, the two had talked together in low tones, about the lay of the land and the limited possibilities ahead of them. Somewhere at their backs they could hear motor vehicles passing through Muir Woods. Not many. This was a deserted part of the forest, and their number had diminished as day turned to night. But there was a road somewhere back there up the slope. Both men were sure of that.

In the opposite direction, downhill, beyond the sequoia trees looming opposite their captor, was, Hank said, a steep, sheer drop, one he'd seen as they arrived.

Frank had never noticed. He'd been too worried by that stage to take much notice of anything except Jimmy Gaines. Now, though, thanks to his brother's acuity, he could tell the drop was there by the way the just-visible foliage faded to nothing in the mid-distance, and from the faint sound of running water somewhere distant and below. There was a creek maybe. It was difficult to tell. Even more difficult as dusk gave way to the pale sheen of the moon, which made the area beneath the high, dense tree cover seem even blacker than before.

Neither man felt at home in the forest. All they had between them were two small flashlights and some vague idea of where the road might be. That would have to be enough. If they could escape Jimmy Gaines and his old black gun, they would head up-hill, back towards the Lost Trail, then try to find headlights that might lead them back to the city and civilisation.

If…

Jimmy Gaines threw his last cigarette into the black void ahead of him, where it vanished like a fire-fly on speed. Then he came tearing towards them, swearing and stomping his big boots on the damp, mossy ground.

"Why can't you keep your noses out of things that don't concern you?" the old fireman demanded.

The gun was in his right hand. Hank had cut both their sets of ropes and left them there so Gaines wouldn't see what had happened. Frank wondered whether that mattered so much. A gun was a gun.

"We're sorry, Jimmy," Frank said. "We didn't know."

"But you still came looking!"

"Blame me." Frank nodded at his brother. "Not him. He's not very bright. Besides, it was always me who got to you. You don't need to bring Hank into this."

"Hank, Frank, Tweedledee, Tweedledum..." The gun was getting higher and starting to look more purposeful. "You're both the same. What business of yours is it, anyway, what Tom and me get up to? He's a good guy. It was Josh who got him into all this shit. Josh and *them*."

"What shit?" Hank asked.

The gun rose and pointed at his head.

"There you go again," Gaines moaned. "Mouth on overdrive. I suppose you think I might as well tell you now it doesn't matter. All this movie shit. Those bastards from Hollywood who ate those two kids up and spat them out. They were doing OK when they just stuck to being computer geeks. Somebody would've come along and bought the company when the money ran out. They didn't need to move in those damned circles..."

The weapon wavered.

"It's got nothing to do with us," Frank agreed mildly. "Our Italian lady said she could help Tom. That's all. So we thought maybe..."

Gaines let out a despairing wheeze. "I don't want

to die in jail. I don't deserve that. I was just looking for a little security when I retired. That and a little companionship."

"We won't tell them," Frank insisted.

"We don't even know what's going on, do we?" Hank asked meekly. "We just thought we were doing your friend a favour, Jimmy. Hasn't he gone to see our nice Italian lady?"

"Never mind where he's gone. None of your business."

"I couldn't agree more there, Jimmy," Frank said. "But she's going to think it's a little odd if Hank and I don't turn up for our regular coffee tomorrow morning. She's like us. Inquisitive."

Gaines moved and a shaft of moonlight caught his face. It was taut, anxious, locked in something close to a snarl.

"As if I don't know you two. Always the smart-asses. You wouldn't tell someone what you were doing before you went out and did it. Not if you figured you'd get some brownie points at the end when you turned round and said, 'Look at us. Look at the Boynton brothers. Look what clever bastards we are.'" He bent and leered in Frank's face. "You didn't tell her where you were going, did you? Or any of this stuff. Admit it. You were always lousy liars, both of you. Don't try that on me. I've known you too long."

"We didn't tell her," Frank agreed. "All the same . . . two and two."

"Screw two and two. If Tom can get a few days free

once he's spoken to the police, that's all we need. We'll be gone. They say Laos is nice." He grimaced. "If that jerk Jonah hadn't locked up the money so tight, we'd be gone by now anyway." He laughed, not pleasantly. "I owe you that, boys. You provided us with a way out. It's a pity..."

The gun arced through the air, from Frank to Hank and back again. To give Jimmy his due, he didn't look keen on any of this. "Tell you what. Let me do you one last favour. You choose who gets to go first."

"Him," Hank said promptly, nodding at his brother. "He got to come into this world seven minutes before me. Only right I get to even things up a little. *After*...we could talk."

"What?" Frank bellowed with heartfelt outrage. "*What?* Because I'm seven minutes older?"

Hank screwed round trying to look at him. "It's only fair. Given the circumstances and everything."

Frank shuffled up against him, remembering not to disturb the loose ropes. "He'd have just *killed* me! And you want to *talk* to him?"

"Who else am I supposed to exchange my final words with?" Hank objected. "The frigging chipmunks?"

"Generally speaking, chipmunks are only active by day," Gaines pointed out. "Too many predators at night. Also—"

"Shut up, Jimmy!" the Boynton brothers yelled in concert.

Gaines shuffled in his big forest boots. "Maybe it wasn't fair of me to offer you a choice," he said a little mournfully. "I mean, it's not like I'm proud of this, you know. It's just...needed." The gun swung towards Frank, and Jimmy Gaines said, "Oh hell..."

It was the loudest noise Frank had ever heard. Like a sonic boom that rang throughout the forest. Unseen creatures skittered across on the ground around them, crashing through the leaves.

Hank had caught Jimmy Gaines's shin hard with his foot as the weapon was coming round. More through luck than anything else, the gun was rising upwards, above them both, when the explosion came.

The recoil on the old handgun seemed tremendous, and the upward forty-five-degree angle pushed it all back into Gaines's shoulder. The force bucked him away from them, onto the slight slope towards the redwood that had, until recently, been wreathed in his cigarette smoke. One stumbling step behind took over from another. Soon Gaines was running backwards downhill, arms flailing and cartwheeling through the air, old gun flying high into the moonlight, trying to stay upright, screaming and swearing until finally he toppled over.

The two brothers got up and watched, helpless. Momentum could be a terrible thing. He'd fallen past the lip of some projecting plateau in the forest floor and flipped over the edge like a tree trunk rolling downhill. In the gashes of light visible through the sequoia branches, they could see Jimmy Gaines's body tumbling round and round on the moss and grass and rocks as the incline grew steeper and steeper, and the trees got more slender and scarce.

They stood together in silence. Then there was a long, solitary cry and Jimmy Gaines's shape disappeared from sight altogether.

"Damn," Hank muttered, and pulled out his little flashlight. The battery was low. The light was the colour of the wan moon above. Frank got his instead and ordered him to turn it off. They might need it later.

They held hands like children to make sure they didn't lose their footings, stepping gingerly down the slope towards the place where Jimmy Gaines had vanished.

After a little while Frank put out an arm to keep his brother back. The incline was turning too sheer. There was no point and they both knew it. Jimmy Gaines lay somewhere below, a long way, close to the tinkling waters of the creek that they could now hear very clearly. Frank doubted even a skilled mountain rescue party could reach him quickly.

He pointed his little light back up the hill. They waited for a minute or two. Then there was the faint sound of some kind of vehicle and the flash of far-off headlights.

"You walk carefully, little brother," Frank Boynton warned, still holding on to his arm. "This has been a very eventful day."

A loud and repetitive electronic beep burst out of the lush undergrowth beneath the beam of his flashlight, one so unexpected it made Frank jump with a short spike of fear.

"My phone," Hank said. "See? I told you there was a point to having different rings."

Frank picked it up, looked at the caller ID. Then he said, "*Pronto.*"

THERE WERE NO OTHER VEHICLES IN THE PARKing lot by the bridge. Costa got out and walked to the edge of the bluff overlooking the Pacific. Fifty years before, somewhere below, a fictional Scottie had seen Madeleine Elster fall into the ocean and had dived in to save her, sealing his and her fate. The movie he'd watched with Maggie wouldn't leave his head. Or what had happened after.

In the distance to the right there were lights in the Marina and Fort Mason, where the Lukatmi corporation was now a dismembered corpse. Further along, a vivid electric slur of illumination marked the tourist bars and restaurants of Fisherman's Wharf. A few boats, some large, bobbed on the water. It was the noise that surprised him, rising into the starry sky, the gruff, smoke-stained roar of a constant throng of vehicles on the highway behind. Their fumes choked the sea breeze rising over the headland; their presence almost blotted out the beauty of the ocean.

The Mediterranean couldn't compete with this scale. Maggie had been right that night she bit into the poisoned apple. In San Francisco the world felt bigger, so large one might travel it forever without setting foot on the same piece of earth twice. This idea appealed to her. Costa found it disconcerting. There was, and always would be, a conflict between two people like them, between his insistence on staring at a small, familiar place, seeking to know it—and by implication himself—better. And Maggie always fleeing, always looking to lose herself entirely in something vast and shapeless, to pull on any passing identity she could find before the next film, the next ghost, entered her life.

He climbed the steps of the viewing platform. Alcatraz stood like a beached fortress across the dappled water of the Bay. It was now two minutes past eleven. Tom Black was late. Perhaps he'd never show. Maggie was right about that, too. He should have called the SFPD.

All the same, he wished this were his case, not theirs, and, most of all, not the Carabinieri's. So many opportunities had been lost through Gianluca Quattrocchi's insistence that the core of the investigation lay within the cryptic poetry of Dante. The *maresciallo* had taken a wrong turning from the start. How did *The Divine Comedy* begin?

"'For the straightforward pathway had been lost,'" Costa said quietly to himself.

Criminal cases, like lives, could so easily follow a false route, a deceptive fork in the road that seemed so attractive when it first emerged. Everything was an illusion.

His phone rang.

"Costa."

"You're alone."

The voice was young, concerned, and American, mangled by the bellowing rumble of traffic behind it. He couldn't be far away.

"Is that a question?"

"Not really."

Tom Black sounded uncertain of himself, aware of that fact, desperate to hide it.

"Listen. There's an unlocked bike at the back of the parking lot. Take it, then go to the pedestrian gate on the bridge. Buzz the security people. They'll let anyone through with a bike. Ride across until I meet you. Don't try to walk. They don't allow pedestrians at night. You won't even get past the gate."

"We could just meet here."

"I need to see you first. I need to make sure you're alone."

The line went dead.

Costa walked around the parking lot until he found the bike. He had the same unsettling feeling he'd had in Martin Vogel's apartment: that he wasn't alone. Maybe it was Tom Black watching him. But then...

He tried to shoo these thoughts from his head. The bike was an old road racer model, with lots of gears and even more rust. He wheeled it around the footpath and reached the gate. There was a button there, and a security camera. He hit the buzzer, a voice squawked something impenetrable from a hidden speaker, and then the barrier swung open on electric hinges.

Wondering how long it had been since he climbed on a bike, Costa got on the saddle and rode slowly onto the bridge, alongside the northbound traffic in the adjoining lane a few yards to his left. The noise grew so loud he could scarcely think straight. In the middle of the great span he paused. It was an extraordinary view. The entire southern side of the city was visible, and the communities on the far side of the Bay. The bridge was well lit. He could see all the way along the pedestrian footway to another closed gate at the Marin end.

He waited a good minute for the phone to ring.

"I'm in an old Ford wagon doing twenty in the southbound lane going back to the city. If I like what I see, I'll slow up to a stop when I'm in the middle. Jump the barrier, cross the road, and get in the back. You with me?"

In the distance on the far side, he could just make

out a vehicle being driven with the kind of caution one expected of the elderly. It was hugging the inside lane and getting passed by everything on the bridge.

"Where are we going?"

"For a drive and a talk. Yes or no?"

When the car got closer, Costa abandoned the bike, stepped over the low iron barrier, waited for a gap in the traffic, and crossed to the other side.

It was an old, battered station wagon and it slowed even further as the driver saw him. The thing was scarcely at walking pace by the time it got close. Costa began to run to match its speed. He found the handle, threw open the back door, and leapt in.

10

THE VEHICLE STANK OF TOBACCO AND AGE. IT wasn't the kind of transport he would previously have associated with Tom Black.

Physically, he was a big, powerful man. Costa looked at the man's shaken, lost face in the mirror as they pulled away. He seemed different now Josh Jonah was gone. Uncertain of himself. Desperate. Black had to struggle with his shaking hands to take out the card to get them through the toll gates on the southern end of the bridge.

"What do you want?" Costa asked, then listened and found himself in fantasy land.

Tom Black had a list, one so ludicrous it was impossible to know how to begin the task of bringing him down to reality. He wanted immunity from prosecution. He wanted access to his frozen funds. A lawyer before being asked any questions by the police. A phone call to his mother in Colorado. Finally...

The figure in the front seat turned round and looked at Costa hopefully, with an ingenuous schoolkid's hope in his eyes.

"I have a ticket for the premiere tomorrow. I want to be there."

Costa shook his head and laughed, aware of the scared young eyes watching him.

"You find this funny?" Black demanded shrilly.

"How else am I supposed to feel? You're wanted for murder and more financial crimes than I can put a name to. Now you want me to make sure you have tickets for the cinema?"

"Lukatmi..."

"Lukatmi didn't pay for that movie, Tom! That's the point. Why don't you just drop me off and I'll find a cab home. This is a waste of time."

They followed 101 off the bridge, cutting into the city past the Palace of Fine Arts, where the lights were still on in the exhibition tents, then on to Lombard, where the highway turned into a broad city street. Then Black turned down towards the waterfront, past the bars of Fisherman's Wharf. It was just lazy driving, the kind you did when you wanted to think or convince yourself you could stay out of harm's way forever.

"That ticket's mine, man. I want to be there. It was part of the deal. I'm owed."

They passed a parked police car on North Point Street. Costa watched the way its lights came on afterwards. Discreetly he turned his head to glance through the rear window and saw it move into the road.

"Who does this vehicle belong to, Tom?"

"I'm not bringing anyone else into this. Don't even think of going there."

"Is it stolen?"

Black turned round and looked at him like he was crazy. Then, to Costa's dismay, he lifted his right hand and showed him something. It was a handgun. A black semiautomatic.

"*This* is stolen. That's all you need to know."

"You don't look like a gun person to me. You don't look like someone who could fix all this on your own, either. Who gave it to you? Is he following us?"

"Shut . . . up!"

Costa sat back. They were on the Embarcadero now. He liked this road. It led to the Ferry Building, a piece of architecture that had caught his eye the moment he first saw it. The tall clock tower reminded him of Europe.

"So what do you say?" Black persisted.

"Pull over, give me the gun, promise to tell the nice people in the San Francisco Police Department everything you know, and it's possible I can keep you alive. Maybe even out of jail. I need to know who wants to kill you."

The semiautomatic came up again.

Costa put up his hands and said, "Fine. We're done here."

They passed Lombard Street and another patrol car pulled out into the road. They were holding off, Costa thought. Waiting for orders.

"Pull the car over, Tom. I'm getting out."

"I want..." He looked ready to crack.

The Ferry Building was approaching. There was no traffic coming in the opposite direction. Costa knew what that had to mean. Soon they could see it. A line of police vehicles straddled the road, blue and red lights flashing.

"You told them, you bastard!" Black yelled, and the weapon was up again, jerking wildly in his free hand.

"I didn't tell them anything. Do you think they would have waited till now?"

"Then...?"

"What about the guy who gave you the gun? The one who set this up? Put that bike out for me? Did he follow us, too?"

"Got to know who to trust..." Black whimpered. "Got to *know*."

Up the street uniformed men stood by the patrol

cars. Costa snatched a look at the beautiful, illuminated clock tower and realised where he'd seen something like it before, where the architect must have got the idea. It was the Giralda in Seville, the Moorish tower attached to a Catholic cathedral that had consumed the mosque that went before. All generations pillaged what they inherited. Roberto Tonti had robbed from Dante. A murderer had somehow found inspiration in a film that was half a century old.

"Give me the gun and I will deal with this," Costa ordered.

They were edging closer to the roadblock. Costa could hear Gerald Kelly's voice booming through a bullhorn, all the commands Costa would expect of a situation like this.

Stop the car. Get out. Lie down.

"I'm dead," Tom Black mumbled at the wheel.

"If you step out of that door with a gun in your hand, you will be."

The vehicle rolled to a halt twenty yards from the police line. Costa couldn't begin to guess the number of weapons that were trained on them by the dark figures crouched next to the line of vehicles blocking the street beneath the tower of the Ferry Building.

"If you're in jail for a couple of years, what's it matter? You'll still be alive. Still got a future in front of you. Maybe there's a lawyer who can get you off. Money talks. You'll find some."

Black turned round and stared at him. "That's

what Josh thought. He just wanted to pay off that blackmailing bastard Vogel once and for all."

"See? That's a start. Keep talking and you'd be amazed how popular you can get."

"You don't understand the first thing about what's going on here, do you?"

"True. So tell me."

He looked out the window, lost, forlorn. "Once you sign up with these people, you never get free. It's a contract, right? A *contract*. Break it and you die."

"Is that what happened with Allan Prime?"

"I don't know what happened with Allan and neither did Josh. It was never supposed to end that way. It was just a deal. Don't you see?"

The weapon was near, but not enough to snatch.

"Give me the gun, Tom. I'll throw it out the window. Then we crawl out of here and go straight down on the ground, faces in the dirt, hands out, not moving a muscle until they tell us. That way we both stay alive."

"Just like the movies," Black mumbled sarcastically.

He was so close. One more minute with this man and he'd be there.

"What's wrong with the movies?" Costa asked.

The man at the wheel stared at him with eyes that were dark, bleak, and full of self-loathing.

"They screw you up. They..." Costa could scarcely make out the words. "They screw everyone. Scottie.

Me. I never thought this'd happen. Not when we went to Jones..."

He threw back his head, closed his eyes.

"Jones? Who...?" Costa was starting to ask.

The bullhorn burst into life again. This time it was loud and close enough to shake the vehicle.

"Get out of the car," Gerald Kelly's metallic voice bellowed.

Black leaned out of the open window, abruptly furious, waving the weapon around, screaming, "Shut up, *shut up, shut up!* Lemme think."

Costa sat back and watched him subside. They had time. Getting the weapon off this scared young man might take an hour. More maybe. But it was achievable.

"We know about James Gaines," Kelly shouted. "We need you to come in. You and your accomplice. Get out of the vehicle."

Something changed in Tom Black's demeanour. His face hardened. Costa's spirits sank.

Black thrust his head out into the night. "What the hell have you done to Jimmy? This has nothing to do with him. Blame Josh and me. Not Jimmy."

"Who's Jimmy Gaines?" Costa asked.

He didn't get a reply. Black was screaming into the street again.

"You bring Jimmy here! I wanna talk to him. This isn't his doing. I want him free."

Kelly didn't come back on the bullhorn straightaway. That was odd.

"Let's just get out of the car like they say," Costa began. "This will be so much easier in someone's office, where it's warm and they have coffee and lawyers and people who can help you."

"I can't bring you Gaines," Kelly said, and there was an edge to his voice even through the electronic medium of the bullhorn. "There was an accident. Let's not have any more."

Costa stiffened back into the old, uncomfortable seats of the station wagon and watched Black fumble at his phone, calling someone who didn't answer, and that made the young man more furious than ever.

"An accident…an accident…what the hell does that mean?"

"If we talk to them…"

It was no use.

"Bring me Jimmy Gaines!" Black screeched out the window.

There was a pause. Then Gerald Kelly's piercing, metallic voice said simply, "We can't. He's dead."

Costa closed his eyes and wondered why words always had to give way to deeds. Why he couldn't talk people out of things. It had cost Emily her life. It had almost robbed him of his sanity. He'd done everything he could to reason with Tom Black, and might have managed if Gerald Kelly—a good, intelligent police officer, Costa didn't doubt that—hadn't intervened with the wrong words at the wrong time.

He rolled over on the backseat and thrust himself

deep down into the floor space. He could smell what was coming in the stink of sweat and fear and panic that was rolling off the man in the front.

The driver's door opened and Black was out, screaming obscenities. Costa steeled himself for the sound. It didn't come. Not immediately. Kelly was shouting. So was Tom Black. Then...

A single shot. One loose round begets a host.

When it began, he forced his fists into his ears to keep out the volley of gunfire enveloping this quiet, beautiful patch of the city outside the Ferry Building.

It was the same, always. In the grounds of the Villa Borghese as an actor posing as a Carabiniere was brought down because he didn't understand how jumpy police officers get when they see what appears to be an armed individual intent on violence. In the grubby gardens surrounding the mausoleum of the emperor Augustus, where his wife died.

There was a short, high scream, then the shooting ended. It was replaced immediately by that angry, taut chorus of shouts that followed almost every act of violence he had witnessed. A part of him felt he could hear the life of Tom Black depart the world, a single human soul lost for eternity, for no good reason Costa could imagine. He had no such recollection of the moment of Emily's death. That instant was black and bleak and empty and would always remain so.

Crushed facedown in the rear seat of the vehicle,

hands now tight on his head, waiting, he was aware of them tearing at the doors, screaming at him, wondering themselves whether he was armed, too, and might take a life of their own.

Strange voices assaulted him, strong hands gripped his arms. Costa felt himself dragged from the backseat and flung facedown onto the ground. He thrust out his arms as they ordered. The gravel scraped his cheeks. A couple of them aimed kicks, one brutally painful, deep into his ribs. He grunted and didn't move, not an inch. After a while the noise and the violence subsided. He heard Kelly's voice say to another man, "Let's see what we've got."

They used their feet to turn him.

Bloodied hands still up over his head, Costa opened his eyes to see the SFPD captain's shape obscuring the grey stone tower of the Ferry Building.

"What in God's name are you doing here?" Kelly asked, shaking his head in amazement.

"I was trying to bring you a witness. I did my best. Sorry."

To his surprise Kelly held out his hand and helped him upright. He had a strong grip. It hurt when it pushed the gravel further back into Costa's torn palm. Cops stood over the body of Tom Black, looking at it, shaking their heads. Sirens were wailing somewhere along Market Street.

Kelly offered him a clean handkerchief. "There's blood on your face. You might want to get it off."

Costa wiped his cheek with the back of his hand.

He felt detached from the situation, as if it were happening to someone else.

"Did he tell you anything?" Kelly asked.

He tried to remember. "I'd have to think about that."

Kelly put an arm around his shoulder and walked him towards the terminal doors. A small crowd had gathered behind the barrier erected by Kelly's men. The traffic was beginning to back up along the Embarcadero.

"Please," Kelly said. "Think hard."

"How did you know he was in the car?"

"Your pathologist called us. Some guys she knows were playing PI and got themselves kidnapped by this Gaines character. Seems he and Black were good friends. So good, Gaines thought he'd get Black out there to cut some deal with you, and then pop off these friends of hers in the meantime." Kelly shrugged. "Didn't work out that way. Afterwards, they called her. And she, being a sensible, helpful lady, called me."

The SFPD captain scratched his grizzled head. "It never really occurred to me you might have got there first."

"We keep trying to do you favours. It doesn't buy us any credit, does it?"

"Not much."

Nic Costa closed his eyes and tried to imagine himself back in Rome. It was impossible.

"Did you happen to witness Tom Black taking a shot at us?" Kelly asked out of nowhere.

"I was in the back of the car with my head in my hands. I didn't see a thing."

"Sensible man." Kelly sighed. "I didn't see Tom Black use his weapon," the cop said. "In fact I'd say the first shot I heard took him down, and that didn't come from us."

PART 6

1

H E WAS WOKEN BY THE PHONE. IT WAS MAGGIE wanting to know what had happened. The incident outside the Ferry Building was all over the morning news. *Inferno* had hit the headlines again.

It was past nine and Costa still felt exhausted. Outside the window of his bedroom the light on Greenwich Street looked different, less bright, more diffuse. The only sound in the house was the noisy throb of the boom box of the Mexican decorators who'd spent most of the previous week painting the front of the building next door.

"You could have been killed," she said, and he flinched at the accusation in her voice.

"Tom Black asked to see me. Alone. He didn't wish me any harm. If he'd listened to me, he'd still be alive and we might have a clearer idea of what's been going on."

"And that makes it all OK?"

"Sometimes. He sounded as if he needed help."

"And now he's dead, too."

The memories of those last moments on the Embarcadero were starting to flood back. "I don't understand what happened. I'm sorry. I know you liked him."

There was a moment's silence on the line.

"Not really. Tom was a sad man. He hung around me for a while like a lot of men do, not that he seemed terribly convinced. I think he felt he was supposed to do that kind of thing. If Josh had told him to jump off the roof, he would have. Tom didn't have the courage to ask for what he wanted, which makes him stand out from most so-called associate producers I've met."

"Tom Black was a producer?" The job was news to him.

"Associate producer. Lukatmi put in money, didn't they? Collect enough tokens, you get free candy." She hesitated. "Did they have to shoot him?"

He thought about Gerald Kelly's odd question, then said, "I didn't see what happened. Black was a man with a gun who looked ready to use it. Just like that idiot in Rome. I tried to talk him out of it. I failed."

"This is getting to me, Nic. I can't wait to get the hell out of here. There are a couple of events over the weekend and then I'm gone."

"Do you know if you've been paid yet?"

"What the hell does that matter?" she asked, incredulous.

"Maybe it doesn't. Have you?"

She sighed. "Only what I got at the start. Sylvie, my agent, is foaming about it. This is partly my fault. I let

Simon deal with the money stuff when it all got complicated."

"Complicated?"

"Not enough money to pay the bills at Cinecittà. People asking for favours. Don't take your fee now. Take it later, in installments. That kind of stuff. Normally you get it before the movie starts shooting. Not partway through. I didn't want to know. Simon was in Rome. Sylvie was in Hollywood. Like she should care. She still gets her cut. Why's my money important?"

"It probably isn't."

"Did Tom say anything about what happened?"

"Nothing useful."

"You wouldn't tell me, would you? Even if he did."

This conversation always came up, in every relationship he'd had. With Emily it had been easy. She'd worked in law enforcement, too. She understood.

"No. I wouldn't."

"OK. I'm starting to get the picture."

"I wish I was. When will I see you?"

"Tonight, I hope. At the premiere. Will you be working?"

"If you can call it that. Babysitting a set of glass cases. We're irrelevant here. Come Saturday, when the exhibition goes back to Rome, we don't even get the rent paid."

She waited, then said, very slowly, "I thought we had an understanding. Barbados. Remember?"

There was always that gap between what was said

in the spur of passion and what was felt in the cold light of day. Costa didn't doubt his emotions there for a moment. He wanted to be with Maggie Flavier.

"Barbados," he said. "Let me talk to Leo."

"Do that. And another thing. An actress can't walk down the red carpet at a movie premiere on her own." A pause. "Do I really have to ask?"

"I'm working."

"Two minutes of your time. That's all it takes. Then you can go back to standing around your glass cases. Two minutes."

He didn't know what to say. He was trying to picture it in his head, all those images of glittering affairs on the TV, shots of the Oscars, celebrities laughing and joking... The sea of paparazzi who had been trying to capture them all along, given what they wanted, on a plate.

"If you'd prefer not to..." she began.

"There's nothing I'd rather do in the world."

"Really?"

"Really. I will smile for the cameras and wear a flower in my lapel. I will hold your hand, if that's not too forward. Be my director. Tell me what to do."

There was a low, throaty giggle on the line.

"I'd rather leave that till later, if you don't mind. The photographers will go to town. You realise that, don't you? We'll be a couple, official. Privacy will be confined to the bathroom from now on, and I can't always guarantee that."

"I can live with it if you can."

"You say that now..."

"Yes. I do."

"If that's true, you'll be the best damn man I've ever known," she said huskily. "Got to go..."

He tried to imagine her in the Brocklebank building, wondering what she would wear for the premiere. Who she might be. Herself? Or someone stolen from a wall in the Legion of Honor?

Costa walked downstairs. The small house was empty. On the table was a handwritten note, scribbled in a familiar, precise hand.

I say this as much as a friend as your commanding officer. To absent yourself on a whim last night, without informing any of us of your intentions, was stupid, selfish, and unacceptable. I do not wish to see you today. Try to amuse yourself in a way which causes no one any concern or harm.

Falcone

He read the message twice, then screwed it up into a tight ball and threw the thing into the kitchen bin. Once again there was no coffee. Costa sat down with a glass of orange juice and called Sylvie Brewster, Maggie's agent. He had to talk his way through three assistants to reach her, and then she said, "You're asking me to discuss the financial affairs of a client? And you're not even an American cop with a warrant or something?"

"I'm a friend. I'm concerned."

"Now I know who you are. You're that one. Nic."

"This is important. It may explain why she was attacked."

"Whoever did that thing to Maggie deserves to be eaten alive by rats. What can I tell you, love?"

"I don't know anything about the movie business. I don't understand how a film can go into production, go as far as having a premiere, and still the cast haven't all been paid. Is that normal?"

"No," Sylvie Brewster replied, and nothing more.

"Then how did it happen?"

He heard a long groan and then the sound of someone sucking on a cigarette. "OK. You will never pass this on to another soul, right?"

"Agreed."

"I haven't a clue. The first thing I heard about it was when the deal was already done. I went nuts, but it was too late. They'd had some financial crisis. Tonti and that evil bastard Bonetti had set it up. They said that if I tried anything, I might be running the risk of bringing the whole damn thing crashing down. Not just no money but no *movie*."

"Could they make a threat like that?"

"They thought so. Dino Bonetti broke every rule in the book. Those bastards took Maggie to one side in Rome. Leaned on her. Begged her. Next thing I know, she's signed some papers and it's all settled."

"Have you seen those papers?"

"Nope. And if I didn't love Maggie, she'd be an

ex-client now. To hell with my cut. This is not the way the business is supposed to work."

"Simon Harvey organised the deal, didn't he?"

"So I hear. Can't get into directing, so maybe he fancies himself a producer now. He'd better not come near my clients again—I'll claw his eyes out. Unless he's got funding, in which case we'll do lunch." She laughed.

"Thanks for the insight."

"I'll tell you something else, too, Nic sweetie. I was talking to Allan Prime's agent the other day. This is a small world. I wanted to commiserate."

"Prime made the same deal," Costa guessed. "Outside the usual rules. No money on the table. No money anywhere."

Sylvie Brewster sounded impressed. "Maggie said you were a smart one. Be kind to her while it lasts, won't you, babe?"

Then she was gone. Costa went to the waste bin and retrieved Falcone's note. He was still reading it, half furious, half ashamed, when Teresa came back with two bags full of groceries.

She saw what he was doing and said, "Well, look on the bright side. At least you escaped getting it face-to-face. Leo was pretty mad at you. Even for him."

"Sorry. I'll have to find him and apologise."

"No rush. Leo Falcone's life consists of a series of small explosions. It always will. Particularly when he keeps getting knocked back. A woman who doesn't fall for his well-oiled charms. We had to come all the way to California to find one."

She didn't say it with much relish.

"Is he upset?" Costa asked.

"About Catherine? He's beside himself. I think the poor thing's actually smitten. I'd like to say it serves him right for treating Raffaella Arcangelo so badly." She screwed up her face. "But I don't feel that way. Must be getting old. It's difficult to work up the energy to be vindictive these days. He'll get over it when he's back home in Rome." She took the note from his hands and put it back in the bin.

"Look. Leo wrote that thing out of hurt more than anything else. It's forgotten now. You should do the same. Don't expect me to make you coffee, either. I'm not stopping. I have identical twins to scold. And for that I do have the strength. Jesus..."

Costa didn't say a word.

She sat down opposite him and grumbled, "Oh for God's sake, what do you want?"

"I want to talk this through."

Teresa put a finger to her cheek, gave him a questioning look. "Let me make a suggestion. You have been granted the day off. There is, it seems to me, someone in your life again. You're in a beautiful city most people would pay good money to visit. Why not go out and enjoy yourself? See the sights. Take Maggie to lunch. Do something normal for a change."

"I do normal things all the time," he objected.

"That is the stupidest thing I've ever heard."

She left without another word. Costa thought about what she'd said. He'd never invited Maggie for a coffee, let alone a meal. In Rome it would have been different. No, he corrected himself, in Rome it *will* be different.

He was reaching for the phone when it rang.

"We need to meet," Gerald Kelly said. "Right away."

2

TERESA LUPO HAD SUMMONED THEM TO THEIR usual table at the café on Chestnut. She couldn't work out whether to feel mad or relieved. Hank and Frank sat there sipping coffee and picking at a couple of doughnuts, staring at the ceiling as if pretending that nothing had happened. Their hands were covered in scratches. Hank's right cheek was red and inflamed from what he said was a reaction to poison oak. Frank's eyes were watery and bloodshot. They looked a mess, and as guilty as a couple of schoolboys caught pilfering from the neighbourhood store.

"What the hell were you thinking?" she wanted to know.

"That maybe we could help," Frank responded.

"It was his idea," Hank jumped in.

"Don't try that with me," she warned. "You two work as a pair. I'm not stupid."

"We did help, didn't we?" Hank seemed quite offended. "In a messy kind of way."

The death of two men had clearly upset them, in spite of Jimmy Gaines's murderous intentions. It was impossible to escape the consequences. The shooting of Tom Black had headlined the morning TV news, and the recovery of Gaines's body from a ravine in the Muir Woods hadn't been far behind. Hank and Frank had spent half the night being interrogated and then, on the advice of the SFPD, found themselves somewhere private to stay in order to avoid the attentions of the news crews. "Somewhere private" had turned out to be a cheap motel in Cow Hollow, just round the corner from where they lived. Frank called it "hiding in plain sight." Hank described the decision as pure laziness.

"If they hadn't shot that poor boy…" Hank grumbled. "He could have told them something."

She was not going to take this nonsense. "Someone who comes racing towards armed police holding a gun is asking for trouble. Don't blame anyone else for that. Least of all yourselves."

"So is that it?" Frank asked. "Is it over? It was Josh Jonah, Tom Black, and Jimmy Gaines doing all this stuff? Along with that photographer guy who got killed?"

Teresa shrugged. "Criminal investigations are

based on assumptions," she said, toying with some strange Middle Eastern pastry the café owner had thrust upon her. "They have to be. It's how we make progress. We assume that when a series of killings occur inside the same circle like this, it's all down to the same individual or group of people."

"That makes sense," Hank agreed.

"But what if the assumptions are wrong?" Teresa asked. "What if one person killed Allan Prime and another one tried to poison Maggie Flavier? They don't look like the same person's handiwork to me. Not for a moment."

Frank looked uneasy. "I don't like complicated ideas. There's a gratifying shortage of people willing to go around knocking off their fellow human beings. What are the odds of them all turning up in one place like this, all at the same time?"

Hank nodded. "I'm inclined to agree. If this were fiction..."

"It isn't fiction!" she hissed. "If you'd got killed last night, you'd have known that."

The brothers stared at her, eyebrows raised in the same surprised, amused expression.

"You know what I mean. Don't ask me what people think right now. I have no idea."

"What did Tom Black tell your young friend?" Frank asked.

"Not a lot. Yes, there was a conspiracy to hype the movie. No, they didn't think anyone would get hurt. That's about it."

Hank finished his doughnut, wiped his fingers daintily on a napkin, and said, "I still don't know why Jimmy wanted to get us out of the way. Why he couldn't just let us go once Tom was in police custody. He must have known it would come back to him in the end."

"He'd have been gone the moment he was out of Muir Woods," Frank muttered. "Murderous bastard…"

"Yeah, but why?" Hank shook his head. "Jimmy didn't like the idea of shooting us. And he didn't need to kill us, did he?"

Frank scratched his nose. "No," he agreed. "He didn't."

Teresa watched them struggle with this idea, then suggested, "There has to be some reason. Something you knew…"

"Like what?" Frank demanded. "We were wise to the fact Jimmy knocked around with Tom Black. We knew Jimmy was gay, or at least hung around in those circles. That's no big deal. Nothing worth killing for."

"Frank's right," Hank added. "No answers there."

"Then it must have been something you said."

The two men grumbled to each other, then folded their arms in unison and gazed at her.

"Think about it," she urged. "When you went to see Gaines at Lukatmi. He surely wasn't thinking of popping you two in the Muir Woods the moment you turned up."

"He looked pleased to see us," Hank agreed. "Turned a touch cooler when we told him why we came. Not that *that* helps us any. He was keeping a big secret. Only understandable."

"Think back," she told them. "Was there some point in the conversation when his mood changed?"

The brothers looked blank.

"What about later?" Teresa persisted. "On the way to the woods? When you got there? What did you talk about?"

"*Vertigo* and how it wasn't really shot where everyone thinks it was," Frank answered. "Oh, and Thoreau. Tom Black loved *Walden*. Those secrets don't merit killing two old colleagues."

"He'd already made up his mind by the time we got there," Hank said. "It was in his eyes."

Frank nodded. "You're right. He was odd with us even before we crossed the bridge. I can't believe we were so stupid to just walk into that forest with him."

She didn't like seeing them like this. "Never look back, boys. Stupidity is God's gift to the world, ours to do with as we please. You're dead tired. Are you going to go back to that motel of yours? Come round to our place if you like…"

They didn't budge. Something she said had set Hank thinking.

"This is insane," he said finally.

"What is?" she asked.

"The moment. When Jimmy Gaines got a look in his eye. I think I got it."

"You have?" Frank asked.

"Maybe. Remember at Lukatmi? When he wanted to take us off for coffee?"

"So?" Frank said, shaking his head.

"You made some crack about there being no insurance against stupidity. Jimmy looked at you funny the moment you used that word. He asked what you meant." Hank leaned forward. "Remember what you said?"

Frank grimaced. "I told him he knew exactly what I meant. It was just a saying."

"He didn't get the joke, brother. Not at all."

The three of them looked at each other.

"Insurance?" Teresa asked, bewildered. "Is that the best you've got? I've spent the last two weeks screaming at people about how the human race doesn't go around murdering itself in defence of poetry. They, in return, have been yelling at me for having the temerity to suggest it might have something to do with a 1950s movie. Now you're throwing *insurance* my way?"

Hank called out for more coffee and added, "Barkev? Is it OK if we use your machine out back?"

The café owner walked to the rear of the room and opened a door to a tiny and very tidy office where a smart new computer sat on a clear and well-polished desk.

"I don't imagine either of you has ever read much Robert Louis Stevenson except for *Treasure Island* and *Kidnapped*," Hank stated.

Teresa exchanged glances with Frank. "I think I can speak for both of us when I say no," she responded.

Hank got up and stretched his scratched and swollen fingers, as if readying them for action.

"There was a book called *The Wrong Box*. He wrote it with a friend. Read it years ago. Funny story, comedic funny, that is. Cruel and heartless, too." He peered through at the office. "Guilty people get touchy, I guess," Hank Boynton said. "They see spooks around every corner. Get twitchy at the slightest, most innocent of things. Maybe..." He looked at them, still working this out for himself. "Just maybe, it's all in a name."

3

GERALD KELLY OWNED AN ORDINARY BLACK sedan and drove it sedately through the city by a route so circuitous Costa couldn't begin to identify any of the neighbourhoods they passed. This was a conversation the SFPD captain had wanted with someone for a long time. Listening to him spend the best part of an hour outlining what he knew, it was obvious why. Without Gianluca Quattrocchi's conspiracy theory, homicide had precious little left to

work on. There was a genuine crime inside Lukatmi—
a missing fortune, and offshore agreements that were
impenetrable to the U.S. authorities, and probably
would remain so now the two founders of the company were dead. But those entailed financial offences
and fell to a different team of investigators, probably
federal ones. Kelly was a homicide man through and
through, and in that field he was struggling for daylight.

They travelled slowly down a long straight street.
At the end the Pacific Ocean sat in a pale blue line on
the horizon.

"What do you think Black was trying to tell you
last night?" Kelly asked.

"That there was a conspiracy within *Inferno* designed to generate as much publicity as possible. As
far as he was concerned, that's all it was. He said Allan
Prime wasn't supposed to die."

Kelly reached the intersection, pulled to the curb,
and stopped. "Don't you love the sea?" he asked. "It's
so beautiful. I could sit here for hours. Used to when
I was a street cop. You'd be amazed what you get to
learn that way." He looked at Costa. "Or maybe you
wouldn't. Here's something that came in from the
overnight people. James Conway Gaines. Former fireman who wound up working security at Lukatmi,
who seems to have become some kind of lover-cum-
father-figure for Tom Black. He had three convic-
tions for violence, bar brawls, the usual. Some rough
gay places mainly. Also . . ."

Kelly's mobile phone rang. He took it out of his jacket, answered the call, told someone he was busy and would be back within the hour.

"Jimmy Gaines was in Italy for two weeks right when all this fun began. In Rome. We found an entry in his passport and stubs for some fancy hotel that ought to be beyond the reach of someone on a security guard's wages. Flew back the day after Allan Prime died."

He wound down the window and breathed in the fresh sea air. "James Conway Gaines was crew, too, but for the publicity stunt, not the movie set. Just like our dead photographer friend Martin Vogel. Gaines fell over a cliff. Pretty clear it was an accident and those two friends of your pathologist got lucky. But why did Vogel get killed?"

Costa thought of the conversation in the back of Gaines's station wagon. There were so many questions he wished he'd asked.

"Vogel was blackmailing Josh Jonah. However much he got paid to start with, it wasn't enough. Jonah went round to see him. Maybe to kill him. Maybe to reason with him and it turned into a fight. Maybe..."

He couldn't shake the memories.

"I still think there was someone else there that night."

Kelly watched a gull float past on the other side of the road, almost stationary in the light marine breeze.

"I know you do. And I wish there was one scrap of evidence in that burnt-out mess to back you up. So let's assume it was the fight idea. I don't see those two geeks getting into the hit business. Dino Bonetti, on the other hand…"

"Everything we have on Bonetti we gave to you. Our people in Rome had plenty of information. The mob connections. The history of fraud."

"Yeah. We had stuff of our own, too. Does it help? I don't know. The guy's a movie producer. Most of that business is clean. Some parts are as dirty as hell. Bonetti's been dining with crooks here and back in Italy for two decades or more. There was a time when the Feds were thinking of refusing him entrance into the U.S. on grounds of his connections. Not that it happened. Maybe a movie wouldn't have got made or something."

"What about Tonti?" Costa asked.

"We all know he's got mob links. His wife's left him, so maybe brother-in-law Scarface isn't too happy. But I don't buy it. This is California, not Calabria. It's not worth going to jail for wasting an in-law who's a jerk. Tonti's Italian by birth, living here, and he's got friends with records. Doesn't add up to much." He waved his arm along the seafront. "There's a dozen restaurant guys not a mile from here I could say the same thing about. We have no proof, only guesses. I'm sick of those."

He started the car and took a right along the

seafront road. Ahead was an expanse of green hillside. It looked familiar.

"Also," Kelly added, "there's the health thing. Roberto Tonti has advanced lung cancer. He wasn't hopping in and out of Martin Vogel's apartment when the shooting started. The guy's got maybe three or four months, max. Little movie industry secret, one they'd like to keep quiet while they're raising dough to make a sequel. Yeah, I know. Sometimes a dying man feels he's been given the right to kill. We'd need a little more evidence than that, though. And a motive." He shook his head. "Killing Allan Prime got these guys what they wanted. Why did they need more than that? How rich do you have to be? If it had ended with Prime, maybe Lukatmi wouldn't have collapsed, not with all that nice publicity to keep it afloat."

He stomped on the horn as a skateboarder crossed the empty road directly in front of them.

"Kids." He peered at the ocean as if wishing he were on it. "Am I missing something?"

"Carlotta Valdes," Costa stated.

They began to climb uphill. Costa had a good idea where they were headed. They drove past golfers playing through wisps of fog drifting in from the sea and drew up in front of the elegant white building at the summit. The Legion of Honor looked just as he remembered it. Images of the paintings it held, Maggie's ghosts, flitted through his head.

Kelly turned and pointed a finger in his direction.

"I was not forgetting Carlotta Valdes. By the way, please tell your boss Falcone that I am mad as hell at him for mentioning that damned movie in the first place. So Tonti worked with Hitchcock fifty years ago. What's the connection?"

Costa took a deep breath. "Think about it. They're the same story. *Inferno* and *Vertigo*. A lost man looking for something he wants. An ethereal woman he believes can provide some answers." He thought of what Simon Harvey had told Maggie. "For both of them, it ends in death. Beatrice waits for Dante in Paradise. Scottie sees the woman he's created in the image of Madeleine Elster die in front of his eyes, and stands alone in the bell tower, staring down at her body. He's lost everything. Including the vertigo that's been cursing him, that got him into the case in the first place."

Kelly seemed unmoved. "You're starting to sound like Bryan Whitcombe."

"Not really. If someone's obsessed with one, it's understandable he might be obsessed with the other. There's a connection. It's obvious when you think about it. What it means..." His voice trailed off. He'd spent hours trying to make sense of the link. Something was missing. "I can't begin to guess."

Another memory returned. "Tom Black said something. About how the movies screw you up. Screwed up Scottie. Someone called Jones..." He shook his head, trying to recall Black's jumble of words.

"Scottie's in *Vertigo,*" Kelly suggested. "Is there a guy called Jones in the movie, too?"

"There was an actor. He played the creepy coroner. He's long dead."

Kelly gave him the kind of look Costa had come to expect from Falcone.

"Are we shooting in the dark or what? I'll check if the name Jones means anything inside the movie crew. You sure you heard it right?"

"Not really."

"Let's deal with something practical, shall we? Where's Carlotta? Back in Rome and paid off? Dead?"

"You tell me."

"*Cherchez la femme.* We don't have one. Not anywhere." He caught Costa's eye. "Except for Ms. Flavier. We're supposed to think someone's tried to kill her twice, except neither time was quite what it appeared on the surface. Personal feelings apart, do you think it might possibly be her? I checked Quattrocchi's files. Carlotta Valdes turned up at Allan Prime's home first thing in the morning. Maggie Flavier was at home in her apartment until two that afternoon. Alone. No witnesses. That name could have been a joke."

"Whoever it was made a real death mask," Costa pointed out. "Does that sound a likely skill for an actress?"

"Maybe. Have you asked?"

"No. No more than I asked whether she poisoned herself either."

The captain didn't flinch. "If you wanted to put on some kind of show, isn't that the way you'd do it? Carrying a hypodermic along with you and a tame cop to help out?" He leaned over the seat and said, in a low, half-amused voice, "You don't mind me saying this, do you?"

"No," Costa answered, refusing to rise to the bait.

"You don't think it hasn't run through the minds of your colleagues, do you? They're not dumb."

"The Carabinieri were wrong when they told you Maggie had no alibi for that morning. She had flowers delivered around ten. Ordered them herself. Signed for them herself. We have a copy of the receipt back in the Questura and a statement from the deliveryman. Little details like that probably never occurred to Quattrocchi. I took the deliveryman's statement myself before we even left Rome. Maggie could not have been the woman who signed herself in as Carlotta Valdes in that apartment in the Via Giulia. It's simply impossible."

The man in the driver's seat creased with laughter. "Jesus...*Jesus*...And I picked Gianluca Quattrocchi..."

He started the engine. They drew away, in the opposite direction down the hill. The Golden Gate Bridge emerged in the distance. The car was headed for the Marina. He'd seen this road before, in *Vertigo*.

"I've got to get back to the office. I'm enjoying

myself too much here," Kelly said. "You want to know the truth? There's only one thing we're sure of right now. There was a conspiracy to hype *Inferno*. Somehow, somewhere along the way, it turned murderous."

Costa shrugged and said, "Any way you look at it, one of three people has got to be at the heart of this case. Roberto Tonti, Dino Bonetti, or Simon Harvey. If they'd been cab drivers or office clerks, they'd have spent a couple of days in Bryant Street being sweated until they couldn't sleep. Instead..."

"Not going to happen, Nic. Tonti and Bonetti are Italian citizens. They insist Gianluca Quattrocchi is present if we so much as ask them the way to the bathroom."

"And Harvey?"

"I leaned a little hard on Harvey right at the beginning. One hour later I'm getting calls from God down asking me why I'm wasting my time. There's not a scrap of hard evidence linking them to the case and you know it." Despite his words, Kelly still looked interested. "You think you can do better?"

"I can try."

"How?"

"By getting in their faces. The way I'd do if they were plain ordinary human beings like everyone else. When they don't want it. Before they can call up a lawyer."

They had reached a bluff overlooking the bridge. Kelly pulled in.

"Now, there's something you don't see often," he muttered, pointing at the ocean.

A long white, smoky finger of mist was working its way across the Bay ahead.

"I'll take you out there someday. We call that place 'the slot.' It runs from the bridge to Alcatraz. Windy as hell sometimes, and you don't have a clue what's going on until you're in the middle of it." He shook his head. "Fog? Now? I'd expect it from the west. And later. But hell. Welcome to summer in San Francisco."

He took off his jacket, removed the tan holster, and held it out, gun first, to Costa.

"Expecting things to turn out like they should is something stupid people do. If you plan to go visiting, and I hope you do, I would like you to have this."

Costa didn't reach for the weapon.

"Men who work with me do so armed," Kelly insisted. "I've lost three officers in my career and that's three too many."

"It's illegal for me to carry a weapon."

"I'll look the other way. I know this city and I have my rules when dealing with it. We both understand there are still people out there with blood on their hands. I'd hazard a guess they'll shed a little more to keep us from finding out what exactly has gone on here. This is not a negotiation, Nic. You take the gun or I drive you home and you stay there." The handgun didn't move. "Well?"

Costa grasped the cold butt of the weapon, felt its familiar weight.

Kelly turned on the radio and kept the volume low. Strains of Santana drifted into the car.

"Oh," he added, as if it were an afterthought. "One more thing. That crossbow that killed Allan Prime. Unusual object." He looked at Costa. "A Barnett Revolution. It's a hunting crossbow, made for killing deer. Very powerful. Not generally available in Italy. It was bought used through eBay. Guy paid cash and met the seller in a parking lot in South San Francisco one month before Prime died. He wore a hat and sunglasses. That's as good a description as we could get. My guess is it got shipped to Rome along with some of the equipment they took out for that event there, not that I can prove it."

"A month?"

"None of this happened on the spur of the moment, did it? Now here's one more interesting thing: we recovered three shells from Tom Black's body. Two of them were ours. One wasn't."

Kelly squinted at the bright horizon. "The shooter was in a parking lot across the street. I guess he must have been following you from when you came off the bridge. When he saw the roadblock, he pulled off, set up position, then popped one into Black as he walked towards us, and another through the windshield of a squad car just to make sure we returned fire. Clever guy. I'd put money he was the ghost in

Vogel's apartment, that he set up that meeting, shot them, and got panicked when you arrived."

He looked at Costa. "That makes two occasions when he could have had you in his sights. Consider yourself damned lucky. And don't lose that gun."

"Anything else I should know?" Costa asked.

"Here's the last remaining fact I have. We have the bullets and we have spent shells from the Embarcadero. They're from a .243 Winchester. Whoever he is, he had a long-range hunting rifle." Gerald Kelly winced. "The kind you use for shooting deer. Which is not my idea of sport, though it's a little bit more humane than a crossbow, I guess."

4

HANK HAD A PAIR OF HALF-MOON GLASSES FOR sitting at the computer. Frank, similarly afflicted, preferred a pair of modern square plastic frames. Both men squinted at Barkev's Mac and made baffling complimentary remarks on its newness and speed. These things seemed important in San Francisco. The average pair of sixty-year-old Roman twins newly out of the fire department would probably have struggled to do much more than send an e-mail. The Boynton brothers sailed through a sea of information sources in front of them with a speed and ease that reminded her of Silvio Di Capua back in Rome, a thought that gave her a pang of homesickness.

Finally Hank found the page he wanted, and once they'd read it, Teresa said, "One more coincidence. It has to be. We're talking nearly four hundred years ago."

"Let's see." His fat fingers clattered across Barkev's pristine keyboard. "Yep. It's a coincidence. Lorenzo di Tonti. Born in Naples. Got into trouble there. Moved to Paris. Died penniless."

"Offspring?" Frank asked.

"Two," his brother replied, placing a large finger directly on the screen.

Teresa scanned the article next to a black-and-white portrait of a man with long, flowing black hair and elegant nobleman's clothes.

"So Roberto Tonti can't be related," she declared when she skimmed to the end.

His fingers ran over the keyboard again.

"Seems not. Even the name changes. Lorenzo became *de* Tonti when he moved to Paris. Both sons wound up over here. One died penniless of yellow fever in Alabama. The second helped found Detroit and died in disgrace. Was calling himself de Tonty by then. They didn't have a lot of luck, these guys, did they? Mind you, all that from an argument in Naples. Interesting lives. Makes me feel quite small."

"So," she repeated, "Roberto Tonti the movie

director can in no way be a descendant of Lorenzo di Tonti the dubious seventeenth-century banker."

"Right," Hank said. "But does that matter? Use your imagination. Roberto certainly does. It's his job. Lorenzo invented the tontine that's named after him. Who doesn't Google themselves these days? How many other people have surnames describing an idea that's killed a good number of idiots over the years?"

Tontine.

She vaguely knew what the word meant. It reminded her of old stories of tortuous conspiracies and unbelievably clever detectives. All the kinds of things real-life law enforcement agencies never met in the mundane world of hard, cruel fact.

"I've got to be honest." Hank looked uncomfortable. "I looked up Tonti a few days ago. Type in 'Tonti' and pretty soon you get to 'tontine.' I apologise for not mentioning any of this earlier. It seemed irrelevant. I thought the same about tontines, too. Maybe I was wrong."

She went through another page he'd found, feeling a welcome mild rush of excitement and possibility.

Teresa dimly recalled a tontine as an agreement between a group of individuals to share some kind of bounty, usually a crooked one, leaving the illicit prize to the last surviving member of the circle. This proved fundamentally wrong in many respects. Lorenzo di Tonti, the man who shared Roberto's name—though not, it would seem, his blood—hadn't set out to make his fortune creating a secret profit-sharing scheme for criminals. He was an ambitious banker trying to establish a new form of investment vehicle of general benefit to those who had the wherewithal to take part in it.

Teresa read the details and tried to recall what little she knew about investing for the future. Money was never one of her strong points, which was probably why the true tontine appeared eminently sensible. Each member made a contribution to the fund. The total was then invested in legitimate enterprises. Any dividends from those holdings were shared equally among the members of the scheme, until the penultimate one died, at which point the entire sum, dividends and capital, fell to the ownership of the last in the group.

The only flaw she could see was the obvious one: there was a substantial incentive on the part of tontine members to murder one another in order to ensure they claimed the richest prize. According to the documents Hank found, this had happened, and not just in fiction either. Tontines were made illegal in most countries by the nineteenth century, and passed on as fodder for novelists.

"Fine . . ." she said quietly. "The connection being?"

Hank found another article, one from the *Financial Times* the previous year.

"I remembered this one because it made me think. Take a look."

It was a long and very serious piece about the nature of life insurance.

"You see the author's point?" Hank said. "If you leave out the temptation-to-murder part, what old Lorenzo actually invented was the very first pension scheme. The only difference is he didn't let newcomers in, so that big final payout remained. In practical terms it's not much different from what happens today." He nodded at his brother. "We get a fire department pension. The pot for that depends on the stock market or something magical, I guess. When one of our colleagues bites the dust, that's one less mouth to feed. We all profit from each other's deaths. We always have. Lorenzo just said all that out loud, and put it in a way that tempted a few people to bring on some of those deaths a little earlier than might otherwise have happened."

"So there was a tontine," Teresa suggested. "And the people who were trying to hype *Inferno* were all in it."

"That's a possibility. Plus Josh Jonah and Tom Black, and Jimmy Gaines. Jimmy wasn't the most sophisticated of creatures. I doubt anyone could have sold him on a tontine. But if they said it was some kind of fancy insurance, one that might give him and Tom Black a tidy return each . . . ?"

"What did Jimmy Gaines have to put into a movie?" Frank asked.

Hank shrugged. "A little muscle, maybe, like that

photographer guy. What you have is what you contribute. And what you take out is…"

There he was struggling. Frank looked sceptical.

"Imagine this is true," he said. "Why would they do it? They're making a movie. What these people need is money. Money pays people. You don't pay people, you don't get the job done."

"They didn't pay people," Teresa interjected. "That's the point. The money wasn't there. Nic told me Maggie is still owed most of her salary. Lots of other people, too."

"I still don't see it…" Frank sighed.

But she did. Or at least she thought she might.

"Imagine you're Allan Prime. They come to you. The movie's nearly finished. You've been working for six months, but the big reward is still down the line, when it comes out. They say there's no money left to pay you what's owed. But if you're willing to exchange your fee for something else…"

"Insurance?" Hank suggested.

Frank shook his big, tired head. "Prime would tell them to take a hike! It's the movie business. Getting paid's the first thing any of them would want."

"But if you won't get paid anyway?" she persisted. "If they say you take this deal or the whole thing collapses? And everything with it? The merchandise cut, the residuals from the TV and DVD rights, the cosy promotional tour around the world? If there's no movie, Allan Prime loses a lot more than his fee. He loses everything that might come after."

Frank still wasn't happy. "I still don't see how someone like Jimmy would get mixed up in something like that. What the hell would he know about the movie business?"

Barkev came in with some more coffee. Teresa gulped hers down quickly.

"They weren't dealing with the movie business," she said resolutely after Barkev left the room.

The two brothers watched her and didn't utter a word.

"The movie people were dealing with Lukatmi. Don't you see? We've been asking the wrong question all along. When Roberto Tonti needed real money, he went to the mob. They stumped up enough to keep the production alive, barely, but it still couldn't be finished. We're pretty sure of that. Dino Bonetti has been taking finance from criminals for years. You don't need to be a genius to understand they'll certainly be expecting their return. Lukatmi was different. They came in later, when Tonti saw the whole project collapsing. Everyone's turned him down. He's desperate. And Lukatmi turn up offering..."

What? It was clear there was precious little money behind the doors of their hangars at Fort Mason by that stage. Josh Jonah and Tom Black hadn't bailed out *Inferno*. They didn't have the cash.

Frank—practical, logical, rational Frank—got there first, naturally.

"I know what I'd do. I'd go quietly to all the people I owe money, not just the big guys like Allan Prime.

I'd say, skip your salary and we'll give you something else. Something that might be worth a whole lot more than some risky horror flick if you play along."

She wanted to pinch herself. It was so obvious.

"This wasn't about investing in a movie," Teresa said. "It was about cutting your losses. About keeping *Inferno* alive and getting a chunk of the next big dotcom float coming round the corner. One that could make you richer than you could ever dream of, even in Hollywood. Josh Jonah and Tom Black were paper billionaires. Allan Prime couldn't even contemplate money like that, and he was a huge movie star. So you put together a secret little scheme to hype *Inferno* to the heavens and make Lukatmi even more lucrative at the same time."

Frank was scribbling down some notes. "Whatever paperwork's involved is squirreled away in one of these funny-money places in the Caribbean," he said. "A limited number of members with the payout based on status. Obviously it can't be equal. Allan Prime's going to expect a whole lot more than poor little Jimmy Gaines, that's for sure. Martin Vogel thought his efforts merited a bigger cut and started blackmailing Josh Jonah. But it's still a fund. A secret one. It has to be. You can't invite in more members, or you go to jail. You get it?"

Not quite yet, she thought.

"It's a tontine by default as much as by design," Frank explained. "When the numbers start to fall because people are dying, where else can the money go except to the original members? Tonti could have sold the whole thing to these people without saying the word 'tontine' once. It was exactly what he said it was. What Jimmy got told. Insurance."

Hank put down his coffee cup. He had a sour expression on his face. "This world sickens me. All these people screwing one another. Jonah and Black thinking they were robbing the movie crowd so's they could keep their tin-pot company afloat. The movie people kidding themselves they'd all get rich on some dumb kids' dotcom dream. Yuck…"

He looked at the door and yelled, "Barkev! I need a beer!"

The dark face appeared. "Hank," the man said, "this is a café. If you want a beer, go find a bar."

"That I shall. Someone going to join me?"

Teresa stared at him in astonishment. "We are about to get some insight into this case, finally, and you want to go to a bar?"

"You can think of a better time? What's there left to talk about? Half these people are dead. Josh and Tom and Jimmy. That photographer. Allan Prime. Anyone else who's involved…why would they do anything now? What for? The money's gone. Lukatmi's worthless. Their grubby little deal won't get them a penny. That's as much justice as any of us can expect."

She caught his arm. "You're missing the point. This is offshore. It can't be part of Lukatmi anymore, otherwise they'd be able to find it. From what

The Dante Killings ❧ 401

Catherine Bianchi told me, even the federal people think they'll never trace where the company's assets really ended up." She needed to get this clear in her own head, too. "That part of things is not dead. It's very much alive, out there somewhere. Just reversed. Lukatmi's the turkey and *Inferno*'s the golden goose. One that's in the names of a diminishing group of people, who, between them, now own a chunk of the biggest movie in decades."

"Do the math," Frank suggested. "Say there's four of them still alive. One dies. Your share just went from…" He paused to do the sums in his head. "Twenty-five percent to thirty-three."

"Two left and you just doubled your money," Teresa added, pulling out her phone. "Winner takes all. It's worth killing for now more than it ever was."

5

THE CALL CAME THROUGH AS KELLY WAS DRIVing him through the foot of the Presidio. Costa got dropped off on Chestnut and met Teresa and the Boynton brothers in a tiny café he'd never even noticed before. Outside the grubby windows the light was changing. Fog was reaching the city, bringing with it a filmy haze that dimmed the bright blue sky.

Teresa and the two somewhat eccentric twins spoke of what they'd discovered. Costa listened.

When they were finished, Teresa said, "We thought you ought to know."

He took a deep breath, smiled, and said, "It's a good theory."

"That's it?" Teresa asked, incensed. "That's all you have to say?"

"You can't base a case on some information you've picked up on Google."

"Nothing else fits," insisted one of the brothers. "Does it?"

"Just because it fits doesn't make it true. Without some evidence, or a confession, which seems just as unlikely, we've nothing."

"A confession of murder," the other brother said. "Sure. No one's going to own up to that easily. But . . . am I really the only one who sees this?"

"Yes, Hank," Teresa said. "I believe you are."

"You don't need to get someone to own up to killing one of these people," Hank said. "All you need is to get them to own up to the deal. The insurance scheme. The tontine. If he—or she—does that and gives you the names of the members, you've got a short list. Someone on it has to be your man."

Teresa stared at him. "Why on earth would anyone confess to that?"

"Because they can't all be murdering bastards. This was an accidental tontine, right?" Hank looked at Costa. "Tom Black told you that himself, didn't he? They surely didn't start out to kill people. Why would they? Just to get a movie made? Someone somewhere's got to have a conscience. Even in the movie business. Either that or they've got to be scared. Looking around at the others wondering, 'Was it him? Am I next?' No sane human being's happy in that kind of situation."

"Know anyone who fits the bill?" Teresa asked Costa.

"I'm not sure," he replied. "Thanks for your time."

Then he threw some money on the table and left.

6

COSTA WALKED OUT ONTO CHESTNUT AND LOOKED west, towards the flat green that fronted Fort Mason. The temperature seemed to have fallen a few degrees in the brief time he'd been inside the café. Gerald Kelly was right about the weather.

In the early days after they'd arrived in San Francisco, he'd checked the whereabouts of everyone involved in *Inferno*. Everyone except Maggie, since that felt somehow prurient. Roberto Tonti lived just a few hundred yards away in his bleached white mansion opposite the Palace of Fine Arts. Dino Bonetti usually took a suite in the Four Seasons on Market.

And Simon Harvey had a rented apartment on Marina Boulevard, not far from the Lukatmi building.

Someone somewhere's got to have a conscience.

So how do you prick it?

He phoned Maggie. She was trying on some clothes for the premiere in a downtown store, surrounded, she complained, by plainclothes police. The two of them made small talk, then she asked, "Why did you really call, Nic? It wasn't to check what I was going to wear tonight, was it?"

"I need to know something. A straight answer, Maggie. It's important and it's not what it sounds."

"That has an ominous ring to it." He heard her move somewhere more private.

"Was your relationship with Simon Harvey ever more than professional? If so, is it over? And if it is, how does he feel about that?"

He could hear the sharp, disappointed intake of breath down the phone. He could imagine the pain this question caused.

"Oh, Nic. You're not going to do this to me all the time, are you? Ask about the past? There are a lot of questions and not many answers you're going to like."

"It's never going to happen again. And I wish I didn't have to ask now. But I do. It's important."

"To you?"

"In the sense that it concerns your safety...yes. Someone tried to harm you."

"Not Simon, never Simon. That's ludicrous…"

He hesitated. He really didn't want to know. "You're certain of that?"

"Yes. I am. We had an affair five years ago while we were filming that pirate nonsense. It lasted a few months. Then he joined the long line of ex-lovers who couldn't take my behaviour any longer. I hurt him, Nic. A lot. I know because he's told me more than once. He thought…Simon thought he could save me from myself. Some men do. It still pains him. From time to time he tries to pick up the pieces. Why do you think he was there in the sanatorium that day? Why do you think he gets so awkward when you're around?"

"I'm sorry I had to ask."

"I'm sorry, too. Don't ever do it again."

The phone went dead.

7

SIMON HARVEY'S APARTMENT WAS ON THE ground floor of a Spanish-style block close to the yacht moorings that adjoined the eastern face of Fort Mason. The fog was now rolling in from the Bay with a steady momentum. There were three uniformed SFPD cops outside the door. They didn't give him any trouble once they saw Costa's ID. Kelly must have put round the word.

Harvey didn't answer the bell straightaway. When he did, he didn't look like a man preparing for the movie event of his career.

"What the hell did I do to deserve this?" He kept the door half open, blocking Costa's way.

"I thought perhaps I'd need a publicist, now you're setting the paparazzi on me."

Harvey's hair was shorter, freshly cut. The vaguely hip, student-like appearance was gone. He was trying on a tuxedo over a pair of jeans and a white dress shirt.

"Does this look like a good time to you? I'm getting dressed."

"It's a good time for me..." Costa began.

Harvey swore and began to close the door. Costa slipped his foot in the gap and his arm up against the wood.

"What the hell is this?" Harvey yelled. "Some Roman punk can't just come here and start harassing me." He glared at the three uniforms by the front gate, beyond the small, immaculate lawn of the garden. "Hey. *Hey.* Do I get some protection here? *Well? Do I?*"

One of the men turned briefly and shrugged.

Costa leaned forward and said, "Just a minute of your time, sir..."

"You don't deserve a *second* of my time—"

"Simon," Costa interrupted, "I *know.*"

The pressure on the door relaxed a little. Harvey's bright, intelligent eyes narrowed. "What's that supposed to mean? You know what?"

"I know about the scam. The tontine that Roberto Tonti had you and Dino Bonetti run up. The one that got *Inferno* made even though you didn't have the money. Just a treasure chest offshore, one part Lukatmi, one part *Inferno*. All under-the-counter, half of it worthless, half—"

"—worth what? Worth killing for? That's crap." Harvey scowled at him. "You really are something else. You mess with one of my stars. You almost get her killed. And now you stand on my doorstep accusing me of murder. Get the hell out of here."

Costa launched himself forward, pushed Simon Harvey hard back through the entrance, kicked the door shut behind, and held him tight against the wall, elbow to his throat. This close he could smell some rank, harsh spirit on Harvey's breath. It seemed rather early in the day for vodka.

"I don't care about you," Costa murmured. "Not for one moment. I don't care who it was turned murderous. Or that he may still have your name on the list of people standing between him and the pot of gold waiting in Grand Cayman."

"Get out of my home—" Harvey began. Then he shut up.

Costa had never done this before but there were lots of things he'd never done until San Francisco. He had the service revolver hard against Simon Harvey's right temple. He was looking into the publicist's ter-rified face, searching for something.

"Do you know what it feels like? To get shot? I do. It hurts. Not the way you think. It's a big hurt. It aches and aches. Long after the blood's gone. Long after the scars. It's not like the movies. Life isn't. It's real and cold and hard. If you lose someone you love, the taste of it stays with you forever."

"Don't threaten me. I could make one phone call..."

Costa stood back, breathing hard. Then he hol-stered the weapon.

"Make the call. Didn't you hear me? I *know*. I know you didn't just cut yourself in on this deal. Somehow you got between Maggie and her agent and put some part of her fee into that grubby little scheme of yours. That's why she's wondering where the money is now. What's she going to think when she finds she got robbed by some..." He waited to let the words have some power. "...old boyfriend? One who still won't let go?"

"You're remarkably out of your depth."

"Maybe," Costa admitted. "Doesn't it bother you, though? The idea that this isn't over?"

"Of course it's over. The Carabinieri said so. Those creeps from Lukatmi did it. Jonah. Black."

"The Carabinieri are wrong. What if someone gets to Maggie first? Would you even care?"

"What the hell are you talking about? Where'd you get this crap?"

"Maggie told me. About you two. And the money."

Harvey stared at him, remembering something. "Big deal. She tell you anything else? About what it was like? What she did?"

"No…"

"You've got all that ahead of you, friend. Nothing I can do will warn you off it, either. Listen. I am not a thief."

"What else do you call it?"

"I call it looking after people who can't look after themselves. I call it keeping her alive, making sure the last movie she was ever going to get didn't fold beneath her. That's the truth. Maggie's career has been on the skids for years. *Inferno* was her only chance to keep her name up there. If it never even made it to the screen…" There was a distant look of resignation and regret on his face. "You weren't there. You can't begin to understand. Some of us put in years for that movie and there it was, ready to fall apart. No fairy godmothers on the horizon. Everything was in hock. Our homes, our reputations. *Everything*."

Costa waited.

"And if you tell anyone I said that, I'll call you a liar to your face," Harvey rasped. "In a police station. On the witness stand. Anywhere. This is America. We've got lawyers who could free the Devil if he got found eating babies on Main Street. Give it up. You can't win. Not with me. Not with Maggie, either. You're way out of your league. Cut your losses." He nodded at the door. "Now get out."

"Best I know my place," Costa said, not moving.

"If that's the way you want to see it."

He took out the weapon again and lifted it. The barrel was inches from Harvey's throat.

"You're not listening to me," Costa said. "Maggie knew nothing of all this. You made her a part of it. You put her in danger. Because of you, she nearly died." The shadow of the weapon fell towards the window. "Whoever murdered Allan Prime is still out there. He murdered Martin Vogel and Josh Jonah. He shot Tom Black dead before the police could get to him."

The blood drained from Harvey's face. "What the hell are you talking about? The cops shot Tom."

"No. He was killed by a single bullet from a distant gunman. They've recovered the shell. They know what kind of rifle he used. A hunting weapon. Like the crossbow that killed Allan Prime."

"This is not possible, not possible. The Maggie thing…it had to be an accident. I couldn't…" Harvey was shaking his head like a man on the brink.

"There are no accidents. None. Every time someone in this deal of yours dies, the rest of you get richer. I don't care what this madman does to you. But…if it's Maggie he finds this time…"

"Not going to happen, not going to happen." Harvey's eyes were closed, screwed tight shut. "It's inconceivable…"

"If it does—it doesn't matter where or when—I will find you. I will walk up to your dinner table in whatever fancy restaurant in New York or Cannes or L.A., anywhere..." He nudged the barrel of the gun back towards Harvey's temple. "...and then in front of your Hollywood friends I will shoot you through the head."

Costa lowered the weapon. He put it back in Gerald Kelly's leather holster. Then he turned towards the door.

A hand touched his arm.

"Don't go."

Simon Harvey was slumped against the wall. He looked drained, lost, defeated.

Then he turned, picked up a bottle of Grey Goose from the cocktail cabinet by the window, poured himself a large glass, and said, "Sit down."

8

I T WAS NEVER SUPPOSED TO TURN OUT THIS WAY," Harvey murmured, gripping the glass. "The whole thing was just something to get us through. Out of the mess."

He sat on the sofa opposite Costa, staring at the mirror on the side wall, as if trying to convince himself. "Maggie wasn't the only one with everything to lose. Roberto's dying. There was never going to be another movie. I wasn't sure he'd live long enough to complete this one."

"I didn't realise the movie business was so sentimental."

"Don't patronise me!" Harvey screeched. "I've worked with these people for years. They're more to me than a paycheck. Even Roberto. Sure, he can be an asshole. They all can. But he's an artist, too, one of the last. The people he worked with—Hitchcock, Rossellini, De Sica. We don't see men like them anymore. Those days, when it was all about film, nothing but film, they're over. When I looked at Roberto..."

His bleak eyes never left Costa's face. "You won't understand, Nic. I grew up with all those movies from the fifties. Roberto *lived* them. You could talk to him, about how Hitchcock would chase the light he wanted, how Rossellini could coax a performance from some two-bit actress who didn't have the talent to speak her own name. *Inferno* was always going to be his last movie, and when he dies, that piece of history dies with him." He gulped more vodka.

"When he dies, all we'll have left are kids who think you can direct a movie with a computer and a mouse. Maybe *Inferno*'s a piece of shit. But there's still some art in there somewhere. I see it, even if no one else does."

Outside, the fog shrouded the Bay. Costa couldn't even see the cops by the gate anymore.

"It wasn't supposed to happen," Harvey said flatly.

"But it did. Maybe it will again."

"No. It won't. I guarantee that. I'll make sure of it. This has gone far enough."

"You need to make a statement."

"Yeah, yeah, yeah," he grumbled, waving Costa down. "And in return...?"

"I can't negotiate on behalf of the SFPD. You need to talk to them direct."

"Fine. But only after the premiere. Not before. Roberto's owed his moment. Maggie, too. We all are."

"Whose idea was it?" Costa asked.

"I said after—"

"I know. But I want to hear it. Just for me."

"Just for you." Harvey shook his head, bitterly amused by some internal thought. "Do you have any idea how long I've wanted to tell someone this?"

"I'm starting to," Costa said honestly.

"I don't even really know when it started. I was drunk at the time. I figured *Inferno* was dead. We'd been everywhere. Dino had begged every last penny he could out of his mob friends, and they were starting to get ugly, thinking the whole thing was about to turn into a train wreck. Maybe it was him, maybe Roberto. Maybe both. I don't even know. I just woke up one morning and the money was there. We got the movie, and maybe down the line we got paid, too."

Harvey scowled at the glass and put it on the table in front of him, half finished. "How do you say no to something like that? We all knew Roberto was sick. He told us he was rolling in his fee as collateral, knowing full well he'd never live to collect it. Lukatmi was going to go sky high. Instant profit for all of us the moment he croaked, even if the movie bombed."

"Whose names were on the contract?"

Harvey stared at him as if it were an idiotic question. "What contract? What do you think this was? A corporation? Some listing on the New York Stock Exchange? It was just some grubby little deal to breathe life back into a dying movie. These things happen all the time—"

"Who...?"

"I didn't know all the names. I didn't want to. Allan put in the balance of his fee. That took a little persuading, but Dino offered to sort out a few personal issues he had somewhere. What's a producer for? I waived what I was owed. Same with Dino. Josh and Tom put in some special form of Lukatmi stock and a little cash just to keep the wheels turning. Those of us on the movie side thought that would turn out to be the pot of gold at the end of the rainbow. How dumb can you get, huh? We thought we were robbing the geeks when the truth is it was the other way round. Robbing murderous geeks, too..."

He cleared his throat then, looked at Costa. "And now you're telling me that's not the case? That Black and Josh didn't do it?"

"I don't think so. Do you know anyone who hunts?"

"In the movie business? Are you kidding?"

"What about the people you used?"

"I made damned sure I stayed clear of that side of things. Fraud's as far as I was prepared to go. Dino handled the rough stuff. He seemed comfortable with it. He had the contacts. Tom and Josh knew some guy from Lukatmi who came in as crew. All I did was get Martin Vogel on board. That creep would screw his mother for five bucks. The only other thing I handled was Maggie. I gave her a few drinks and talked her into signing her cut away into some fictitious offshore production company. She didn't have a clue what she was doing. Money's never been her thing. I had her name on the paper before her agent knew anything about it. Nothing anyone could do after that."

His phone rang. Harvey took it out of his pocket, looked at the number, then turned the thing off.

"She wasn't going to get robbed, either. I'd never let that happen to her. All of us figured we'd get what we were owed at the very least. Maybe more, if Lukatmi's stock went through the roof. Dino handled the money and contract side of things. He could do that better than anyone. I didn't understand a word of what he was doing. All any of us cared about was the fact this gave us a chance to make *Inferno* happen."

He looked at his watch and shrugged. "I've got to get dressed soon. Really."

"Who put it all together?" Costa pressed.

"We just did what we'd been doing all along. I'd

been hyping *Inferno* from the start. Would the academic community be pissed off by it? Was the thing cursed? The media loved all that crap. The story had legs. So we decided to build on it. This idea that someone was stalking the movie and leaving clues straight out of Dante. We forged a few e-mails." He stiffened. "Someone hired that guy to wear a Carabinieri uniform and create some kind of incident the day of the premiere in Rome. No one was supposed to get shot."

"Allan Prime..."

"I damned near told you all this then. But that would have killed the movie stone dead. All I knew was that Tom and Josh had cooked up something to get us some publicity. They never told me what. I don't know about the others. Afterwards..."

He fell silent.

"What?" Costa asked.

"I thought the rest of them didn't understand it, either. Allan was supposed to disappear for a while, get that death mask nonsense made, then put on that little show in front of the camera as a stunt and get rescued by the cops. They were going to portray it as some kind of warped attack. Allan was in on the plan. They told him all about it. That's what they said. They had no idea why he got killed. They thought maybe something went wrong..."

"He was murdered, deliberately, in cold blood, in front of millions of people. It almost kept Lukatmi alive."

"Josh said it was never meant to happen. That's all I can tell you."

Harvey tapped his watch. "When the premiere's over, come and see me and I will make a statement. I'll want a lawyer there. This has gone far enough already. I don't want anything else on my conscience. Besides…" He caught his own reflection in the mirror and the traces of a smile creased his face. "…it's a hell of a story, isn't it? Biggest I've ever spun. Could make a movie someday."

Something was still missing.

"There was a woman involved," Costa said. "She went to Prime's apartment the morning he died. She made the mask. She left with him."

Harvey waved away the idea with his hand. "I don't know about any woman. Except for Maggie, and she didn't know the first thing about what was going on. Can't help you there."

Costa kept his eyes on him and said, "The woman called herself Carlotta Valdes."

Simon Harvey blanched. He said, "What?"

"Carlotta Valdes? Do you know the name?"

"Of course I do! *Vertigo*. It was shot right here. Roberto worked on it. He's talked about it, often."

"What do you think it means? That the woman used Carlotta Valdes's name?" Costa asked.

"That some punk in this nightmare still has good taste in movies."

9

T HE SECURITY CORDON RAN FROM 101 ALL THE way down to the waterfront stretch of Marina Boulevard. Bright red barriers and yellow tape blocked off all the normal entry routes. Photographers and TV camera crew who hadn't managed to beg media accreditation wandered the perimeter like mangy starving lions. Uniformed SFPD officers stood at the two entry checkpoints, ruthlessly checking the credentials of the lines of men in evening suits and women wearing elegant, stunningly expensive dresses. Once they were approved, the guests were then forced to walk through a portable airport-style metal detector to check for weapons, an unusual addition to such an event, Costa thought, and one that clearly engaged the attention of the photographers. All stood shivering in the chilly mist.

The queue of expensively clad bodies was steadily working through the system. Costa walked round the entire enclosed area once, then stopped by the lake that fronted the main structure of the Palace. Even this close, he could only just make out the domed roof of the structure across the water. Soon that would be gone. *Inferno* would be launched, appropriately enough, in a miasma of San Francisco fog. He wondered if the grey cloud might even seep into the gigantic tent erected for the private screening, and if it did whether those at the rear of the seats would have much of a view. Perhaps that wasn't the point. This was an occasion to be seen at more than anything. The lines of sleek dark limousines drawing up by the checkpoints contained more than a few faces he had come to recognise from the TV since he'd arrived in San Francisco, politicians and media figures, actors and celebrities, a constant stream of beautiful women on the arms of men in impeccable evening dress.

He looked ruefully at his own crumpled dark blue suit, bought from the usual discount store in Vittorio Emanuele, near the bridge to the Castel Sant'Angelo. Costa tightened his tie into a half-passable knot, which was as good as it got. When no one was looking, he stepped into a nearby flower bed, stole a red rose from one of the bushes there, and placed it in his lapel. Then he took out his Roman police ID card and, after the uniform on the gate checked with Gerald Kelly, made his way into the world premiere for Roberto Tonti's *Inferno*.

After a brief search he found Falcone, Peroni, and Teresa in the tent that housed the main historical exhibits from Florence. The three of them looked bored and out of sorts, yawning next to a set of glass cabinets displaying illuminated medieval manuscripts. Only a handful of visitors had wandered into the place. The rest were outside, with the stars and the free drinks. Compared to those, some old documents seemed insufficient to warrant anyone's attention.

Falcone cleared his throat and said, though with precious little in the way of displeasure, "I was under the impression, Soverintendente, that you were off-duty today."

"I am." He flashed the envelope Maggie had sent to the house on Greenwich Street. "Someone sent me a ticket for the main event."

"Lucky you," Peroni observed.

"Thanks."

"I meant," the big man went on, "lucky you getting away, after all that nonsense last night. It would be nice if we knew where you were sometimes, Nic."

Costa shrugged and apologised. "I hadn't really expected things to turn out the way they did. Also..." He wondered how much to tell them. "...I was hoping for a little gratitude from Gerald Kelly when I brought him Tom Black. It wasn't the fault of the SFPD that things went wrong."

Not at all, he thought, remembering the hunting weapon, and its link to the crossbow that had killed Allan Prime.

Teresa reached up and did some more work on his tie. "If you're on a date, and I suspect you are, Nic, you really ought to take a little more time with your appearance."

"Been busy," he said, fighting shy of her hands.

They caught the unintentional note of satisfaction in his voice.

"Good busy or idle busy?" Peroni asked suspiciously.

"Good."

He left it at that.

Falcone looked at him and asked, "How good?"

There was no way to say it except simply.

"Possibly as good as we're likely to get. When the show's over, Simon Harvey wants to make a statement. He'll confess to being a part of a financial conspiracy to hype *Inferno* by making bogus threats to those involved, with their knowledge usually. They needed the money. They needed the movie to be a success. Also…"

"No details, not now," Falcone said, suppressing a wry grin.

Teresa smiled. "Will he name anyone else, perchance?"

"Allan Prime. Josh Jonah. Tom Black. Dino Bonetti." He paused. "And Roberto Tonti."

"A tontine?" she asked.

"Effectively. Harvey says that Tonti made his illness one of the lures. It was obvious he wouldn't survive to pick up his share, so all the others believed that would give them an instant profit. In return, he was allowed to make his final movie."

Falcone pointed a finger at him. "What did I say about details?" He glanced around. "Harvey's told you all this already? And you say he's willing to repeat it all?"

"After the premiere. He feels they're all owed their moment of glory. After that, though, he's had enough. He's a decent man."

Peroni huffed and puffed and grumbled. "*Now* he's decent! And if he changes his mind?"

Costa pulled out the tiny MP3 player he'd bought from Walgreens on Chestnut on his way to Harvey's apartment. It had been tucked into his jacket pocket, set to record, throughout their conversation. The histrionics with the gun had been intended, in part, to make Harvey so nervous he might not notice its presence. For twenty dollars the thing did a good job; Nic had checked through the little earphones on the walk back to the Palace of Fine Arts. He still didn't quite recognise his own voice, particularly in those moments when he had the gun in his hands.

"If he changes his mind, then I just give this to Gerald Kelly and let nature take its course. The entire conversation is recorded, from beginning to end. I'm not sure how much of it will pass the evidence rules in America..."

They were grinning like Cheshire cats, all three of them.

"I mean that about the evidence, Leo. It would be best all round if the man confesses..."

"Let me worry about that." The inspector hesitated, then asked, "No more names to give me?"

"Maggie Flavier was defrauded of her fee. She

never knew a thing about what was going on. Harvey's admitted that. At the very least Kelly can charge them over that."

"At the very least," Falcone agreed, then took the audio player from Costa's fingers. "Thank you very much."

Costa stood his ground. "And you intend to do what with it, sir?"

Leo Falcone stiffened, straightened his own tie, and looked outside the door at the swirling mist.

"I intend to find Captain Kelly and tell him what you've just told me. I want to leave this place feeling we did our job as well as could be expected in the circumstances. Not in the middle of some argument over who deserves the credit."

"And me?" Costa asked.

Falcone frowned, as if the question were ridiculous. "You're off-duty and you've got a date. Make the most of it. As for you two…" He glanced at Peroni and Teresa, then waved at the glass cabinets and their ancient manuscripts. "…watch this stuff, will you?"

10

FALCONE FOUND GERALD KELLY ALONE A LITTLE way from the mob of photographers and reporters jostling one another by the red carpet runway to the premiere. The tent was now a ghostly grey shape in the fog. Through the open flaps, he could just make out the brightly lit stage with mikes clustered thickly in front of the screen, like the podium for some cut-rate copy of the Oscar ceremonies. A half-familiar face from the TV was scheduled to start a warm-up for the evening. Then there would be the movie, and, some three hours later, a closing speech from Roberto Tonti.

The Roman inspector wished to see none of it. He knew his own force could take no part in what followed, even if the crucial information were to come from them in the first instance. This was Gerald Kelly's case, one that would, if it came to court, be prosecuted through the American authorities, not those in Italy. If Falcone could return home with the missing mask of Dante Alighieri, then he would be content, though he did not expect this happy conclusion to be reached.

"Are you planning to watch the movie?" Falcone asked as the American police officer arrived.

"Not if I can help it," Kelly said.

"I understand." The American had a very piercing gaze. "Are you pleased with the arrangements, Captain?"

Kelly frowned. "As much as anyone could be. The glitterati don't like going through metal detectors, but they can learn to live with it. We're doing what we can."

Falcone thought of how Maggie Flavier had been poisoned by someone working in a catering truck, an individual with a fake name and no ID. There were limits to how much security one could put in place for events of this nature. Without months of preparation and the vetting of everyone concerned—neither of which had been practicable—some loopholes had to remain.

He didn't mention this because he knew Gerald Kelly understood the problem just as well as he did. Instead, he told Kelly briefly what he had learned from Costa. He passed on the audio player, then requested that he attend any interview with Simon Harvey to ask the necessary questions about the missing death mask of Dante Alighieri. After that—barring any new discoveries—the work of the Roman state police in San Francisco would be done. They could return home on the weekend with some sense of achievement, even if the public prize would doubtless fall to others.

This news did not appear to surprise the American police captain, which Falcone found odd. But Kelly thanked him politely for it, agreed to Harvey's conditions, and asked for Falcone to meet him with the publicist at the temporary police control truck after Roberto Tonti's closing speech. Then he said no more.

Taking the hint, Falcone left to amble idly around the crowd, determined not to return to a tent full of glass cases and mouldering pieces of paper.

Finally, not consciously realising that this was what he intended all along, he found her. Catherine Bianchi stood beneath the dome of the Palace, a radio in her hand. She wore a dark suit that was tight on her slender figure, and she might have been mistaken for a guest herself had she not spent so much of her time alone, scrutinizing the crowd with the careful attention he knew all good police officers possessed.

"Leo?" she said as he approached.

"It's a foul evening for a movie premiere. They should have chosen a theatre."

"It's only a movie. A few hours of fantasy, then it's over." She smiled at him. She looked different somehow. More at ease. More ... alluring perhaps. Falcone found this odd and a little disconcerting. He had scarcely given Catherine Bianchi a second thought all day, possibly for the first time since he had arrived in San Francisco.

"I'm through at nine," she said. "I know a warm

place for dinner. We should go to North Beach. You've been avoiding Italian food ever since you got here. It's time to try something new."

He laughed. "I don't think I've done anything else but try new things since I got here, have I? And now…"

"Now you're going. I can see it in your face."

"Is it that obvious?"

"You're very transparent, Leo. You all are. Peroni. Nic. Teresa. I'll miss that. It's unusual. You're unusual."

"Perhaps. Perhaps we're just out of place."

"When do you go?" she asked.

"Sometime this weekend, I think. I haven't given it much thought, to be honest. Nic said something about wishing to tack some holiday on the end. It's fine by me. I have some reports to deal with in Rome. Internal reorganisation. You know the kind of thing."

"They're transferring me downtown," she told him. "Bryant Street. I'll miss the Marina. It's my little village."

The distant quacking of the waterfowl on the lake echoed through the mist. There was a burst of laughter and applause from the stage, now almost invisible in the fog.

"You'll never leave Rome, will you?" she asked.

"No more than you'd leave San Francisco."

"Kind of makes things hard, doesn't it? When two people are fixed in their ways like that?"

"We have what time we have. We do with it the best we can."

A part of him had sought this woman's affection with an ardent desire he'd not known for a long time. Now that Italy beckoned, that passion had dissipated almost as quickly as it had arisen in the first place. Yet there was a look in her eyes...

"I'm sorry if I offended you, Catherine. That was never my intention."

"I wasn't offended. I was flattered. But you try too hard, Leo. And also..." She looked a little guilty. "I have a rule. I don't date cops."

He blinked. "Ever?"

"Ever." She was smiling at him. "At least I haven't since I made the mistake of marrying one briefly a decade or so back."

"Ah..."

"But we could have dinner in North Beach to-night. Since you go home so soon...We're free as birds. After the premiere...?"

Falcone felt briefly lost for words. Then he tapped his watch and said, rather more bluntly than he wished, "I'm afraid I can't fit you in. Business, unfortunately. It may go on for a while. We should meet for a coffee sometime. That would be good."

The radio burst into life. She held it to her mouth and began speaking. He could see she hadn't even touched the press-to-talk button. Their conversation had come to a close.

Falcone walked to the cordoned area, found a

quiet place with a seat. He was acutely aware of something that surprised him. He would miss this city. He would regret, too, the overzealous and childish way he had chased Catherine Bianchi without ever once asking himself what she might seek in return.

Cries of surprise and a ripple of applause drifted through the mist from the nearby runway into the premiere.

Falcone walked to the edge of the crowd, close to the road, and, with the deft elbows of a Roman, worked his way politely but forcefully to the front.

The cameras and the reporters had only one thing on their mind, and that was the couple walking slowly along the red carpet.

Leo Falcone stood behind the yellow tape, and found himself beaming with a mixture of pride and emotion at what he saw. Nic Costa looked as if he belonged with the beautiful young woman on his arm, even though his cheap Roman suit seemed somewhat shabby next to her flowing silk gown, a flimsy creation for such a chilly, fog-strewn night. Not that Maggie Flavier, being the consummate actress she was, showed one iota of discomfort.

As the reporters shouted her name, she simply smiled and waved and held herself like a star for the cameras, her small hand always on Costa's arm. The young police officer held himself with quiet, calm dignity.

As they slowly passed, Falcone, to his own

amazement, found himself crying out, "Soverintendente! Soverintendente!"

The couple stopped. Nic Costa turned and stared
at him with a quizzical look.

"*In bocca al lupo*," Falcone shouted, with a sudden
and entirely involuntary enthusiasm.

"*Crepi il lupo!*" Maggie Flavier cried back joyfully at
him.

And then they moved on.

In the mouth of the wolf. Foreigners always found it a
curious way to wish someone good luck. He was
impressed that Maggie Flavier knew the correct response. *Let the wolf die.*

The wolf had hung around Nic Costa long
enough, Falcone thought as he watched them disappear into the mist.

11

GIANLUCA QUATTROCCHI WORE HIS FINEST
dress uniform with a white carnation in the
collar, determined to look his best at this final glittering event before his return home. He had already
rehearsed in his head the report he would give to his
superiors. Of the uncooperative intransigence of the
American authorities, unable to relinquish their grip

on the case sufficiently to allow the Carabinieri to do their job. Of the meddling of the state police, constantly obstructing and interfering with Quattrocchi's investigation. He would single out Falcone by name, in the knowledge that to do so would get back to the higher echelons of the state police and perhaps earn the man the reprimand he deserved.

There was, for Gianluca Quattrocchi, a point at which a failed case turned from a mystery demanding solution into a disaster requiring containment. The death of Allan Prime and the sequence of events that had followed now fell entirely in the second category. It would be for the American authorities to pursue whatever slim, time-consuming half-leads and connections they could find in the financial affairs of the two dead men involved in the dotcom bubble of Lukatmi. The Carabinieri had neither the time nor the resources to become involved in such work, not least because any resulting case would surely be tried in America and benefit the Italian authorities not one whit.

This was not the outcome Quattrocchi sought. He had, for a while, genuinely believed that the Canadian professor, Bryan Whitcombe, who had pressed himself upon the Italian authorities with such adamant enthusiasm, might hold some insight into the case. That idea had waned lately, and he'd even begun to find the man somewhat creepy. Whitcombe had turned up for tonight's premiere in a garish white suit and taken to bearding starlets with his lascivious gaze. The man had even announced to the media that he intended to write a book on the affair of "Dante's Numbers," as he had dubbed it. According to that morning's papers, an outline for the work was now being hyped around American publishers by one of the book world's more notorious agents. Law enforcement work often had unforeseen consequences. The elevation of Bryan Whitcombe to the status of unlikely media star was one he could never have predicted.

None of this did much for Quattrocchi's mood as he sipped his free champagne. He began quietly to plan his exit from the proceedings so that he might miss the screening altogether, merely returning for the closing ceremony. Then he saw Gerald Kelly, a man for whom he felt no affection whatsoever, stomping towards him like a bulldog intent on its victim.

"We need to talk," the American snapped. "Somewhere private."

Quattrocchi followed to an empty area close by the lake and listened. As he did so he felt the bitter taste of envy rise in his throat.

The SFPD captain was right to tell him of this development. He was in charge of the Italian investigative team. Falcone should have come to him first with this news, and allowed Quattrocchi to pass it on to Kelly.

The American finished with the suggestion

Quattrocchi join him and Falcone for the interview with Simon Harvey after the premiere.

"Of course I'll be there," Quattrocchi insisted. "We're joint investigating authorities in this case. It would be highly improper to commence without me."

Kelly glared at him. "You know, I never got around to saying this to your face until now. But this is our country, not yours. We interview who we like, when we like, and I don't care whether that pisses you off or not."

"And Tonti? What do you propose with him?"

"I'm feeling generous. And I don't want this freak show getting any worse. He's a sick old man. He's not going anywhere. He can turn up with his lawyers at Bryant Street in the morning. No reporters. No leaks. Not a word to anyone."

The *maresciallo* nodded at the pack of photographers now corralled into a specific section of the secure area by the stage outside the screening tent. "You think they'll be happy with that?"

"I don't care what they'll be happy with. That's the way it's going to be."

He stalked back into the crowd.

Americans amazed Quattrocchi. Their incapacity for a little common deviousness from time to necessary time was quite bewildering.

He found Roberto Tonti in the center of a group of movie company executives. The man looked more gaunt and haggard than he had two weeks before.

His eyes were invisible behind sunglasses as usual. His grey hair appeared stiff and unreal. The director was finishing a cigarette as Quattrocchi arrived. Immediately he lit another and said nothing as the suits around him gossiped and argued.

Quattrocchi got next to him and said in Italian, "Tonti, it is important we talk."

"I doubt that very much."

The Carabinieri officer nodded at the men around them. "Do they speak Italian?"

There was a slow, shallow intake of breath, then Tonti replied, "They're producers. Most are still struggling with English and it's their native tongue."

"Listen to me well. Once this premiere is over, it is the intention of the San Francisco Police Department to arrest you on suspicion of fraud and conspiracy to murder."

Tonti took a long drag on the cigarette, looked at him, and said nothing.

"They have a witness," Quattrocchi persisted. "A member of your . . . tontine. He has already told them of your arrangement. The man has agreed to make a statement, doubtless in return for some kind of immunity."

"Who?" Tonti demanded.

"This is not an appropriate time."

"I wish to avoid embarrassment this evening. You must understand that."

"Of course. All the same . . ."

"Shut up. I am thinking."

Gianluca Quattrocchi fell silent. There was something chilling in the authority of this man. Something decidedly odd.

"What do you have to offer me?" Tonti asked at last.

"You're an Italian citizen. If you give yourself up to my authority, I can arrange these matters through our courts, not theirs."

"You don't understand Americans. They don't like to lose."

"Captain Kelly is feeling sentimental. He will invite you for an interview tomorrow morning. Were you to leave the country tonight after the premiere and arrive in Italy in due course... It would not be difficult. A private jet would have you in Mexico in a couple of hours. After that, what could the American authorities do?" Quattrocchi coughed into his fist, praying none of this conversation would ever go any further. "Extradition proceedings take years. You will receive much fairer treatment in your native country, surely. If you plead guilty to some minor financial transgression, we can spin things out for a long time..."

"I'll be dead before summer turns." Tonti spoke with a matter-of-fact certainty.

"Then die in Rome, where you belong. In bed. In your home, not some prison cell in California."

"Without a name I shall not agree to this."

"I cannot..."

"Without a name I shall go to the Americans this

instant. I shall tell them everything, and inform them of your approach and your offer. Perhaps they can better it."

Quattrocchi's temper had stretched to breaking point. The premiere would begin in a matter of minutes.

"I believe they have an appointment with Simon Harvey," he muttered. "I did *not* tell you this."

"Of course, *Maresciallo*. This is kind of you."

"No. Merely practical." He tried to fathom the expression in the man's haggard features. "So we have an arrangement?"

"How could one deny the Carabinieri?" the director replied effusively. "It would be impertinent, no?"

Gianluca Quattrocchi did not expect thanks from this individual. Nor did he anticipate or enjoy condescension.

"I shall endeavour to make your time in Rome as comfortable as possible," he replied stiffly, aware that he was speaking to the long, thin back of Roberto Tonti as the director turned to the suits and evening gowns, the mayhem of the premiere of *Inferno*.

12

THEY WATCHED THE MOVIE FROM THE DARKNESS of the VIP seats at the front. Not long after the start he felt her head slip onto his shoulder, her hair fall against his neck. Costa turned his head a degree or two and stole a glimpse at Maggie Flavier. On the screen she stood five metres high, the ethereal beauty Beatrice, Dante's dead muse, offering hope as the poet faced the horrors and travails of Hell's circles, just as the idea of the unworldly Madeleine Elster had appeared to bring solace to the lost and fearful Scottie. For most of the movie, the real woman behind Beatrice was fast asleep against him, mouth slightly ajar, at peace. He scarcely dared breathe for fear of waking her. However loud the commotion on the screen, she seemed oblivious to it all, slumbering by his side like a child lost in a world of her own.

He felt happy. Lucky, too. And like her, he scarcely took any notice of the overblown cinematic fiction that had brought them there. Costa's thoughts turned, instead, to the events of the past few weeks, and the growing conviction that the roots of this genuine drama lay, somehow, in the fairy tales these people created for themselves.

The conspiracy had sprouted from the ability of men like Roberto Tonti and Dino Bonetti to invent some fantastical story out of dust. Costa still failed to understand how that trick had come to shift from a desperate marketing ploy into a murderous actuality, but the seeds were there from the outset in the way those involved danced between one world, that of everyday life, and another in which fiction posed as fact.

Maggie was an unwitting part of that fabrication. In ways he didn't wish to understand, it had damaged her.

This dark, unsettling thought dogged him as the movie finally came to an end. Costa was about to nudge her gently awake as the lights came up. There was no need. Her head was off his shoulder even before the waves of applause began to ripple around the audience.

By the time Roberto Tonti was striding onto the stage with Simon Harvey by his side, most of the audience was on its feet. In the way of things, Costa found himself following suit. Maggie rose next to him. He leaned down and asked her when the cast would join Tonti on the platform.

She had to cup her hand to his ear to make herself heard over the din. "This is Roberto's moment. We were all told that. He's the director. We're just his puppets, remember?"

It still seemed unfair, Costa thought, half listening to Harvey run through a fulsome tribute to Allan

Prime, followed by a lengthy homily about Tonti's determination to see the project completed. The years of struggle, the script revisions, the financial difficulties, the threats, the tragic events of recent weeks. Above all, said Harvey, the fight for artistic and creative control, without which the movie in its present form could never have been conceived, least of all made.

It was florid hyperbole delivered with a straight face. Within the space of the next thirty minutes, either Harvey would be making a statement to the SFPD incriminating Tonti in the conspiracy that had brought about at least four deaths, or Falcone would be handing over the audio evidence to justify his arrest and interrogation on those same charges. One way or another the riddle would be brought to some kind of resolution.

Then Harvey stepped back. Awkwardly, with a pained, sick gait, which a cynical part of Costa's mind felt might be faintly theatrical, Tonti shuffled to the microphone. He stood there alone, listening, only half-smiling, to the wall of clapping hands, catcalls, and whistles of the crowd.

It was tedious and artificial. Costa was becoming impatient, wishing for an end to this show. As he fought to stifle a yawn, something caught his attention.

A woman was walking towards Roberto Tonti from the far side of the stage. In her hands she held a gigantic bouquet of roses, carnations, and bright, vivid orchids.

Costa blinked, trying to convince himself this was not some flashback out of a dream, or a night in front of the TV in the house on Greenwich Street.

She was of medium height and wore a severe grey jacket with matching slacks and a white shirt high up to her neck. Her build was full, almost stocky; her hair was perfect, dyed platinum blonde, unyielding, as if held by the strongest lacquer imaginable. As she turned to present the flowers to Tonti, Costa could see that the wig—it could be nothing else—was tied back into a tight, shining apostrophe above the somewhat thick form of her neck.

In spite of the weather she wore a pair of black plastic Italian sunglasses, so large they effectively obscured her features. Yet Costa knew her. She was the character from *Vertigo*. Kim Novak as Madeleine Elster. Or rather a fake Madeleine who posed as the doomed wife Jimmy Stewart's Scottie came to love and hoped to save.

It also occurred to him that she matched exactly the description of the woman calling herself Carlotta Valdes who had visited Allan Prime in the Via Giulia, ostensibly to create a death mask.

He found himself fighting to get through the cordon around the stage. Maggie gasped as he clawed his way forward.

"What are you doing?" she asked.

"Stay where you are. Don't go near the stage."

He pressed forward and the large hand of a security guard shoved him hard in the chest. Costa fell backwards. He stumbled and found himself guided by Maggie back into a seat.

"Nic," she said, exasperated, "you can't go up there. Roberto owns that stage. No one's going to take it from him. Those bouncers wouldn't let God himself through unless He had a pass."

The crowd was still on its feet, whooping and cheering.

"There's something wrong," he muttered, and dragged out his Rome police ID.

She gazed at the plastic card in his fingers and said, "Well, that's going to work, isn't it? For pity's sake, what's the matter?"

He struggled to his feet and wondered, for a moment, whether he was going mad. The woman was gone. Roberto Tonti stood on the stage, with Simon Harvey a few feet behind him. The ailing director held the gigantic bouquet and waved and nodded to the joyful, over-the-top roar of the crowd.

"Five minutes of this," Maggie whispered into his ear, "and we're out of here. I promise."

He prayed more than anything she would be proved right.

The tall, gaunt figure on the stage mouthed something into the microphone. Costa knew what it was. A single word in Italian, an exhortation, a command.

Silenzio.

13

"ONCE UPON A TIME, IN A LAND FAR AWAY . . ."
Roberto Tonti began.

He clutched the bouquet to his emaciated chest, then he removed his sunglasses and tried to squint at the audience beyond the blazing floodlights.

"You come to me for stories." The old man's voice sounded distant and hollow and sick. "Children begging for gifts. Did you get them?" The noise of the audience diminished slightly. Tonti waited. He took hold of the microphone and, in his hoarse, weak voice, tried his best to bellow, *"Did you get them?"*

The strained sound of his words, the accent half American, half Italian, carried into the night with a deafening clarity. The space inside the tent turned abruptly silent.

"Did you appreciate the cost?" he croaked. "Allan Prime. A wretched actor. A weak man. Nothing to be missed. He died. Why not? Where's the loss?" He spat out his words. "See what I must work with? See how I make something precious out of clay? What do you want of me? What else do you expect?"

Maggie murmured in Nic's ear, "I can't take this anymore . . ."

She slipped away from him, and still he couldn't tear his eyes from the stage.

Simon Harvey stepped towards the director. Tonti stopped him with a single magisterial glance.

A low murmur of disquiet and astonishment began to rise up from the crowd.

Tonti reached into the bouquet of flowers and withdrew something that stilled every voice in the room. A small black handgun emerged from the orchids and the bloodred roses. He cast away the bouquet, held the weapon high for the benefit of the camera rigs hovering over the stage, wandering around him like robotic eyes, fixated on a single subject.

"Watch me," he said to the giant, peering lenses. "Focus, always, always."

Costa scanned around the crowd. Gerald Kelly was at the edge of the platform with a group of uniformed officers, holding them back for the moment.

Tonti's skinny, weak arms waved, as if beseeching them for something, some kind of understanding.

"Listen to me. Listen! This once I tell you the truth. Some impertinent hack once asked Fellini..." The tip of the black barrel caressed his cheek, like a thoughtful finger. " *'Che cosa fai?'* What do you do?"

"Enough, Roberto..." Harvey said, and took another step closer. The gun drifted his way. The publicist froze.

"Fellini answers... *'Sono un gran bugiardo.'* I am a big liar. Pinocchio writ large. See my nose! See my nose!"

Tonti was clutching his own face, laughing, and the movement brought about a spasmodic cough that briefly gripped his frail frame.

"Fellini, Hitchcock, Rossellini... Tonti, too. This is what you demand of our calling. That we are liars, all, and the more distance we put between your dreams and the miserable mundanity of your sad little lives, the better we lie, the happier you are."

The man's voice was cracking with emotion, and it was impossible to say whether it was anger or grief or some deep-rooted sense of fear.

"Mea culpa. Mea culpa."

His hands fell to his sides, and he bowed low before the audience.

"I am the director. All you have seen of late, on screen and off, is my creation. From Allan Prime dead in the Farnesina to some pretty little clotheshorse choking for life from a poisoned apple. This is my doing, my direction. Listen to me now..."

He coughed again, and it was raw and dry and rasping.

"No man gets a better final scene than this. Better than any I gave any of these two-bit hacks. See..."

He indicated the cameras, following his every moment. "See! This is the last of Roberto Tonti. Greater than any of you. Any of them."

Kelly had nodded to his men. They were starting to make their way onto the stage. Tonti knew what was coming, surely.

"Not Dante Alighieri, though," the old man added. "Listen to me, children. Listen to the final words of *Inferno,* that I never gave you on the screen, for they are beyond your comprehension."

He drew himself up, closed his eyes, and began to recite, slowly, in a sonorous, theatrical tone.

> *"The Guide and I into that hidden road*
> *Now entered, to return to the bright world;*
> *And without care of having any rest*
> *We mounted up, he first and I the second,*
> *Till I beheld through a round aperture*
> *Some of the beauteous things that Heaven doth bear;*
> *Thence we came forth to rebehold the stars."*

Roberto Tonti paused and gazed at the rapt, still, silent crowd in front of him.

He was shaking with laughter, and his eyes, now open and dark and alert, glistened with moisture as they fixed on the camera lenses ravenously following his every move.

"'Through a round aperture...to rebehold the stars,'" Roberto Tonti repeated, and swept his arm along the rows of glitterati and celebrities before him. "Such as they are."

Simon Harvey was getting closer, hands out, pleading for the gun.

"Yet," Tonti continued, "each and every story deserves a twist, some small epiphany at its close."

Without warning he swung to face Harvey. The

publicist froze, looked at the director, and asked, "Roberto?"

"Traitor."

The word, the final key in the ninth circle, the last of Dante's Numbers, came out in a flat, unemotional tone.

He began to fire, repeatedly, deliberately, into the torso of the flailing, tumbling publicist.

A woman screamed behind Costa.

When the gun clicked on empty, Roberto Tonti stopped and took one last disgusted glance at the shattered body on the stage.

Then, seizing the microphone, he gazed up at the cameras.

In a calm, disinterested voice, he ordered, "And... *cut.*"

PART 7

1

IT WAS SATURDAY MORNING. THE WEATHER WAS warmer. August beckoned. Costa woke in Maggie Flavier's apartment, then drove to Greenwich Street to help the rest of them pack. Their flight home would be late that afternoon. He would travel to Barbados the following Monday. There were still some private business events on Maggie's calendar. The job never seemed to disappear completely. Simon Harvey's death continued to stand between them like some unspoken obstacle. Perhaps time would deal with that, time and a move to a different place, one with no connections, no memories. He was unsure.

But at least the case appeared to be, if not closed, at least partly resolved, probably as much as it ever would be. Roberto Tonti had scarcely ceased speaking to Gerald Kelly and his team since he was taken into custody. The SFPD had passed on the details to Falcone, since Gianluca Quattrocchi had been recalled to Rome with his officers to face an internal inquiry. Quattrocchi's private approach on the night of the premiere was only one of the revelations the director was now minded to disclose. He had also confessed to being the originator of the tontine scheme to save the troubled movie in Rome, and to diverting Harvey's secret publicity scam about fictitious threats to the production into a real and murderous conspiracy. His motive, he said with no apparent shame, was purely selfish. *Inferno* was by no means a guaranteed success, even with Harvey's incessant hype. Something else was needed and, as Tonti knew this was the last movie he would ever make, he was prepared to go to any lengths in order to find it.

He had named Josh Jonah, the photographer Martin Vogel, and the Lukatmi security guard Jimmy Gaines as the principals in the plot to murder Allan Prime. Vogel had arranged the poison for Maggie Flavier. Jonah had then approached the photographer after being blackmailed over his involvement in the plot. Tonti had promised them Prime would be the only victim. He had hoped that would be the case, and that the halfhearted attempt on Maggie Flavier's life, which he had not expected to be successful, would merely gain yet more publicity to keep the movie in the headlines. The deaths of Jonah and Vogel he regarded as accidental, if fortuitous. He claimed to have shot Tom Black—who had never understood the true nature of the scheme—himself, from a viewpoint near the Embarcadero, and then disposed of the weapon.

Dino Bonetti's role remained unclear. The producer had disappeared the night of the premiere and was now the subject of arrest warrants for fraud and attempted murder. Tonti, however, steadfastly refused to discuss his involvement in the conspiracy, dismissing it as minor. The credit, as he saw it, was to be his.

In spite of the man's age and frailty, he remained in custody, though Kelly was minded to waive any objections to bail provided Tonti surrendered his passport and reported to the police on a daily basis. The medical reports indicated that he had, at most, a few months to live, and would never face trial. There was no question, either, that the man would wish to flee to Italy, in spite of Gianluca Quattrocchi's promises. The truth, Kelly felt, was that Roberto Tonti had achieved what he wanted.

The SFPD phone lines had burned with calls from TV networks and newspapers pleading with Tonti to go on air or give lengthy press interviews. From the major newspapers to the prime-time celebrity shows, he was, suddenly, in demand. This, it seemed, was worth a succession of lives, none of which the dying man deemed of any great value. Only his own reputation, his legacy, mattered, and by force of circumstance, that would always be tied to a single movie, Roberto Tonti's *Inferno*.

Hank and Frank Boynton had been round for breakfast when Falcone returned from Bryant Street to brief them on what he'd heard from Gerald Kelly. All of them at the table—the Boyntons, Teresa, Peroni, and Costa—listened intently, and then the Italians stayed silent.

Hank, however, raised a forefinger and said, by way of objection, "But just a minute—"

"Not now, Hank," Teresa stopped him, mid-sentence. "We're finished here."

"But—"

"Not now."

"The movie business," Frank grumbled. "He couldn't take being behind that camera all his life, watching others get the fame. What was that line from Dante he spouted after he killed that poor bastard in front of everyone?"

"'Thence we came forth to rebehold the stars,'" Costa said.

"Envy. Greed. This insane craving for fame." Frank Boynton shook his head then got up from the table. "Come on, brother. These people have things to do." He looked at Teresa. "That invitation to Rome still stands?"

"Whenever you boys want it."

"Good. Have a safe journey home. All of you."

They watched the two men leave. Ten minutes later Catherine Bianchi arrived and offered them one last drive round the city before a farewell lunch in the Marina.

2

COSTA ALMOST FELL ASLEEP IN THE MINIVAN AS it wound through a city landscape he felt he now knew well. The views across to Marin County, the great bridge, the hulking island of Alcatraz... It would be hard to shake San Francisco from the memory for many reasons, good and bad. Then he remembered he had something to return. It was sitting in a plastic grocery bag he'd brought along for the purpose. When they stopped at a light, he reached forward and placed it on the console between the front seats.

"That belongs to Gerald Kelly. Tell him thanks but I didn't need it."

Catherine Bianchi took a look at the handgun in its leather holster. "Lucky you."

Her dark eyes wandered to the tall lean figure in the passenger seat. Something had changed between these two. Falcone sat next to her looking relaxed and perhaps a little bored. He was no longer the ardent pursuer and had already talked wistfully that morning of work back in Rome. Yet, as his eagerness waned, Catherine Bianchi's, it seemed to Costa, was beginning to surface, rather too late in the day.

"Is everything good?" she asked with a brittle, edgy ease.

The question was principally aimed at the man next to her. He scarcely seemed to notice.

They were travelling along Union towards Russian Hill, trying to make a left turn, when, after her third attempt to start a conversation, Catherine finally lost patience.

"Listen," she snapped. "I may never see any of you guys again. Ever. And all you can do is sit there moping. What the hell is the matter now? What did I do wrong?"

"Nothing," Falcone remarked, turning to look at her.

"Then why are you . . . all of you . . ."

She muttered something beneath her breath, then added, "You might at least look a little grateful this mess is over. That someone's in custody, admitting to the whole damned thing. Loose ends all tied up. Case closed." She glanced at Falcone. "Tickets home all booked."

The Italians squirmed uncomfortably on their seats.

"The loose ends aren't all tied up, Catherine, and you know that as well as the rest of us," Teresa said before anyone else could. "All that's happened is that Tonti's stuck up his hand and said, 'Send it all my way.' Which is very convenient in the circumstances. But . . ."

"But what?"

She was too late. The dam had burst. Peroni got in next, aware, perhaps, that there was likely to be a queue.

"I was under the impression we weren't going to talk about this. But since we are, let me say just one thing. Tom Black was shot from a considerable distance by someone using a hunting rifle. Either Roberto Tonti is quite a marksman or he got very lucky. Have you seen his eyes? How he shakes? I don't believe he could do that. Not for one moment."

He was getting into his stride. "Also . . . how did he know Tom Black was in that car with Nic in the first place?"

"He says Black called him beforehand asking for help," she snapped.

"But why?" Peroni asked. "If Tom Black knew Tonti was behind the whole thing . . . Oh, I give up."

Falcone smiled pleasantly in the passenger seat and said nothing.

"Carlotta Valdes," Costa added abruptly. "Who was she? Where is she now?"

Catherine Bianchi turned around, looking cross. "He won't tell us, Nic. The guy's just confessed everything and that's that. Are we supposed to lose sleep over it? Whoever that woman was, she didn't do much. Maybe roped in Allan Prime and brought Tonti a gun on-stage at the Palace of Fine Arts. One more fake ID among many. Trust me. Kelly's people have checked. They could spend a lifetime chasing someone who was nothing more than some two-bit courier. And they even will, for a little while. But not for long. Do you blame them? Don't you have priorities in Rome, too?"

"It's the name," Costa emphasised, not quite knowing what he meant, struggling to place a memory. "Why that name?"

"Because of Hitchcock," Teresa insisted. "As I've been trying to tell you all along. Tonti worked with him. It was all here..."

The vehicle came to an abrupt halt by a busy junction. Catherine Bianchi slammed her hands angrily on the steering wheel.

"You people make me want to scream. Why, in God's name, do you have to make everything so *complicated*?"

Falcone finally took his gaze off the ocean horizon. "We didn't. We never had the chance. The fact that film was made here—"

"This is San Francisco! Movie central!" she yelled. "Haven't you noticed? Watch."

She jerked out into the street, cut left onto another road, then bore right again.

"*Dirty Harry,*" she chanted. "*Bullitt. Mrs. Doubtfire, The Joy Luck Club*..."

"Eastwood and McQueen—" Teresa cut in.

"Shut up! *Harold and Maude, Freebie and the Bean, Pal Joey*...Am I making my point here? It's not all dark and bloody. Remember *The Love Bug*?"

The Italians stiffened and glanced at each other.

"*The Love Bug?*" Teresa asked eventually. "You mean the kids' movie?" She winced. "The Disney one?"

"The Disney one."

"Like *Bambi*," Costa murmured, still trying to place the recollection that was haunting him, one that was buried somehow in that dark night that had ended in bloodshed outside the Ferry Building on the Embarcadero.

He was amazed to see that the road they had entered bore the name Lombard, just like the broad highway that became Route 101 as it swept towards the Golden Gate Bridge. Here, however, it was narrow and residential. Then they crossed a broad cross street and Lombard became a one-lane road that turned into a crazed series of steep switchbacks winding downhill past grand Victorian mansions and newer apartment blocks.

"Tourist time," Catherine announced as she wheeled the big Dodge easily around the tight hairpins, the vehicle grumbling over the brick road. "America's crookedest street. Architecturally speaking, of course. Most of the people around here are upstanding citizens, with plenty of cash, too."

The street straightened and became smooth asphalt once more. She pulled in by the junction at Leavenworth and looked back over her shoulder at the winding lane behind.

"Recognise anything?" she asked. "That little Beetle Herbie came down here. Lots of movies came down here. After L.A., this city is the biggest movie stage in the world. So what's the big deal if someone steals the name of a movie character now and again?"

Costa wasn't looking back. His eyes were fixed straight ahead, seeing something he recognised. There was a city map in the seat back; Costa took it out, scanned the index, found what he wanted, ran his finger across the ganglion of streets that criss-crossed the crowded, confined peninsula of San Francisco, a complex patchwork of neighbourhoods, each running into the next, overlapping, obscuring the obvious.

"Drive on, please," he said. "Ahead. Indulge me."

The view ahead changed shape, becoming more like the one he expected. Costa asked her to stop at the next junction. Opposite was a plain two-storey house with scaffolding along the side obscuring the long windows of what must have been some kind of living room. The curtains were closed. A builder was working on the exterior, setting up a cement mixing machine.

Tom Black's words kept coming back to him.

They screw you up … they screw everyone. Scottie. Me … I never thought this'd happen. Not when we went to Jones …

There was a scene in the movie … Jimmy Stewart's character stared out from his living room window towards the Bay Bridge, admiring this very view fifty years before from the building across the road. This was Scottie's old home on Lombard, the very building Hitchcock had used. The front, with its long living room window, was on a street called Jones. Someone who didn't know might think that was its real address.

Tom Black hadn't been talking about a man, Costa realised, cursing his own stupidity. He'd been remembering a place. Somewhere he'd met a movie-obsessed individual who'd stolen his name from *Vertigo*.

He climbed out of the car and walked across the road. The builder was a big man, his hands smeared with plaster, his face wary, full of suspicion.

"I was wondering if Scottie was in," Costa asked as if it were the most natural question in the world. "I heard the lucky bastard got some nice old car from somewhere. He promised to show it to me when I was in the neighbourhood."

The man looked him up and down carefully. "Only his friends call him that. Never seen you before."

"Been a while."

"Mr. Ferguson went out this morning. I don't expect him back while I'm here, and I'm here all day."

"The car?"

"Remind me . . . ?"

"Green. Jaguar. Nineteen fifties? Scottie said it was a beauty."

That broke the ice.

"Oh, it's a beauty, all right. I guess that's why it hardly ever gets out of the garage. Bad luck, though— it's not here today."

"Where . . . ?"

"I don't know." He took off his hard hat and scratched his head. "Maybe it's at that theatre of his. Don't know . . ."

"The theatre?" Costa asked.

"That weird little dump on Chestnut, down the Marina. The one with the tower. How the hell Scottie manages to make a cent out of that . . ."

Costa picked up a steel-headed mallet from the side of the concrete mixer.

"Now," the builder said, "let's not do anything hasty . . ."

The door looked so old he felt sure Jimmy Stewart had touched it. People made things well back then. It needed three swings to smash through the hardwood slab.

3

THE PACKAGE ARRIVED AT TEN, ALONG WITH THE man from the movie festival offering to give her a ride to the event. Maggie Flavier glanced at the box in his hands and asked, "Costume?"

He was in his early thirties, sturdy and very clean-shaven, with soft, pale skin that belied his heavy, calloused hands, worn jeans, and white T-shirt. A pair of thickset black plastic sunglasses sat on his face.

"The festival people said..." he began.

"They didn't mention anything about a costume to me."

She didn't know what they'd said. She couldn't remember. This engagement had been on her schedule for weeks. Her agent had arranged it while she was filming in Rome.

He took off the glasses. Bright blue eyes. Too blue. She wondered if they were coloured contacts. Hangers-on at the fringes of the business sometimes had affectations, too.

"If it's a problem...forget it. They went to a lot of trouble to get this dress. They said it was important. But if they screwed up..." He shrugged.

"What am I supposed to be doing?"

"My name's John," he said, smiling pleasantly, and holding out his hand. "John Ferguson."

She shook it. He had the strong grip of a workman.

"What am I doing today, Mr. Ferguson?"

"Marina Festival of Fifties Noir. Sponsored by the local organic supermarket, a bank branch, and an arts foundation. Opened by Miss Maggie Flavier. Fifteen minutes in public, a couple of smiles, and you're done." He peered at her. "You do *know* the Marina Odeon, don't you?"

"Sorry. Movies are work, not leisure. Also, I never quite hit the Marina scene. It's a ways from here."

"Ah..."

"Noir?" she asked.

"We open with *Touch of Evil* and close with *The Asphalt Jungle*. Talk about doing things backwards, but I just fetch and carry. Programming's someone else's job."

He put down the large cardboard dress box and extracted a slip of paper from his jeans pocket.

"According to my schedule you cut the ribbon for the opening at one-thirty, then we show the Welles film at two. You don't need to stay after that, if you don't want to. We have one reporter and one TV crew. No one else will be allowed inside. We got the message from your agent about not wanting too much press there." He glanced at the clock on the wall. "And if we get there quick, no one's going to be outside either. The festival people would like to get a few words from you first for some DVD they're putting together. Just a few questions..."

He nodded at the box. "It's all for charity, you know. Gorgeous dress. I got the limo around the corner."

"Why do I have to wear the dress?"

"Came from some society lady in Russian Hill. Of the period, or so they say." He sighed and shrugged again. "I'm just the messenger here. I'm sorry. After all this awful stuff I read about in the papers, I understand if you don't feel up to it. If you want to cancel, just say so. I can tell them... It's no problem."

"No, no..." Maggie hated letting her fans down.

It seemed so selfish, given the money and acclaim she got in return for what, in truth, was a small amount of talent and a lot of luck.

She opened the box, took out the garment, and found herself wondering for a moment whether to believe what she had in her hands. The dress was a long, voluminous silk evening gown, low cut, the kind of thing glamorous women wore in old movies. It was a dark, incandescent green. The same green as the one in *Vertigo*. It was so beautiful she could scarcely take her eyes off it.

"What is this?"

"They said it's a copy of one Janet Leigh wears in *Touch of Evil*."

That was a film she did remember. The sight of Orson Welles's fat, sweating face looming out of the Mexican darkness was hard to forget.

"I thought that was made in black-and-white."

"Well, I guess the movie was. Not the clothes. What do I know? Don't shoot the messenger, remember?"

She hesitated. The death of Simon Harvey and the dark succession of events that preceded it had exhausted her. She felt tired and uncertain about the trip to Barbados. Uncertain, too, about what might come afterwards...

She remembered Scottie's nightmare from the movie, of falling into a deep, shapeless abyss. Vertigo. It wasn't just fear of heights. Vertigo was fear of the unknown, too.

"We need to go, Miss Flavier," the man insisted, gently. "If you want to. The limo can't wait forever."

One last appearance, and then some space. Some time to think about who she really was, what she really wanted...

"Do you want me to put it on now?" she asked, looking at the dress in her hands.

"Nah. There's a dressing room at the theatre."

He carried the box carefully in his arms, following her all the way down to the parking lot.

"We're just around the corner," he said, beckoning her to the back of her apartment block.

They turned a corner and she saw the car.

The green Jaguar gleamed in the half shade, sleek and old and full of memories. She remembered the smell of the leather and the drive with Nic up into the heights beyond the Legion of Honor.

"What the hell is going on here?" she started to say, swinging around to look at the driver.

The sunglasses were back on. He'd dropped the big cardboard box. He was grinning at her. There was no one near, not a window overlooking this place.

He was getting something out of his pocket.

"It's the final act," the man who called himself John Ferguson said. Suddenly he was on her, strong arms around her neck, a hand pushing some cloth that stank of damp, corrosive chemical into her face.

She tried to struggle. Then she tried to breathe. Her arms flailed wildly, to no purpose. She could hear him laughing.

As she started to fall, she could just make out the sun, bright and wild in a pure blue Californian sky. The world started to turn dark. For one short moment the sun glittered high above her. Then the cloth came down once more. She couldn't breathe. She couldn't feel. He held the thing over her mouth, choking her until she submitted and fell into the dark.

4

ONCE INSIDE THE HOUSE, COSTA WASTED FIFTEEN seconds fumbling for a light switch, then he threw open the curtains on the long flat panes that covered the corner of the room abutting Lombard and Jones, revealing a view that, through ancient venetian blinds, took him back to Maggie Flavier's apartment, watching *Vertigo* for the second time in a matter of days, both of them feeling the past tapping on their shoulders like some hungry ghost.

This wasn't just the same building. It was the very room they'd seen in the movie, with its beautiful hillside vista out to Coit Tower and the ocean. The furniture had been carefully selected from the same era: a pale fabric sofa, long, low chairs of 1950s design. Even a small TV set with manual rotating dials and switches and a bulging, pop-eyed screen. An old-movie channel was playing on it: something black-and-white, the sound turned down as if the room needed to be inhabited by the cinema even when no one was present. It was a sanctuary, a kind of temple, and it was instantly obvious what was being worshipped here.

The walls were plastered with movie posters from floor to ceiling. All from the fifties to seventies. American, English, Italian...

Teresa went round them methodically, finger on the old paper, checking the names.

"Roberto Tonti worked on every one of these," she murmured. "Whoever this man is, he knows his stuff. Tonti doesn't even get a credit on the *Vertigo* poster, but it's up there along with all the Italian horror flicks he directed. We have a fan here. *The* fan."

"Rome." Falcone was busily rooting through documents on the antique desk next to the TV. "He went there one week before Prime died and returned home the day after. Just like Martin Vogel and Jimmy Gaines. Look—plane tickets in the name of Michael Fitzwilliam, the bill for a hotel near Termini, cards for restaurants and bars. A receipt for a pair of sunglasses from Salvatore Ferragamo in the Via Condotti." His grey eyebrows furrowed in bafflement. "Ferragamo don't make *men's* sunglasses, surely..."

"So we've found one more member of the tontine?" Catherine Bianchi asked.

"It would appear so. Ferragamo..."

"You're right. They don't make men's sunglasses." Peroni emerged from a spacious walk-in closet with something held almost tenderly across both outstretched arms. It was a set of women's clothing fresh back from the cleaners, pressed and spotless inside plastic wrapping. A grey jacket with matching slacks. The same clothes they'd seen worn by the woman who handed a bouquet of flowers, with a gun inside, to Roberto Tonti on the stage by the Palace of Fine Arts. The same clothes apparently worn by the mysterious Carlotta Valdes when she appeared at the apartment of Allan Prime in the Via Giulia.

"He keeps his ladies' things in the same cupboard as his men's stuff. There's makeup and a mirror. This is a bachelor apartment with a difference. Also, there's this…"

He held up a photo of a man in hunting gear, his booted foot propped on a dead deer.

"When he's not wearing lipstick, he likes to go shooting. There's a locked firearms cabinet next door that could house a couple of rifles."

"OK," Catherine Bianchi said. "*Now* I am calling Kelly."

From the bottom drawer of the desk, Falcone retrieved what appeared to be a plastic garbage bag wrapped with duct tape. He picked up a pair of scissors and cut the fastenings. From within he pulled out something swathed in white tissue paper.

As they watched, he unwrapped the death mask of Dante Alighieri.

The mask seemed very old and fragile, brilliantly lit by the bright Californian sunlight, a place Dante could never have guessed existed. Costa looked at the closed eyes, the face in peace after so much pain, the long, bent nose, the thin-lipped, intelligent mouth, and knew in an instant that it was genuine.

"This is our case, too," Falcone said with obvious satisfaction. "Call Kelly. Tell him we need an immediate check to find out this individual's real identity, and a discreet distribution of his description."

He gave her the kind of look he gave policewomen in Rome, one she hadn't seen before.

"I do not want to see this in the media. Not even on a police station wall. If this man can change identities so easily and convincingly, he'll be gone the moment he hears."

"Yes, sir . . ." she said caustically. "Anything else?"

Falcone ignored her. Teresa Lupo had returned from the kitchen.

"We need forensic," she said. " 'Scottie' may be finicky about his fancy clothes but his work gear is stuffed into one big pile in a basket just like any other bachelor slob." She looked at them. "There are items in there with what I'd swear are bloodstains on them. And a pair of jeans that still smell of petrol. Martin Vogel's apartment. There's a lot here, Catherine . . ."

"OK, OK, OK. I'll call . . ."

But she still didn't. She looked at them.

"Who the hell is this nut? And how does he fit into the tontine?"

Costa walked over to look at the shelves in the corridor. There seemed nothing unusual among the collection of personal belongings. Souvenirs, from Mexico and Italy, some small pieces of pottery, a few photographs in cheap plastic frames. Everything was so ordinary. If you took away the posters and the incriminating evidence, this would simply be the apartment of a wealthy bachelor with a penchant for 1950s style.

He moved closer and picked up one of the photographs. It showed a tall, erect figure with a full head of dark hair, standing on the waterfront near Fort Point, beneath the grand span of the Golden Gate Bridge, squinting into the sun. He had his arm around a tall, spindly boy of perhaps ten or eleven. Neither was smiling. The man was a younger Roberto Tonti. The boy wore faded shorts, a cheap T-shirt. His hair needed cutting, his face was frozen in an expression of fear and anger.

There was a hook on the back of the frame. He unlocked it and took out the print. It was sufficiently recent to have a printed date still faintly visible on the rear: *8-24-87.* Scribbled in thick, grey pencil, an adult hand had written a line Costa recognised …

Said the good Master: "Son, thou now beholdest
The souls of those whom anger overcame."

The *Inferno* … "Does Roberto Tonti have children?" he asked Teresa.

"Only married once. Without issue, as they say."

"That we know of, anyway," Peroni said, studying the photo. "That's a man and his son. Take it from me. They don't see each other much. They don't like each other much. But the same blood's there and they both know it. You can see it in their faces."

Costa thought he could make out some slight physical resemblance in the two narrow, lost faces.

"Scottie...Ferguson," Peroni went on. "Whoever lives here is Roberto Tonti junior, living and working under another name just a mile or so from his father. He must be thirty or more by now."

Catherine Bianchi was finally starting to punch the buttons on her phone. She looked up at them, excited, maybe a little anxious, too.

"Better not touch anything else, folks. I'll be collecting unemployment if they realise I had this guy under my nose all along and never even noticed."

Costa replaced the photograph. "No one would have noticed. That was the point. He was just one more extra in his father's scheme."

A player who, like the others, ceased to discern the line between what was real and what was invented. Everything in the apartment—the posters, the photos, the movies on the TV, the frantic scribbling on the walls—spoke of obsession. A compulsion that had prompted this man to take at least two false identities, one of them the name of Jimmy Stewart's character in an old movie in which his father had been a minor technician, to buy an old green Jaguar and lend it to an actress in the hope of…what?

He thought of the mythical Scottie dogging Madeleine through the San Francisco of five decades before, peering at her compulsively through the windshield of his car as his curiosity turned to an irresistible desire, until the moment she fell in the ocean and then woke naked beneath the sheets in a scene meant to take place in the bedroom of this very apartment.

Some memory tweaked an anxious nerve. In *Vertigo*, Scottie had watched the sleeping, naked Madeleine avidly from the sofa in the living room, through an open door. The real door was closed.

Costa opened it and stepped over the threshold. The room was almost pitch black. Just the barest fringe of light seeped through what must have been a large window opposite, one blocked by heavy opaque blinds.

He found the switch and flipped it. In his astonishment he was scarcely aware that the others had followed and stood behind him, stunned, too, into silence.

This was the bedroom from the movie, copied with a precise and compulsive eye for detail. There was the same set of bureaus by the door, four small framed paintings on the facing wall, a plaid chair in red and white and brown.

And the bed. A double bed with a high walnut veneer foot. The sheets and pillows were as crumpled as they had been when Madeleine Elster was woken from beneath them by a phone call, puzzled, but not entirely ashamed of her nakedness after being rescued by Scottie from the Bay. In his own mind Costa half believed he could smell the ocean at that moment, rising from the creased linen.

But it was the walls that worried him. They were covered in photographs. Not of Kim Novak or anything else from *Vertigo*. It was Maggie Flavier, everywhere, so altered in some that he barely recognised her until he found the courage to stare into the frozen eyes of the figure they depicted and see that same mixture of courage and fear and resignation he had recognised in her from the start.

Some were so old they must have predated her acting career. There was one in which she stood with a group of schoolgirls outside Grace Cathedral on Nob Hill, not far from her home. Maggie was immediately recognisable even though she couldn't have been more than thirteen. Just another child among many, prettier, more striking than the rest, with a woman behind her, pale, sick-looking, a hand on her shoulder.

Costa turned away and forced himself to look at other photos. Maggie as a bright-faced girl on a farm, as a poverty-stricken teenager, as a rich young lady in an English mansion. And then the new images. The adult woman: her beauty strangely marred, as she moved through a series of roles that, seen in this cruel, linear fashion, in this gloomy private shrine, only underscored her fall from the innocence of childhood into a fragile, haunted maturity. No longer smiling, but looking now into the camera with a hatred that was sometimes pure and vitriolic, her face stared back at them from the walls. And her body, too, in some of the more lurid shots, blown up to display every open pore, every inch of her skin, its minor imperfections, the faint, discernible penumbra of blonde hair rising above a posed, bare arm.

There was scarcely an inch of the room that wasn't covered with her presence in one way or another. The photographs spanned, as far as he could make out, almost two decades, from child to woman. Costa couldn't take it anymore. He turned away, trying to grasp the memory that lay just out of reach.

When he tried to call her, there was no answer. He phoned Sylvie Brewster, her agent.

"It's Nic," he said urgently. "Where's Maggie's appointment today? I need to know."

"You mean you didn't think to ask over breakfast?"

"Please..." he begged.

The woman put him on hold for a moment, then came back and told him. Costa knew already somehow, and what he'd do. There could be no more police standoffs. Because of the police, the actor Peter Jamieson had died outside the Cinema dei Piccoli. So, in a way he still didn't fully understand, had Tom Black.

The rest were still in the bedroom. He could hear

their quiet, low voices, Falcone's more prominent, more commanding.

Kelly's team from Bryant Street couldn't be more than a few minutes away.

Without saying a word Costa walked over to the desk, found Catherine Bianchi's bag, and took the keys to her Dodge. Quickly, silently, he walked through the open door and down the stairs.

The sun was brighter than ever. The builder was back at work. Costa slid into the driver's seat and worked the unfamiliar automatic vehicle out into the road. As the minivan wound round the side streets back to Chestnut and the long straight drive to the Marina, his hand reached over into the passenger side, found the glove compartment, flicked it open, and fumbled inside.

Gerald Kelly's gun was still there.

5

SHE WOKE BENEATH THE WRINKLED SHEETS OF AN uncomfortable old double bed pushed hard against the corner of a cramped office that smelled of damp and sweat. As she tried to clear the fumes of the drug from her nose and throat, choking and nauseated, Maggie Flavier felt at her own body automatically, fingers trembling, mind reeling. She ached. She felt … strange.

Then she opened her eyes, knowing what she'd see. John Ferguson, whoever he was, sat opposite, his arms leaning easily on a chair back, watching her squirm as she tried to force herself upright on the stiff mattress. It took one look at herself to confirm what she suspected. She was now wearing the strange green dress and nothing else. He must have stripped her while she was unconscious, then put on the old silk garment.

She tried to move but something stopped her and it hurt. Rough brown rope, the kind construction people used, gripped both her wrists. He'd tied her to the iron bed-head, loose enough to let her move a little, but not much. Not enough to get off the bed entirely.

He had an expression on his face that suggested he knew the panic that was running through her head, and a part of him liked it. But there was some uncertainty there, too.

"I told you it was a nice dress." He reached for a packet of cigarettes tucked into the sleeve of his T-shirt, took one out, the last one, lit it, scrunched up the pack, and threw it on the floor. The smoke rose into the blades of a rotating ceiling fan performing lazy turns above them.

"Who are you?" she asked. "Where the hell am I?"

"You had an engagement. Don't you remember?

Booze and boyfriends getting to the old grey cells now?"

"There'll be people here soon. Just let me go now and I'll forget this ever happened."

He closed his eyes for a moment as if he despaired of her.

"That's what I love about movie people. You're all so damned wrapped up in yourselves you never check stuff out, do you? Someone calls and says"—he put on a high-pitched girl's voice, like Shirley Temple on drugs—" 'Miss Flavier. Oh, *Miss Flavier*. We love you so much you just *got* to come open our little noir festival in some flea-pit movie theatre you wouldn't normally' "—the real voice came back—" '*deign* to set foot inside.' And you don't even think to check it out."

He flicked a finger at the face of his watch.

"Why I say, I say . . ." She recognised the new voice. It was a cartoon character, fake Southern gentleman Foghorn Leghorn. " . . . I *say*, boy . . . festival folk don't turn up till four in the afternoon. Till then ain't nobody here but us chickens."

He leaned forward. "I hope you enjoy my voices, Maggie. I've been working on them for a while. All my life, if I'm being candid."

She hitched herself up on the bed, knees together beneath the sheets, taking the rope as far as it could go before the harsh hemp began to bite into her skin, and said, "Your voices are very good."

"We have scarcely scratched the surface, dahling . . ." he groaned lasciviously.

She recognised this new look. It was one she'd known since she was a pretty little teenager. He was staring at her as if she were meat.

"Here's a question," he continued. "You wake up stark naked except for that dress and you realise some guy you don't even know put it on you. At least there *is* a dress. Not like Madeleine, huh? There she was all… *bare*… in Scottie's apartment… nice apartment by the way, play your cards right and one day maybe you get to see it. Well?"

"Well what?"

"Why didn't Madeleine scream? Some complete stranger takes her home, puts her in his bed, takes her clothes off…"

She didn't rise to the bait. This flustered him.

"I mean he must have *looked*, didn't he? Maybe more than just looked. How would you know? If you were out cold like that?" A pink flush briefly stained his cheeks. "How would you know… If… if… he'd d-d-done the *real thing*. All the way. You must know, right? You'd feel something. I guess."

She still didn't say anything.

"But what about if he just kind of… fiddled around?" He sniggered. "Got some touchy feely in there." He shook his head, laughing out loud now. "You ever think of that? Jimmy Stewart perving all over Kim Novak while she was out like a light and him all hot fingers, runny, runny…" He was licking his hands, slobbering all over them. "…runny… runny. And she never even knows."

He stiffened up on the chair and stopped laughing.

"Or does she?"

John Ferguson, which was, she now recalled, the real name of the character Jimmy Stewart played, leaned forward and screamed at her, *"Does she?"*

"They were actors. None of it was real."

His face, which had seemed so ordinary, wrinkled with hate and disgust.

"Now who's being naive, Miss Flavier? You of all people. Telling me a little of the story never makes its way into real life. Truly, I am *shocked*." It was a new voice, that of a doctor or a prim schoolteacher.

Beside the bed there was some kind of storage cabinet. On it stood film cans lined up like books next to a small office desk with a phone on it, a cheap chair, and not much else. A dusty window almost opaque with cobwebs. A door opposite that led ... she had no idea where. They had to be in the movie theatre. But even so, she could only picture one part of it in her head: the big white bell tower looming over Chestnut.

If she could just get to the door, fight him off long enough ...

"What do you want?" she asked.

He shook his head as if that was a way of changing something, whichever character possessed him.

The voice altered again.

"You talkin' to me? You talkin' to me? You talkin' to *me*? Then who the hell else are you talking ... you talking to *me*? Well, I'm the only one here. Who the fuck do you think you're talking to?"

Taxi Driver.

"I don't know who I'm talking to, but I don't think it's John Ferguson," she said quietly. "Or Travis Bickle."

His head went from side to side in that crazy fashion again. He blubbed his fingers against his lips and made a stupid, childlike noise.

"Yeah. That's the problem. *You don't know, Maggie.* And you should. Because knowing means you get to answer the conundrum."

"The conundrum?"

"You know. *The* conundrum."

She stared at him, baffled. He sighed as if she were a stupid child.

"The fuck-you-kill-you conundrum," he said, wearily.

Maggie Flavier's mind closed in on itself, refused to function.

"You do know what that is, don't you?" he said.

"Tell me," she said softly.

"Fuck you *then* kill you? Fuck you *or* kill you." He placed a finger on his lips, hamming a pensive pose. "Kill you *then* fuck you, even?" He giggled. "Though if I'm honest, the fuck-you part is a little moot. Let's face it: whatever way things work out, that's gonna happen."

He leaned forward, looked very sincere, and added, "I've been waiting a very long time for that, Maggie.

Keeping myself…pure. While you got banged by anything that grabbed your fancy."

There had to be a weapon somewhere. Or something she could use. A kitchen knife. A ballpoint pen. Anything she could stab him with when he came close.

"Who…" she asked, very slowly, "…are…you?"

"Like you want to know."

"I do."

"Really?"

"Really."

He shrugged, got up, walked over to the little desk, rudely swept away a pile of papers from the surface, and then scrabbled around until he found what he wanted. Then he came back, sat down again, eyed her once more. Maybe not quite so hungrily. Not quite.

"My name…my *real* name," he said quietly, "is"— the voice became liltingly Irish now—"Michael Fitzwilliam. 'Fitz' in the Gaelic sense, meaning bastard, *sans père* for you froggies, illegitimate, mongrel, wrong side of the blanket, born out of wedlock, or even love child, if you happen to be of a humorous or gullible disposition."

She found it hard to breathe. She was remembering something from a very long time ago.

"Sure and the name has jogged a little memory now, I'm thinking."

It was a terrible Irish accent and meant to be.

He had something in his hand. She didn't want to see it. But there was nowhere to run, and she felt hot and tired and weak beneath the old dress that was tight in the wrong places.

Michael Fitzwilliam—Mickey, hadn't they called him that?—threw a piece of fabric on the bed and she couldn't not look at it, couldn't take her eyes away.

Notre Dame des Victoires was on Pine Street, four blocks from the Brocklebank Apartments, though that wasn't why her mother chose the school. It was the only one in the city that offered daily classes in French conversation and writing.

She stared at the school badge, faded with age, pinched between his fingers. A white fleur-de-lis inside an oval shield with a red and blue crown at the centre. She thought of the name Mickey Fitzwilliam again. Now the memory had a face attached to it, that of a sad, lonely, unexceptional child, one who bragged constantly of his famous father yet always refused to name him.

"I'm so sorry," she whispered.

His head lolled around his shoulders, his eyes rolled in their sockets, a bad comic actor's "come again?" routine.

"Is that it? 'I'm so *sorry.*' Me, the poor little bastard you all laughed at, teased, and fucked with. No dad. No money. Just a drunk for a mom and a…"

She could hear it before he even spoke, rattling around her head from across the years.

"…a st-st-st-st-st-stutter…"

Mickey Fitzwilliam, who so wanted to be the same

as the rest of them and never could. She'd made sure of that.

"I'm sorry," she said again.

"You will be. You've got to be. *Really* sorry, Maggie. Not acting sorry. I know the difference. I had a director for an old man, and in between times when he was pretending I didn't exist, I got to watch him and learn. Got to know how he worked. Got to learn your *tricks* over the years. Can't fool Roberto Tonti's kid now, can you? Not some two-bit actress who got where she is by handing out a quick fuck on the casting couch to any wrinkled old producer who demanded one."

"That is not *true*!" she screamed.

He sat there, smiling, unmoved. "No. It's not true. So what *really* got you where you are, Maggie? Do you remember?"

She'd heard that question a million times, from a million different showbiz hacks.

"A little luck," she said automatically. "A little bit of talent."

Mickey Fitzwilliam gazed at her, then shook his head. "You've got to remember better than that, Maggie."

He reached down beneath the foot of the bed and his hands came back up with a knife in them. The blade was long and clean and shiny.

"It's what the fuck-you-kill-you conundrum hangs on."

6

I T WAS SATURDAY MORNING, SHOPPERS' HELL. THE
traffic started bad and got worse. He was still ten
minutes from the theatre when it finally ground to a
halt. Up ahead, through the snarl of cars, he heard
the wail of a siren and his heart fell. Then a couple of
very shiny red fire engines battled their way into the
angry mass of stalled machines blocking the breadth
of Chestnut. Costa pulled the Dodge over to the side
of the road and climbed out.

People were coming out of stores and offices to
stand in the street to gawk. There was a cop there, in
uniform, looking bored.

Costa caught his attention.

"Can you tell me what's going on?"

"Fire down at Fort Mason. Stupid contractors
lousing up or something. Or maybe the insurance.
That place always was bad news."

A fire. Not an emergency call to the little theatre
further down the road on Chestnut. Maybe he had
still had time.

"Is the street going to be blocked for long?"

The cop grimaced. "Sadly, my psychic powers just
fail me there, sir. You can't dump your vehicle like

that, by the way. You'll have to wait for this train wreck to clear just like everyone else."

He'd put on Gerald Kelly's leather shoulder holster. The black handgun sat snug against his chest. If this cop had been any good, he'd have seen it already.

"Thank you, Officer," Costa said meekly, and went back to sit behind the wheel of the Dodge.

When the stocky blue uniform crossed the road, wending his way through the choked cars and buses, he climbed out again, looked down the street, past the idle bystanders clustered on the sidewalk. In the distance, crowds of shoppers milled on the sidewalk outside the stores, wandering into the road, darting in between stalled cars the way Romans did in the Corso on a Saturday afternoon.

He took one look at them, saw the cop was returning, looking angrily at Catherine Bianchi's abandoned Dodge, and then began to move, falling into a steady pace as he wound through the growing throng of bodies, on into the Marina.

7

SHE DID REMEMBER. IT WAS ALL THERE. JUST HIDden, waiting to be let out into the light of day like an old poltergeist freed from the basement.

It must have been September. She could still feel the heat. Seventh-grade boys and girls, out on a trip to Crissy Field, doing the things schoolkids did. Working a little. Playing a little. Teasing…

Maggie Flavier could still picture herself on that bright distant morning, thin as a rake but tall for her age and with a look about her that turned men's heads. She tried not to notice. She felt alone and a little unhappy in San Francisco. This was her mother's idea, not hers. To flee Paris and an estranged father, to try to find some new life halfway across the world in a city where they knew no one, and had, as far as the young Maggie could see, no clear idea of what the future might bring.

She'd danced at the stage school in France, and men looked then. Her mother had watched and taken note.

They were so kind in the church school on Pine Street. They smiled a lot and listened to her. They didn't mind she hated trigonometry and algebra and preferred to dress up and play on the stage instead, always inventing something, stories, characters, voices, situations, imaginary people she created to fill the void inside.

These small and seemingly useless talents mattered, her mother told her. Because of the *auditions*. She spoke the word as if it possessed some magical power. As if it could save them. The young Maggie had no idea how. All she understood was that she possessed a burning, unquenchable need to be noticed, to be applauded. By her peers. By her mother, more than anything.

The notes had been coming for weeks, always unsigned, always written in a crude childish hand on cheap school notebook paper. They were, young Maggie thought, beautiful in a simple, babyish way. Flowery language. Sometimes bad French. Sometimes, she thought, better Italian, which she recognised from lessons in Paris. They were never coarse or dirty, like some she'd received, and some the other girls sent from time to time. All they spoke of, carefully, indirectly, was love. As if there were an emotion somewhere waiting for her to discover it, like a hidden Easter egg, a secret buried in the ground. Something ethereal, something holy, distinct from the hard, cold physical reality of the life she knew. She didn't really understand the words or the poetry, some of it so old she found the verses unreadable. So she threw them away mostly, until the last.

Had this unseen admirer written, simply, *Margot Flavier, je t'aime, je t'aime, je t'aime,* then, perhaps, she would have tried to understand. But nothing was that clear and sometimes the language was so florid, so odd, she thought it was a joke. Sometimes it scared her a little. She was young, she was exiled in a foreign land, with a strange and unhappy mother who wished to push her into a career about which she felt unsure, not that her doubts mattered for one moment.

Naturally, she told the girls. Barbara Ronson.

Louise Gostelow. Susan Shanks. The trio who ran the class.

Naturally, when the final note arrived, they had an idea.

That last message came the day after she'd gone to the first successful audition of her life, taking time off school for the short flight to L.A. with her mother, spending hours reading the scripts, trying to make her fast-improving English bad again for a group of men and women who seemed to demand that. Afterwards, when they waited at LAX for the flight home, her mother had made a call on a public phone. When she returned, her face glowed with a happiness Maggie had never seen there before. Maggie had the part. Françoise in *L'Amour L.A.* A life mapped out in a single day, not that she knew that then, not that she felt anything much at all, except pleasure that this had produced joy in her mother.

Maggie had been surprised. She thought she'd fluffed her lines and failed the audition.

The next morning, she came into school and found the note tucked into the seam of her locker. It read, *Tomorrow at Crissy Field I will reveal my love.*

Barbara and Louise and Susan had gawped at the scrawled, nervous handwriting, giggling, and then concocted the plan.

Out on the hot, dusty sand dunes of the Marina the following day, they'd played it out. While the rest of them walked with Miss Piper, making notes about the grass and the lizards and the birds, Maggie had detached herself, looking distracted, knowing full well what would happen.

Finally the teacher headed for the public washrooms, ordering them to wait. Maggie walked to one of the small huts owned by the park service and stood in its shadow, out of the burning sun. It took only a minute. Then he was there, staring at her, his plain face getting redder and redder, voice tripping over itself, his eyes, which were not unattractive, skittering over the pale, drifting sand, avoiding hers.

"Maggie…"

At that moment she didn't even remember his name. He was just *that boy*. The one with the stutter and the cheap clothes, the one whose father was something big and famous, not that anyone was allowed to know his name.

"Oui?" she'd asked.

He bowed his head, held out his hands, and tried to speak.

All that came out was "I lu…lu…lu…lu…"

It happened so swiftly she didn't have a chance to intervene, even if she'd possessed the courage. The three girls burst out from their hiding place and formed a ring round him, hands locked, eyes wild with glee, chanting, mocking.

Strapped to an old, hard bed in some place she thought was a shuttered movie theatre in the Marina, the adult Maggie Flavier could still hear that heartless song, see them dancing round him, a jeering circle of coarse, hard cruelty, eyes wild, voices cackling, taunting, chanting rhythmically...

I lu...lu...lu...lu...

I lu...lu...lu...lu...

I lu...lu...lu...lu...

She could see the way he'd stared at her, see how his bewildered eyes filled with tears.

Then the boy ducked beneath their arms and she'd watched, heart beating wildly in her chest, as he tore away down the beach towards Fort Mason, shrieking with shame and fury until his cries mingled with those of the gulls that hung in the sea air as if pinned to the too-blue sky.

She didn't speak much to Barbara and Louise and Susan afterwards. She blamed herself for showing them the letter in the first place. She wished, more than anything, to apologise to the boy. But it was impossible. Mickey Fitzwilliam never came to school again. He had no friends, and the teachers, when she asked, refused to tell her where he lived. For a while he was a burden on her conscience. Then other things intervened. Trips to L.A. to the TV studios. Work. A career. Her mother's growing frailty.

From that point to now...

She tried to imagine the distance, the journey, and couldn't. Not for herself. Certainly not for Mickey Fitzwilliam.

8

"I LU...LU...LU...LOVED YOU," HE STUTTERED, clutching the old school badge.

"We were thirteen. We were just children."

"I loved you!" he roared.

She couldn't think of anything to say.

"Did you never ask yourself why it was *that* day? Why then?"

"I was a child. I didn't ask myself anything."

"He was the p-p-producer. Roberto. My dad." The head was shaking again but there was only one voice left now, a young, frail one that sounded hurt and damaged. "He gave us money. He came by from time to time. Didn't want to see me. He just wanted my mom. That's all."

"I don't understand..."

"He wanted to give me something. To ease his conscience. So I told him about you. About how you danced and acted and sang. About how beautiful you were. How your mom wanted to get you into show business. Everyone knew that. I got him to give you the audition. I begged him to give you that part. That was me."

"Thank you," she said simply.

"You were good, even then. Everyone wanted to look at you. They couldn't stop."

She whispered, " 'But 'oo can blame Françoise?' "

"Don't play those games with me," he snarled. "I saw you. On the TV. Going around town. You never even noticed me. I *watched* you." He stared hungrily at her. "I watched you change. All those nice parts in the beginning. The good girl. Sweet dreams and apple pie. Then... That first time you... t-t-took off your clothes."

"Mickey..."

"Do you know what that did to me? Do you even care?"

She shook her head and said, "I did not know you then. I do not know you now. If I had..."

"While you were banging half of Hollywood, I was there. Didn't touch another human being. Not once. Waiting."

"Mickey, please..."

"I stood outside the TV studio all night long sometimes. I knew what was going on inside. None of those bastards loved you. Not your actors and your rich guys and your pimps. Not some stupid Italian cop..."

"Stop this now!"

"I watched you every day of your life. On the screen. In the papers. On the Net. I was right there next to you in a store, an elevator, at the movies. You never noticed, did you? Never had a clue what you owed me. Why the hell do you think Roberto cast you for *Inferno* in the first place, huh? Some washed-up has-been dodging in and out of rehab so fast even the papers had given up on you? Why'd he pick *you* of all people?"

"Because I can do my job," she insisted, mainly to herself.

"So can a million other pretty women, all of them younger than you. I asked him. I *begged* him. One more favour for the bastard son. Keep him quiet. Ease an awkward little situation. Got to say that about my old man. He still has a Catholic sense of guilt somewhere, even when he's murdering people. You know when he came along and wanted someone else removed from that sweet scam of his, to keep up the coverage in the papers?"

She didn't want to listen to this. She didn't want to think about it.

"I screwed it up on purpose. I sent out Martin to get that almond stuff knowing you had that hypo-dermic handy."

"I could have died."

"If I'd wanted it, you would have. Don't you *see*?"

It was the last thing she needed, but the tears were beginning to prick in her eyes. "In God's name… what is it you expect me to do?"

"Fuck-you-kill-you…" he whispered. "Lu-lu-love you. I waited so long for this. Twenty years. I didn't want you to hate me. I *made* you, Maggie. I *rescued* you. I still can. There's just the three of us left now. Me, you, and my old man—and he won't be around much longer. Millions and millions and millions of dollars. It could last a whole lifetime. For the two of us."

"What are you talking about?" she asked, exasperated. "I don't understand..."

"*The scam,* dummy. The one that jerk Harvey wrote you into when you were too bombed to notice. Once my old man's dead, there's a place in the Caribbean we can fly, walk in a bank, pick up the whole bundle, everything that was meant to go to him, to Harvey, Martin, those Lukatmi losers... It's all ours, Maggie. No more work. No more worry. You don't need to go down on some jerk in a director's chair. I don't have to slave away in construction until my old man calls and tells me to go do his dirty work. Everything will end perfectly. Don't you see?"

He didn't stutter when he felt confident. He didn't even look terribly threatening.

"Talk to me some more," she said. "Come closer."

Mickey Fitzwilliam laughed nervously, then patted down the sheets at the foot of the bed. He sat down, very stiff, very nervous.

"See, Roberto said this whole thing was really all for me in the end. The money. The tontine. All I needed was to cut the numbers a little."

He snickered like a child and looked, briefly, proud of himself. "Well, a lot actually. Josh and Martin... that was pure improv. They came by my place bleating about how it was all going wrong... how *scared* they were. Pissed me off. Next day I just sent Josh a stack of letters demanding money and made it look like they came from Martin. Easiest thing in the world. Morons. They thought I was there to, like, mediate. You believe that? Then that idiot Tom Black calls me when he's on the run."

Another voice, high-pitched. Terrified.

"'Scottie, Scottie, ya got to help me. Like you promised...'"

A dark, malevolent gleam flashed in his eyes.

"I hate dumb people. Told my old man afterwards. Know what the great Roberto Tonti said? That I got lucky. That I oughta shut up. He'd take care of it. See me right. Call that luck? Does anyone get that lucky?"

"I'd call it fate."

He smiled. "Me too. This was *meant* to be, Maggie."

He scanned the room as if he was looking at something he despised.

"Roberto gave me this theatre. My inheritance. Bullshit. He couldn't make any money out of this dump. All these things...they were supposed to be his way of saying sorry. I'm not stupid. It was always about him. That scam was...his pièce de résistance. His big moment. Going out in a big blaze of glory. Look at me, Ma! Top of the world! All those years behind the camera. All those years watching actors get the applause. It ate him alive..."

"I saw that."

"You did?"

"It was obvious. Tell me more."

He inched a little closer and looked at her left leg, bare, half askew on the bed.

"I never touched a woman before. Not till today. When you were sleeping."

Maggie Flavier gave him a stern look. "That's not nice. Touching a woman when she doesn't know."

"I'm sorry. I just..." He shook his head. "I couldn't stop looking at that movie after my dad gave it to me back when I was a kid. *Vertigo*. It was the first piece of work he did in America, you know. I watched it right away, to please him. Said it was his movie, too, in a way. Then I saw you and you lived in the same place. It was like..."

He ran his tongue over his lips as if they were dry. "I'd watch it every day. Twice, three times sometimes. Got it in French and Italian, too. I could sit here and tell you every second, read you every line."

He gazed at her, frankly, greedily. "After a little while it was you I saw, not some dumb old actress no one's ever heard of. You in that car. In that dress." He blushed again, looked younger. "In bed, in that apartment. *My* apartment. Bought it with my own money. Robbed a bank in Reno. Self-made man. Wasn't taking everything from Roberto. I got my dignity." He squeezed his eyes shut. "That movie... it kind of got inside me."

"They do sometimes."

He edged closer still and, as she watched, gingerly put his hand on her knee, looking all the time, anxious for her approval. His fingers closed on her skin, squeezing, as if she were some kind of lab specimen.

"Not hard," she told him. "That's not nice." She held up her arms, with the rope dangling from the wrists. "*This* isn't nice."

She leaned forward as if to kiss him. The rope was just short enough to stop her. She moved back into place with a sigh.

"A woman can't make love tied to a bed. Not a good woman. That's what hookers do. Dirty women. I don't want to be a dirty woman. I won't do that. Not for anyone."

"I-I-I d-don't want that, Maggie. I *never* wanted that. All that fuck-you-kill-you stuff. Jesus…All I wanted was to be with you. Like we should have been from the beginning. Now we've got the money, we can…"

His words drifted into the nothingness of acute embarrassment.

"We can what, Mickey? Tell me. Please."

"We can be like normal people. A couple. We can live where we want. Paris, maybe. On a desert island. Or a farm in the country with a-a-animals…" He squeezed his eyes shut and blushed. "Kids maybe. All in good time. We don't have to do it right now. I don't expect that. I just…sometimes. Sheesh. Sometimes I'm not *me*."

He took his hand off her knee, then mumbled, "We don't even have to do *it* till after we're married.

I'd like that. It would be the right thing. In the circumstances."

"In the circumstances..." she echoed, cursing herself for letting a little of her fury show, glad he didn't notice. "I can't kiss you if my hands are tied, Michael. Can I call you Michael? Is that OK?"

"If you like."

He looked at her, mouth open, a little idiotic. Then he went back to the chair, scrabbled on the floor, came back with the knife, and sat next to her on the bed.

"The reason I never messed with girls is my old man told me. They screw with you. They fuck your head. They gobble up your whole life, until one day there's nothing left."

"Some girls. Not all." She held out her hands. "It depends how you treat them."

"Yeah."

He reached over and sawed through the loop of rope on her left wrist, then her right.

"I didn't tie them tight, you know. I didn't want to hurt you. Not ever."

"I realise that."

She took his right hand, the one with the blade, slipped forward, angled her body against his, heard his breathing catch, turn short and excited.

"Are you going to hold a knife even when you kiss me, Michael?" she crooned.

"Oh..."

He looked at the thing, shamefaced, then released

it. She heard it clatter on the floor, and then, before he could even look at her again, Maggie Flavier was on her feet, trying desperately to remember some of the things she'd learned in the few self-defence classes she'd taken a couple of years before.

But her mind was a blank, so she did what came naturally. She jerked back her arm and elbowed him so hard in the face that the blow sent something electric running up and down her funny bone, and she screamed.

Mickey Fitzwilliam crumpled, clutching at his nose. Blood leaked out between his fingers. He was moaning and whimpering like a child.

She didn't wait. She ran to the door, jerked on the handle. The door didn't budge. There was an old-fashioned key in the lock. In her mind's eye she was already rushing outside, into the bright, safe world, screaming at the top of her lungs for all her life was worth.

The trouble was the key wouldn't turn.

He was curled on the floor near the bed, snarling at her, a different Mickey again, the one who'd been there when she regained consciousness. The one who snatched her, stripped her, put her inside someone else's old dress, dreaming, dreaming, dreaming.

He didn't care that snot and blood were pouring down over his lips, dripping off his chin.

"Guess that solves our conundrum," he said in a nasal slur.

9

H E WAS STAGGERING TO HIS FEET, STUMBLING toward a glass cabinet on the wall. It was marked *In Case of Fire* and contained an axe, set diagonally against black fabric, like some kind of museum exhibit.

Mickey Fitzwilliam smashed his fist through the glass. Blood shot out from his fingers as the pane shattered. He didn't seem to notice.

Praying to any god who might save her, Maggie scrabbled at the key. It finally turned. The door opened and she dashed through. It was pitch dark. Her hand flailed against the wall, her fingers somehow found a switch. A dazzling light burst on her from a single bulb that dangled from a wire not more than a hand's width from her face, momentarily blinding her.

Escape had taken her into a small, square room entirely without windows or furniture, nothing but plain whitewashed brick. A rickety-looking wooden staircase rose against the white, dusty wall opposite. A dark corridor led off to the right, maybe to nowhere.

A picture came into her mind's eye, one kept there

from the times she'd driven down Chestnut on the way to the shops or Roberto Tonti's grand mansion opposite the Palace of Fine Arts.

She knew where she was instantly. Inside the fake bell tower of the Marina Odeon, the one pretending to be the *campanario* of San Juan Bautista.

Breathless, trying to think straight, she ripped the key out of the lock and slammed the old wooden door shut, enclosing herself in the tiny room. Hand shaking, fingers fumbling, she got the key into the lock on her side of the door and managed to turn it. She pressed her cheek to the edge of the door frame and whispered, "Michael, Michael..."

There was no reply.

"You're sick," she said deliberately. "Let me help you."

Was she serious? Was she acting? She'd no idea.

"I can help. There are doctors..."

Silence. She tried to catch her breath. She looked up the narrow wooden staircase winding up the interior of the fake bell tower.

Face against the wood, trying to sound calm and in control, she said, "Talk to me, Michael. Please..."

The axe blade crashed through the flimsy old timber, inches from her face. She shrieked. The sharp, gleaming metal withdrew, and he began battering again, repeatedly, maniacally, tearing a ragged hole through the panel, sending splinters and dust everywhere.

She retreated to the other side of the tiny chamber,

staring at the growing breach he was tearing in the last barrier of defence she possessed. The world was closing in on her and it was one that seemed to be composed entirely of clips from movies, half-remembered lines of dialogue, flashes of recognition that veered between fact and fiction.

The next thing she knew, she was stumbling down the dark little corridor, praying there might be some way out at its end. She had plunged into darkness. Her fingers crawled along the damp plaster, seeking a switch. Finally they found one; she flipped it and felt a raw, painful scream leap into her throat.

Ahead of her was a naked man. One part of her panicking mind could recognise and name him, although he looked so different, so altered. Dino Bonetti was trapped upright in some kind of tall glass cabinet, the kind they had in restaurants for desserts and ice cream. The producer was still alive, barely, moving a little, mumbling wordlessly. At his feet was a round paper object the size and shape of a football. It seemed to be spewing a constant stream of yellow and black shapes that flew in and out, only to find themselves cornered in the cabinet alongside Bonetti. A cloud of furious wasps buzzed around him, crawling across his florid, swollen face as if feeding, pulsing thick, like a living carpet, on his chest.

His fist banged weakly on the padlocked glass. He could see her, just. There was a putrid, vile smell leaking from somewhere. She edged back, towards the foot of the tower.

As she stumbled against the door joist, there was a brutal, vicious crack. Mickey Fitzwilliam was through, his face a rictus of amused savagery, so close she could feel the spittle from his mouth fall like hot rain on her skin as he leered crazily through the gap.

There was nowhere else to go. She stumbled towards the staircase, knowing somehow what role he would choose next: Jack Nicholson in *The Shining*, a performance twice removed, an actor mimicking something else from the real-unreal world of show business.

"'Here's J-J-Johnny!'" Mickey Fitzwilliam screamed.

10

AT THE END OF HIS LONG RUN TO THE MOVIE theatre, Costa found the front door locked and not a light on anywhere. He opened a low wooden gate and worked his way to the back of the building.

There was no obvious entry point at ground level, only rough plaster walls and the white tower rising three storeys or more into a cloudless sky. Close by—this he hardly dared look at—stood an old cemetery headstone over a grave marked out by pansies and daisies. A grey urn was positioned before it, filled with red roses. A green sash was wrapped around the stems.

Out of breath, lost for a way inside, he heard a scream, then another.

Then he heard Maggie's voice. A man's name, over and over again.

Michael, Michael, Michael . . .

He knew in an instant where she was: behind the fake adobe wall, just a few short steps away, trapped with the man who'd covered the walls of his bedroom with two decades of her portraits.

Next to the base of the tower was a small window so grubby and littered with cobwebs it was opaque. He searched the trash-filled backyard until he came across an old, discarded sink, hefted it in his arms, stumbled through the rusting junk back to the building, then, with a desperate lurch, threw the thing through the glass. It landed on the far side with a muffled crash. Picking up some rusty piping, Costa roughed out a gap through the shards of glass remaining, wrapped his fingers in a handkerchief, reached inside and pulled himself through. He found himself spread-eagled across an old office desk, reached ahead, gripped the edge of the wood, and dragged himself forward until he was mostly free of the spikes and scattered glass.

There was a bed in there, the sickly sweet smell of sweat, and a misshapen red puddle on the grimy floor.

Some second sense made him turn. A man stood

in a doorway at what appeared to be the foot of the stairs of the tower. He had a bloodied face and hands and wore an expression of surprise and contempt.

His right arm held a long, fireman's axe, which, as Costa scrambled from the desk, began to fly, turning, turning, turning, towards him through the air.

Costa found himself dropping like a sack onto the hard concrete floor. Bells chimed, pain flooded into his temples. Maggie was there, somewhere beyond his assailant, screaming. He'd landed on his right shoulder, which hurt like hell. Maybe something was broken. After a brief, sickening moment of blackness, Costa found himself amidst a sea of shattered glass trying weakly to recover the gun from Gerald Kelly's leather holster inside his jacket. He rolled and came face-to-face with the axe. The blade had driven itself deep into the wood less than an arm's length away from his head. The fall, painful as it was, had saved him.

When he got half upright, onto a single knee, gun in hand, with a clear view back towards the tower, he was alone.

Costa staggered towards the tower, his head throbbing, his body convulsed in a single painful ache.

"Police!" he bellowed, stumbling through with the kind of unguarded, careless bravado that would have got him screamed at in the state police academy in Flaminio. *"Police!"*

Laughter drifted unseen down the rickety staircase.

Maggie cried in an echoing scream, "What do you *want*?"

There was a noise to one side, down a gloomy corridor, a sound like someone rapping on glass. Costa glanced that way automatically, seeking its source. What he saw sent his mind reeling. At the end of the narrow passage, illuminated by a single swinging bulb, stood an upright glass cabinet. Inside, a naked man was banging weakly against the glass door. Around the trapped man's bloated, livid body swarmed a thick, angry cloud of buzzing insects.

"No time," Costa murmured, and pointed the gun at the cabinet. He heard a thin frightened screech from the figure locked inside, then saw him fall, shrieking, arms clasped around his head, to the cabinet floor.

Costa fired twice. The cabinet exploded. Glass, wasps, and finally the bloodied, torn husk of a human being tumbled outwards, into the hot, fetid air.

Costa couldn't wait to see any more. Maggie had gone ominously silent. Trying to take the stairs two steps at a time, he stumbled and fell, splinters tearing at his fingers, the pain ricocheting through his shoulder. The gun slipped rattling from his grasp. Back at the bottom again, he recovered the weapon and scrabbled up the staircase.

"*What do I want?*"

Not Maggie's voice. A man's voice this time.

Costa staggered ever upward, round and round the twisting corners of the staircase, until, panting, exhausted, he reached some bright, sunny platform, clinging onto the banister for support, aware that, once again, he wasn't alone.

Maggie crouched in the far corner, clad in an old-fashioned dress the colour of an emerald. Above her stood the bloodied man, a knife in his hand, his face twisted with pain and fury.

"Put down the knife," Costa snarled. "Stand away from her. Do as I say and no one will get hurt."

The man across the room didn't even seem to hear him.

"What do I *want*?" he asked again. "To be happy, Maggie. Is that so freaking much, huh?"

The blade was high over her, frozen, gleaming. A spiralling swarm of wasps rising from below was beginning to work its way into the room.

"You're sick, Michael. I'm sorry, so sorry. Please, please, listen to me…" She was weeping, choking, and there was more than fear in her voice, Costa thought; there was regret there, some kind of recrimination and self-hate. "Let me help. Let me help you…"

Costa snatched a frenzied glance around him. Ahead was a single arch the height of the room, open to the blue sky, with a ledge outside so narrow only a bird could stand on it.

"How can you possibly help me?" the man with the knife demanded.

Maggie, crouched in the grime on the floor, knees bunched before her, arms around them, was a tight, terrified ball of misery.

"I'll do whatever's needed," she said in a low, weak voice. "Whatever..."

Costa raised his gun. He aimed straight through the shaft of bright sun that separated them. A cloud of yellow and black insects danced in the dusty golden air.

"Move away from her," he ordered. "Do as I say."

"He's sick..." Maggie whispered. "Please, Nic, can't you see he's..."

A voice came into Costa's head, and it was Emily's, repeating the words she'd uttered moments before his hesitation ended her life by the side of a crumbling monument that stank of cats and the homeless, a rank, pungent stink that would never leave him.

"Don't beg," he said, so quietly he knew this was for himself, not her. "Never beg. It's the worst thing you can do. The worst..."

The knife didn't move. The weapon in Costa's grip didn't waver, not even when something small and dry crawled across his extended hand, paused, and thrust its sting into the soft, taut flesh between his index finger and thumb as he gripped the gun.

A hot, sharp spike of pain that he barely noticed.

The man ahead moved, just a fraction, turning to

look at Costa, something new, a look of doubt maybe, in his eyes. Another vicious yellow and black creature crawled across Costa's forehead, stabbed its poison into him, got crushed in an instant as he swept its carapace into his skin with the back of his hand.

"You know…" The voice didn't match the tortured face of the figure with the knife. It was anonymous, anybody's, nobody's. It drifted dreamily around the bell tower. "I was thinking…"

Costa's first bullet struck him in the left arm, near the elbow. The shattered limb jerked like that of a rag doll. The jumping man screamed. So did Maggie Flavier.

The second shot flung his body hard against the rotting wall and, for a moment, Costa didn't know where he'd hit him. So he kept on firing, jerking on the sweaty trigger constantly, desperate to empty the weapon into this husk of a man as the pained shape jerked and shrieked across the room until he came to block the searing California sun at the long bright archway, still upright, just, still holding the knife.

"He's *sick*…" Maggie screeched through her hands, beseeching someone, him, the wounded man.

Costa scarcely heard her. All he heard at that moment was his dead wife's voice and the buzzing of a million tiny wings.

"Drop the knife."

It was spoken quietly, calmly, and he didn't wait for a reaction.

He pointed the gun across the room, dead straight,

hand steady, and pulled the trigger. The shot caught the man who called himself John Ferguson in one life, and Carlotta Valdes in another, full in the chest. The impact blew him out of the tower, backwards into the unforgiving brilliance of the day.

The room went quiet. He could hear her weeping and knew, in a sudden revelatory instant, there would never be anything he could say to heal the hurt.

Costa crossed the room. He walked out onto the narrow ledge three storeys above the tiny garden that sat among the junk and debris in the shadow of the bell tower of the Marina Odeon.

Heights didn't scare him. Nothing scared him much anymore. Only the big unknowable things, life and closeness and the fragile bond of family. He stood in the high open arch of the counterfeit *campanario* of an imaginary Spanish mission house and peered down over the dizzying, exposed edge.

Below, on the bright grass, next to a shattered grey urn strewn with scarlet roses, a broken body lay exposed before the headstone of Carlotta Valdes, like a corpse that had worked its way out of the grave below.

If you liked

The Dante Killings

Read on for an exciting look at
David Hewson's riveting new thriller

City
of Fear

Coming from Delacorte in May of 2010

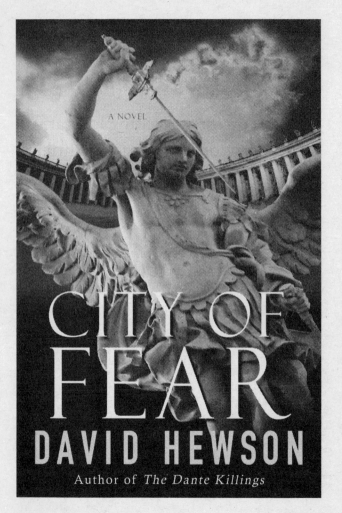

A NOVEL

CITY OF FEAR

DAVID HEWSON

Author of *The Dante Killings*

CITY OF FEAR
On sale May 2010

1

THE GARDEN OF THE QUIRINALE FELT LIKE a sun trap as the man in the silver armor strode down the shingle path. He was sweating profusely inside the ceremonial breastplate and woolen uniform.

Tight in his right hand he held the long, bloodied sword that had just taken the life of a man. In a few moments he would kill the president of Italy. And then? Be murdered himself. It was the fate of assassins throughout the ages, from Pausanius of Orestis, who had slaughtered Philip, the father of Alexander the Great, to Marat's murderess, Charlotte Corday, and Kennedy's nemesis, Lee Harvey Oswald.

The stabbing dagger, the sniper's rifle . . . all these were mirrored weapons, reflecting the man or woman who bore them, joining perpetrator and victim as twin sacrifices to destiny. It had always been this way, since men sought to rule over others, circumscribing their desires, hemming in the spans of their lives with the dull, rote strictures of convention. Petrakis had read much over the years, thinking, preparing, comparing himself to his peers. Actor John Wilkes Booth's final performance before he put a bullet through the skull of Abraham Lincoln had been in *Julius Caesar,* although through some strange irony he had taken the part of Caesar's friend and apologist, Mark Antony, not Brutus as history demanded.

As he approached the figure in the bower, seeing the old man's gray, lined form bent deep over a book, Petrakis found himself murmuring a line Booth must have uttered a century and a half before.

"'O mighty Caesar . . . dost thou lie so low? Are all thy conquests, glories, triumphs, spoils, shrunk to this little measure?'"

A pale, long face, with sad, tired eyes, looked up from the page. Petrakis, realizing he had spoken out loud, wondered why this death, among so many, would be the most difficult.

"I didn't quite catch that," Dario Sordi said in a calm, unwavering voice, his eyes, nevertheless, on the long, bloodied blade.

The uniformed officer came close, stopped, repeated the line, and held the sword over the elderly figure seated in the shadow of a statue of Hermes.

The president glanced around him and asked, "What conquests in particular, Andrea? What glories?

What spoils? Temporary residence in a garden fit for a pope? I'm a pensioner in a very luxurious retirement home. Do you really not understand that?"

The weapon trembled in Petrakis's hand. His palm felt sweaty. He couldn't speak.

Voices rose behind him. A shout. A clamor.

There was a cigarette in Dario Sordi's hands. It didn't even shake.

"You should be afraid, old man."

More dry laughter. "I've been hunted by Nazis." The gray, drawn face glowered at him. Sordi drew on the cigarette and exhaled a cloud of smoke. "Played hide-and-seek with tobacco and the grape for more than half a century. Offended people—important people—who feel I am owed a lesson. Which is probably true." A long, pale finger jabbed the evening air. "And now you wish me to cower before someone else's puppet? A tool?"

That, at least, made it easier.

Petrakis found his mind ranging across so many things: memories, lost decades, languid days dodging NATO patrols beneath the Afghan sun, distant, half-recalled moments in the damp darkness of an Etruscan tomb, talking to his father about life and the world, and how a man had to make his own way, not let another create a future for him.

Everything came from that place in the Maremma, from the whispered discovery of a paradise of the will sacrificed to the commonplace and mundane, the exigencies of politics. Andrea Petrakis knew this course was set for him at an early age, by birth, by his inheritance.

The memory of the tomb, with its ghostly painted figures on the wall, and the terrible, eternal specter of the Blue Demon, consuming them one by one, filled his head. This, more than anything else, he had learned over the decades: Freedom, of the kind enjoyed by the long-dead men and women still dancing beneath the gray Tarquinia earth more than two millennia on, was a mayfly, gloriously fleeting, made real only by its impermanence. Life and death were bedfellows, two sides of the same coin. To taste every breath, feel each beat of the heart, one had to know that both might be snatched away in an instant. His father had taught him that, long before the Afghans and the Arabs tried to reveal the same truth.

Andrea Petrakis remembered the lesson more keenly now, as the sand trickled through some unseen hourglass for Dario Sordi and his allotted assassin.

Out of the soft evening came a bright, sharp sound, like the ping of some taut yet invisible wire, snapping under pressure.

A piece of the statue of Hermes, its stone right foot, disintegrated in front of his eyes, shattering into pieces, as if exploding in anger.

Dario Sordi ducked back into the shadows, trying, at last, to hide.

2

Three days earlier . . .

"BEHOLD," SAID THE MAN, IN A COLD, TIRED voice, the accent from the countryside perhaps. "I will make a covenant. For it is something dreadful I will do to you."

Strong, firm hands ripped off the hood. Giovanni Batisti saw he was tethered to a plain office chair. At the periphery of his vision, he could make out that he was in a small, simple room with bare bleached floorboards and dust ghosts on the walls left by longremoved chests of drawers or ancient filing cabinets. The place smelled musty, damp, and abandoned. He could hear the distant lowing of traffic, muffled in some curious way, but still energized by the familiar rhythm of the city. Cars and trucks, buses and people, thousands of them, some from the police and the security services no doubt, searching as best they could, oblivious to his presence. There was no human sound close by, from an adjoining room or an apartment. Not a radio or a TV set. No voice save that of his captor.

"I would like to use the bathroom, please," Batisti said quietly, keeping his eyes fixed on the stripped, cracked timber boards at his feet. "I will do as you say. You have my word."

The silence, hours of it, had been the worst part. He'd expected a reprimand, might even have welcomed a beating, since all these things would have acknowledged his existence. Instead . . . he was left in limbo, in blindness, almost as if he were dead already. Nor was there any exchange he could hear between those involved. A brief meeting to discuss tactics. News. Perhaps a phone call in which he would be asked to confirm that he was still alive.

Even—and this was a forlorn hope, he knew—some small note of concern about his driver, Elena Majewska, everyone's favorite, shot in the chest as the two vehicles blocked his government car in the narrow street of Via delle Quattro Fontane, at the junction with the road to the Quirinale. It was such a familiar Roman crossroads, next to Borromini's fluid baroque masterpiece of San Carlino, a church he loved deeply and would visit often if he had time during his lunch break from the Interior Ministry building around the corner.

They could have snatched him that day from beneath Borromini's dome, with its magnificent dove of peace, descending to earth from Heaven. He'd needed a desperate fifteen-minute respite from sessions with the Americans, the Russians, the British, the Germans. . . . Eight nations, eight voices, each different, each seeking its own outcome. The phrase that was always used about the G8—the "industrialized nations"—struck him as somewhat ironic as he listened to the endless bickering about diplomatic rights and protocols, about who should stand where and with whom. Had some interloper approached him during his brief recess that day, Batisti would have glanced at Borromini's extraordinary interior one last time, then walked into his captor's arms immediately. Anything but another session devoted to the rites and procedures of diplomatic life.

Then he remembered again, with a sudden, painful seizure of guilt, the driver. Did Elena—a young, pretty single mother who'd moved to Rome from Poland to find security and a better new life—survive? If so, what could she tell the police? What was there to say about a swift and unexpected explosion of violence in the black sultry velvet of a Roman summer night? The attack had happened so quickly and with such brutish force that Batisti was still unsure how many men had been involved. Perhaps no more than three or four, to judge from the pair of vehicles blocking the way. The area was empty. He was without a bodyguard. An opposition politician drafted into the organization team was deemed not to need a bodyguard, even in the heightened security that preceded the upcoming summit. Not a single sentence was spoken as they dragged him from the rear seat, wrapped a blindfold tightly round his head, fired—three, four times?—into the front, then bundled him into the trunk of some large vehicle and drove a short distance to their destination.

Were they now issuing ransom demands? Did his wife, who was with her family in Milan, discussing a forthcoming family wedding, know what was happening?

There were no answers, only questions. Giovanni Batisti was forty-eight years old and felt as if he'd stepped back into a past that Italy hoped was behind it. The dismal seventies and eighties, the "Years of Lead." A time when academics and lawyers and politicians were routinely kidnapped by the shadowy criminals of the Red Brigades and their partners in terrorism, held for ransom, tortured, then left bloodied and broken as some futile lesson to those in authority. Or dead. Like Aldo Moro, the former prime minister, seized in 1978, held captive for fifty-six days before being shot ten times in the chest and dumped in the trunk of a car in the Via Caetani.

"Look at me," a voice from ahead of him ordered.

Batisti closed his eyes, kept them tightly shut. "I do not wish to compromise you, sir. I have a wife. Two sons. One is eight. One is ten. I love them. I wish you no harm. I wish no one any harm. These matters can and will be resolved through dialogue, one way or another. I believe that of everything. In this world, I have to." He found his mouth was dry, his lips felt painful as he licked them. "If you know me, you know I am a man of the left. The causes you espouse are often the causes I have argued for. The methods—"

"What do you know of our causes?"

"I . . . I have some money," Batisti stuttered. "Not of my own, you understand. My father. Perhaps if I might make a phone call?"

"This is not about *money*," the voice said, and it sounded colder than ever. "Look at me or I will shoot you this instant."

Batisti opened his eyes and stared straight ahead, across the bare, dreary room. The man seated opposite him was perhaps forty. Or a little older, his own age even. Professional looking. Maybe an academic himself. Not a factory worker, not someone who had risen from poverty, pulled up by his own boot laces. There was a cultured timber to his voice, one that spoke of education and a middle-class upbringing. A keen, incisive intelligence burned in his dark eyes. His face was leathery and tanned as if it had spent too long under a bright, burning sun. He would once have been handsome, but his craggy features were marred by a network of frown lines, on the forehead, at the edge of his broad, full-lipped mouth, which looked as if a smile had never crossed it in years. His long, unkempt hair seemed unnaturally gray and was wavy, shiny with some kind of grease. A mark of vanity. Like the black clothes, which were not inexpensive. Revolutionaries usually knew how to dress. The man opposite him had the scarred visage of a movie actor who had fallen on hard times. Something about him seemed distantly familiar, which seemed a terrible thought.

"Behold, I will make a covenant . . ."

"I heard you the first time," Batisti sighed.

"What does it mean?"

The politician briefly closed his eyes. "The Bible?" he guessed, tiring of this game. "One of the Old Testament horrors, I imagine. Like Leviticus. I have no time for such devils, I'm afraid. Who needs them?"

The man reached down to retrieve something, then placed the object on the table. It was Batisti's own laptop computer, which had sat next to him in the back of the official car.

"Cave eleven at Qumran. The Temple Scroll. Not quite the Old Testament, but in much the same vein."

"It's a long time since I was a professor," Batisti confessed. "The Dead Sea was never my field. Nor rituals. About sacrifice or anything else."

"I'm aware of your field of expertise."

"I was no expert. I was a child, looking for knowledge. It could have been anything."

"And then you left the university for politics. For power."

Batisti shook his head. This was unfair, ridiculous. "What power? I spend my day trying to turn the tide a little in the way of justice, as I see it. I earn no more now than I did then. Had I written the books I wanted to . . ."

Great, swirling stories, popular novels of the ancients, of heroism and dark deeds. He would never get round to them. He understood that.

"It's a long time since I spoke to an academic. You were a professor of ancient history. Greek and Roman?"

Batisti nodded. "A middling one. An over-optimistic decoder of impossible mysteries. Nothing more. You kidnap me, you shoot my driver, in order to discuss history?"

The figure in black reached into his jacket and withdrew a short, bulky weapon. "A man with a gun may ask anything."

Giovanni Batisti was astonished to discover that his fear was rapidly being consumed by a growing sense of outrage.

"I am a servant of the people. I have never sought to do anyone ill. I have voted and spoken against every policy, national and international, with which I disagree. My conscience is clear. Is *yours*?"

The man in black scowled. "You read too much Latin and too little English. *'Thus conscience does make cowards of us all.'*"

"I don't imagine you brought me here to quote Shakespeare. What do you want?" Batisti demanded.

"In the first instance? I require the unlock code for this computer. After that, I wish to hear everything you know about the arrangements that will be made to guard the great gentlemen who are now in Rome to safeguard this glorious society of ours." The man scratched his lank gray hair. "Or is that *theirs*? Excuse my ignorance. I've been out of things for a little while."

"And after that you will kill me?"

The man seemed puzzled by the question.

"No, no, no. After that *he* will kill you."

The man nodded toward the back of the room, then gestured for someone to come forward.

Giovanni Batisti watched and felt his blood freeze.

The newcomer must have sat silent throughout. Perhaps he was in the other car when they seized him at the crossroads.

He looked like a golden boy, a powerfully built youth, naked except for a crude loincloth. His skin was the color of a cinematic Mediterranean god. His hair was burnished yellow, long and curled like a cherub from Raphael. Bright blue paint was smeared roughly on his face and chest.

"We require a sign," the man in black added, reaching into his pocket and taking out an egg. "My friend here is no ordinary man. He can foretell the future through the examination of the entrails and internal organs. This makes him a . . ." He stared at the ceiling, as if searching for the word.

"A haruspex," Batisti murmured.

"Exactly," the man agreed. "Should our act of divination be fruitful . . ."

The painted youth was staring at him, like a muscular halfwit. Batisti could see what appeared to be a butcher's knife in his right hand.

On the table, a pale brown hen's egg sat in a saucer with a scallop-shell edge.

The man with the gun said, in a clear, firm voice, *"Ta Sacni!"* Then he leaned forward and, in a mock whisper behind his hand, told Batisti, "This is more your field than mine. I think that means, 'This is the sanctuary.' Do tell me if we get anything wrong."

The golden boy stepped forward and stood behind him. In his left hand was a small bottle of San Pellegrino mineral water. His eyes were very blue and open, as if he were drugged. He bent down, gazed at the egg, and then listened, rapt, captivated, as the man in black began to chant in a dry, passionless voice, "Aplu. Phoebos. Apollo. Delian. Pythian. Lord of Delphi. Guardian of the Sibyls. Or by whatever other name you wish to be called. I pray and beseech you that you may by your majesty be propitious and well disposed to me, for which I offer this egg. If I have worshipped you and still do worship you, you who taught mankind the art of prophecy, you who have inspired my divination, then come now and show your signs that I might know the will of the gods! I seek to understand the secret ways into the Palace of the Pope. Thui Srenar Tev."

Show me the signs now, Batisti translated in his head.

The youth spilled the water onto the table. The knife came down and split the egg in two.

The older one leaned over, sniffed, and said, "Looks like yolk and albumen to me. But what do I know? He's the haruspex."

"I cannot tell you what you want to know," Batisti murmured. "You must appreciate that."

"That is both very brave and extremely unfortunate. Though not entirely unexpected."

The naked youth was running his fingers through the egg in the saucer. The man pushed his hand away. The creature obeyed, immediately, a sudden fearful and subservient look in his eye.

"I want the code for your computer," the older one ordered. "You will give it to me. One way or another."

Batisti said nothing, merely closed his eyes for a moment and wished he retained sufficient faith to pray.

"I'm more valuable to you alive than dead. Tell the authorities what you want. They will negotiate."

"They didn't negotiate for Aldo Moro. You think some junior political hack is worth more than a prime minister?" He seemed impatient, as if this were all a tedious game.

"You've been out of the real world too long, Batisti. These people smile at you and pat your little head, caring nothing. These," he dashed the saucer and the broken egg from the table, "toys are beneath us. Remember your Bible. *When I was a child, I used to speak like a child, think like a child, reason like a child; when I became a man, I did away with childish things. For now we see in a mirror dimly . . .*'"

Batisti recalled little of his Catholic upbringing. It seemed distant, as if it had happened to someone else. This much of the verses he remembered, though.

"'*But faith, hope, love, abide these three,*'" he said quietly. "'*And the greatest of these is love.*'"

"Not so much of that about these days," the silver-haired man replied mournfully. "Is there?"

Then he nodded at the golden boy by his side, waiting, tense and anxious, for something to begin.